PRIMAL DEITY

3

Containment

ALLEN OZARK

Edited by Bella Fox

Published by Sumner House Publishing

ISBN: 978-1-7334656-4-9

In loving memory of my friend

Robert Phil (Racartron) Sumner

1939 - 2016

Dedication

I first noticed her in algebra class, sitting right in front of me, wearing a cute white sweater and a blue, suede skirt. I thought, *if only I had the chance.* Turns out that day, our teacher was absent. Lucky for me, the substitute teacher was away from our classroom so much that she was pretty much out as well. So, I did what any savvy, eager young man would—I took a chance on making the pretty girl in the blue, suede skirt laugh. I didn't even know her name, but I knew if I could just make her laugh, she'd succumb to my gentlemanly charms. So, I sat behind her and cracked joke after joke. Boy did she laugh. In fact, she laughed so hard, she just about fell out of her desk.

For more than two decades I've managed to keep her laughing—most of the time. Twelve years after giving me the best gift ever granted a man—my son—she made lightning strike twice. And now, with each stroke of key, as I carefully craft the next chapter of Alex Southerland's life, I do so with a full heart, imprinted with a smile that may very well last an eternity. This book is dedicated to my wife and my baby daughter, who has spent the last three years stealing my heart. Daddy loves you.

PRIMAL DEITY

3

Containment

Chapter 1

Years ago, my dad sat me down and told me what he believed to be the defining characteristics of a gentleman. That day, I'd gotten in trouble at school for fighting a terribly annoying boy, who reeked of corn chips. I told the boy he smelled like funky old feet. After turning beet red, he walloped me good. My head was ringing, but I focused and did what I imagine any 12-year-old girl would—I hit him square in the face with my lunch tray, and then did my best to cut his head off with it. Our school principal was concerned that I, knowing the boy had to go to the hospital, had little remorse for my part in the fight. He wanted me to feel bad. He nearly bored me to death for at least an hour with a dissertation on what "good people" do and don't do. By the end of our time together in his office, he was thoroughly horrified that I was not ashamed of my actions. At home however, it was a totally different story.

I remember sitting on the sofa in the living room, waiting for Dad to come home. Mother stood across the room, staring at me with her arms crossed, mumbling something to herself and rolling her eyes. I could only imagine what she was saying, but surely it was nothing good. When Dad got home, he entered the living room and set his duffle bag down on the floor. He walked over and whispered something in Mom's ear, and then he made his way over to me. He took a knee down in front of me and put both his hands on my knees. He started by calling me *Porkchop*. I always loved when he called me that. He said, "Porkchop, a gentleman is a man smart enough to know that fighting solves nothing, yet cruel enough to know that once fighting starts the offender must be dealt with the harshest of blows. In this family, man, woman, child or dog, we're all gentlemen. Understand?" I nodded, and Dad smiled that big Southerland smile of his. Unlike Principal Brown, he didn't scold me for an hour. He didn't ask why I did what I did. He didn't even put me on punishment. He told me to defend myself at all times. He told me to fight. And, without saying another word, he gave me the permission I was looking for to unleash hell on humanity for years to come.

As Dad hugged me tight that day, I opened my eyes and looked back at my mother. For the first and possibly last time ever, she seemed happy that I was her baby girl. My mother was many things, some not so bad and some awful, but at the core she was just like Daddy—a fighter through and through. I'd like to think in that moment, the three of us were existing in perfect harmony. We were fit and strong and ready to defend our family, hand in hand, against all enemies. Obviously, that was a long time ago. Everything's changed now—everything, except me. I took a lot of crap off my mom, but I don't take anything from anyone now. Don't get me wrong, I do my best to avoid drama, but when the fighting starts, I fight cruel and hard. Deep down inside, I'm still the gentleman Dad described all those years ago. My blows are harsher than ever, and the people who make the mistake of thinking I'm just a lady never see me coming.

I think one of my greatest strengths is knowing where I've come from and who I am. I've never had a problem with that, and I stand proud of the woman I am today. True, I'm a little rough around the edges, but that's also what makes me unique. I think it's safe to say I've grown for the better over these past few years. For example, my infamous, red-hot temper—the one that got me in so much trouble back in Atlanta—well, it's not so hot anymore. Also, I rarely curse, I shower daily and dress like a lady, which would've made Momma proud, rest her soul. Most importantly, I don't wake up hostile, angry, and uncooperative anymore. I used to get out of bed with a full-blown hate-on, ready to fight whoever or whatever crossed my path, but not anymore. And, just for the record, none of this is by accident either. I've worked very hard to find my inner peace.

Greek mythology is one of my first literary loves, and through my compulsive reading habit, I discovered the

Primal Deities. When I delved into who they were, suddenly my life made sense. Primal Deities are the ancient deities who created the gods. They came from the Primal Chaos, a void that predated the dawn of the Universe. The Primal Chaos was dark and empty much like me before I broke away from my mother's talons and breathed my first breath of air in the real world. Primal Deities have unmeasurable power and can create other deities. Mine created me in her own image and filled me up with her untamable spirit. She revealed herself to me and wrapped me up in her enigma to make me whole at a time when I'd lost all hope. I loved her for her gesture of kindness, and she loved me in return. She gave me extraordinary gifts, and I gave her a fitting name—Blondie. Unfortunately, all her gifts would not be bestowed upon me without me paying a high price, mostly with my sanity. For the majority of my life, this ancient, wicked being has commanded my every unforgivable move, and wreaked havoc wherever I went, but no more. Blondie is history. Technically, she's still kicking around inside me against my will, but I think the important thing here is that she's no longer steering the ship.

For the longest, I thought I was cursed. I tried to rid myself of Blondie, but at this point I've just accepted the fact it's never going to happen. She's my Primal Deity, and through good or bad, for better or worse, we're stuck together until death do us part. There's really no sense fighting who you are anyway; that's self-loathing. Pitting all the reason in the world against an ounce of her insanity is futile. You can't win. And, there's no such thing as locking that slut up either. Trust and believe, even if you could—and I have—she just grows more belligerent and unbearable than ever before. Witnessing the manifestation of Blondie within me from the inside out was like watching a wild, hungry panther being locked in a cage made entirely of raw meat. That panther clawed and bit and chewed its way out, consuming every ounce of flesh until its belly was distended. Any time you let that animal out the cage, she's hell on wheels for days.

It may come as a surprise, but I have a history of following Blondie's lead without question or challenge.

What can I say, I'm loyal? But I'm done playing the victim. No more internal alcohol baths for this country girl. No more sex for supper and violence for midnight snack—not for me—not for some time. See, Blondie and I have come to an understanding. When she tries to trick me into doing something, we both know I shouldn't, I simply refuse her sultry advances. Sure, she yells and calls me names, but I just ignore her. I finally realized I have a choice in what happens in my life. It also occurred to me I've been literally arguing with myself since childhood, but shrink after shrink, Blondie is still onboard for the ride. I can't force her out, but I don't have to let her control me either. When I feel pressured, I remind myself whatever Blondie commands is not really a command, it's a suggestion, and usually a bad one. Sometimes I take her words to heart, but more than not I don't. She hates she can't manipulate me anymore, and she calls me pathetic, but this drastic change in our dynamic is largely responsible for my newfound peace. After all these years, finally I'm in control.

Looking back, I think I've learned more in the past few years than ever, but there's still a lot to discover about life. On the other hand, I've learned just about all I care to know about death. I think back on David, Dominic, my mother, and I—it's a subject I'd just soon avoid. The funny thing about death though is that just the threat of it helps you see things in a different light.

Growing up, I loved watching Sesame Street. That adorable little show had a letter of the day in each episode, and they would repeat it throughout the show. It was great to learn the alphabet, and there was always an important lesson. Even with all the iPads and technology today, the Sesame Street way is probably still one of the best learning methods for kids. Like my daddy used to say, *repetition is the mother of learning*. Maybe that style of learning works on adults too for all the words they tend to forget like honor, truth and loyalty. I guess if I had to pick a word of the day, it would be *time*. And, the lesson would be, *time is precious; you don't have a second to lose*.

You can always get certain things back in life—material items, friends, money—everything but time. Time is this insanely precious gift we get with no training whatsoever. We don't even get a dingy ole user manual to thumb through. By the time we figure out what to do with our time, poof, it's all gone. If you do something stupid or embarrassing, you may get smarter, you may regain your composure, and you may even find your pride again, but you will never, ever get your time back. As usual, the all-knowing Alex Southerland is a day late and a dollar short because none of this dawned on me until death finally came calling.

For the record, I've had some pretty close calls, and I'm usually all overly dramatic about it like, *oh my God this is the end*, but I knew it wasn't my time. I've stared directly at death, but only from a safe distance. This time's different though. This time, I'm in a real pickle.

Oddly, despite the way I've lived my life, I always imagined my untimely demise would be sweet and tender. I dreamed I'd be in some big, strong, handsome man's arms, my limbs dangling about, and I'd be all sweaty, but still cute. He'd tell me I'm beautiful just before I fade away peacefully. This sexy stranger of a man would catch feelings for me postmortem, but not the creepy kind. He'd slowly shut my eyelids with his fingertips, and as a single tear streamed down his cheek, he'd yell, "WHY HER LORD? SHE WAS SO YOUNG!" Sure, it sounds like a joke, but it's my joke, and I'm sticking to it. Speaking of jokes ... all those years I wasted beefing with family, pissing off friends, and doing a bunch of screwed up mess no person in their right mind would ever do ... I'm just saying, if I could get a "do-over," I think maybe things would be different.

Date:	Unknown.
Time:	Unknown.
Location:	Unidentified military facility.
Stat-rep:	Critical Mission Failure.

It's hard to believe I'm still doing Keller's stupid updates in my head, but it's the one thing that's keeping me sane and alert. I still feel I have a mission to complete, but with all my heart, I fear death's close proximity. I can smell it. I smell her, Karla Charles, a young girl who died a horrible death years ago in Atlanta. I'll never get the smell of her corpse out of my memory. I've lost all hope, and I've begun replacing life's sweetest memories with darkness—cold, empty darkness. I've run this same game enough times on the opposite side of the table to know how it all plays out. I'll die a horrible death before I let them use the people I love against me.

I'm a real tough cuss, and I keep telling myself to hold out, but one look at the walls and its obvious men tougher than me have been broken in this very room. You take the pain and withstand the pressure as long as you can, but everyone breaks eventually. It's just a matter of time. Thing is you can't give them an inch of anything, or they will take a mile out of your hind parts. Blocking out memories and feelings, good or bad, about my family just might keep them safe and me alive. I calm my mind and do my best to block the few blissful moments of my life from my thoughts. Now, I have to put all my remaining energy into the seemingly impossible task at hand—staying alive.

Who knew I'd end up like this, betrayed by the unexpected, captured by God knows who, beat to hell for no good reason, and bound to a cold metal chair? It seems I'm destined to breathe my last breath alone in a wet, dark dungeon. Damn the Navy. I should've listened to Momma and gone to law school.

My plastic zip-tie restraints are digging deep into my flesh. My wrists and ankles sting like hell, but that's the least of my concerns. I can't feel my legs anymore. It won't be long now. My body's shutting down. Mentally, I'm fit and strong. I still have my wits about me, and as always, I refuse to give up, but apparently my useless meat-sack of a body didn't get the memo.

It's a good thing there are no mirrors around because I'm a hot mess. Both my eyes are swollen almost completely shut, and every inch of my face is numb from the relentless barrage of unprovoked attacks I've been subjected to daily. They take turns beating me like a man. I've been punched so many times my bottom lip won't close up, and it's got to be cut pretty bad because I can stick my tongue down in it.

My mouth's bleeding badly. I can feel a steady stream of blood running from my chin onto my chest and down into my navel. I'm naked and all alone. My body's sticky with dried blood, and I feel stiff and cold. *Jesus, I smell bad too.* My life's approaching the bitter end, I can feel it. To be honest, it can't happen fast enough.

"God, help me," I whisper. In hindsight, I should've had my butt in church more than the preacher. Maybe my ex-boyfriend, Bill, was right after all. *Imagine that.* There was a guy on the SEAL team I supported back in the day, who was a bible-thumping Jesus freak to say the least. I remember once he told me, "Alex, hell may not be some dark fiery place in the afterlife. It could be right here on earth. Only thing that'll get you through is your faith." *Well Hector, is faith gonna miraculously zap me out of this fucking chair? I don't think so!* And where's the rebel-killing preacher now? Who knows? Hector's probably behind the pulpit ass-raping some underage male prostitute. The holy rollers do dirt and always seem to get a second chance. *Focus, Alex … Focus.*

The door swings open and a burst of light from the hallway pours into my holding cell. My eyes are shut, but they're still extremely sensitive to light. I hear chatter out in the hallway. It's hard to make out what they're saying, but unless my hearing's failing—along with everything else—it sounds like they're planning a major offensive, against who, I can't say, but I'm certain I heard them mention Riyadh. Whoever they are, I know they mean business.

I'm all banged up. To say I need medical attention would be an understatement, but no matter how bad I hurt, I have to stay sharp. When you're captured, gathering as much intel about the facility and personnel as possible can be extremely useful if you ever get out alive and in one piece. A well-trained operative can use the smallest detail as a bargaining chip, even under extreme pressure. I'm trying my best to pay attention, but the pain's an easy distraction, and it's not the only one. I'm not alone anymore.

"Who's there?" I ask.

"You're going to be okay," whispers a soft voice from below.

I stick my nose out and sniff the sweet aroma of Bvlgari Jasmin Noir. It overpowers the smell of dried blood in my nostrils. It's her; the only one in the bunch that doesn't smell like starch, brass, and shoe polish. I don't know who she is, but she's kind to me the way I imagine an angel would be. In fact, I believe she is an angel—my angel. I know that sounds like bullshit, but the thought gives me hope, and I need at least one glimmer of it. Truth is though she's just the quiet before the storm. Angels always show up right before the demons wreak havoc. I mean, you can count on them to warn you the evil bastards are coming to tempt or trick or filet your buttocks over a pit-fire grill, but you can forget about them hanging around to fight with you. If you're lucky and survive the incident, a few angels may be kind enough to show back up and help you pick up the pieces, but don't count on that either. It's amazing how the good ones rarely stick around for battle. They be like, *Hey, I warned you! I told you what was coming. Oh, you want me to stay and fight? Nope, not my job!* Then, they conveniently flee the scene. Kinda reminds me of my dad. He used to disappear as soon as my mother decided to rearrange my face. Then, he'd come back after the coast was clear with his handy little first aid kit. Even that thing had a big dent on the side from where Momma used it one day to "discipline" me as she called it.

I'm lucky to have survived middle school, but I have to attribute that all to my dad. He made me tough as nails. I'm pretty sure he wanted me to be a boy because my mother claimed he didn't want to have more than one child, but they kept at it. All in all, I don't think it worked out too well for Dad though because my little brother Chris is all metrosexual and video games. I don't think that boy could turn a bolt if his life depended on it, but he is smart as a whip and quite the looker like his big sister, of course.

It was no secret, Mother wanted perfection from me, but only for things she was most interested in. She never gave a damn about what I wanted. At the end of the day though, Mom was selfish just like everybody else. Nearly everyone I have encountered has all wanted something from me. Funny thing, I don't have a clue what the people holding me want.

They are, however, hell bent on taking something out of my ass one way or another. From the moment they strapped me down, they beat me senseless without asking a single question. Perhaps they are cannibals and are just tenderizing me for a banquet. Either way, it's clear to me they won't stop until they get whatever they want. I guess they figure all they have to do to get me to talk is just hurt me badly, repeatedly, over a long period of time—they should've checked with my ex Bill on that first. *Motherfucker.* Just thinking about him makes me curse and devolve the situation into something far more emotional than I can afford to experience right now. *Dammit Bill, get out of my head.*

The entire time I've been held captive here, all they keep asking me is if I'm ready to cooperate. I can only assume that means they want information of a top-secret nature. So far, I haven't given them a single crumb, but I wonder how long I can hold out. Don't get me wrong, I have a talent for not being the most cooperative person on the planet, but everyone has a breaking point. I don't know how close I am to mine, but the bad men seem to know what they're doing, that's for sure. They don't mess around with me at all. When they ask, they ask hard.

"This will be a little cold," the woman warns.

She presses her stethoscope against my bare chest, but by now I'm used to the feeling of cold metal on my skin, so it doesn't bother me. She checks my vitals and tends to my flesh wounds. I shriek in agony as she lifts my blood-soaked bandages. She dresses my cuts and wipes my bloody face with a soft cloth. Her warm, kind touch feels good, reassuring even. Her presence helps me cope with the situation just a little better. In my heart, I hope she never leaves, but all fantasies aside, she's a misplaced angel in the worst hell I've ever known.

I have plenty of good reasons to be damned for all eternity, so I know from personal experience this woman is completely out of place. She's one of the good ones, but deep down I know that no matter what she says, there isn't much she can do for me. I haven't quite put together who the devil in charge is, but it damn sure ain't her. My gut tells me they work for the United States military. I hope to God I'm wrong.

It's official. I'm a complete failure. I've failed everyone—my family, Tony, Vice President Keller—everybody including myself. My body's coming apart at the seams. There's no way I'll survive another attack I just know it. I can't see a thing, but I imagine Satan's patiently waiting in the dark corner for his little star child. My Bible study is a little out of date, but based on what I remember, I'm destined to bust the gates of hell wide open, wearing a gasoline Snuggie for all the things I've done in my life.

"Everything's gonna be alright," she promises.

I desperately want to believe her—hell, who wouldn't? But, it's all just wishful thinking on both our parts. I have a feeling my captors will never quit. And, the truth of the matter is, I'm more than willing to drown in my own blood before I give those monkeys a recipe for cheese toast, more less betray my country. I don't know what made those men, who've been kicking me around, turn mercenary, but they have no mercy whatsoever—not even for a defenseless woman. And, like my daddy used to say, a man without mercy is itching to kill something. I figure I'll eventually give them what they want, but why wait?

"Kill me," I whisper.

"Don't you say that!" the woman exclaims. "You're going to make it just fine I promise."

"PLEASE!"

She sighs heavily. "I can't do that, but I can make you all better I promise. I won't let them hurt you like this anymore."

The situation's all bad; she knows it and so do I. It'll be a miracle if I survive the night. Everything would be better if she would just pump me full of morphine, but for some stupid reason, she's not willing to put me out of my misery.

I can't believe how negative I'm being right now. It's not like me to be this way, but I'm in bad shape. The woman goes on filling my head with hearts and flowers, and unfortunately, after a few more moments of it, I actually get a glimmer of hope and a new blast of energy. It's like the time-tested Southerland spirit is back on full tilt now, and

I'm ready to break the hell out. Sure, I'm trapped like a rat. Yes, I'm defeated and don't have a single play to make, but that one little spark of hope she just gave me is enough for me to start visualizing a way out. I know if I'm gonna escape I have to play every single card I have. If I don't have one, I have to steal one out the deck on the sly. Then again, maybe I don't have to do anything at all. Maybe she's the card I've been looking for. After all, she is my angel, right?

Even facing the end I'm as stubborn as ever. I really want to give up, but a good sailor once told me, when you've done all you can and you can't fight anymore, don't give up, find someone else to fight for you. My angel or nurse or whatever she is—she's my best shot. In hindsight, I've played it smart with her right from the start. Each time she comes into my cell, I give her another reason to like me. From what she says, clearly, she doesn't like what's going on. I think it's just a matter of time before she'll fight for me; her tone of voice says it all. The way I see it, if I'm so important that they torture me like this, then she's just as important as I am. No way in hell they'd send a rookie in to patch me up the way they're kicking me up and down and all around this cell. And if she's as important as I think she is, they'll listen to her. They need her to keep me alive. She's my leverage, and I have to make my move.

They say the eyes are windows to the soul. There's a lot to see in mine. I need this woman to look in my eyes and see I'm a good person, even with all my flaws. I need her to see how worthy of mercy I am. So, I force my eyelids open one-by-one. It hurts like hell, but I manage to get them both all the way open. My vision's blurry, so I squint and focus. I've never set eyes on her before, but she's just as I had imagined. She may just be a middle-aged woman in a white coat, but she sure looks like an angel to me. Her face is pale and kind. She has long, thick black hair mixed with gray. She looks like a sweet old lady.

"This is a shot," she warns. "It'll make you feel better."

I'm so numb, I don't even feel the needle pierce my skin, but I feel the effects of the drugs in my bloodstream almost immediately. My body goes completely limp.

"You're going to be just fine," she says again. Her voice is soft and soothing.

I close my eyes and drop my head. "Thank you for taking care of me," I mumble.

"It's okay sweetie," she replies, "it's okay."

She keeps reassuring me everything will be fine, but just when I start to buy it, I hear footsteps echoing in the hall. I know what that means. The footsteps grow louder with each passing moment, clicking and clacking, bringing a dark evil closer with every step.

"Help me," I mumble. "Please," I beg, "help me."

"Shhh, hush," she warns.

"Please!"

"There's no way out of here," she tells me. "I can help you, but you have to-"

The clacking of heels comes to an abrupt stop, and so does the woman. She puts a finger up to her lips and mouths the word, *quiet*.

I look up and see two shadowy figures in the doorway. The men watch us for a moment from the hall. Then, they walk in and stand on opposite sides of the woman. She's still kneeling, facing me. The man to my left is extremely muscular, a baldheaded, clean-shaven black man, pressed from head to toe in his polo shirt and khakis. He has no dog tags or any other kind of identification, but he's got an impressive skull and dagger tattoo on his lower left arm. I make a mental note of it. He looks to me like he used to be Special Forces, and judging from his demeanor, he's not here to show off his body art. I can only assume he is here to replace the last guy, who must be out on medical for breaking his fist on the top of my skull.

The look of disgust on the new guy's face tells a thousand stories of pain to come. He stands at ease, gazing upon me like a heap of gutter trash that needs to go out to the curb. Just from his stance, I can tell he's the angry type too, ready to unleash pure seething hatred the best way he knows. This man's ready to kill me, but his buddy to the right is playing a different game. I guess he's the good cop. He is an older white man, tall, well over six feet. His face is closely shaved right down to his chiseled chin, and he has this thick mustache that's strikingly distinguished to say the least. I think I could pick him out of a lineup just off that Magnum P.I. 'stache, and I'm pretty sure I've seen him somewhere before, but with all the hits I've taken to the head, my memory is a little foggy. Unlike his enforcer, he has a head full of hair, silver all over, every strand from root to tip. He's wearing fatigues and desert colored boots. Like Baldylocks, he doesn't have on any tags, and his BDU's show no rank, but my gut says he's the man running the show. He's been in my cell before, hovering from a distance. From what I've gathered, he commands every man in green in this bunker. I figure he's either the man bankrolling the operation or a high-ranking military officer. And, to think torture never happens in America. *Puhlease.* I know better.

"Doctor," he says, smiling directly at me.

She doesn't respond.

"WHAT'S HER CONDITION?" he asks sternly, raising his voice.

She stands up and circles behind me, placing her hands on my shoulders. "I've stabilized her," she replies. "She'll live, but I fear further injury will be fatal. She needs medical attention, and I can't treat her here. If you'll allow me to-"

"Thank you, Doctor."

"I just need a man to help me get her to the medical bay, so I can start-"

"That won't be necessary," he interrupts.

"I don't understand." She quickly maneuvers back in front of me with her hands on her hips as if she's trying to protect me. I think she actually believes she can. I thought she could too, but the way this man is acting, I'm beginning to have my doubts. *Poor Doc ... hell, poor me!*

"With all due respect, Colonel, my job is to do everything I can to keep-"

"Colonel...?" I interrupt. I squint my eyes and look at him again, this time harder than before. "Wait, I... I know you ... Hammer...? Uh, Hammond...? COLONEL HAMMOND! Army Intelligence, YOU GODDAMN MOTHERFUCKER!"

Hammond rolls his eyes and gives the Doctor a cold, evil stare. "Your job's done, Doctor," he says, callously.

"NO, YOU WON'T LET ME DO MY JOB, COLONEL!" She crosses her arms and continues, "You ... you can't do this ... I won't let you do this ... YOU'LL KILL HER! WE NEED TO MOVE HER TO A BED!" Her voice trembles and she's firm with the Colonel, but he is hardly moved by her display.

"Duly noted ... you can leave my interview room now."

"INTERVIEW!" she exclaims. "THIS IS NO INTERVIEW! THIS IS TORTURE ON SOVEREIGN U.S. SOIL AGAINST ONE OF OUR OWN! I'm an officer. I am duty bound Colonel and so are you. I CANNOT JUST STAND HERE AND LET YOU-"

"AND, YOU WON'T!" he yells. "IF IT WERE UP TO ME, YOU'D BE TRIED FOR TREASON...!" Colonel Hammond shouts back over his shoulder, "CAPTAIN!".

A soldier storms into the room. "SIR!" he yells, snapping to attention.

"Escort Doctor Lerner to her quarters, now."

"SIR, YES SIR!" He salutes the colonel, and then grabs the doctor by the arm.

"YOU CAN'T DO THIS COLONEL!" she yells, struggling to break free as the soldier drags her towards the door. She puts up a good fight, but the big man easily overpowers her, and just like that, my angel's gone.

Another soldier walks in with a chair. He slams it down a few feet in front of me. Then, he waits for a nod from the colonel after which he goes back out to the hallway.

I shake my head a little. "That's how they knew," I say, sniffing blood up into my nose. "You bastard, you were feeding us bullshit while giving everything to the enemy."

"You're not as dumb as they say you are," Hammond says, chuckling as he sits down and casually crosses his legs. "So, I need to ask something of you," he says, "but, I'm a little concerned ... as Doctor Lerner so passionately stated, you need better medical attention than you're currently receiving. I mean, you heard what the good doctor said with your own two ears, right? You're going to die if you don't get treatment," he teases. "You know what...?" His tone changes as if he just had an epiphany. "I can help you ... I can get you comfortable quarters, maybe a hot shower. How'd that be?

Would you like for me to do that for you?" he asks softly, grinning from ear-to-ear. It's like this is all a game to him.

I shake my head.

"No...? Sergeant-Major, you believe this one?" he asks, laughing harder than the situation seems to warrant in my mind.

His henchman laughs too. "You ask me, she's not too bright, sir," says the baldheaded man.

"You hear that, Southerland? My man thinks you're an idiot for holding out like this. Obviously, you're a tuff little cunt, but just how much abuse do you think you can take? You're drowning in your own blood. If I was drowning, and someone threw me a lifeline, I would say thank you, Sir, without hesitation. You haven't eaten in a week, and honestly, you look a little cold. I can have a blanket in here before you can blink twice." He sits up and grabs the edge of my chair between my legs. He pulls me closer to him. Then, he lifts my chin and moves my hair out of my face. He smiles and runs his fingers through my sweaty, bloody hair. "I want to help you," he says softly, "I mean that ... I really do. This is breaking my heart young lady. You and I shed the same blood for our country. Nothing I want more than to get you back home where you belong, out of this big mess you got mixed up in. Vice President should've never involved you, but here we are now at this crossroad. That's neither here nor there. I'm going to help you, but I need you to do something for me first, and you're on borrowed time. You've held out this long, but I'm gonna need your answer now. What's it gonna be?"

I shake my head free from his hands.

"Look, either you play ball, or I'll make the last 15 minutes of your miserable life last an eternity."

"Fuck you!" I murmur.

"Say again?"

"Go to hell!" I yell. I spit blood in his face.

A vein pops up in the middle of his forehead, and I witness his frightful transformation from saber-rattling, sinister bad guy to deadly, torturous son-of-a-bitch. He wipes my spit and blood off his face with his handkerchief, and his entire head turns beet red. There's nothing but pure, unadulterated rage dancing around in his electric blue eyes now. He snatches up a fistful of my hair, yanking my head back with extreme force.

"YOUR MISPLACED ALLEGIANCE TO KELLER HAS BETRAYED YOU AND YOU'RE ALL ALONE—NOBODY'S COMING FOR YOU!" he exclaims. Then, he throws my head back with all his might, slamming it against the back of the chair.

I moan in agony.

Hammond sighs heavily and leans back in his chair. "SERGEANT-MAJOR!"

"YES, SIR!"

"HELP HER UNDERSTAND."

"MY PLEASURE, SIR!" yells the soldier, enthusiastically.

Without warning, the baldheaded man knocks my jaw clean off the hinges with the heel of his right boot. My eyes are so swollen I don't even see it coming. The left side of my face explodes on impact. The force from his supernatural spin kick knocks me over onto the ground. I'm in a daze, but lucid enough to know blood's gushing out of my mouth worse than before. I lay still on the floor. My right arm is pinned under the heavy metal chair I'm bound to. To say it aloud it sounds kind of stupid, but I'm actually trying to play dead. Unfortunately, it doesn't fool anyone, especially not G.I. Joe. I fear the worst is yet to come.

The big man paces back and forth, circling my body until he's ready to strike again. He kicks me in the stomach and chest, over and over with everything he has. The steel toe of his boot digs deep into my flesh with every kick, bumping my body against the back of the chair. This time, he takes his time, building up more potential energy than ever before. Then, he delivers a masterful kick that lands with the force of a twelve-gauge shotgun blast. On impact, I hear something that sounds eerily like a yellow number-two pencil snapping in half during a grade school game of pencil-pop. He kicks me so hard, my chair slides back several feet towards the wall. It feels like a grenade just went off inside my chest. I can barely breathe.

After cracking my ribs, Major Pain appears bored with all the kicking, so he drops to his knees and flips my chair onto its back. I'm lying face up. I can see the light in the ceiling for about one second before he straddles me and chokes me with one hand, snarling and grinding his teeth. He has my throat clinched in a death grip and seems to be enjoying every second of it, literally squeezing the life right out of me. *Sadistic bastard.* I start to blackout, but he releases my neck just in time.

I gasp for air, coughing and wincing. "PLEASE!" I beg.

He stands up. "Oh, you think you gettin' off that easy, bitch? Huh?" He chuckles and shows me both fists. He rubs them all over my face, laughing an evil laugh. Then, he pounds my lights out, bashing my face in repeatedly, coating both his fists completely with my blood. "YOU READY TO PLAY BALL NOW?" he asks, yelling at the top of his lungs, and then he hits me. "YOU FUCKIN' PIECE OF TRASH!" he exclaims, and then hits me again. The punches were coming in a one-two boxer style, but then he ups the ante, launching a five-hit Mortal Kombat style combination I'm sure only Roy Jones, Jr. could deliver. The last punch is a wild, swinging right-handed blow that makes me go blind and lose the hearing in my left ear. He grabs my neck and hurls me back into an upright position. I gasp for air as the chair comes to rest on all four legs.

"Kill me," I murmur.

The soldier laughs and swats me one last time with the back of his fist, right across my nose. I feel my face bone crack, and everything goes dim. I fall into a deep, cold darkness. I probably should be thinking about something more profound, but all I can wonder is, "How'd I get myself into this?"

Chapter 2

I hate having that daydream because it's not a dream at all. It was the realest moment of my entire life, and I re-live that nightmare over and over in the depths of my mind more than I prefer. Colonel Hammond did everything short of putting me in the ground that day. I barely got out of that place with all my parts still attached, so being alive to tell the tale is a triumph in itself. At this point, saying I have PTSD is a severe understatement. Strange things seem to be the norm for me. One thing is certain, I never should've put myself in that position. I only have me to blame. I should've seen it coming, but I was too busy trying to just be happy and a little bit normal for once.

After all that happened, it's hard to shake the feeling someone's trying to kill you. Some nights I wake up in a cold sweat. During conversations, I drift off mid-sentence into a dark space that oddly comforts me. I know I'm not losing it, but nothing seems right anymore, and with the way things worked out, I carry a heavy burden everywhere I go. I can't escape it. Most days my heart is broken, and I feel hopelessness in every sense of the word. Today, my last day in court before sentencing, is no different....

"ALL RISE!" commands the seaman standing at attention to the right of the judge's bench. "THE HONORABLE JUDGE SCOTT PRESIDING," he announces.

I jump to my feet, hands trembling. No matter how hard I try, I can't manage to keep still. The entire courtroom stands up around me. I feel all of them staring. I don't need to look around the room, I know they're watching and judging me, and I know why. It's not the first time. It probably won't be the last.

"You may be seated," Judge Scott says calmly as he sits down.

Everyone in the courtroom sits back down too. I look over at my Appellate Defense Counsel and throw him as many daggers as possible. He doesn't seem to notice though because he's too busy shitting bricks. I can't imagine what his problem is—my head is on the chopping block, not his. I swear this man, like others, who shall remain nameless, is as useless as ever.

"Good morning," Judge Scott greets. "This special session of the Navy Discharge Review Board has been sanctioned by the Secretary of the Navy and the Office of the Judge Advocate General's Corps, United States Department of the Navy, in conjunction with the Federal Bureau of Investigation's Office of Professional Responsibility. It is being conducted based on the outcome of two independent investigations conducted by the Criminal Investigation Division and as a result of charges brought against the appellant in the case the United States versus Lieutenant Denise Alexandria Southerland, O-3, U.S. Navy. This is not a trial. It is a special Navy court-martial procedure for capital offense. Lieutenant Southerland, your actions, under the authority of the Naval Special Warfare Command in support of Naval Special Warfare Development Group DEVGRU, and more recently those that led to the death of a high-ranking government official, have been deemed rebellion against the supreme authority of the United States during wartime. There will be neither cross-examination, nor will you have an opportunity to argue a defense. However, this panel reserves the right to ask any questions it deems necessary during this special proceeding, including questions regarding your involvement in the disappearance of FBI Deputy Director Anthony Crane, who is currently missing and presumed dead. You are hereby ordered to establish a timeline of events before your sentencing tomorrow. This court will record every detail, big or small, beginning with your assignment in Los Angeles, California. Your testimony will in no way impact the outcome of this court-martial, however you are still under oath ... do you understand?"

I lean forward and speak clearly into the microphone on my table. "Yes, Sir."

"Very well ... please state your full name and rank for the record."

"Special Agent Denise Alexandria Southerland, FBI ... I have no military rank."

Judge Scott and his peers seated on opposite sides of him all look at me with the most disgusting of expressions.

"Lieutenant Southerland," Scott responds in a snappy, impatient tone, "I was assured you'd cooperate with this panel. Have I been misled?"

"Your Honor, I am not a Naval Officer. With all due respect, I am unclear as to why charges are being brought against me here. I received an honorable discharge from the Navy years ago."

"Let the record show the appellate refuses to state her rank, forcing this panel to commence with sentencing. Lieutenant, you are hereby remanded to-"

"WAIT!" I exclaim. Honestly, I don't have a choice. I have to play along for the time being, so I yell out my name and rank. "Southerland, Denise Alexandria ... Lieutenant, United States Navy, sir!"

Scott sighs heavily. "Thank you, Lieutenant. You have been tried and convicted of the following charges ... four specifications of wrongful use of cocaine, three specifications of wrongful distribution of cocaine, one specification to wrongfully introduce cocaine onto an installation used by the Armed Forces, and an act of treason involving the assassination of the Vice President of the United States of America. Do you have any questions before we proceed?"

I look over at my attorney, who just so happens to be right in the middle of a fucking daze. I clear my throat loudly and nudge him. Finally, he springs into action.

"Uh, y-yes," he stutters, clearing his throat, "Your honor ... if ... if I may...?"

"Go ahead, Lieutenant Saunders," replies Scott.

"My client received an honorable discharge more than 10 years ago. If it pleases the court, I respectfully raise an assignment of error as the convening authority was disqualified from forwarding the charges in question based on the fact the appellant was not and is not a Naval officer. There's no real evidence of any wrongdoing here. We believe the referral of these charges was improperly influenced, and ask that these baseless military charges against Agent Southerland be overturned and she be released on her own-"

"Duly noted, Lieutenant Saunders, however-"

"But your honor, we need a thorough investigation by law enforcement and not a military hanging based on-"

"Careful, Counsel," the Judge warns, "Vice President Keller's body was just buried days ago, and this court will bring his assassin to justice, swiftly."

"Your honor, my client is not a military officer and she has a right to a fair, civilian-"

"Duly noted, Lieutenant Saunders," the judge repeats sternly and slowly. "Vice President Keller, in his efforts to give Lieutenant Southerland clearance to Special Access Programs, reinstated her as a Naval officer and bridged her service, thus making the prior discharge null and void. Lieutenant Southerland was and is still a Commissioned Officer. As a result, all activities engaged in during the specified period of time were taken in consideration. We have carefully reviewed the record of trial, the appellant's assignment of error, and the Government's response. This court concludes these findings are correct in law and fact and that no error materially prejudicial to the substantial rights of the appellant was committed. Your client's lack of cooperation during her trial is the reason for this special hearing. It is imperative we work to establish a complete and accurate record of events, and I encourage your client to exercise extreme caution in withholding details from this convening body. Lieutenant Southerland, I need not remind you that you have been convicted of treason, punishable by death for killing the very man who believed in you and gave you the power to bring the terrorists to justice. You abused your power, and your actions weakened the stability of this great nation. You have a lot of sins to atone for. We cannot change the past, but now it's time for you to start doing the right thing. And, you can start by telling us about your assignment in Los Angeles."

My lawyer just throws his hands up and shrinks back down on his chair. That fool all but said, *oh well, fuck it, I tried!* I was never even a commissioned officer. Keller screwed me big time, and I know it sounds bad, but I'm glad I shot him. He worked a number on me, but this bastard of a defense attorney, Saunders, is the icing on the cake. I would've been better off with a team of well-dressed chimpanzees defending me instead of this jackass. As usual, I'm on my own.

I clear my throat. "Your Honor, I was recruited by Vice President Keller to track down and neutralize a known terrorist."

"Peter Tesh?" asks Scott.

"Yes, your Honor, that's correct," I confirm.

"Please continue Lieutenant."

"I immediately began working the case. First, I developed a plan, and then I spent several weeks establishing an identity and using my new security clearances to build a convincing cover."

"And what was your cover?" asks Scott.

"I was to enter the Los Angeles branch of the DEA, using a DOJ inquiry as my cover to identify and make contact with a suspected mole in the department. My objective was to acquire this asset and use the asset to infiltrate Tesh's criminal network."

"Lieutenant...." Scott holds up a plastic evidence bag with a document inside. "This is a writ from the U.S. Attorney General's office authorizing this investigation. What concerns this panel is U.S. Attorney General McNamara's statement says he never authorized such an investigation. Can you explain this?"

I sigh and reluctantly reply, "The writ's a forgery, sir."

Everyone in the courtroom gasps as if they never heard of such a thing happening in the U.S. government.

Scott shoots his glasses down to the tip of his nose and looks over the top of his frames. "Say again, Lieutenant."

"The writ was not authentic," I reply. "Vice President Keller gave me complete autonomy. He instructed me to accomplish my task by any means necessary, and so I did. I didn't know who I could trust. Alerting the Attorney General would've only complicated things. I had a 50/50 chance no one would attempt to verify it ... ... you may not approve of my choices, but there are no current protocols for handling this type of secret, undercover investigation, and I had no handler ... no one had my back."

Scott shakes his head and jots down a note. "Very well. Please continue."

"I used FBI Deputy Director Anthony Crane's credentials to establish a profile and background in the DOJ-"

"Without his authorization?" Scott asks.

I nod.

"The appellate will respond yes or no."

I lean forward a little more. "Yes sir, without his authorization, without his knowledge, and without asking him to provide his credentials to me. I flooded the network with a fake Trojan. When the virus was removed from Deputy Director Crane's computer, it embedded a key logger in his system, which I used to compromise his FBI login."

"I see a pattern emerging here, Lieutenant," says Judge Scott, frowning. "...Continue."

"Once everything was set, I waited for the right time to fly out to L.A. Weeks passed with no activity, but I finally got word of a planned drug raid after the Colorado incident. It was the perfect opportunity to insert myself into the situation without raising suspicion. I had a contact inside the Department of Justice make a call to notify the DEA of my intent, and I left ASAP. I arrived at LAX Tuesday morning. This operation took months of planning and prep work. I'd been traveling back and forth and was able to secure an apartment three months prior."

"Lieutenant, you had advance knowledge of a covert U.S. Drug Enforcement Agency raid?" asks the judge.

"Yes."

"How—rather who leaked this information to you?"

"A contact in Justice," I reply.

"And, who is your contact in Justice?" asks Scott.

"Classified, sir."

"Say again lieutenant."

"I'm sorry your honor, but that's classified."

"NOT FROM ME!" he snaps.

"Sir, unless everyone here has SAP level five clearances, I cannot give you this information in an open forum. As it has been stated, I am still a Naval Officer, and I am duty bound."

Scott looks frustrated. "I take it when you say, "a contact," this means you have put yet another Justice Agent in jeopardy. Is that correct, Lieutenant?"

"I repeat, Sir, this incident involved a contact in Justice."

Judge Scott shakes his head. "We'll come back to this later," he responds. "So, you went to your apartment?"

"No, I took a taxi from the airport straight to the DEA office...." I pause for a moment.

Scott takes off his reading glasses and puts them down on the desk. "Lieutenant is there a problem?" he asks. "LIEUTENANT!"

The sound of his bellowing voice shakes me out of my trance. "Sir, my family ... I was told I'd be able to see my family this morning, but I have not been allowed to see them yet. When can I see them?"

"As soon as we're done here," he replies, unconvincingly. "So, you arrived at the DEA ... what happened next?"

I touch my face, picking at my scars with my fingernails. "Yes," I continue, "the cab driver stopped at the front gate. I paid him and walked over to the security officer in the guard shack. I waved my ID and he buzzed me through. I walked into the building up to the front desk, and officially started my investigation...."

As I recount my story to the court, I relive it all again for the millionth time....

So, there I was, walking my pack of lies right into the lobby of the U.S. Drug Enforcement Agency's Los Angeles office.

"Can I help you?" asked the security officer behind the desk.

I flashed my phony shield and matching ID. My cover was pretty thin, but it was the best I could pull together with limited resources.

The guard picked up a clipboard and studied it for a moment. Then he glanced back and forth at me and my ID a few times. "I'm sorry, but you're not on the access list."

"The gate buzzed me through. Check again, please."

"Hang on a minute...." He grabbed his radio, frowned, and then spoke into it. "Bravo-one to control."

"Go ahead Bravo-one," came a man's voice over the radio.

"I got a Justice Agent here requesting access, but she's not on the list."

"What's the name?"

"Johnson... Anna Johnson."

"Roger that, Bravo-one, standby...."

"This'll just take a second," the guard whispered to me.

I gave him a disgusted look, but it didn't seem to faze him at all.

"Bravo-one..."

"Go ahead," answered the guard.

"Agent Johnson is cleared for access, repeat she is cleared for access, over."

"Roger that," he replied. "Sorry Ms. Johnson ... can't be too careful nowadays, you know?"

"Indeed," I spun the login sheet around and clicked my pen to sign in.

Then, he took the clipboard, inspected my signature for a moment, and then wrote my badge number on the same line.

"Here, take this to the door on your left," he said, placing a small yellow slip of paper on the counter in front of me.

"What's this?" I asked.

"You need that to get a proxy card." He looked up with a toothy grin and gave me a badge with the word *Visitor* written across the bottom. "Once you finish up in there, come back and I'll get you an escort."

"Thanks." I took the visitor badge from him and the slip of paper off the counter. I stuffed the badge in my pocket and walked away from the desk.

"Uh ma'am, you need to put that on your jacket."

I didn't even acknowledge him. I just walked over to the administration office. Inside was a very helpful young lady, who did what I hadn't seen a government employee do in years—she worked fast. It didn't take long at all to get my proxy card. She told me it granted access to the entire facility, so instead of going back to the security desk for Barney Fife to stick me with a babysitter, I took the liberty of snooping around on my own.

I quickly found myself surrounded by fine government workers at their best. Each floor was full of busy suits. I casually roamed around, looking for a place to dig in and get started. I took the elevators up floor-by-floor, getting a feel for the layout. Around eight o'clock, I saw a group of agents hustling towards a large conference room up on the fourth floor, so naturally, I followed them....

"Why did you follow them?" asks Judge Scott.

"Instinct, I guess." My head is full of thoughts that are just all over the place. I pause for a moment, and then continue telling my story to the court....

I entered the room and blended into the crowd. I spoke to a few people as I floated around the room. I was smart enough not to stick that visitor's badge on, but I wasn't wearing any other ID. It was obvious I didn't belong, but they didn't seem to care enough to ask who I was, so I didn't volunteer any info either. After a few uncomfortable stares, everyone turned their attention to a news broadcast playing on the monitors mounted on the front wall.

"This is David Anderson reporting live from an abandoned warehouse in Long Beach. At approximately 2:30 a.m., reports of gunfire led police to a chilling scene. Officers discovered the bloody remains of civilians and undercover agents killed in what appears to be a drug bust gone bad. I caution our viewers, the images you're about to see are of a graphic nature. Viewer discretion is advised. As you can see over there, bodies are scattered about this facility. We've been ordered to keep our distance, but sources indicate crucial evidence may have been removed from the scene. Police Chief, Greg Thomas was unavailable for comment; however, DEA Chief, Joshua Carter, released the following statement... *Today, a terrible act claimed the lives of civilians and law enforcement agents. Federal agencies have joined forces with local authorities to process the crime scene as quickly as possible. We're utilizing all considerable resources to quickly process evidence and bring those responsible to justice."*

The report sparked heavy conversation all over the room, but I zoomed in on a young man with the heavy southern accent, who was running his mouth a thousand miles an hour.

"Looks like the same M.O.," he said to another agent.

"Maybe," the agent responded, "either way, I doubt they'll find anything ... hey, Collins, what's this thing with DOJ?"

"No telling," replied Agent Collins, "Assholes never lifted a finger to help us before and every time we try and get a warrant it takes an act of God. I guess now they wanna get a piece of the action after we done all the hard work ... idiots."

"So, what, you're not in the loop?"

"Nope," replied the cowboy, "they've got some dimwit coming to get in our way ... some black girl, and I hear tell she's a real piece of work."

"Can't be that bad," the other agent said.

"Uh, hello," interjected another agent, "why does she have to be the black girl?" She made air quotes. "Why can't she just be a DOJ agent?"

"Hell, I dunno, 'cause maybe she's got a big ole booty like Vanessa!" he snickered.

"You're such an asshole!" she exclaimed.

"Collins, you watch way too much porn dude."

He grinned really big, "Man, there's this one of 'em, does nothing but white guys, and good Lawd that's a whole lot of...." He realized I was in earshot and promptly shut up.

I cut my eyes at him, giving the *I'm black and I'm proud* look, but based on his response, or lack thereof, I'm not sure he decoded the message.

I walked off and headed to the other side of the room towards the only man who was seated at the time. Way I saw it, if he wasn't checking out the report like everybody else was, he already knew, which made him the smartest man in the room. I decided to go over and make friends. I paid close attention to his uniform. He was an Army man, highly decorated, and I checked his rank—a Colonel, and he looked familiar to me. I've seen some sharp Army boys, but this man's uniform was stellar to say the least. Not a thread was out of place. As I drew nearer, I leaned in for a closer look at his name tag. Turns out the man was Hammond, someone I'd been trying to find a way to get to for months. There he was right under my nose. Whatever was going on, it was serious. If he was there, I was definitely in the right place.

"Good morning, Colonel Hammond," I greeted.

"Ma'am," he replied. He stood up and offered me the seat beside him.

"Thank you." I sat down and crossed my legs. "You're quite the gentleman."

He smiled but didn't respond. He just sat back down. I tried to strike up conversation about the breaking news. "That's some serious stuff there," I said, but I was wasting my time.

Hammond's lips were sealed. He just nodded and declined to comment.

After about 15 minutes, two men walked in. They spoke briefly, and then the tallest and younger of the two called the meeting to order.

"I'm sure by now you've all seen the reports. We're waiting for a late arrival. Thank you for your patience. Take your seats, and we'll get started momentarily." He made a call on his cell phone as everyone assembled and sat down. I wasn't close enough to hear his conversation, but he appeared to be getting more frustrated by the moment. He ended the call and waited a few extra minutes before starting the briefing. "We've been waiting for Agent Johnson from Justice," he announced. "She's somewhere in the building, but we can't delay any further ... Chief Carter?"

In hind sight I probably should've announced myself but being a fly on the wall was way more fun.

Carter stepped up to the podium and adjusted the microphone down to his level. "Thank you, Deputy Administrator, Farrell. Department heads, supervisors ... we've been working this case for more than a year. As you just heard, there've been further casualties. Truth is, we've exhausted nearly every DTP resource, and the situation continues to escalate out of control. Our crime scene unit's been deployed to Long Beach. Army Intelligence Colonel James Hammond and Forensic Scientist Dr. Helen Chiles will bring you up to speed ... Colonel."

Hammond stood up and walked to the front of the briefing room. "Thank you, Chief Carter," he said, settling in behind the podium. "On One, November, the DOD, DEA Joint Task Force for Drug Trafficking Prevention, DTP, launched a campaign to bring down a known drug lord and American terrorist. The operation ended prematurely in Colorado with an ambush on DTP agents during an exchange. Early morning satellite imagery showed helicopter drops of unidentified militia at various points along the Colorado, New Mexico border. Army Intelligence was unable to track their activity. Our operatives were attacked sometime during the exchange. Additionally, our surveillance units encountered visual impairments or system failures moments before the attack. Fortunately, we have a transcript of communications. Careful review of these transcripts indicates the presence of unidentified assailants post exchange. Several operatives are still missing and presumed dead. Dr. Chiles?"

Chiles walked up and stood beside him. "Thank you, Colonel ... crime scene processing was unsuccessful. The environment was sanitized quickly and effectively. In short, someone went through a great deal of trouble to cover their tracks. No exotic explosives were used to gain entry to the facility, and no trace of the intruders could be found within a 20-mile radius. The trail was cold in a matter of hours. We expanded the search grid and found the remains of a rare cigar. We were able to extract some DNA and a partial latent, which places Peter Tesh just 30 miles from the scene. Tesh is the leader of a militant extremist group, codename *Alluvion, Sons of Noah*. Tesh's proximity to this crime was not a coincidence. Tesh is a former-"

"We've been following their activity for some time now," interrupted Hammond.

Dr. Chiles, seemed confused, but she held her peace as the Colonel continued.

"To date, there've been 13 more attacks on DEA exchanges. In each case, evidence was removed from the scene moments after the attack. We've lost valuable personnel and millions in Federal buy money. An increase in bombings, ransoms, and other threats indicates rapid growth in street-terrorism and possible cell expansions inside our borders. Soon, the enemy will have at their disposal enough resources to launch a number of deadly attacks, and we cannot allow that to happen. Their capture is necessary to preserve the lives and freedom of those we've all sworn to protect ... Chief Carter."

Carter moved back to the microphone. "Analysts are working around the clock to identify additional persons of interest, but Peter Tesh is still our principal target. We will have a representative from the Department of Justice on site for the next few days. Upon her arrival, Agent Farrell and I will meet with her before making new DTP assignments. Many of you are not trained for DTP, so you'll need to get up to speed quickly if selected. Make no mistake this is our only priority! We're losing good agents and credibility, so don't let me catch you dragging your feet. Any questions...? Then, let's get moving, team."

"COLLINS," shouted Farrell as the other agents filed out of the room.

"Sir?" replied the same loudmouth cowboy who was clearly fascinated with big, black asses.

I walked towards them as inconspicuously as possible while they huddled.

"What are you working on?" Farrell asked.

"I figured I'd push the lab guys processing the bodies to get a rush on it, and-"

"Forget that for now. I need you to locate Agent Johnson. We need to put DTP back online."

"I can pull in my old team. Sullivan's already working a special op for this case anyway. She's got firsthand intelligence. Matter of fact, she's due in from the field tonight. I can pull our old techies and tactical team members too."

"Okay ... yeah, that makes sense ... put it together young man, but locate Johnson first."

"But, sir I-"

"No buts, just do it."

"This is bullshit," Collins mumbled as he turned away.

"Time is short Mr. Collins," said Farrell, "what's on your mind, son?"

Collins turned back around. "Well Sir, I don't think we need some asshole watchdog from-"

"Careful, son," Farrell warned.

"Sorry, sir, but they can't be trusted. All they do is try to make cases against good agents. All I'm sayin' is we lost a lot of good agents. DTP is down to less than four, and I just don't think we need anybody from the outside, looking over our shoulder on everything we do. All that's gonna do is slow us down, you know? Plus, the first thing they'll want is to try to take over, and I can't let-"

"Don't worry about it," said Farrell, "that's not happening."

"I wouldn't be so sure about that," I interjected.

They both turned and looked as if they'd been caught pissing on the back of a luxury car in uptown New York by NYPD.

I continued with my farce. "Agent Collins, you've violated a number of agency policies," I said. "You botched this thing up and good."

"And, just who the hell are you?" he asked with a smug look on his face.

I noticed Carter approaching out the corner of my eye. I took a deep breath and flashed my phony badge. "Agent Johnson, Justice."

Collins looked me up and down for a second. Then, he turned back to Farrell and continued whining. "Sir, all I'm saying is that I just don't think we need this right now."

Neither Farrell nor Carter seemed to have his back.

"You don't have a choice, Mr. Collins," I said. "I'm taking over this investigation, effective immediately. Chief Carter, I need to speak to you in private."

"We've been expecting you, Agent Johnson. Come with me. We can talk in my office." He turned around and headed for the door.

Carter, ancient in appearance, actually seemed to be a nice guy. He was a kind-looking old man, short and stocky, but he had a commanding presence, and everyone seemed to respect him. He wore a black suit with a silver tie and a strategically positioned matching handkerchief in his outer jacket pocket. He had a full head of white hair too. Rumor was he started out as a Special Agent and rose up through the ranks fairly quickly. At first glance, I had a hard time imagining him out on the streets running down criminals, but you know it's always the little ones you have to watch out for.

I followed Carter out into the hallway and down the corridor. He walked extremely fast. I had to sprint a bit to catch up to him. I chased him into his office with Agent Farrell hot on my trail. Carter cornered his desk and sat down on his chair. I stopped short and turned back towards Farrell, who was just coming in through the door.

"Chief Carter, I was hoping we could speak in private," I said, looking back over my shoulder.

"Agent Johnson, my people don't want you here and neither do I," Carter replied sharply.

Well, I didn't see that coming. Nice old man my ass.

Carter continued my tongue-lashing, saying, "You're here because some oversight committee thinks we failed to make progress on this case. But I suggest you tread carefully, Johnson. My people are on this and you don't have the authority to take over anything. Now, as far as Jack's concerned, he knows where all the bodies are buried, so I suggest you either get started or get the hell out of our way.

It may be a foreign concept to you super smart folks over at Justice, but we actually have real work to do here."

I thought really hard for a moment about how best to respond. My cover was thinner than a piece of notebook paper, so yes, I did have to tread carefully. Carter was holding all the keys, and at the same time blocking all the doors. The only thing I could do was play ball or my mission was over.

"Mr. Farrell," I respectfully greeted, offering a handshake.

He smiled. "Jack ... please, call me Jack."

We shook hands. He was handsome for an old white guy. He had a strong, chiseled chin and distinguished silver hair, but he was more than just a looker. I heard guys at the Bureau talk about him before. They call him *Big Jack*. Like Carter, his reputation preceded him too. He was a seasoned agent, well respected throughout the department and known for his involvement in high profile Colombian Narco-Cartel cases. Farrell was DEA to the core, and based on my research, he didn't mind stepping on any inter-departmental toes either, so I didn't expect him to be too excited about me being there. I sat down at the desk across from Carter.

"I understand you're here to make a report," said Carter, "but, you don't have the authority to take over my investigation, so I suggest you get that out of your head right now."

I pulled a tri-folded document from my inner jacket pocket and held it up. "This is a writ from the U.S. Attorney General's office, authorizing my review. I've been ordered to suspend all DTP field operations until further notice."

"WHAT?" Carter exclaimed.

"Your guys made a big mess out in Long Beach," I replied. "Folks back in D.C. are concerned you don't have what it takes anymore, Chief Carter. To be honest, I'm beginning to wonder myself considering this warm welcome I'm receiving. I mean, are we on the same team or not? Look, I'm authorized to shut you down this second, but I was hoping maybe we could work together instead."

Jack suddenly lost his permanent smile. He snatched the paper from my hand and read it carefully. While he muddled through the misleading fine print, I walked over and sat down face-to-face with Carter.

"I see benefit in our collaboration."

Carter raised an eyebrow. "Collaboration?"

"Or cooperation, if you prefer. Make no mistake, I'll shut this train wreck down faster than you can say *unemployment line* ... but, I'm willing to bet you're sharp enough to sort this out in a way that benefits us all. Nobody works their way up to the top without making friends. I need a friend right now, Chief."

"Jack...?"

I spun around in my seat and watched Farrell's reaction to my below-board document.

He looked at Carter and shook his head. "Sorry Josh ... she's got total oversight for 72 hours."

I spun back around to Carter. "It'll be extended based on my evaluation," I warned. I have never lied this much in my entire life, and that's saying a lot.

"Goddammit!" exclaimed Carter, slamming his fist down on his desk. "My people stay on this case you got that?" he yelled, pointing his finger at me.

"If they cooperate, they stay in the field," I replied.

Carter thought for a moment, and then made one more demand. "Jack maintains tactical command."

"He reports to me."

Carter became even more irritated. "Now wait just a goddamn minute-"

"It's okay," Jack responded, smiling again. By then his smile looked far less genuine than before.

"FINE!" Carter was, as grandma used to say, fit to be tied. He rubbed his face with his hands a few times. "Jack ... set up a briefing and move Johnson into a vacant office in your area. Make sure the others have availability and coordinate with them too-"

"Actually, Chief Carter," I interrupted, sticking a finger in the air, "I'd like to start without the team. I'm gonna need a complete briefing and access to all restricted files ASAP."

"Anything else you require, Agent Johnson?"

"Not today, Josh." I smiled.

He frowned big time as if I'd violated some kind of unspoken man-rule by calling him by his first name.

"Jack...?" Carter's tone was growing harsher by the moment.

"I'm on it," said Farrell. Then, he walked out.

I wanted to continue talking, but Carter's phone rang. He answered it and waved me off as he whirled around in his chair. Obviously, that little gesture meant *we'd talk later*, as in next Julember, so I just hopped up and darted out of his office after Farrell.

"JACK!" I yelled, waving for him to slow down.

He looked over his shoulder like he wanted to run for his life, but he eventually stopped and waited for me.

"Jack, I-"

"Deputy Administrator," he interrupted.

"Well, what happened to Jack?" I asked.

"Respectfully ma'am, you fucked that up!"

I gasped. "Excuse me?" I responded, preparing to apply as much fake outrage to the situation as I felt it warranted.

"What can I help you with, Agent Johnson?"

I could see Jack's attitude was deteriorating. Apparently, he and his butt-buddy Carter had worked so long together they shared the same menstrual cycle.

"I understand you're the man around here," I said. "So, why don't you tell me what's really going on?"

"Justice wants you here, so we welcome your input," Jack retorted.

"You know that's not what I mean," I replied.

"In case you haven't noticed, Johnson, we got a lot going on, so for God's sake, get to the point."

"I need to know what I don't know."

"Try Google!" He started walking again, so I ran up beside him.

"Jack, I'm not leaving until I find the truth. We've got people dying. It's an all-out war on the streets, so like I say I need to know what I don't know, which means I need to know what you know."

"Pick up today's newspaper, and you will know everything I do."

"That doesn't speak well for DEA, DOJ relations, Deputy Administrator. The Attorney General and I expected more cooperation from you. Should we give him a call?" I asked, smiling and hoping he would not call my bluff.

Jack cut his eyes at me. "What makes you think I'd cooperate with you?"

"I read your file."

"Don't believe everything you read," he grunted.

"Well, I must say it's extremely hard to believe what you read in the newspaper after seeing a supposedly dead DEA Agent on a LAX surveillance video a couple of hours after this poorly executed bust. You got some bad apples up in here ... so, is it a cover up or something worse?"

Jack stopped in his tracks. We'd walked a few feet past his area. Perhaps I got under his skin a little.

"This way Johnson," said Farrell, backtracking to his door.

We entered his area and he introduced me to his assistant.

"Johnson, Delores, Delores, Johnson," said Farrell callously as if I wasn't important enough to warrant a proper introduction.

Delores jumped up to shake my hand. "Welcome Agent Johnson, we've been expecting you."

"Nice to meet you, Delores," I replied as we shook hands.

She seemed nice, but with my luck that day, there was no telling. Hell, if you told me that Carter's little fun-sized, Napoleonic ass would turn out to be a mean ole bastard, I would have argued you down. Maybe that was DEA standard operating procedure—reel you in with kindness, and then gouge your eyes out.

Farrell opened his door and waved me in. "Have a seat," he said, "I'll be with you in a moment."

I walked in and sat down. I could hear Farrell and Delores talking behind me, but they were shuffling around so much paper I couldn't make out what they were saying. After a few minutes, he came into the office and shut the door. He took his jacket off and hung it up. As he walked over to his desk, I tried to establish control over the conversation before he could settle in, but that turned out to be a disaster.

"You guys got a real cluster-fuck going on here," I criticized. "So, you wanna tell me about the drug raids?"

"You know what Johnson I can follow orders, even from somebody like you-"

"That's good to know, Agent Farrell,"

He frowned at me. "Look, you need to understand there's a unified chain of command here. See, if I support an initiative, this agency supports it. You following me?"

"I think I see your point," I replied.

"So, Agent Johnson, you first."

"What are you talking about, Farrell?" I asked.

He leaned back in his chair and clasped his hands together, interlocking his fingers. "You know what I mean," he said. "Tell me about the demolition suits Customs lost. Then, and only then, will I tell you about the raids."

"Mr. Farrell, I-"

"Tell me about the suits," he interrupted, "otherwise, I'm gonna have to ask you to leave. I got a lot of work to do, and-"

"FINE!" I snapped. He was being an ass, but at least he seemed willing to do a little horse trading with me, so I told him everything I pretended to know. "Two years ago, Customs stopped a shipment of electronics. They found 30 experimental demolition suits welded under a false sub floor in a container. The material couldn't be identified, but they were definitely high tech."

"So, they seized them?" asked Farrell.

"Yes."

"Coffee?" Farrell offered.

"Now you're talking, boss!"

He pressed the intercom button on his phone, "Delores...?"

"Yes Mr. Farrell?" she answered.

"Can you bring in some coffee?"

"Cream and sugar for Agent Johnson?" she asked.

"No, black please," I responded.

"You get that, Delores?"

"Yes, sir," she replied. "I'll be right in."

"Thanks," he hung up. "So, how'd you get involved in all this?" he asked.

"We tied a dock manager to the container violation. He was running a big-time smuggling operation. We indicted him, and he said he could lead us to his source, so we cut him a deal."

"Were you able to track down the manufacturer?"

"Not exactly. Our guy hung himself in custody."

Farrell's left eyebrow shot up to the ceiling. "Let me guess, no leads, right?"

"We monitored some chatter and kept watch on a few web sites, but these guys are smart. They jump from site to site using high encryption. Best option we had was to put the demo suits in play and hope for the best."

"Let me offer up one more good guess here ... your transport got hijacked."

I smiled. "The truck got hit as soon as it left the Bonded warehouse."

Jack rubbed his chin. "This is one hell of a mess. You think the suits are military?" he asked.

"I doubt it ... maybe something your buddies at Langley conjured up or stole from another country."

"My buddies...?"

Delores knocked twice before entering with the coffee. She placed a full cup on the table in front of me, and then filled up the mug on Farrell's desk. That little mug looked as if it'd made it through the war.

"Let me know if you need anything else," she said.

"Thanks Delores," Farrell replied.

We sipped our coffee and continued talking.

"Okay Jack, now you know what I know ... so, it's your turn."

"Ever heard of Will-Clark Pharmaceuticals?" he asked.

I took a big gulp of coffee. "Sounds familiar."

"In 2002, the Williamson-Clark Corporation, a New York based pharmaceutical company, made significant advances in a drug called Chemotin. Treatments administered to patients with early stage cancerous developments were a documented success. Didn't take long for the market to respond. The medical community watched as the company continued R&D of this wonder drug, but the lab got raided a year later right after receiving a major shipment of hazardous drug manufacturing materials. Dr. Gerald Williamson, CEO and head of research, disappeared a week before the robbery after liquidating all his assets. He's been missing ever since."

"You got a file on Williamson?"

"Yeah, hang on..." Farrell unsuspended his laptop and printed an electronic file. He gave me the stack of papers and I browsed the file while he continued.

"Soon after, the company folded, and his partner, Elena Clark, disappeared too. No connection's been made between the robbery and the disappearances, but drug activity and violent crimes have since increased over 48% on the west coast. We suspect the stolen goods went straight to the suppliers. We've been working to recover the equipment and get the poison off of the streets, but can't get to the major players unless-"

"Wait, I don't follow you," I interrupted. "I understand drug activity is up, but that was a small-time smash-and-grab. What does this have to do with the current crisis?"

"Here's what makes this thing dangerous," he explained, "the actual research and patented technology used to produce Chemotin was stolen. So, the perps have the ability to manufacture a host of synthetic products they pass off to junkies as designer drugs. People who don't die after one hit eventually lose their marbles. This poison is worse than the real thing sad to say, but they're moving it by the truckloads and pushing the dealers' backs against the wall."

"So, why not work with the drug dealers?" I asked. "They've got skin in the game and should want to protect their turf."

"These new players are not fucking around, Johnson. Drug lords have been getting knocked off left and right. The rest are running scared. They won't talk to us anymore."

"What about the victims?"

He raised an eyebrow. "Victims?"

"You said people were dying, right? Somebody's got to be concerned about that."

He shook his head. "Not really. People treat addicts like the scum of the earth around here. Nobody's missing them and the other addicts are just looking for that next fix. There was a guy so fucked up over on the east coast, he stripped naked and went into the street and ate a homeless man's face clean off."

"Like a zombie?"

"Cops shot him at least four times and he was still growling back at them," Farrell said. "This thing is bad—real bad. It's up to us to do something about it."

I thought for a moment. "There's no way in hell those idiots would understand how to work the suits more less the lab equipment, and I'm pretty sure designer synthetic drugs are out of the question ... you think it was an inside job?"

"Maybe," he replied. "The FBI launched an investigation into the executives' disappearances, but the case was closed due to insufficient evidence. I'm assuming that's why you're here?"

"How's that?" I asked.

"We believe Dr. Williamson and Peter Tesh are one in the same ... here take a look at Williamson's photo ... ... and, now Tesh."

I examined both photos closely. "Hmm ... ... minus the beard, I can see the resemblance," I said. "Wait that's a surveillance shot at LAX ... FROM A MONTH AGO!" I was blown away.

'Bingo," he said.

"How the hell do these people travel so freely?"

"And, that would be the six-million-dollar question of the day," said Farrell. "So, what do you think Johnson?"

"I'm not sure ... I mean, with the prospect of curing cancer, Williamson probably had enough drug materials on hand to supply the northern hemisphere, and I'm guessing enough money to buy his own private island. According to this file, he has a PhD in Chemistry and degrees in Biology, Criminal Psychology, and wow a Harvard Law Degree? Who the fuck is this guy? If he really is Tesh, then we're up against a well-funded criminal genius. You pull in his former business partners? At least tapped their phones or checked their financials?"

"Can't get a warrant on circumstance." Farrell sighed.

"Well, Williamson's supposedly dead. You could trace his financials, right?"

"Already got a couple of guys on it. It's a long shot, but it may give us a better idea of what we're dealing with. Oh, I almost forgot, hold on for a second...." Jack pressed the intercom button on his phone. "Delores...?"

"Yes, Mr. Farrell."

"Delores, I need a conference room starting in two hours ... probably for most of the day. As soon as you can, go ahead and-"

"Just a moment, sir," interrupted Delores. I could hear her clicking keys on the computer keyboard. "Okay, I've reserved briefing room 423-A for the day."

"Thanks Delores."

"No problem, Sir," she replied.

"Oh, and Delores..."

"Sir?"

"Get a hold of Keller and Pearson for me."

"For the conference?" asked Delores.

"For whatever kind of meeting you can pull together," he replied, "we'll work around their schedules."

"Right away, sir."

"She's good," I remarked.

"Couldn't make it through the day without her." Jack smiled, but then he got quiet for a moment.

I figured his silence was my cue to keep talking. "Who's Pearson?" I asked, but he didn't respond. "So, Mr. Deputy Administrator-"

"Call me Jack."

Suddenly we were back to Jack. I call that progress. I smiled. "Jack, who's Pearson?"

"CIA Director Pearson."

"Oh...? Okay ... but didn't-"

"Don't ask," said Jack.

"Don't tell," I retorted. "So, what about the missing DEA agent?"

"Classified until further notice," he said.

"Jack, you know I have clearance."

"Listen, Johnson-"

"Anna."

"Anna, give me a few hours to sort out some internal issues. I'll bring everyone up to speed during the briefing and I'll give you additional insight afterwards."

"You're my new best friend, Jack!"

"I typically kick my friends out of my office while I'm working."

"Don't have to tell me twice ... later, Jack." I stood up, grabbed my coffee and headed to the door.

"Oh, and Anna..."

"Yes?" I turned back towards him, my hand still on the door handle.

"Delores will set you up in the office next door."

"Thanks."

I pulled his door shut and walked over to Delores' desk. Before I could say a word, she started handing me all kinds of stuff—paperwork, pass codes, meeting schedules and more. She also threw in a boat load of overwhelmingly large case files. Then, she made a few calls to facilities management, and within the hour, I was resting comfortably in my new office.

My new home away from home—away from home—had a wall-sized world map and a window with a view, overlooking the city. I used the login information Delores gave me to access the network and stumbled around in the system for a while. After that, I reviewed the case files, which were completely out of control. There was entirely too much information to absorb in a short period of time, but I read as quickly and carefully as possible.

Time flew, and before I knew it, Delores was knocking at my door. She stuck her head in and told me the first meeting was at 11:00 a.m. I'd been sitting there for nearly two hours. It was already a quarter till, so I grabbed my stuff and headed out. I walked around the corner to room 423-A.

Vice President Keller caught me just as soon as I stuck my face in the door.

"Agent Johnson," he greeted, "thanks for joining us."

I walked over and shook his hand. "It's an honor to meet you Mr. Vice President."

"Please call me Jim," he responded. "Johnson, this is CIA Director Pearson."

"Pleasure to meet you, sir."

"Agent Johnson."

Pearson shook my hand as if I had the plague. I swear I saw him wipe his hand on his pant leg afterwards. We chitchatted for a few minutes while we waited for Jack and Carter. Finally, Carter arrived, followed by Jack shortly thereafter. Those two were joined by a government issued umbilical cord.

"Mr. Vice President, Director Pearson, thank you for being here on such short notice. I apologize for the delay."

"Busy time for you, hey Josh?" asked Keller.

"Nothing we can't handle, sir," Jack interjected.

Keller frowned, but pretended to be interested in Jack's opinion. "Agent Farrell," he greeted, grabbing Jack's hand and shaking it firmly.

"Deputy Administrator now isn't it, Jack?" said Pearson. "Congratulations."

"Thank you, Director Pearson, I-"

"Time's a wasting!" exclaimed Keller.

Jack smirked. "Gentlemen, please have a seat." He walked to the podium at the front of the room.

I purposely sat down next to Director Pearson who seemed more than willing to protest. After a few moments of uncomfortable silence, Jack began the briefing. I noticed Pearson staring me down from the corner of my eye, but I ignored him and paid close attention to Jack.

"Our nation's primary defense against drug trafficking has been under attack for over a year now. The casualty rate increases as this threat continues unchecked. Last Tuesday, we attempted to bring down a major cell of the Alluvion criminal network. Our primary target was Carlos Nelson, an upper echelon personality we believe to be responsible for a number of recent bombings and kidnappings. The exchange was compromised. We lost good U.C.'s and approximately $20 million in federal money. Satellite imagery from Tuesday's been processed." Jack directed our attention to the main screen. "Analysts identified each of our agents and marked their positions throughout the series." Then, he pointed to a mark labeled "SA-P.H." with his laser pointer. "This is Special Agent Pamela Harris at 2:05 a.m., pre-exchange. This is the warehouse at 2:07," said Jack, advancing to the next image. "The heat blast on the side of the warehouse is most likely from the explosive used to gain entry. Now, at 2:08 a.m., the smaller starburst pattern heat sources are automatic gun fire. At 2:09 a.m., you see Harris firing close range on an unidentified person. Seconds later, the body's down and remains in the same location we later found Jeremy Taylor, Peter Tesh's number one errand boy we believe acted as a liaison between the synthetic drug suppliers and the street dealers. Harris shot Taylor and then opened fire on her colleagues. She exited the building with Carlos Nelson at 2:19 a.m. In the interest of national security, we notified the department Harris was K.I.A. Immediately following the firefight, a crew moved in and cleaned the scene thoroughly. Investigators say they extracted bullets from victims and the environment. Not a single shell or fragment of anything was left behind. Survivors were removed from the scene. They left Taylor behind to die. When first responders arrived, his vitals were weak, but they were able to stabilize him. Taylor suffered a close-range contact wound to the head and was airlifted to the hospital. He survived a surgical procedure in which his damaged skull was repaired. Amazingly, he was coherent just hours after surgery. He agreed to testify in exchange for immunity, but he was killed Wednesday morning during transport...." Jack cleared his throat. "We don't know exactly how his killer knew he was alive or how they got word of the planned transfer, so we must proceed with caution and minimize security leaks. We're down to a single lead. Intelligence indicates the old Will-Clark building in New York contains a stockpile of narcotics and weapons that can put us back on the trail of Alluvion. We need to check it out. DTP staff is down significantly ... Agent Collins is pulling in new team members and heading to New York tomorrow. Any questions so far?"

I looked around and no one seemed to have a pulse, so I dove right in. "You said Taylor was Tesh's number one guy?"

"That's correct, Agent Johnson."

"Why was he targeted?" I asked.

"ATF arrested Taylor in March on a stolen weapons charge. During interrogation, Taylor confessed to three murders and his involvement with Tesh. He instantly became a valuable FBI asset and ATF turned him over to Justice. The Bureau cut him loose and put him back on the streets as their C.I. Taylor continued to increase rank, becoming privy to actionable intelligence. We were able to identify vulnerabilities in the Alluvion Network and were planning to move fast, we just needed a little more intel. Tesh must've smelled a rat and sent Harris in to flesh him out. While onsite, she gained access to information that led to Taylor. Her boyfriend, John Baker, has been taken into custody for questioning. She's been moved to the top of the FBI's Most Wanted list, and photos are out on the wire to law enforcement agencies across the country. This infiltration is one hell of an embarrassment for the agency, so specific details are on a need to know basis. Any other questions?"

"Well, yes," I spoke up. "Why isn't the FBI here?"

"DTP is DEA, DOD territory. The FBI is overwhelmed right now, with counterterrorist activity."

"Ooookaaay, but, isn't Tesh a terrorist?"

Jack shook his head, "We don't have all the answers, Johnson."

"I understand," I replied, "so, what's the connection between Harris and Tesh?"

We believe Pamela Harris is Elena Clark. Disguised as a well-respected law enforcement officer from Chicago with an impeccable record, she infiltrated the DEA. Her identity was expertly manufactured, and, unfortunately, our background investigation didn't raise any red flags ... ... anything else?"

"Just one more thing ... since this is a DEA, DOD task force, what's Director Pearson's involvement?"

"Director Pearson is-"

"We're here to help, Agent Johnson," interrupted Pearson. "This is a national crisis, and teamwork will increase the potential for success."

"So where do we go from here?" I asked.

"Isn't this your investigation now, Agent Johnson?" asked Pearson.

I could tell they'd been talking, so I figured I'd take the high road. "I'm merely soliciting input from the team."

"I'm sure you need more time to look over the case files and meet with DTP," said Jack.

"I don't want to slow down progress. I'll review the case files and meet with the team now ... gentlemen." I gathered my things and walked towards the door.

"Johnson, I need to spend some time with these guys," said Jack, "so I'll see you back in my office in about an hour."

"Okay Jack, I'll be in my office."

"Hang on there, Johnson," said Keller. "May I have the pleasure of walking you back to your desk?"

"I'd be honored, sir."

"Call me Jim," he reminded, smiling.

I nodded. "I'd be honored, Jim."

"Jack my boy, give me a little time," said Keller, "I got me a date. I'll be back in 15."

"We'll be here," said Jack.

Jack sat down with Pearson and Carter. Keller and I walked out of the room together and strolled down the hall, side-by-side with a mob of Secret Service Agents behind us. And, what do you know? I spotted a familiar face—Agent Stephen Billings, the chicken-cooking Secret Service Agent that delivered me into Keller's den of iniquity in the first place. What a coincidence.

"Johnson, huh ... that's cute," said Keller, chuckling softly.

"I thought you may think so."

"I'm sure my wife's maiden name had nothing to do with that."

"Of course not." I smiled really big. "But maybe if I get into hot water, I can just say she's my mom."

"Well ... Johnson," Keller rolled his eyes, "you are quite the smartass, but I think you handled yourself just fine back there."

"Thank you. I'm glad you approve."

"Any problems so far?" he asked.

"No, and I don't foresee any." I entertained his question but was hoping he'd just cut to the chase.

"So, we are making progress, right?" he asked, speaking slowly.

"I'm not sure what you mean."

"You identified a target yet? Can't just be Harris, we know she wasn't working alone in here. And, it damn sure ain't the boyfriend."

"I'm not sure what you mean. I just got here."

He stopped and motioned violently for secret service to back off. As soon as they did, he lunged for me. He grabbed my elbow and pushed me to the wall.

"Cut the bullshit," he whispered. "President thinks this is a wild goose chase. For God's sake, he wants to pull the plug on this operation ... so do I ... Peter Tesh could be out of the country by now."

"You're hurting my arm!"

He realized he was holding on too tight and immediately let go.

I rubbed my elbow. "For all I know the President's right!" I exclaimed.

"Lower your voice!" he commanded.

"Look, if the President wants me out, then I'm out," I said softly, "but Farrell knows more than he's letting on I can feel it. I'm on to something here and you know it, or you wouldn't be up in here leaning on me like this. Jesus, Jim, you wanna blow my cover?"

Keller sighed. "Look, Alex ... the President's a good friend, and I respect his opinion, but I'm not ready to throw in the towel just yet. You may not think so, and maybe I don't show it, but I have confidence in your ability. Maybe you're right. You got good instincts, sailor. Perhaps we should continue as planned."

"I agree ... thank you."

"Don't thank me, Alex, get the goddamn job done!" he snapped. "You don't have a single friend in the White House, and I don't have to remind you about that tax evasion charge, do I?"

I rolled my eyes and shook my head. "This is bullshit, and you know it, I took care of those taxes already!"

"Well, it seems all those amendments your CPA filed haven't made their way to the right department at the IRS yet."

"Fuck you, you goddamn sick old bastard!" I gave him a mean stare. "You're making me fuckin' curse again!"

He smiled really big. "You got 'til Monday, sailor. One mistake, one screw up and you're not just off the case, you're out of here in handcuffs. I make myself clear?"

"As a bell," I replied, sarcastically.

"You know what's at stake!" exclaimed Keller as softly as his emotions would allow.

"No, Jim, I don't. I don't know what's at stake. What's really going on? I thought I was after one man ... turns out it's a whole damn army with spies and tradecraft and shit. So, what are you not telling me?"

He shook his head. "Stay focused! Smoke out the mole, Southerland. Find that bastard Tesh and put a bullet between his eyes. Everything else is secondary. You think you can do that sometime this century?"

I squinted and stared him directly in the eyes. "I'm working as fast as I can."

"The next school full of children he kills will be on your head, agent."

We stared each other down for a moment after that low blow, and then he finally sighed and apologized.

"I'm sorry, I-"

"Don't," I interrupted. "Don't patronize me."

Keller nodded. "I am. You're the only one I can trust. We are in this together. Just be selective of what you share. If you come across anything that gives you pause, you'll best serve your country by contacting me directly young lady. Understand?"

"Yes."

We started walking again and the Secret Service agents caught up with us. We spent the rest of our stroll in complete silence. Finally, we arrived at my office.

"Well, it was a pleasure meeting you. Good luck Miss... was it Johnson?" he asked, putting on a show for Delores' benefit.

"Yes, Mr. Vice President, Agent Johnson."

He smiled again. "Well then, good luck Agent Johnson."

"Thank you, sir."

We shook hands one last time.

Before leaving, Keller walked over to Delores and touched her shoulder. "Delores, it's always a pleasure."

"Thank you, Vice President Keller." She smiled.

Then, Delores and I watched as he disappeared into the hallway. Once he was gone, I stepped inside my office and closed the door. I stared out the big window trying to figure out my next move.

Chapter 3

There I stood in my new DEA office, doing absolutely nothing at all. It seemed like I'd been standing in the same spot for nearly an hour when my cell phone rang, but it had only been a few minutes. "Go," I answered.

"Guess who," asked the caller.

"Oh, I've never heard this voice before," I replied, chuckling. "And why are you calling in the middle of me doing something very, very important?"

"I got something for you," said the caller. "What?" I asked.

"A car," he replied. "I've got some guys bringing it to you right now."

"Thank God, I don't have to take a cab home."

"There's something you need to know about the car. Secret Service Agent Billings just contacted me, and-"

The intercom rang. "Hang on," I interrupted.

"No, it's important, there's a-"

"Hold on just a sec." I pressed the intercom button on my desk phone. "Go ahead Delores."

"Agent Johnson, Agent Farrell is back and would like to see you in his office."

"I'll be right out." I hung up and returned to my cell phone call. "Hey, I gotta go," I said.

"No wait-"

"I'll call you back later, I promise!"

I hung up the phone. I could have sworn I heard Jack say he would be back in an hour. It'd only been like 15 minutes. *What the hell is going on around here?* I sprung up from my desk and hurried into Jack's office. He had a troubled look on his face.

"You alright Jack?" I asked.

"Yeah ... look, I've gotta leave. Take off and we'll get started in the morning, say eight o'clock sharp?"

"You sure?"

"Yeah, I have to take care of something." He said.

"Am I okay to take a few files?"

"Take whatever you need," Jack replied. "Here's my card. Call my cell if there's a problem with security."

"Will do. Thanks."

"I'll see you tomorrow 8:00 a.m. sharp," Jack reminded. Then, he left in a hurry.

There was no reason to hang around, so I grabbed my things and headed for the security desk. I dropped off my visitor's badge, signed out and exited through the front door. Outside, I noticed a young man holding a clipboard, standing next to a black Mercedes parked in the tow away zone.

"AGENT JOHNSON?" he yelled, waving. "ARE YOU AGENT ANNA JOHNSON?"

"YES," I replied, waving.

"I HAVE A DELIVERY FOR YOU." He pointed to the car.

"Oh, oh yes." I quickly skipped down the stairs to meet him.

"Sign here near the x." He handed me the clipboard and pointed to the signature line at the bottom of the release form.

I scribbled the most illegible signature I could, and he handed me the keys.

"Thanks."

"You're welcome," he replied. "Here's your copy." He smiled and handed me the yellow carbon copy. Then, he jumped in the back of the SUV parked behind the Benz.

Those guys didn't hang around. They pulled off immediately and sped out of sight. Bureau boys can be so dramatic.

I pushed the unlock button on the handle of the little funny shaped, laser cut ignition key. The parking lights flashed, and I walked around to the driver side door. I peeked inside of the AMG SL500 and saw it had been set up with the usual law enforcement gadgets, warning lights and all, which was a plus for driving on the 405. I wasn't sure why Tom sent me the car, but I trusted him with my life, so I didn't hesitate to take possession of it. Mr. Procurement and I had history. He gave me hell years ago back in the Atlanta Field Office, but he always looked out for me, so whenever he asks me to test out some equipment, I don't give him any shit. Besides, that Mercedes was fly as hell. I made a mental note to call Tom and see what he wanted to tell me about Agent Billings. I probably should've called him back immediately, but at that point, the only thing on my mind was getting home and taking a hot shower. It was my first day on the ground. Whatever Tom had going on with Billings, I was sure it could wait till later.

I hopped in and put the key in the ignition. As soon as I started the motor, I pressed the convertible top button. I powered on the stereo as the roof retracted, and started scanning for a decent radio station, but that was a waste of time. I got frustrated after about five or six seeks forward and immediately made a mental note to unpack my pirated CDs as soon as possible. Yes, despite the fact I used to put people behind bars for piracy, I was and still am public enemy number one on that front. Good bad or indifferent, I've been a pirate since the mid 80's. I always did my job, but I never agreed with the laws or the big record labels and their bullshit. Sure, I can afford to pay for music, but stealing it off the internet reminds me of cracking old Commodore64 games, and I just start to feel a bit nostalgic every time I do it. Why, the very thought of engaging in such electronic criminal activity makes me quite randy. I think if the agency took one look at my iPod, they'd have a goddamn cow.

Desperate for good radio, I gave the seek button one last try. Thankfully the tuner landed on what seemed to be a pretty decent jazz station, so I adjusted my mirrors, put the car in gear and sped off towards the freeway. I headed straight for my apartment.

I got home and parked in my self-proclaimed, reserved space. I was surprised no one had taken it for themselves since I had been gone for so long, but clearly, they all feared me, so enough said. I hopped out of the car and climbed the stairs up to the top level. There were only two apartments per floor, and mine was on the right. I opened the door and walked straight into a big surprise. "Oh God, that's nasty!" I exclaimed, "I hate spider webs!" I hadn't been there in a while, so the place was pretty dusty too. I'm slightly obsessive compulsive, so even though I didn't feel up to it, I had to clean up and fast. I figured I could shower later. There was no way I was going to stay the night in that filth. I hung up my jacket, kicked off my shoes and plugged in the vacuum cleaner.

I made the place sparkle from top to bottom. Afterwards, I just took it easy for the rest of the day. With all that cleaning, I'd worked up a serious appetite. I may be all petite and sexy, but I can eat. I don't play that *I'm so dainty I can't pick up a fork* mess. I hadn't eaten much at all that day, so I ordered myself Chinese food—Mongolian beef with the little crunchy noodles under it. Whenever I get that stuff, it reminds me of my ex Bill. For some reason, I was really missing him that day. He and I would do this crazy thing where he'd be like "Alex, what do you want to eat?" as soon as he walked through the door. And of course, I'd fool around for 20 minutes, talking about different food options until he got tired of my mouth. Bill knew me like the back of his hand. At that point, he'd say two little words, *Mongolian beef.* All I had to do was exhibit the faintest little smile on my face and he'd tear out the door to go get it. We enjoyed a lot of good times together, but we also had a lot of bad ones. Honestly, I regret shutting him out of my life. He ended up making a certain moo-cow, whore-of-a-sister, who shall remain nameless, a real good husband. In fact, they're still married to this day. I always saw Bill as the biggest, dumbest fuckup in captivity. Who knew he'd actually make a good husband and father? Guess we can put that on my long list of bad calls.

When the food arrived, I tore open the unmarked white plastic bag, ripped back the top on the little Styrofoam takeout plate and dug in. I worked my chopsticks like a judo master while looking over the files I'd brought from the office. After dinner, I crashed on the sofa. I should've prepped for my next meeting with Jack, but I needed a break, so I stayed up late watching Reno 911 reruns. I like the lieutenant in the little booty shorts—he's hilarious. I watched the show for a while and eventually fell asleep on the sofa.

Unfortunately, I overslept the next morning. It was Wednesday, and I got up feeling extremely exhausted. I'd slept all night, but not for more than 15 minutes at a time. My insomnia was beginning to get the better of me, and it was worse than ever. I can never seem to get enough rest. I shook off my sleepiness and showered in a hurry. Under normal circumstances, I'd spend all morning doing something clever with my hair, but I didn't have time, so I just let it hang and got dressed. I rushed out to the car and just before I got in, I noticed an unmarked police car in the parking lot. Inside were two cops. I had a hunch as to why they were there, but I didn't have time to deal with them, so I burned rubber out of the parking lot and hit the 405. Traffic was thick, but drivers fled from the sight of my big Benz emblem and the flashing blue lights on my dashboard.

"Come on, move bitches!" I yelled at several drivers on my way in.

I finally got to the building and passed through security around 8:35 a.m. Down the hall, I noticed a man in a navy-blue suit near the elevators. He was standing there by himself sipping coffee from a DEA mug. He looked up, noticed me, and then pressed the elevator button. Then, he just stood there and stared. The elevator arrived, but he didn't get on, so I got curious and started really checking him out. He had a nice shape for a white boy—at least it looked that way from a distance. At age 34, with my lack of social life, my vagina is like *RED PHONE RINGING!* Sometimes I feel I missed out on my wild teen years although I've done more than my share to make up for it as an adult. But, every time I notice a good-looking man and he notices me, it just reminds me I'm getting older every day, and I'm still hopelessly single.

So there this dashing gentleman was, standing near the elevator, waiting just for me. I felt so special. He was checking me out too, so I kicked on my sexy *Blondie* walk— it gets them every time. Sure, I'm a little on the scrawny side, but I got a fat ass ... ... okay, maybe I just have nice hips, but that doesn't matter because I was working every bit of what my momma gave me for this stranger's private viewing pleasure. I worked it, and I kept on working it until I got close enough to make out his face and realized it was just Agent Farrell. I damn near tripped up. Either he was fine as hell yesterday and I didn't notice, or lack of sex had me totally screwed up in the head. One would think Blondie and I would be on our best behavior in the middle of a high-stakes, undercover operation, but for some reason, she decided to get all chatty. I tried to tell her to shut her trap, but there's no reasoning with her, ever. I could hear her, prancing around in the depths of my mind, daring me to make a move.

"Look at what you are doing for your country," she said, convincingly. "You deserve this. Shoot your shot, baby!"

It would seem a desperate woman requires very little persuasion. *Fuck it*. I dropped my Starbucks cup in the trashcan between the elevator doors and moved my hair out of my face. Then, I lined myself up in front of Farrell perfectly, posing like a supermodel.

"Jack," I greeted in my deep sexy morning voice, "you look very handsome today."

"You're late, Johnson," he replied callously. He reached over and pressed the elevator butoton again.

Seriously! That man acted like we were talking over a fucking intercom. And, the face he gave me, oh, my God. I couldn't even begin to fathom what his little nasty-ass attitude was all about. Either he wasn't a morning person, or something happened yesterday to change things between us. I'd built up a rapport with him, but it seemed to be crumbling fast because Jack was being quite the salty codger.

"You alright Jack?" I asked. "Something happen?"

"I'm fine," he said in the driest tone imaginable.

I could tell he was lying. Something was definitely off. I didn't want to push him too hard though, so I just shut up. We stood in silence waiting for the elevator to come back. Finally, it reached our floor and the doors opened.

"After you," said Jack, holding the elevator doors open.

I stepped inside and pressed the button for our floor. Jack moved to the back and leaned against the rail. The doors closed, and I watched him in the reflective gold surface of the doors. His eyes were all over my ass, but I don't think it was intentional. He was wound so tight, I doubt he even realized what he was doing. His mind was clearly elsewhere—that or he was starting his "man-period."

The second-floor bell chimed, and Jack nearly jumped out of his skin. He must've realized he'd been staring at my booty the whole time because he had this look on his face like he felt the need to apologize. Personally, I didn't think so. After rudely dismissing my sexy walk in the corridor, he at least owed me a booty-ogle. I was starting to feel like I was losing my touch.

The elevator stopped at our floor and we walked out together. Jack gave me this weird blank expression and then he sighed.

"How 'bout we get started in your office in 15?" I asked.

He looked down at his watch. "Quarter till?"

I nodded. "I'll see you there."

Jack headed for his office, and I stepped inside the lady's room to refocus. After 10 minutes of staring in the mirror, I still hadn't pulled it together. Truthfully, I had no realistic plan—at least not one that made any sense. I had been shooting in the dark, fishing for Vice President Keller. Under normal circumstances I would have every possible outcome planned out and written down with multiple scenarios, strategies and options, but not this time. It was freaking me out too, but I just had to suck it up and do what I do best, which typically involves me flying by the seat of my pants. Whatever I did the day before to win him over, I had to do it again because I was facing a totally different Jack that morning, and Keller was itching to drop me in a deep, dark hole. It was almost a quarter till. Time was running out, so I pumped up my confidence and stormed out the bathroom.

Down in the DTP area, Delores, unlike Jack, was bright and sweet just like the previous day.

"Welcome back, Agent Johnson, it's good to see you again," she said, smiling.

"Good morning, Delores," I replied.

"A man called several times for you, but he didn't leave a message."

"Thanks, I'll be in Agent Farrell's office for a while. You mind coming in and getting me if he calls back?"

"Sure, no problem," she responded.

Jack's office door was open, so I walked in and sat down. He finished a phone call, and then directed his attention to me.

"Okay, what's up Johnson?" he asked.

The soft, sexy approach didn't work at all back at the elevators, so there was no point in trying to play it safe. I decided to just go ahead and take the gloves off.

"Jack ... can I still call you Jack?"

"Please."

"Jack, do we have a problem?"

"I don't know, do we?" he replied.

See, I knew something was up. "Well, yesterday, you and I were making progress," I responded. "Unless I'm missing something. But now, today, your tone makes me think we somehow managed to hit the reset button. So, what's up?"

"I've got bosses just like you. I'm not from Washington, but that doesn't mean I'm slow on the uptake."

"Come on, Jack, what's the deal? Be straight with me."

Jack frowned. "You first."

"What...?"

"I've got people over at Justice," he said. "Nobody in Washington has ever heard of you."

I paused for a moment. "So, maybe we have a lot to talk about."

"I just need to know who I'm working with," he said.

"Working for, you mean?" I reminded.

He rolled his eyes. "For the moment."

We stared each other down for nearly a minute.

"Can we talk about this later?" I asked politely.

He shrugged his shoulders like a little kid, so I took that for a *yes*. One thing was certain, somebody had gotten to him. But I didn't know how much he knew, so I had to be careful.

"Okay, I've been going over the case files, and-"

"That why you're late?" he asked, smiling.

"Nope ... I overslept."

"Least you're being honest about that."

"I'll take that as a compliment, Jack." I smiled too.

"Listen, whatever you find in the case files you can just put it in your report," Jack said, still seemingly irritated. "I've got bigger issues to worry about. Collins pulled together a new crew of DTP Agents. They're leaving for New York today."

"Then I guess we should pack."

"We?" He raised an eyebrow.

"I'm going to tag along," I replied.

He hesitated to respond for a moment. "Okay, good. Keep me posted and let me know if you need-"

"Actually, I need you there too, boss man," I interrupted. I tapped my bright red nails on the top of his desk as if it were a done deal already. I may not be a card-carrying salesman, but I know how to "assume the sale."

"No-can-do, Johnson," he snapped, "I've got a meeting this evening."

"Okay then, see you tomorrow?"

Jack started acting nervous. He shook his head. Then, he opened a drawer and pulled out a stack of employment dossiers. He pushed them to the edge of his desk in front of me. "Look Johnson, I'm the Deputy Administrator of the DEA ... I can't run out into the field just because you think I look good in a suit and you can't manage-"

"You do look good in a suit, Jack," I interrupted.

His face turned beet red.

I gave him the nicest smile ever. "But, that's not why I need you up in New York. If you want me out of your way quickly, then I need a high-level perspective out there on the streets, not a subordinate's skewed point of view."

"Collins will be there."

"You mean the bright-toothed racist? I don't think so, Jack."

He placed his fist in front of his mouth. I knew he wanted to laugh.

I threw my hands up. "Come on, Jack, it'll be fun!"

"Fine, I'll meet you on the ground tomorrow."

"Fantastico!" I opened the folder on the top of the pile in front of me. "Everybody here?" I asked.

"All except for Alonzo Parrish," he replied. "His file's classified."

"Spook?" I asked.

"Who knows?"

"Nothing from Internal Affairs?" I asked.

"Yeah, but everything's redacted," said Jack.

"Look, I'll assemble the team for you. How much time do you need?"

"Go ahead and start pulling them in. I'll check these out while I wait."

"Some of these guys are still in debriefing," said Jack. "I'll expedite them and meet you in situation room three. You know where it is?"

"I'll find it, thanks." I gathered up the employee files and stuffed them under my arm. I walked out of Jack's office with my head ready to pop. There was no telling what I was getting myself into with this team Collins pulled together, but I knew no matter what, I had to stay sharp. If they had even an inkling of who I really was, they would've already pulled the plug on this operation, so in my mind I was still good to go, but I had to walk a thin line. Whoever the mole was, they would lead me straight to Tesh, my walking *get out of jail free* card. I had to keep my cover intact at all costs.

Funny thing about all this, if they'd just thought to give the Attorney General a quick phone call, I would've been in the slammer faster than you could say *butt-fuck*. Luckily for me, government workers rarely verify anything. It's like people in horror films never look up when we all know damn well the evil, blood-sucking werewolf is hiding up there, hanging from the chandelier, waiting to pounce on the little redhead and satisfy his hunger. All I had to do to infiltrate the DEA was flash a phony badge and a paper-thin, forged document, and they gave me access to the Deputy Administrator and everything in between. No wonder there's a mole. Good thing I was not an assassin.

So far, things were going my way. I was making progress fast with Keller's secret mission. I had DEA's top leadership believing all my *porky pies*, and I was on my way to meet with the DTP team. I was confident I'd be pressing the barrel of my pistol to Tesh's temple in enough time to make it back to my office at the FBI by Monday morning. It's getting to the point where it's hard for me to keep all these lies straight in my head. I'm looking forward to telling a few less of them soon.

Chapter 4

I'm not naïve. Hijacking DTP would not be easy. For all I knew, I was walking into an ambush. I searched around for Situation Room Three. After wandering around for about five minutes, I finally found it. I walked in and took a seat up front. I scanned through the team members' files for almost an hour. Then, the agents started rolling in. Collins was first to arrive.

"Ms. Johnson, I'd like to apologize for-"

"Not necessary, Mr. Collins," I interrupted.

"Let me know if I can be of assistance," he said, humbly.

Collins was a thick-necked country boy, who must've won Mr. Alabama or something. He had blindingly bright teeth and spiked, buzz-cut hair, brown with blonde streaks. Our last encounter left a bitter taste in my mouth, but he was behaving for the moment. He sat down and I continued reading the files. After a while, I broke the silence.

"Agent Collins, I'll be riding along with you to New York today. Can you introduce me to the team?"

"My pleasure," he responded. "Oh, here's a copy of everything we got so far." He walked up and placed a massive three-ring notebook on my workstation.

"Thank you," I said.

After a while, a few more agents walked in. Collins met them mid room and began the introductions. "Ms. Johnson, we got a few stragglers, but the bulk of us are here, so I'm gonna get started." He paused a few seconds, checking for my objection, but then quickly continued. "Listen up y'all, this is Special Agent Anna Johnson. She's here from Justice—been with us about a day or two now. She's here to help DTP and will be joining us up in New York City. I imagine she's got a lot of experience in situations like this, so we're lucky to have her."

Judging from Collins' tone, he was not convinced about that last statement. In fact, I think that was a low-key jab at me.

"Agent Johnson, this is our team ... Adriana Rodriguez, ex-Army MP, and a damn good sniper. She spent years with them Airborne fellers, special operations and stuff like that. She's good with explosives and one helluva marksman, or markswoman I guess."

I closed my files and walked over to her.

"Pleasure to meet you, Agent Johnson," she said. She was thin and very pretty with long wavy black hair and a thick Latin accent.

"Pleasure's all mine, Rodriquez." We shook hands.

"This is William Davis," said Collins. "Army Delta Force. He finished a second tour in Afghanistan before coming back and going over to DOD. We pulled him over to DTP a while back. He can master just about any computer device."

"Call me Bill," he said. "Nice to meet you, Johnson."

"Likewise, Bill."

Bill was a well-dressed older gentleman with a few distinct streaks of gray and a very firm handshake.

"Over here is Terence Slade, Navy SEAL team leader, special warfare out of Mississippi. I'll just say he's never let us down."

I almost laughed when I realized who was standing in front of me, but I managed to hold it in.

"I'm not as dangerous as my file says, L.T.," he joked.

"I'll be the judge of that, sailor!"

We shook hands and stared at each other for a brief moment. I knew what he was thinking, and he I, but we didn't utter a word about our history.

"Ms. Johnson," interrupted a very short, glamorous-looking young woman. She pushed Slade out of her way and shook my hand. "I'm Stratton, and it's good to meet you."

"Thank you, Stratton, it's good to be here."

After those words came out of my mouth, she practically disappeared.

Collins leaned over and whispered, "That's Nicole Stratton ... former spy. We call her Nick. Well connected, but paranoid. She can pass a polygraph like I never seen before, lying her ass off," he said laughing, loudly. "It's rather spooky, no pun intended."

I guess he was trying to be funny. "I appreciate the heads up."

He smiled, and then directed my attention to another team member. "Agent Johnson, meet Alonzo Parrish. He's got Top Secret, Black Ops clearance, so I can't tell you much about him, but he's one of the best interrogators we've seen 'round here."

"Perhaps a personal demonstration is in order?" said Parrish, a very tall dark-skinned black man with a shiny baldhead and a perfectly trimmed goatee. His voice was "Barry White" deep.

"That won't be necessary, Mr. Parrish," I responded.

"So, have you seen my file?" he asked.

"You looking for fans?"

He grinned and winked at me before walking off. Parrish went to his station and sat down. Then, four more agents entered the room.

"Just in time guys," said Collins. "Agent Johnson, meet Kevin Rhodan, Maxwell Burtram, Dr. Timothy Hughes, and Vanessa Sullivan."

"Welcome to the team," greeted Sullivan. "I apologize for my appearance I was pulled in late last night. I've been debriefing ever since and haven't had a chance to change."

"I understand," I said, smiling, and I did. I completely understood what it's like coming in from the field and being held up in a little debriefing room for eight plus hours. What I didn't understand was how she survived all night in that Vegas Nights, hooker getup. It looked painfully uncomfortable.

Sullivan was taller than me with flawless brown skin and a tiny waist, but she was unusually thick in other places—and don't get me started on her heels—they were sharp to death. She seemed to have an endless supply of confidence too. Basically, she was the exact opposite of me, except for the confidence of course. I'm bright, skinny, and maybe not intimidated by her, but definitely a little jealous. *Bartender, oh bartender, one shot of hater-aid please. Make it a double and keep 'em comin'.* In hindsight, I think I was hating on Vanessa Sullivan with a passion for no good reason right from the very start. I'm usually not like that, but Blondie can be a jealous bitch sometimes.

"Don't ask me how, but this gal here, she can get just about anything," said Collins, touching Sullivan's arm. "Anything you ask for, she finds a way to get it every single time, go figure."

"I'm extremely good at what I do. Like the man says, anything you need I'll take care of, boss," said Sullivan, who at the time was sizing me up like Olga the hard-hitting cellmate.

It wasn't what Sullivan said as much as it was how she said it. The whole "staring at my tits" thing didn't help either. I just tried to dismiss it.

"Thank you, Agent Collins," I said. "So, what is it that you do again?"

Collins smiled a toothy grin. "Well, I'm Thomas Collins, but everyone calls me Tommy."

"Yeah, well I call him Tom, 'cause that's the only way I can remember his name," said Burtram.

"Ah, like the drink?" I asked.

Burtram chuckled. "Yep. Ladies and gentlemen, Tom Collins!" He made little six guns with his hands and pointed them at Collins.

Everyone laughed.

Collins continued, "Like I was sayin', we've all been on different cases, but we work together a lot too. Lucky for me, we work well with one another. I'm team lead. Honestly, all I really have to do is just keep us moving in the right direction. So far nobody's took me out yet."

"WE KEEP TRYING, BUT HE'S TOO DAMN BIG!" exclaimed Burtram, jokingly.

Everyone laughed. They all seemed to have a good rapport with one another. They were acting like old classmates at a 10-year high school reunion. With everything bouncing around in my head, it was refreshing to see.

"Thanks, Burtram, I needed that," I said, smiling. "So, how about you?"

"Please, call me Max," he replied. "Basically, Kevin and I-"

"She asked about you, dumbass!" Kevin interrupted.

Max ignored Kevin and continued, "BOTH KEVIN AND I really just profile criminal behavior. Dr. Hughes is the one you want to watch out for—thinks he's some kind of genius."

"Shut up, Max!" Hughes said.

Max kept right on. "Yeah, he claims to have doctorates in electrical engineering and computer science from Georgia Tech, but we don't believe him, and he refuses to bring his diplomas in to settle the matter. Perhaps you could use your DOJ influence to persuade him? He started out in medicine too, and despite his aversion to it, he stitches up wounds and gives CPR like an ER actor. He's our unofficial on the job medic. Speaking of jobs, Vanessa is a total-"

"Say something stupid, Maxey!" dared Sullivan.

"Hey, don't call me-"

"Thank you, Burtram," I interjected. I figured it best for me to jump in there since the situation was rapidly devolving. "Thank you, Agent Collins, for the introductions. Everyone, please have a seat."

They all sat down. I returned to my workstation and scanned back over their files one last time, then I proceeded.

"Some of you have already contributed to this case, and I applaud your efforts to date. Contrary to popular belief, I'm not stepping in here to trap anybody. I'm just here to observe, so I'll try not to get in the way. Mr. Collins?"

"Thank you." He waited for me to sit down. "Okay, let's get started ... recent developments put Dr. Gerald Williamson and Elena Clark of the Williamson Clark Corporation at the center of our investigation. Davis, Rhodan, and Burtram, you're already on background, right?"

"Yeah, we're running financials," replied Davis.

"Good, crank up the heat and expand your search. Compile me a list of friends and associates on both. Pull records and search assets of everyone you identify."

"We'll need a warrant for that," warned Rhodan.

"Not today," Collins responded. "But, still check with me before you follow up on anything solid, and as always, keep me posted on your progress."

"You need the list by tomorrow?" asked Rhodan.

Collins replied, "Just get it to me as soon as you can."

"We're on it," said Burtram.

The three of them stood up and walked out.

"Collins, I understand you'll be pulling in more agents?" I asked.

"Negative ma'am. We lost half of DTP and the other half is out on medical. I pulled these guys in today. They're all we got, so we'll have to make do. You have any field experience?"

"Yes, I do. Actually, I'd like to review your operational plan on the plane."

"It's in the notebook I gave you."

I picked up the notebook and turned to the page for his plan.

He asked, "You good...?"

"Yes, I'll let you know if I have questions."

"Alright then. Team, you know the drill. Delores set up flight and hotel, but we'll need equipment and transportation on the ground."

"I'll get with Vincent Oakley on weapons, vehicles and equipment," said Dr. Hughes.

"Good deal, Doc," replied Collins. "Team take the rest of the day off and spend some time with your families. Report to the airfield at 1900. Personnel will be available to load the plane. Briefing's at 0800 tomorrow during breakfast ... any questions?"

"What about the cases we're working now?" asked Parrish.

"All on hold indefinitely. Bury 'em."

"Fine by me," Parrish replied.

"Any other questions..." asked Collins. "All righty then ... you're dismissed. Go do something fun for a change."

The team exited the room and Collins closed the door after them. I just watched as he strutted back over to me like a cowboy at the O.K. Corral. I could tell he'd just packed his bags for a power trip.

"Something on your mind, Agent Collins?"

"I consider myself a pretty smart feller," he snapped. "Here's what I can't figure is why you're really here."

"I'm just working to complete my evaluation. Nothing more, nothing less."

"BULLSHIT!" he yelled. "Look now I know you are not just here to evaluate us ... that dog ain't gone hunt, lady."

Jack entered the room.

Collins frowned and ran his fingers through his spikey hair, but it was so stiff with gel, it didn't even move. "I've got my orders," he said, "and ain't nothing I can do about that. But I won't let you put my folks in jeopardy. Get my drift?"

"Just so we're clear Mr. Collins ... whether my time here exceeds 20 years or a single day, I call the shots, and you will follow my direction, or you won't see this case to the end. Having said that, I'm assuming tactical command on the ground in New York."

"WHAT!" He instantly got pissed.

"That's right, I'm taking over. You disobey a direct order for any reason, I don't care if you just botch up my coffee order, I will bounce you out of there faster than you can remove my heel from the crack of your ass."

He didn't respond. He just stood there with his mouth open. We locked eyes for a moment, and then he snapped his gaze away.

"COME ON JACK, SHE CAN'T DO THIS!" he exclaimed.

"That's enough, Collins," said Jack.

"But sir, I-"

"It's not up for discussion, son. Like it or not, we have to play this one by the book, so get moving."

Collins didn't challenge Jack. He left the room immediately.

"Kid's got balls," I said, chuckling.

"Yeah, but he's one of the best we got. Besides, yours are bigger and shinier!"

Jack laughed really hard, but I didn't think it was funny.

"Look, don't read too much into it," Jack said. "I doubt you'll have any problems with him. Besides, I'll be onsite as soon as possible, remember?"

"Yeah, that's comforting," I replied, sarcastically.

Jack frowned. "So, what's the deal tomorrow?"

I held up Collins' plan. "Looks fairly straight forward to me. The Will-Clark building is the target. We're conducting a search of the premises. Once we get a good list from the techies, he's got them splitting into two-man teams to interview ex-board members, investors and employees."

"So, this plan meets your expectations?" Jack asked.

"Why yes it does, Mr. Farrell," I replied, smiling.

"Good." Jack was about to say something but paused just before it came out. "Anything else?" he asked instead.

"No," I responded. "Unless there's something else I should know about?"

"Not that I'm aware of," he replied.

"Then, I'll see you on the ground in New York, Jack?"

"Looking forward to it." He tapped me on the shoulder a few times and then left the room.

It was a little before noon, so I left the office to go home and pack. I went down to the parking lot, hopped in the car and started the motor. I dropped the top and pulled out of the deck, headed towards the freeway. As usual, traffic was sick. After sitting on the 405 for an hour, I started watching the clock hard. I needed to get home and pack but hadn't moved from the same spot in 20 minutes. Glancing across the sea of cars, all I could think about was the mysterious one I was driving. I kept wondering what Tom was trying to tell me earlier about Agent Billings and what he had to do with the car. *Weird.* Hell, Tom all but acted like it was the most important thing of the day. My curiosity was growing out of control, so I grabbed my cell and called Tom's office, but he didn't answer. I tried again and got nothing, so I pulled over on the shoulder of the road and checked my messages. I actually had an email from Tom that read, *IMPORTANT: package in car.*

"Package? What package?" I said aloud.

Obviously, Tom didn't just want me to test drive the car for him. He was trying to get something to me. I put the car in park and started poking around the interior. I looked in the glove box, checked the center console, and then ran my hand under the dash, but came up with nothing. I peeked inside all the little compartments, but didn't find anything in them either, so I opened my door and stepped out to check under the seats. The driver and passenger side both looked clean. I popped the trunk and checked it too. I even lifted up the spare tire, but as far as I could tell the car was clean. I thought something may be in the engine compartment, so I popped the hood and looked around in there too but didn't see anything out of the ordinary.

Now, I may be crazy, but I'm not stupid. Tom never called like that before. My gut told me there was something about the car that was waiting to be discovered. I should've talked to him while I had him on the line, but I was too busy trying to placate to Farrell's overly sensitive ass. Hindsight is always 20/20. At that point, I just needed to get back in touch with Tom to find out what's going on. I tried his cell phone again, but it just rang and rang and never went to voicemail. It was not like him to ignore my calls. I sighed heavily and tried his cell one last time. After about four rings, someone finally answered.

"Hello," said a woman.

I hesitated to reply.

"Hello...?" she answered again.

I cleared my throat. "Yes, I'm trying to reach Tom ... is he available?"

"There's been an accident," she replied.

"I don't understand," I said. "What accident? I just spoke with him earlier today."

The woman went silent all of a sudden.

"Where is he?" I asked.

"Who is this?" she snapped.

"WHO THE FUCK ARE YOU LADY?" I yelled back.

She went silent again, but I could hear someone whispering, saying, *we almost got it*. They were tracing the call. It reeked of standard FBI bullshit, so I hung up quickly and switched SIM cards.

"FUCK!" I exclaimed. "Accident? What accident?" I thought about it for a second, and then calmed down a little. There was no telling what Tom was up to. Maybe he stuck himself with a paper clip, or maybe he just got in trouble yet again for doing something he shouldn't have done. Tom was a rebel like me. If he is being investigated, or worse, if he is in custody, and they are tracing his phone calls, then something really serious is up. Tom's a character, but I've never known him to take unnecessary risks. Whatever he wanted me to see, it was worth his job—maybe his freedom. I needed to find whatever it was before my paper-thin cover became the next victim of those nosey Bureau bastards. That's the last thing I needed. I could see Tony, going straight into cardiac arrest, or at least serious shock over this entire mission, which of course hadn't been cleared with him. Tony most likely would've told Keller to go fuck himself with a sick dick, but I needed to earn my freedom back and the crafty VP was holding my golden ticket. Nobody had juice like Keller. I'm sure Tony would've fought for me, but I probably would've been spending Christmas behind bars.

I had to figure things out fast. I thought hard for a second, canvassing the day's events in my mind. Once I had all my thoughts in order, I was even more convinced something was stashed in the car. I didn't have much time before we had to leave for New York, so the situation called for someone who was good at finding stuff other people didn't want found fast. I needed the help of a damn good thief. There was only one man I knew I could trust to do it without 20 questions—my oldest, dearest, trusted acquaintance—a devil in his own right. I closed the hood, jumped back in the driver seat and merged into traffic. I flipped around at the next exit and headed south towards Long Beach.

It is true that I tend to shamelessly spend more time with hardened criminals than I probably should, considering I am an FBI agent. However, I am a paranoid sailor, and up to this point in my life, I can count the number of times a righteous man has done right by me, and I can count the number of men I trust on one hand—my dad, my boss, my ex, and my boy from high school. Now, Daddy's dead, rest his soul, my boss is off limits for his own protection, and my ex was one hell of a mechanic, but he's out of state and also a lying, cheating, illiterate ass-hat, so that's a no go too. However, I've always been able to count on my homeboy from school.

If there was something to be found in the car I was driving, my homeboy would find it. But he'd also probably try to sell whatever he found to the highest bidder, so I knew I had to proceed with caution. Taking the car to him was probably the worst idea I had at the time, but it was the best option nevertheless. There was just one small problem. The last time we were in the same room together, we didn't get along amicably. We still speak from time-to-time when he needs me to get him out of a jam, but we haven't seen each other in years. Luckily, he's in a bit of hot water again and had been begging for me to pull some strings. He didn't know it, but I had already decided to help him. Honestly, I'll always do whatever I can for him. For the life of me, I can't say what it is, but through all our ups and downs, something keeps us together—something real. We may be on opposite sides of the law, we may fight, and sometimes we literally threaten to kill each other, but we're always there when the chips are down—always.

In situations like this, the what and the why are always the easiest parts of the equation. When you need to get something dirty done for the greater good of humanity, sometimes, you have to get out on the dance floor and samba with Satan. If you don't like that idea, my advice is, get used to it because, most times, that's the only way you get what you need. You just have to learn to deal with the fallout afterwards as best you can. Usually the end justifies the means. The big problem is how. In this case, my friend was just as paranoid as I was, and I had been ghosting his calls after I told him I would help. He might've acted up if I just dropped by unannounced—maybe think I'm running a sting operation or getting ready to raid him. It's always better to be safe than sorry, so I figured I'd call first. I grabbed my phone off the passenger seat and dialed his number. He answered straight away.

"Yeah, hello," he said nonchalantly

"Malik?"

"Yo, hold on, hold on ... MAN PUT THAT SHIT BACK IN! THAT MUFUCKA GOTTA BE READY BY THREE ... yeah hello."

"Malik," I repeated.

"Yeah, who the fuck is this?" he snapped.

"It's me," I said softly.

"What?"

I spoke up and said it again, "It's me."

"Awe shit, now you wanna talk?"

I knew it.

He continued on his tirade. "You can't pick up when I call, but now you callin' me? What you want? Matter fact, fuck dat, these bitches is all up on me man! What up wit' dat? Yo, we had a mothafuckin' deal!"

"Malik, I got your back. You asked for my help, and I will help as agreed, but-"

"YO THIS SOME BULLSHIT, MAN!" he exclaimed very emotionally. "You think I'm going back to prison, YOU OUT YO FUCKIN' MIND, BITCH!"

"Oh, so now you gonna talk to me like that, Malik? I'm just a bitch now, huh?"

He was silent for a moment. "Nah, man I-"

"Do we have a problem, Christopher?" I asked.

"Whatever man, don't be callin' me by that shit, yo."

"That is your name ain't it big gangsta Chris?" I giggled.

He laughed too. "Whatever dude. The fuck you want? I'm busy gettin' my hustle on."

"I need your help, big hustler ... and, I'm on my way."

"On your way? You fuckin' beat me with a cane last time you saw me, kickin' me and shit, calling me bitch-made ... then you play like you wanna do some shit for me, but that's just to help yo ass, and on top all that you ain't called in I don't know when, wit' yo' ole bullshit cloak and dagger messages back and forth. But now yo ass want something and you can just be on yo' way? This some bullshit."

"Malik, every time we talk, you start rehashing that old ass shit ... that was ages ago."

"IT WAS LAST FUCKING WEEK, RED!"

"Whatever! Look, get over yourself. And, while you trippin' I called you on your birthday and Christmas. Just 'cause you out doin' a bunch of shit you ain't got no business doing don't have nuthin' to do with me. I call you all the time, nigga. Shit, you the one who act like you got a goddamn broke-up index finger."

"Man, you need to get these mufuckas up off me 'cause-"

"NO MALIK! I BEEN KEEPING THE HEAT OFF YOUR ASS FOR YEARS. YOU STAY INTO SHIT, AND I ALWAYS LOOK THE OTHER WAY, SO NOW IT'S MY TURN. YOU HELP ME FIRST, AND THEN I'LL SET YOU STRAIGHT."

"Man, I don't know 'bout that shit."

"Well you better think fast. From what I hear, them white boys down there itchin' to run up in dat ass. So, what's it gonna be? You in or out?"

"Man Red, you trippin' yo. See I know the deal ... you always looking for me to do some shit, but when yo' boys wanna put the hook in the crook, that's when you look the other way."

"What are you talking about, Malik?"

"I'm tellin' you I can't do no mo' fuckin' time, Red!"

"You know what, Malik, you a selfish ass. I kept LBPD and the Feds off your back for years, and you swore up and down you were gettin' out the game. What, you makin' this a lifetime career now?"

"Maybe."

"You're unbelievable. I watch your back and this is how you repay me? I do for you, but you never do for me! After all that shit you caused in Atlanta!"

He got quiet again.

"Look, you owe me from the last time I delayed the inevitable!"

"College girl," he mumbled.

"Yeah, nigga, I said it—the in-e-vi-ta-ble," I repeated slowly, "GET A FUCKING DICTIONARY!"

He laughed loudly.

"Look Malik, I can't stop this thing from going down. You know that. And, don't try to make me feel guilty either. You brought all this on yourself going for the million-dollar boosts. You think LBPD gonna overlook that shit forever? The only reason it's gone on this long is because I said you were cooperating with me on an investigation. But since you haven't given us shit—and you haven't—there's not much I can do now. LBPD's gonna get a warrant, so you need to get yo shit together, nigga. I'm puttin' my ass on the line just giving you a heads up."

"You right, baby. I 'preciate you. I just need more time you know ... I mean, we got history you and-"

"Malik," I interrupted, "you are my boy, but you been free from the people for years. Now your rent's due. One way or another it's going down and soon."

"Ain't no other way?" he asked.

"I'll put in a good word with the D.A."

"HELL NAW RED!" he exclaimed. "I told you I can't do no fuckin' time, man!"

"This call's getting long, Malik."

"Yeah whatever ... ... fuck you want anyway?"

"I need a brand-new black AMG 500SL with a clean V.I.N."

"Is that it, your highness?" he asked, sarcastically.

"No smartass! I need you to switch out all my gear without screwing up anything. Then, I need you to search the car front to back. Think you can handle that?"

"As usual, you want me to do yo lil dirty work. What you looking for anyway?"

I thought about it for a moment. "Anything that shouldn't be there."

"Okay cool, then let me cut it up, Red."

"HELL NO! I need the car back."

"You want that shit done fast, it's gone take longer if I gotta put that bitch back together. I'm just sayin', I got to go scout a mufucka out, I got to steal that bitch, and transport it back, I-"

"Did you just say the word *steal* on an open line with me, boy?"

"Yup!" He laughed. "STEAL, STEAL, STEAL, MOTHAFUCKING GANK THAT BITCH TYPE OF STEALING FOR THE F, B, MOTHAFUCKIN' I!" he exclaimed, letting out the biggest, fiendish laugh ever.

"Whatever, negro—you gonna do this or not?"

"Yeah, it's cool. When you need it though?" he asked.

"Uh, how 'bout right now, big pimpin'?"

"Hell nah, fuck that, Red, I can't do it!" exclaimed Malik.

"So, it's like that?"

"Yeah, it's like that ... ... but, I might be able to put a rush on it if you keep a nigga free, nah-mean?"

"What makes you think I'd do anything for your uncooperative ass?"

Without skipping a beat, he replied, "Because deep down you still love me. That's why you be taking care of me 'cause you know you got mad love for me."

As much as I hated to admit it, he was right. Malik still had my heart even though he had broken it over and over again.

"Red ... yo, Red...!"

"Fine ... I'll pull some strings and team up with LBPD. But you are gonna give me 10 stolens."

"WAIT, WHAT?"

"TEN STOLENS ready for export when we come in ... ... and it's gonna be like next Wednesday, okay? You make sure your black ass is there when I show up too. I'll say you cooperated and make sure you get a deal, but you're shut down permanently, and you gotta give up your little South American buyers too."

"So, I won't do no time?" he asked.

"That's what I said! God Malik you got a one-track mind. So, what you gonna do?"

"Fuckin' crackas don't wanna a nigga to have shit. Bet you ain't comin' down on them white boys back east like this."

"Malik, you're preaching to the choir. I need an answer."

"Yeah ... cool."

"So, we got a deal?" I asked. I needed to hear him say the words.

"Yeah, that's cool we got a deal, Agent Southerland," he said in a high-pitch whiney voice that was surely a stretch for his baritone vocal cords.

"Good, I'll be there in a couple of hours. And, Malik...."

"What?"

"I don't have a lot of time, so no hanky-panky bullshit."

"Yeah whatever man."

"Malik...."

"What?" he asked in a frustrated tone. I could tell I was irritating him.

"Thank you."

"Nah, you ain't got no love for me, man."

"I'll see you soon."

I hung up and continued traveling south. I took the 101 to Venice Beach and pulled up at Malik's around 2:30 p.m. A young man came out and told me to drive around back, so I did. Behind the main building, another guy motioned for me to pull into a large bay. I drove through the doors and parked. There were pieces of cars everywhere and at least a dozen men in coveralls working heavy machinery, removing everything from rims to doors, stereos and convertible tops. From the looks of things, Malik had been busy. He even had a few exotics over in the corner.

"You lookin' for Malik?" asked one of the workers.

I nodded.

"He's in the back," said the young man, pointing to the dimly lit office in the rear of the building.

"Thanks."

"You left the key in?" he asked.

"In the ignition."

"Okay." He hopped inside, started the motor and pulled off.

I walked back and opened the office door. Malik was on the phone, but I stepped inside anyway and closed the door behind me. When he heard the door shut, he looked up.

"Hey, let me call you back," he said. He slammed the phone down and sprung up from his chair. "HEY BABY!" he yelled, grinning big. He ran right up to me and lifted me up off the floor into the biggest bear hug ever given to me by a man. After all that big talk, I guess he was happy to see me.

Malik was dark skinned, six-foot-five, 240 pounds of hard penitentiary muscle, and he smelled good enough to eat. He tried to kiss me on the lips, but I turned my head and made him miss.

He frowned. "So, it's like that?"

I giggled a little. "Put me down boy I said no hanky-panky, remember?"

He set me back down slow and gently. "Yeah, but damn, Red, you finer than eva. I can't help myself."

That made me blush. I pulled my hair back behind my ears on both sides. Seeing Malik kind of messed me up. We kicked it for years, sneaking around behind my boyfriend Bill's back. For whatever reason, I always cheated on Bill. If it wasn't with Malik, it was some other lucky buster. Not sure why I ever got so pissed with Bill for cheating on me ... ... *oh, I remember now, it must have had something to do with him knocking up my whore-ass-of-a-sister in my own fucking goddamn bed, but that's a different story.* If I thought about Bill at that point, I would have started cursing again, and I didn't want anyone to think less of me with the amount of cussing I'd have to do to revisit that fucking shit in the depths of my Christian mind. Keller really messed me up. I had that whole "not cursing" thing under control until his conniving ass showed up.

Malik always took pride in being my number two or three or whatever. In fact, he spent a lot of time cracking jokes at Bill or the *daffodil* as he called him. Believe it or not though, with Malik it was more than just sex. God, we got into all kinds of shit, but then I grew up, I got serious—went to the Navy, got into law enforcement, and we eventually had to part ways for obvious reasons. From that point on, because of where I was at in my life, the only way we talked was as bad cop and two-time felon. I came really close to locking him up myself a few times. He always wanted me to feel bad for him, but he made his choice, and I made mine. Even still, I watched out for him.

"You thirsty?" he asked.

"No thanks. I'm good."

"Nah, you look good, baby." He grinned and showed every tooth in his head like a goofball.

"Thank you." I smiled back and started feeling a little giddy. Malik knew just how to push my buttons. Before long, I was doing that fidgety thing I do when I'm around a guy I really like. I had to put the brakes on that though because I didn't want him to get any bright ideas. This was a business call—nothing more, nothing less.

"I missed you," he confessed.

I sat down on the brown leather sofa against the back wall. He sat down too and put his big strong, muscular arms around me. Malik was a bad boy, but he always made me feel good. On the other hand, I always made him feel guilty, and I saw no need to give up on tradition, so I cut right to the chase.

"You know you wrong, Malik ... you got a Ferrari, a line of Porsches, and I saw a damn Aston Martin back there. What, you thought nobody was gonna miss those cars?"

"Yeah, I kinda fucked up man, I got greedy. On the strength though, I got chips and dip, know what I'm talkin' 'bout!" He laughed, loudly.

"LBPD's coming down hard and fast, Malik, and I ain't talkin' weeks or months here, I'm talking days. I'm giving you a heads up 'cause you're my boy ... you need to get your shit together, but you can't tell your crew, understand?"

"What you mean?"

"Don't you start that shit, man. No point in you trying to do the right thing now," I warned putting up air-quotes. "You can't breathe a word of this to anybody. Not even your little bitch out there."

"But Red, I-"

"What?"

"Red, I'mo be straight witcha ... ... see, I got this one kid, man he ain't bad at all yo, he like 19 and-"

"It's not my investigation," I interrupted sternly. I needed him to understand how much I was putting my neck on the line for him and that there was no room to negotiate. "If it was my case, I'd do everything I could for him, and you know it. But it'd take a miracle for me to jump on board at the last minute and start adding extra confidential informants to the fold. They would be extremely suspicious of both you and me. Hell, we'd be sittin' up in the same cell staring at each other. Keep in mind I'm calling in some serious favors here with my boss, so I have to deliver. Besides, that kid made his choice. He knew the risk."

"So, did I, but you givin' me another chance."

I didn't know what to say really. I just stared into his big brown eyes.

"Check this out Red," he says, pumping up the volume on his infamous *Malik charm*. See, I'll shut this mothafucka down right now, today, I'm talkin' this very second if you leave wit' me." He ran his fingers through my hair.

I looked away. "You know I can't do that," I replied.

"I know you still got mad love for me. Am I right?"

"Malik I-"

He grabbed my head with both hands and pulled me in, gently pressing his lips against mine. I closed my eyes and leaned into him as he pushed his tongue through my lips. I reached around and caressed his back. I love to kiss, and Malik always knew how to make me so hot and wet just from kissing. A rush of passion and memories came over me. I started to feel like there was never any bad blood between us. After a few more kisses, I started to feel how I used to when I heard the sound of his deep, sexy voice over the phone, a feeling I tried to ignore the entire way over. I thought I had will power, but there on that sofa, with his big strong hands all over me, I was powerless to resist the bad man.

With every part of my body, I wanted Malik to take me right there in his office on his dusty leather couch. I wanted to taste him so bad. I needed to feel his body against mine. I longed to take every inch of him deep inside my aching pussy. My desire burned red hot for all of his love. But just when I'd started to fall for his cheap parlor tricks again, the door swung wide open, and an unsuspecting woman stormed in.

"Hey sexy man, I need to—oh holdup—WHAT THE FUCK!" She rolled her neck a few times. "OH HELL NAW! WHO THE FUCK IS THIS GANGLY, BONEY WHITE BITCH YOU GOT UP IN HERE?" she yelled, swinging her arms around like she wanted to fight.

Malik and I looked at each other like, *damn.* I pushed him away and he stood up, with his dick bulging in his pants. He was smiling like a kid caught with his hand in the cookie jar—my cookie jar.

"MOTHAFUCKA!" the half-dressed hoochie mamma screamed. "ERR-TIME I TURN AROUND YOU GOT YO' GODDAMN DICK STUCK UP SOME UGLY ASS HO! I CAN'T STAND YOU NIGGA! SO, WHAT, THIS SWEET BLACK PUSSY AIN'T GOOD ENOUGH FOR YOU? YOU GOT TO GO OUT AND GET SOME STANKIN' CRACKA ASS BITCH. JUST WAIT TILL IT START RAINING UP IN HERE AND HER ASS SMELL LIKE A WET DOG, YOU GONE WANT THAT THEN? SHIT, I'M THROUGH WIT'

YOU NIGGA! THAT WHITE BITCH CAN CLEAN UP AFTER YO' FUNKY ASS AND I-"

"HOLD ON, BITCH!" he yelled.

She threw both hands up. "BITCH? WHO DA FUCK YOU CALLIN' A BITCH, NIGGA?"

"HEY, DON'T BE RAISING YO VOICE UP IN MY MUTHAFUCKIN' OFFICE!" He looked back at me with a sheepish grin. "Wait here, I'll be right back," he whispered.

I just rolled my eyes. Malik walked over, grabbed the girl by the arm and pulled her out of the office, shutting the door behind them. At first, I was going to say something to her, but I realized how much alike she seemed compared to a younger version of me. Years ago, that could've been me yelling at some no-good man, embarrassing myself. To be honest, I felt sorry for her.

Malik and his girlfriend were outside his office, but even with the door shut, I could still hear their foolishness. He told her to go wait in the front office, but she wasn't trying to hear that at all. After a few more outbursts, she finally gave in to his charms—everybody does. I saw them walk off together through the partially opened blinds. I leaned back on the sofa and laughed. Truth be told, I was happy she showed up. My pussy was wet, and my heart was pounding. Malik had a cock that could make Superman cower in his cape and tremble down on the floor in the fetal position. As horny as I was, that fine ass chocolate man was damn sure gonna get anything and everything he ever wanted. Hell, that girl probably saved me at least three months of drama.

After about 20 minutes, Malik finally came back in. As soon as he walked through the door, I got up off the sofa just to be on the safe side. No sense stumbling off into the same trap twice.

"That ho trippin' man. Sorry 'bout that Red, where were we?"

He moved over and tried to put his arms around me again, but I smacked his hands away and started looking at the pictures he had up on the walls.

"Malik, you ain't changed," I said softly.

"What...?"

I let out a big sigh of relief. "It's not even worth it," I replied. "Did you get my ride?"

He frowned up. "So, it's back to business now, huh?"

I shrugged my shoulders. "Well...?"

"Yeah, I got it for yo' ungrateful high-yella ass," he said proudly. "Damn sure wasn't easy though, considering the time frame, but you know we gone make it do what it do, baby."

"Well, I been in here a while already, so it's ready right?"

"Almost," he replied. "I just saw they moved the equipment and all your police shit over."

"And the equipment's working, right?" I asked.

He threw both hands up. "Come on now Red, who you talking to?"

I grinned and rolled my eyes.

"Jimmy back there workin' the V.I.N. now," he said. "He'll swap the plates in a minute. Yo', you mad?"

His dumb, rhetorical question triggered a brief Blondie moment. I walked right into him and rubbed the front of his pants. I tongue-kissed him slowly and massaged his dick through his slacks until it nearly busted out through the zipper.

"I hate you," I whispered softly, and then punched him as hard as I could.

"Damn, that's cold," he said, hopping foot-to-foot and grabbing his crotch.

I walked out of the office, rubbing my knuckles, which were a little tender from punching Malik's rock-hard six-pack. He followed me out walking funny, trying to shake off his hard on. We walked together back up to the middle of the bay. The girl who'd busted up our little moment had wandered back in and was standing nearby, looking like she wanted to cut me.

"I TOLD YOU TO WAIT UP FRONT!" Malik yelled. "THE FUCK'S WRONG WIT' YOU?"

"FUCK YOU NIGGA!" she hollered, "I'LL WAIT WHEREVA-THE-FUCK I FEEL!"

He sighed. "Silly bitch," he said under his breath, "...anyway, like I was sayin'-"

"Malik," I interrupted.

"What?" he snapped.

"Stay focused, this is serious. Now, there may be something in there, something valuable to some really bad guys. You find it, I want you to hide it in the safest place you got, and don't talk to anybody about it. I'll be back Monday."

"Baby, I eat bad guys for breakfast."

"MALIK, I'M NOT JOKING!" I exclaimed.

"I got you baby. So, you gonna be working out here again?"

"For a minute," I replied. "I gotta run to New York, but I'll be out here next week, maybe for a few months. Why?"

"Listen, I need you to be careful out there fightin' crime and shit," he warned.

"Awe, you gettin' soft on me?"

"Soft? Fuck soft I just wanna take you home where you belong."

"And, what about her?"

"Oh, that bitch right there? She just entertainment," he boasted.

"Like I said, you ain't changed boy. I gotta go."

He didn't say another word, he just gave me a big hug, and I damn near melted in his strong arms.

"Go back out front," said Malik. "Jimmy'll pull your new joint around."

"Thanks."

"You know what..." he smiled really big. "What?"

"Never mind."

"No, what's up Malik?"

"Let me swoop you up Monday when you get back so we can talk."

I nodded. "Yeah, I can do that."

"A'ight. Now, get out of here ole big head-ass girl."

I smiled a little. "Thanks babe."

Malik turned his attention back to his woman. They were arguing before I could get out the door. I walked out the bay and headed towards the front of the property. There, I waited outside the front office for Jimmy, all the while thinking about Malik's crazy butt. After a few more minutes, Jimmy finally pulled up. He got out and held the door open for me.

"Thanks Jimmy."

"It's what I do," he replied confidently. "See ya 'round." Then, he jogged back to the building.

Malik and his crew were good. If I didn't know any better, the car Jimmy drove up was the exact same car I'd brought in. I sat in the driver seat with my eyes closed for a minute, thinking about the times Malik and I had shared. Truth be told, I really did miss him. Despite all the bullshit, I was definitely looking forward to seeing him again. I couldn't wait until Monday. After being that close to him, I needed a drink. Scratch that, I needed an entire bottle of something strong.

I cleared my thoughts and got back on the road. The low speed bumper-to-bumper freeway traffic was irritating to say the least, but I managed to endure it. I arrived home after what seemed like 10 hours of *Car Wars*. I parked, grabbed my mail, and ran upstairs. I walked inside the apartment and dropped my keys and cell phone on the entryway table. Then, I grabbed a couple of suitcases out of the hallway closet. I drug them into the bedroom, opened them up on the bed, and started packing. I stuffed everything I could into those two little bags. The weather in Southern California was pleasant, but the Big Apple would not be as forgiving, so I threw a full-length coat onto the bed too.

I needed to do something with my hair, but it was already 4 p.m., so I pulled it back into a pony tail and stuffed it under my shower cap. I took a quick hot shower, and then jumped into the clothes I'd laid out. Talk about multitasking, I was moving at warp speed, stepping into my shoes and fastening a few shirt buttons with one hand while spraying on perfume with the other.

There was no telling the conditions inside our target location up in New York, so I figured it best to prepare for the worst. I collected two Smith and Wesson SW9F's, one shoulder holster, a hip holster, some ammo, and four 17 shot magazines from the safe. Then, I sat down on the bed and filled each clip with hollow point bullets. The shoulder holster, one of the guns and all the extra clips went in the smaller of my two suitcases, but I clipped the hip rig onto my belt and holstered my other gun. I was ready to roll, so I took my coat into the living room and dropped it on the sofa. At that point, it was time to get everything organized and ready for departure.

I walked back into the entryway where I'd left my purse and other stuff. I clipped on my cell, put my keys in my purse and slipped it onto my shoulder. Then, I realized my hip was feeling a little lighter than usual. I pulled out my gun to check it, and man was I glad I did—the damn thing was empty. I set it down on the table, threw my purse on the sofa and ran back into the bedroom.

In my haste, I'd put all four clips in my bag, so I fished one out and went back into the entryway where I loaded my gun. Just before I had a chance to re-holster it, the doorbell rang. Without thinking, I reached over and partially opened the door.

There was a man and a woman standing in the hallway. They looked like cops, so I gave them attitude.

"CAN I HELP YOU?" I yelled.

"Are you Anna Johnson?" the man asked. "Is this your place?"

"WHO WANTS TO KNOW?"

"Detectives Marshall and Dillinger, L.A.P.D Homicide," said the man, flashing his badge up so I could see it. "Can we speak with you for a moment, Ms. Johnson?"

"I don't have time for this shit," I whispered, "I need a fuckin' drink."

"Ms. Johnson...?" he asked.

"I'm busy, but feel free to come back later."

I tried to push the door closed, but he stuck his hand out and stopped me from closing it.

"This'll just take a moment ... may we come in?"

I sighed. "Show me your badge again?"

He held up his shield one more time.

"Does your sidekick have one?" I asked.

The woman moved her jacket to the side to reveal her badge which was clipped to her belt.

I looked at my watch and sighed. "You got 10 minutes."

I swung open the door, and their eyes immediately zoomed in on my pistol. The woman panicked and reached for her weapon, but I stepped back and holstered my gun before she had time to draw.

"PUT A LEASH ON TRIGGER OR SHE'LL HAVE TO WAIT OUTSIDE!" I exclaimed.

"You got a permit for that weapon?" asked Marshall.

"You got a warrant for this visit?"

Marshall's eyes got big. "Do we need to get one?" he asked.

"I'm pressed for time, Detective. You wanna talk, come in, otherwise, have a nice day." I let go of the door and walked towards the kitchen.

Naturally, they came in and cautiously followed me, looking all around the apartment and being nosey. I didn't pay them much attention at all because the thirst-demons were calling, and I had to feed them fast. I took a glass from the cabinet and grabbed an unopened carton of orange juice from the fridge. The date on the juice was old. I must've bought it the last time I was in California, but it was nice and cold, so I didn't care. "You guys want something?" I asked, measuring out a half glass of juice.

"No thanks," said Marshall. Dillinger didn't respond.

"Suit yourselves." I grabbed a bottle of gin from another cabinet and topped off my O.J. Then, I mixed it all together with my finger.

"You drink a lot, Ms. Johnson?" asked Marshall, staring at my glass.

"You know a lot of drunks, Detective?" I retorted, sucking my finger dry.

He gave me a strange look.

"Nice apartment, Ms. Johnson," said Dillinger, "what do you do for a living?"

I ignored her, partly because she tried to draw down on me outside, but primarily because she looked dumb as a bag of hammers.

"Ms. Johnson, you drive a black Mercedes Benz?" she asked.

Again, I completely ignored her, which seemed to irritate her even more. I sipped my drink and rolled my eyes. "Detective Marshall, what can I help you with?"

"What kind of car do you drive?" he asked.

"Oh, I get it ... you're parking police. I'll clear those tickets up right away, no worries." I took an unladylike gulp and set my glass down on the counter.

They both looked like they were quickly approaching wits end with me. I smiled and walked out of the kitchen down the hallway to the bedroom. I returned with my two suitcases and placed them on the floor next to my laptop bag.

"Leaving town, Ms. Johnson?" asked Dillinger.

"You're not too bright are you sweetie?"

Dillinger grew angry. "LET ME TELL YOU SOMETHING I-"

"Ms. Johnson, do you know this man?" interrupted Marshall. He took a photo from his inner jacket pocket and held it up so I could get a good look. It was a picture of some old dude in a white lab coat.

I took a glance and replied, "Nope."

"He was killed last week in a car accident."

"Homicide detectives work traffic? Look, I'm sorry to hear it, but I have an impeccable driving record. I didn't do it. Now, if you'll excuse me-"

"I bet you'd be more cooperative if I drag your Gucci wearing ass down to the station?"

"Hang on Dillinger!" said Marshall. "Ms. Johnson, please take a look at one more photo?"

"Is she always this simple?" I asked.

"Cunt," mumbled Dillinger loud enough for me to hear.

At that point, I was ready to beat her ass, and I didn't mind her knowing. I stepped to her, but Marshall intervened.

"WHOA!" he exclaimed.

"Ron she's armed and uncooperative. We need to take her in."

"Hold on, Dillinger. Listen, Ms. Johnson, we're not here to give you a hard time-"

"You expect me to believe that?"

"Please, just take a look at the photo. Please?" he asked. I cut my eyes at Dillinger, and then reluctantly looked at the picture. I almost hit the floor. It was Jeremy Taylor. Turns out I was actually interested in what they had to say after all. I felt a little like a jackass.

"No," I lied, "I don't know him either."

"You sure?" he asked.

"Positive."

"You don't know him, huh?" Dillinger crossed her arms and frowned.

"That's what I said," I replied.

"So, you don't know him...? I can't believe this shit!" She started fidgeting around and shaking her head. "Then maybe you can explain how the hell you're-"

"Give me a break here, Dillinger," said Marshall, waving his hands, motioning for her to calm down. He turned back to me, "The man in the first photo was Robert Taylor. His brakes were tampered with. He went through a red light and got side swiped by a tractor trailer. He died on the way to the hospital."

"Okay, but what does this have to do with me?"

"We're hoping you could tell us," he responded.

"I don't know what you're talking about," I said, "and frankly, you're starting to irritate me."

"Six months ago, the Taylors reported their son Jeremy missing. Missing Persons hasn't come up with anything yet, but I got a call yesterday from a black and white, says he spotted Jeremy's car in the area. It's a black AMG Mercedes."

"And...?"

"The V.I.N. matches the car outside parked in your space."

"I doubt that."

Sighing with frustration, Dillinger was about to mouth off again, but Marshall preempted her.

"Hang on," he said. "Look, Ms. Johnson, we know you're driving his car."

"I AM NOT!" I yelled.

"Is he here?" asked Dillinger.

I raised my voice even higher. "What the hell are you people talking about?"

"Listen, if he's here, we need to talk to him about his father."

"I live alone, Detective Marshall."

"Is he in back?" asked Dillinger, moving in closer. She had a real fucked up look in her eyes.

"No, you don't understand...." I turned around and walked over to the sofa to get my purse, but then froze in my tracks when I heard a familiar clicking sound behind me.

"DON'T MOVE!"

Slowly, I looked back over my shoulder. Dillinger was pointing her gun at me. Marshall advanced, wide-eyed with one hand extended in a halting position and the other on his gun, which at the time was still holstered.

"WHOA, EVERYBODY JUST CALM DOWN!" he exclaimed.

"I'm reaching for my badge," I said. "Lower your weapon, so I can show it to you without getting shot in the back."

"Put the gun down, Dillinger," commanded Marshall. "PUT THE GODDAMN GUN DOWN!"

She wouldn't budge, so I took a chance. "I'm gonna hold up my badge ... DON'T SHOOT! DON'T SHOOT!" Slowly, I turned around and held up my badge. "DOJ, don't shoot."

"THIS IS BULLSHIT!" she said, dropping her gun to her side.

Marshall rubbed his forehead and sighed. "Dillinger, go wait for me in the car."

"But, Ron, I-"

"NOW!" he yelled.

Her face turned damn near purple. It looked as if she'd stopped breathing. She gave me one more funny look, and then turned and stormed out of the apartment.

Marshall collapsed onto a chair and rubbed his face in his hands.

I rolled my eyes. "Make yourself at home, detective." I walked back to the counter to finish my drink.

"Why didn't you identify yourself?" he sighed.

"I'm working a case. Would you go waiving your badge around like a flag if you were in the middle of an investigation?" I asked. "Come on, you're a detective."

"Guess I deserved that."

"So, are you like your partner? Quick on the draw and wet on the wick?"

He stood up. "I'm smart enough to know you're wearing Manolos, not Gucci."

"So, it's not just police work with you, detective?" I picked up my glass of gin and juice. "At least you're not as dumb as she made you both look." My hand shook a little as I lifted my glass to my mouth. Somehow that old ass orange juice seemed tastier since I'd almost gotten shot. I don't care how many times you have a gun stuck in your face, it's still very disturbing.

I slammed my empty glass down onto the counter.

"So, what do you know about the Taylor family?" he asked.

"That's classified." I grabbed the bottle of gin and poured a little more into my glass.

Marshall rubbed his head with both hands. "Is Jeremy in custody?"

"Classified," I replied, swallowing my shot of gin. It burned the back of my throat like lemon juice on a deep cut.

"You're not making this easy for me, Johnson."

"Special Agent Johnson, and I have many tasks, but none involve making life easy for the L.A.P.D. You people sure as hell don't make it easy for me."

"I'll impound the car!" he threatened.

"Your 10 minutes are up, and I have a plane to catch." I picked up my laptop bag and strapped it along with my purse onto my shoulder. Then, I extended the handle on the small suitcase and rolled it across the room towards the door. "You mind helping a lady out?" I pointed towards the larger bag near the sofa.

Marshall looked over at my large suitcase. "Oh yeah, sure." He picked it up by the handle and followed me to the door.

"Please, Agent Johnson," he said, lugging my suitcase downstairs.

"Please what?"

"Help me out on this one."

"Why should I?" I asked. "I don't know you from a can of paint."

"I'm the guy helping you with your bags, remember?"

I looked back over my shoulder. "I'll give it to you Detective, you are quick on your feet."

He chuckled, but I didn't skip a beat. I kept moving fast down the stairs. Out at the car, I opened the trunk and put my bag inside. Then, I circled around to the driver side while Marshall loaded my other bag. I tossed my laptop and purse on the passenger seat, got in, and started the motor. Marshall closed the trunk and walked around to the driver side window. He knocked on the glass a few times. I pushed the button for the convertible top.

"I'll be straight with you," he said, leaning down over the window as the top retracted, "I got a dead scientist and a missing boy. So far, I got nothing except you. I'd appreciate anything at all you think might be helpful."

"Marshall, I have to go, but here...." I reached down in my purse and pulled out a fake business card. I held it up to his face. "Call me next week and I'll see what I can do on my end, okay?"

"Thank you. I appreciate it," he took the card and studied it for a moment. "Seriously, thank you ... and I apologize for-"

"Goodbye, Detective."

I checked the rearview and backed out of my space. Trigger Dillinger was behind me taking pictures, so I didn't waste any time. I burned out of the parking lot.

As I headed towards the airfield, I tried to process what just happened in my mind, filtering it for any reason to be suspicious, but I couldn't find a single one. It's no secret, in law enforcement, one hand never seems to know what the other's up to, so I wasn't surprised they didn't know Taylor was already dead. I'm not sure DEA would offer up that information anyway with an ongoing investigation. The only real thing that stuck out like a sore thumb was what Marshall said about the father—said he was a scientist—a murdered scientist at that. No one on the inside told me, so they're either just as inept as I feared, or I'm being played.

It was after 6:00 p.m. when I left the apartment, so I had to boogie. Traffic was unusually light. I arrived at the airfield right at 7:00 p.m. All DTP team members were already on board. I parked near the runway, grabbed my bags from the trunk, and ran towards the plane.

"Good evening, Ms. Johnson," greeted a young man, jogging towards me. "Here, let me take your bags."

"Thank you," I said.

"You doing alright tonight?" he asked.

"Yes, I'm fine."

"Remember to check your weapon before entering the passenger cabin," he reminded.

"I'll be sure to do that."

"Enjoy your flight, Ms. Johnson."

"Thanks," I replied.

I climbed up the stairs and boarded the private jet. After logging in, I gave my gun to the agent on duty, who secured it in a safe behind the cockpit. I walked back to the passenger cabin where everyone was already strapped in.

"I see you all made it here alright," I said, standing in the middle of the aisle. "Equipment?"

"On board," replied Hughes, "we got weapons and communications gear stashed in the cargo bay."

"And, transportation?" I asked.

"Vehicles are waiting on the ground at J.F.K.," said Hughes.

"Good work, doctor."

"Ms. Johnson," greeted a flight attendant.

I knew what she wanted. "Yes?"

"The Captain's ready for takeoff. Please take your seat and fasten your seatbelt."

I complied.

"Thank you," she said. "Now, would you like anything before takeoff?"

"A pillow and a blanket," I replied, unable to stop myself from yawning.

She grabbed a couple of pillows and a blanket from an overhead compartment and gave them to me. "If you need anything else, please let me know. My name is Sharon."

"Thank you, Sharon."

I checked around to make sure no one was being nosey, and then pulled out a little bottle of Jack I always keep in my purse in case of emergency. The gin and juice I had back at the apartment merely wet my beak. I had to get something serious in my system. I unscrewed the top and gulped down my drink in lightning speed. Last thing I needed was a bunch of pencil-pushing dickheads talking about me drinking on the job and blowing my cover, but I couldn't wait till I got to the hotel. It was worth the risk.

After that drink, I was all good again. I switched off my cabin light and positioned my pillows right behind my head. I leaned my chair back, unfolded the blanket and pulled it up to my chin. I shut my eyes while the captain made his announcement.

"Ladies and gentlemen, this is your captain, Richard Porter. Welcome aboard. We're proud to provide nonstop service to New York. Flight time is approximately three hours, 30 minutes. Our Inflight Specialist is Ms. Sharon West. Federal regulations prohibit smoking and alcohol on all flights; however, there's plenty of juice and water available, just ask Ms. West. We're third in line for takeoff, so we should be departing in about five minutes. Please ensure all cell phones are powered off and your safety belt is fastened securely. Thank you for joining us, and we hope you enjoy your flight."

Once the tower cleared us for takeoff, we taxied up to the runway. Captain Porter accelerated to takeoff speed and we ascended into the westward bound sky. We did a 180 degree turn over the ocean. I was so exhausted, I dozed off mid-bank. It's strange, I spend most nights in bed staring at the ceiling, but I never have a problem in the air. That night, I slept like a baby.

Chapter 5

Apparently, we ran into some bad weather on the way to New York—at least that's what they told me after I woke up. We touched down at J.F.K. around 11:30 p.m. and deplaned just before midnight. As soon as I stepped outside, the cold New York air hit my face like a ton of bricks. I started feeling nostalgic, but then I remembered leaving my coat on the sofa back in L.A. and I panicked a little. Those homicide detectives were so irritating, they made me forget my coat. It was so cold outside.

There were two Ford Crown Victorias and a black Chevy van parked near the runway waiting on us. I caught a glimpse of them and didn't waste a second. I clasped my suit jacket together in the front, and then ran full speed straight to the vehicles. Thankfully, somebody was smart enough to leave them running with the heat on. I hopped in the driver seat of the first Crown Vic and turned the heater fan up on high. I held my hands right in front of the vents to get them warm. The team loaded up. Nobody wanted to ride with me, but that was cool. I needed some quiet time anyway.

After a while, we finally rolled out and headed for the Four Seasons in Manhattan, a much fancier hotel than I expected a group of government workers should stay in, but who am I to judge. On the way, I tried to clear my thoughts and concentrate on the road, but my mind was working overtime. I couldn't stop wondering about Taylor's father and how they both were connected to Tesh. Maybe he was working for Tesh, but what was he working on? A bomb, bio-weapon? There's no telling, but I knew the faster I found the leak in DTP, the closer I'd be to getting some real answers.

We took the Van Wyck Expressway towards New York and got off on Exit 10 for Grand Central Parkway. By the time we reached the FDR Drive toll, my head was filled with wild conspiracy theories. None of them made sense, but I find it beneficial to play out multiple scenarios in the depths of my mind. We followed FDR Drive south into New York City, home sweet home. By the time we hit 63rd street, I was grinning like a little schoolgirl. The hotel was right around the corner.

We pulled up to the front of the hotel at 12:45 a.m. The team raced inside, but I took my dear sweet time unloading. I didn't turn the heater down in the car at all. I think if I could've turned the temperature up anymore the vents would've singed my eyebrows. I stepped outside the car and enjoyed the freezing-cold, brisk air for as long as my overheated body could stand. By the time I entered the lobby, everyone except Agent Sullivan had checked in and cleared out. When I walked up, she was leaning across the front desk speaking with who appeared to be the night manager. I placed my small bag on the floor right beside the big roller bag and patiently waited my turn.

There was a porter standing nearby with Sullivan's luggage, neatly stacked on a cart. Sullivan thanked the woman she was speaking with and slowly walked towards the elevator, motioning for the young man to follow her.

I moved up to the desk and gave the manager my phony ID.

"Welcome to the Four Seasons Ms. Johnson," she greeted, "how are you?"

"A little tired, but otherwise I'm fine. Thanks for asking."

"You're welcome," she replied. "This will just take a moment."

I waited while she searched the computer.

"I'm sorry Ms. Johnson, but I don't have a reservation for you."

I raised an eyebrow and paused for a moment. "Okay, no problem, I'll take whatever you have."

"Actually, there's a conference here, and ... well ... we're all booked up."

I was about to trip, but then I felt someone breathing down my neck. I turned around and Sullivan was all up on me, violating my personal space.

"Trouble, Boss?" she asked, smiling.

"No." I turned back around. "Can you call a nearby hotel for me?" I asked softly.

The lady behind the desk smiled. "Sure, where would you like for me-"

"That's crazy!" interrupted Sullivan, advancing to the counter.

"They're overbooked, Sullivan," I said. "I'll just get a room down the street and meet you guys here in the morning."

"Absolutely not, you can bunk with me."

"No ... uh, no I couldn't ... well, I'm sure you prefer your privacy, so-"

"Don't be silly, it's a suite," she bragged. "There's plenty of room, and we'll be saving our country money. Come on." She grabbed my small bag and took off towards the elevators.

It didn't take a rocket scientist to know how much I'd regret that decision later, but I was tired and didn't really feel like stumbling around in the cold trying to find another hotel, so I reluctantly gave in.

I tapped my hand down on the counter a few times. "Thanks for your help," I said politely.

She smiled. "You're welcome." Then, she pushed my ID back across to me.

I picked up my ID, grabbed my other bag by the handle, and followed Sullivan into the elevator. We went up to the top floor and got off the elevator. Sullivan's suite was actually more like a mansion than a hotel room. It was definitely one of the nicest rooms I'd been in, and believe me, I've been in some nice ones. I almost got excited, but then I remembered she was probably up to something, so I promptly calmed down before she noticed.

Inside the room, the young porter unloaded Sullivan's truckload of luggage. He really had a job on his hands. While he worked, Sullivan disappeared in the back. I took a moment to look around. I gazed upon the impressive décor for a few minutes before realizing I forgot my laptop in the car, so I excused myself.

"Sullivan, I'm going down to the car, I'll be right back."

"OKAY," she yelled, "THERE'S AN EXTRA KEY ON THE ENTRY TABLE."

I looked at the small console table near the door, and sure enough there was a room key sitting there for me. I grabbed the key, and then took the ice bucket from the counter on the way out. I felt dehydrated for some reason. Maybe the plane ride dried me out—that or a lack of booze. Either way, a glass of ice water was just what the doctor ordered.

I took my time going back out to the car. Once I got to it, I put the ice bucket on the hood, so I could unlock the doors. I opened the back-driver side door and grabbed my laptop bag from the seat. With my laptop strapped up on my shoulder, I closed the car door and pressed the lock button on the remote. The park lights flashed on and off and the doors locked. It was cold out, but the fresh, well-polluted New York air was refreshing. I stood there for a few minutes, reminiscing on the good old days before everything got so complicated, but my hands were beginning to shake a little, so I grabbed the ice bucket and headed back inside.

It took a minute to find an ice machine, but I finally got lucky. I filled up the ice bucket and made my way back to the elevators. Aside from Vanessa Sullivan's strange behavior, I didn't know jack about her. I'm a fairly private person too, so I figured I'd give her the same courtesy I expect to receive in return and announce myself before going back in the room. I opened the door about halfway, and then knocked. "Sullivan...? I'm back," I said, but she didn't respond, so I went ahead and stepped inside. "Sullivan, I'm back," I repeated. I heard her in her room talking softly to someone on the phone.

"I'm not playing your sick little game anymore," she whispered, "I don't care ... Fuck you, you son-of-a-bitch, this is gone too far ... Look, I gotta go." She slammed the phone down. "HEY BOSS," she yelled. "You were gone almost 20 minutes. I was beginning to think you weren't coming back."

"Yeah, I couldn't find an ice machine."

"Uh, it's the Four Seasons not the Holiday Inn Express," she said, sarcastically. "Not too many vending machines around here. We do room service."

I walked up to her bedroom door, which was wide open. I peeked around the corner into her room. She'd changed into casualwear and was putting on some earrings. I stepped inside the doorway with the ice bucket tucked under my left arm.

"Nice room," I said, looking around.

"Not bad, huh?" she replied, smiling. "I keep this place all year round just in case. I actually lived here for about two years, so I know the employees. They pretty much let me do whatever I want. You're over there," she pointed to the smaller bedroom directly across from hers.

I looked back. The door was open, and from a distance, everything inside looked neat and tidy, just how I like it.

"Thanks for letting me stay here tonight. I'm sure there will be some rooms available tomorrow."

"No sweat, boss," she replied. "Listen, the guys and I are headed out. Why don't you let me buy you a drink?"

"Uh, thanks, but no thanks."

"Not interested?" She smiled and said, "Come on, my treat."

"Maybe next time," I responded.

"Not much of a drinker? I bet I know what you want." Sullivan replied, seductively. Then, she laughed out loud.

I instantly lost my grip on the ice bucket. It fell, hit the floor, and the top flew off. Ice cubes scattered all over the carpet into the entryway to her room. I stood there for a moment a little confused. I'm not sure if it was because I thought this woman was trying to run game on me or because I didn't want her to stop. I snapped out of it and dropped down to get the ice. I flipped the bucket right side up and used the top to scoop the ice up.

"You okay?" asked Sullivan, rushing over to help.

She kneeled right beside me. God, she smelled good.

"First time with a woman, huh?" she said, teasing, laughing, and picking up ice with both hands. Each time she dropped another handful into the bucket she laughed loudly.

It was at that very moment I understood exactly what the team meant about her getting what she wanted. She had an overpowering presence. She acted as if she already knew I was captivated by her, and like any good predator, she was making her move. Little did she know, I didn't even like women like that, but oddly, all I could think about was how soft her skin looked and how it might feel against my body.

I'm not bisexual or a lesbian or whatever. I mean, people have a right to do what makes them happy, but gays are sickening to me. Maybe that's not the right thing to say. I just don't respond well to those kinds of advances. I remember my roommate in college tried over and over again. I was young, barely 16-years-old, and I didn't know what I wanted in life. All I ever knew was Bill, for the most part, but there she was telling people I was her girl. I don't roll like that. She never had clothes on in the room, and every time she got drunk, which was just about every night, she'd make a "mistake" and end up in my bed. Whenever she climbed in bed with me, I'd kick that ho right back out onto the floor. She was crazy, but I had to live with her, so I just avoided her as much as possible. I see a lot of dykes out playing husband and wife, especially in California, but that's ridiculous to me. I like man-meat way too much.

I have absolutely no desire whatsoever to be with another woman—never have, never will. But confusing as it may sound, if there was ever to be an exception, maybe Sullivan was it. When I first saw her back in L.A., she made the whole dyke thing make sense to me. Or, maybe that woman was just some kind of vampire that could place you under her trance with one look. Unfortunately, Blondie is much like a chameleon. She'll change her stripes in a New York second if she suspects there's an orgasm waiting at the end of the tunnel or the bottom of a glass. Down on that floor with "Count Sullivan," all of a sudden Blondie was Transylvanian. Apparently, having no interest in women whatsoever was a minor, unimportant detail to Blondie because damn the ice, I wanted Sullivan to lay me down and use me like a prison bitch until there was a big wet spot on the floor between my legs.

I started breathing heavily and even sweating a little down my back. Sullivan had the body of an exotic goddess, the kind of woman you might find downtown working the pole at a popular gentleman's club. She could definitely get it, and I think she was picking up on that, so as soon as the ice was back in the bucket, I launched myself off the floor to get away from her. I may be crazy, but I ain't stupid.

I walked back into the living room and set the ice bucket on the bar. Then, I picked my laptop bag up off the floor and set it down on the table.

"Don't worry about getting more ice," Sullivan said, walking up close to me, "I'll call room service for you, okay?"

"No, um ... I'm fine," I frowned and lowered my head down a little to avoid eye contact. "I'll just grab a coffee."

"How 'bout you just come go with us. Surely they have coffee where we're going." She smiled big again. "Maybe get warmed up and have a few drinks with us? The night is young."

"It's late, and ... I ... I've got a lot to catch up on. You guys go ahead without me."

"Suit yourself, boss lady, I'm out."

She left the suite, and finally, I exhaled. I'd been holding my breath ever since I smelled her perfume down on the floor. She made me so hot, I didn't know what to do, but I knew turning it all over to Blondie would've been a career ending move. It's not just the whole sex with a woman thing either. I was investigating the entire DTP team, and Sullivan may have been suspect number one. No way could I explain that. Blondie was always around for the booty call, but nowhere to be found when my booty got strapped to the hot seat or my head on the chopping block. I had to be smarter. Besides, that was probably Sullivan's plan—get me in the sack and discredit my investigation—my fake investigation. Things were getting complicated.

I felt a cold sensation in my right palm. I held my hand up and realized I was still holding a piece of ice. I rubbed it on my neck and chest to cool down. Then, I went back into the kitchen to put on a pot of coffee. While it brewed, I rolled my bags into my room. Then, I unpacked them and arranged my clothes neatly in the dresser drawers. I put my underwear in the top drawer, and then tops and bottoms down below. I put my guns and ammo in the nightstand near the bed, and then changed into some shorts and a matching top. By the time I returned to the kitchen, my coffee was ready, so I poured myself a cup and sat down at the table. I was just about to take a sip when I noticed the clock on the wall. It was almost 2:00 a.m. Drinking coffee that late was the last thing I needed with my growing insomnia. I just decided to hit the sack.

I poured the coffee down the sink. I stretched and yawned, and then my eyes caught sight of just what the doctor ordered—the wet bar. I must confess, my weakness isn't exactly kryptonite. I grabbed a few of the little bottles and snuck back into my room like a kid with a new toy. Before the door to my room could close fully, I'd already downed one bottle. Then, it was straight to business— drinking, drinking, and more drinking, then flossing and brushing my teeth. I wrapped my hair as best I could with blurry vision, and then I drank one more bottle of whatever it was to help me sleep. I took my shorts and top off, folded them up, and put them back in the dresser drawer. Then, I pulled back the covers and jumped into bed.

The obviously expensive, white satin sheets were nice and cold against my skin. They felt so good. I rolled over on each side, trying to get comfortable. Finally, I settled down on my left side with one arm tucked under the pillow. With my legs curled up almost in the fetal position, I pulled the covers up to my ears and closed my eyes.

The day had taken its toll on me, and the nap on the plane didn't seem to help as much as it should have. I was still tired. When I fall asleep in bed, it's never right away. I can lay in bed for hours and somehow still not fall asleep, but that night I got lucky. I dozed off after maybe 20 minutes.

I couldn't have been asleep for long when I heard my door open. At first, I thought I was dreaming, but then something hit the floor. I opened my eyes and looked at the clock on the nightstand. It was 4:35 a.m. Before I could even process the fact that someone woke me up for no good reason, that same someone pulled back the covers and climbed into bed with me. I was half sleep and a little drunk, so I didn't have it all together, but whoever it was, they didn't belong in my room, and they damn sure shouldn't've been in bed with me.

"Who the fuck...?" I pushed and shoved trying to squirm out of bed, but the prowler grabbed me by the wrists and pulled me back into the sweetest of smells. I knew then exactly who it was.

"Shhhh," whispered Sullivan, pulling me close to her naked body. Her breath was that of a hardcore drunk, which instantly turned me on way more than being down on my knees, picking up ice off the floor with her. Somehow, vulnerable just didn't say it.

"STOP!" My speech was unsurprisingly slurred. I was still drunk. "You're in my fucking room Sullivan. You shouldn't be in here." Admittedly, if my tone was a measure of how much I wanted her to turn me loose, it was less than convincing.

I shoved her, but she didn't stop grabbing on me. She told me to be quiet and proceeded to yank my body all the way into hers. She was so strong. I shivered at the touch of her warm skin. She was nearly suffocating me, pulling my face in between her huge, natural breasts. I moved my head side to side and convinced myself I was trying to break free. Sullivan's nipples were erect and hard to the touch. She ran her fingers down between us and teased my belly button. I tried to push her away, but she wasn't having it. Honestly, neither was I. She squeezed my tits—first one, and then the other.

"Stop," I whispered, softly.

Of all the things that could've gone wrong, that was surely the worst. Despite my efforts to come to my senses, in my mind, all I could see was that psycho slut, Blondie, across the room with her legs spread wide, rubbing her kitty and licking her lips, watching us. Naturally, I gave in. She was the only being in the world who knew just how much I wanted Sullivan to do bad things to me. Yes, Blondie's probably the cause of all the worst things that have ever happened to me, but that never stops her from being right. After spending my entire life being the most vicious, homophobic bitch on God's green earth, at that moment, all I wanted was for Sullivan to take me by force the way Bill used to when I pissed him off.

Sullivan rolled me over and wrapped her legs around me, grinding from behind.

"Oh baby," she moaned, forcing her hand between my thighs. She rubbed my clit and teased it with two fingers.

I felt like I was going to cum already.

"Oh, God! Fuck! No, wait!"

Sullivan was so busy. It was like she had eight hands, all over me, all at the same time. I got hotter and wetter by the moment, but I was still in control up to that point, or at least I hoped so. I knew it had gone too far, and I was going to put a stop to it, but when she squeezed and tugged at my clit with her fingers, I lost it.

"Wait, oh my, you fuckin' ... no ... Sull... STOP!"

Again, I tried to break free, but as it turns out, Sullivan actually had the upper hand. She snatched off my head wrap and pulled my hair down. She continued grinding her pussy on my ass and rubbing my clit with her fingers, faster and harder with every passing moment. She moved my hair out of the way and kissed me right between my shoulders. Then, out of nowhere, she bit me.

"FUCK!" I clinched my pillow.

Sullivan had me completely off kilter. She forced me over from my side down onto my stomach, and then moved under the covers, spreading my butt cheeks and planting her face right between them. My mouth was saying no, but my body didn't get the memo. I hiked my ass up, giving her full, unrestricted access. She spanked me with her right hand and snatched my hair back with the left, making me arch my back while she circled my asshole with the tip of her tongue. Then, she spit on it and forced her tongue inside.

"When you fuck me," Sullivan mumbled, licking, tonguing and sucking my wet asshole, "you fuck me like this." She kissed and fingered and spanked and moaned down under the covers. "Make me your little bitch just like this, oh, mmm, yesss!"

Even with all my surreptitious acts, I was a novice in Sullivan's hands. My God, the things she did to me—I mean, for starters, no one ever spit on my asshole before. I was in virgin territory. Sullivan worked her long-wet tongue inside me, delivering pleasure like I'd never experienced from any man. She worked two fingers inside my dripping wet pussy and continued French kissing my ass. It was all so dirty and nasty, and I loved every bit of it. My thighs trembled as I came uncontrollably.

How could I let this happen was the question in the back of my mind, but at that point it was so far back there, it didn't make one bit of difference. I wanted her to fuck me like a dirty whore, but knowing full well what was at stake, I still made one last attempt to resist her. I reached behind and pushed her head away, but that only seemed to energize her more. She grabbed my wrists, pulling me up and slammed me down onto my back.

"TURN OVER, LITTLE SLUT!" she commanded, pinning me down and hovering over me with her lips just a breath away from mine. I squirmed, but she easily overpowered me. Then, she dropped her mouth down hard onto mine, forcing her way in past my lips and sucking my tongue like a wild woman.

We were both breathing erratically. As she kissed me and whipped her tongue around in my mouth, she straddled my leg and started grinding her clit into my thigh. Her pussy was so hot and wet on me. She delivered a multitude of sloppy, wet French kisses—one after the other, cutting off my air supply. If all that wasn't enough, she spit in my mouth. Yes, that crazy, tall, Amazonian bitch called me a little slut and then proceeded to spit in my mouth. I was horrified and angry, but that shit turned me on immensely.

Sullivan's body moved like an evil, sensuous serpent. I could feel extreme pressure building up. She began moaning loudly, and she slid her fingers inside me again, curling them back, searching for my G-spot. It didn't take her long to find what she was looking for, and when she did, she targeted it and went to work. All of a sudden, it felt like I had to pee, so I frantically tried to get up.

"STOP!" I pushed her several times—I think—but, she just laughed and ignored my wishes.

"Shut the fuck up, bitch," Sullivan whispered. Then, she grabbed my hair and yanked my head back. With her thumb, she rubbed my clit while she hit my spot again and again. I exploded everywhere, all over her and the bed.

"Fuck, shit, g... get off!" I stuttered, pounding my fists into her shoulders. "THE FUCK'S WRONG WITH YOU, SULLIVAN?"

"Ooh, a squirter," she slurred, smacking her lips and sucking her fingers.

"YOU'RE DRUNK!" I stood up, pulling the bed sheet with me to cover up. "GET THE FUCK OUTTA HERE! GET OUT! NOW!"

She stood up and stumbled out. "Good night, baby," she said, strutting out and pulling the door shut.

I ran over to the door and locked myself in. Then, I went back and sat down on the edge of the bed. I put my head in my hands, and yelled, "FUCK!" Then, I laid down, kicked my feet under the covers and slammed my head back on the pillow. There was no way I could get back to sleep after an orgasm like that. I've heard of female ejaculation, but it never happened to me before, and I sure as hell didn't want it to happen at the hands of a sick dyke like Sullivan. I just lay there in the bed confused. I felt violated—maybe not exactly violated—I actually wanted her to pretty much rape me, and listening to Blondie, it seemed like a good idea at the time, but afterwards, the consequences were quite obvious. The truth hurts—it always does. I had to face the facts at that point ... I liked pussy. I liked her pussy ... I just hoped she was too drunk to remember our little encounter.

Considering the situation, my sudden change in sexual preference was the least of my concerns. What if she'd just played me? What if she's the one I'm looking for? Prosecuting Sullivan would just be a fantasy the moment she took the stand and told the jury how I took everything she gave me. Talk about getting fucked after getting fucked. I had a feeling this was gonna end and badly for me, but all I could do was just be cool and wait it out. And as usual, Blondie was nowhere to be found after the fact. *Bitch!*

Chapter 6

Later that morning around 6:30 a.m., I finally climbed out of bed. I was a mess, sweaty all over and sticky down below. I quickly showered and got dressed. If I had it my way, I would have just stayed locked up in my room all morning. I desperately wanted to avoid my new "special" roommate, but I had a job to do, and I was starting to worry less about the consequences of my sexual misconduct. Blondie was back in my head, reminding me that Vice President Keller told me to complete my mission by any means necessary. It wouldn't take much for me to convince him it was necessary to fuck Agent Sullivan to get closer to Tesh. Despite the fact I admire him, he still gives me this sick, old, racist white man vibe. He probably would be just fine hearing about two black bitches rolling around in the sheets. At that point, all I had to do was get over my embarrassment and shame. I took a few deep breaths, and then finally decided to suck it up and venture out into the kitchen. Little Ms. Rapist already made coffee and was pouring a cup as I walked in. We locked eyes, and I gave her my evil frown of discontent.

"Coffee?" she asked, smiling like the Cheshire cat.

I sighed heavily. "Yeah," I replied in a dry tone.

She flipped over another mug and filled it up. "Sugar?"

"No." I put my things down on the floor near the table, and then walked over and grabbed the mug off the counter.

We both sat down at the table and sipped our coffee. I could feel her staring at me, but I didn't want to talk, more less look up at her. It was at that moment I sympathized with my parents. They ate together for years at the same table without saying a single word to each other. That's how I was feeling that morning. I didn't want that bitch to say a goddamn word to me.

"You okay?" Sullivan asked.

I put my cup down. "I'd rather not talk about it," I snapped. I tilted my head back and massaged my temples with my fingers.

"It's nothing to be ashamed of. I think we make-"

"Not interested, Sullivan."

"Yeah, I heard that one before," she retorted.

I held my cup to my lips and blew softly.

"You know, you're pretty hot for a skinny, white girl."

I slammed my cup down on the table, and then I had an epiphany. "Shit, I need to get something before we leave and I'm not sure how to make that happen."

"What?"

"My coat," I replied. "I left it back in L.A."

"Baby, it'll be cold out here today," said Sullivan, "you can't go out with just that on. You'll freeze to death. Here, you can use my coat till you-"

"No, I'll pick something up on the way," I interrupted. "And, don't call me baby!"

Sullivan chuckled a little. "Well, at least let me help ... I could have the manager call one of the nearby shops."

My eyes lit up. "Really?"

"Consider it a peace offering, baby."

I frowned again. "Set it up ... and don't call me baby again."

"Done." She smiled and tried to touch my hand, but I pulled back from her.

"By the way, I don't have to tell you not to-"

"What happens with Vanessa stays with Vanessa," she interrupted.

I rolled my eyes and grabbed up all my gear off the floor. "See you down in the briefing, Sullivan," I said. Then, I walked out the door with my head hung low.

On the way to the elevators, all I could think about was how badly I had screwed up. Maybe it wouldn't impede my investigation, but I was certain I'd be judged for it. It was the last thing I needed, considering everything that was at stake—my freedom and everything else important in my life—not to mention innocent lives.

I reached the elevators and pressed the down button. While I waited for the elevator to come up, I noticed a faint reflection in the doors. I took a closer look and realized somebody was standing right behind me. I spun around quickly for a better look. It was Alonzo Parrish, standing in complete stillness with a cigar in his mouth. He was wearing a long, black leather trench coat and a little round matching black leather Kufi hat. He looked like the token negro in a 1980's private detective television series. *Spenser for Hire* comes to mind.

"Shouldn't let people sneak up on you like that, Johnson," he warned, "makes for a very short life."

"Well, it's early, and the eyes in the back of my head aren't up yet."

"Sounds like paranoia to me," he said. "You're not really from Justice, are you?"

"How's that?" I asked, raising my left eyebrow.

"Just a hunch," he replied.

The elevator doors opened, and I stepped inside. "Now look who's being paranoid?"

He laughed and joined me. "Maybe we should start over?"

"Sure," I replied. Then I changed my voice to a horrible English accent. "Top of the morning to you, Mr. Parrish," I said. Then, I pressed the *L* button for the lobby.

"And the rest of the day to you, Ms. Johnson," he responded, tipping his leather hat.

"Oh, a gentleman I see." I smiled and leaned against the railing on the side.

Parrish moved to the back of the elevator. He pretended to not be watching me, but I saw him in the reflection of the doors, sneaking a peak in here and there. We rode the elevator down and exited on the lobby floor. Parrish walked towards the dining room while I made my way over to the man at the front desk.

"How may I help you?" the front desk attendant asked.

"I left my coat back home, and I-"

"Ah yes, we just got a call from the Sullivan suite. Room 411, right?"

"Yes."

Will you be returning to your room now?" he asked.

"No, I'll be in the main dining room, and then I'll be leaving right after."

"Will you need to be sized?"

"I wear size eight in dresses," I replied.

He leaned over the counter and looked me up and down briefly. "And, is there a particular style you had in mind?"

"Just something to keep me warm today."

"I'll have a representative come right over," he said. "Please, enjoy your breakfast."

"Thank you."

I walked into the dining room over to a large round table. I thought I saw Alonzo go in, but he was nowhere to be found. It was a little early, so I just sat down and waited for the team. After about 15 minutes, they all came in together like a pack of wild wolves. Everyone sat down and we engaged in minor chit chat while we ate. Collins finished his breakfast first, and then wiped his mouth at least 20 times with his napkin. He was so squeaky clean it was almost hilarious. After a few more wipes, he finally started the meeting.

"So, team, are we gonna do some work today or what?" he asked, smiling his bright white smile. He reached down into his bag and pulled out a stack of folders, one for each team member. He passed them out and gave us a moment to look them over.

"Today's target is the abandoned Williamson-Clark facility. Layout's on page four. The building's been closed since '99, so this should be a walk in the park...."

As soon as he said that, there was a simultaneous groan amongst the team, as if they knew he was feeding them a good ole fashion line of bullshit.

"Intel says this location is currently being used to stockpile drugs and weapons," Collins continued. "That puts this op in DTP's very capable hands. It's highly unlikely we'll run across any upper echelon Alluvion, but if we do, we bring 'em in alive for questioning, y'all got me? Nobody shoots the big kids today. We've got a no-knock warrant to search the premises, and this is gonna be a real simple raid. Nothing fancy here at all, folks. We'll enter through the front and search each floor. I've included both missing person reports and a copy of the robbery file. Rodriquez, set up sniper cover in the adjacent building marked on your map. That should give you the best vantage point for the front of the building and the surveillance van unless you have a better idea...."

"Looks good to me," Rodriquez replied.

Collins continued. "Be sure to radio once you're in position. Hughes, I want you to put the van in the location marked on your map. You'll be our eyes and ears, so stay sharp. Inside, Slade and Stratton will secure the first floor. Slade, you get back and cover the rear, and Stratton you're on lobby detail. The rest of you will go with me. We'll break up into teams and sweep each floor. Team one will cover odd ones, and team two will take even. Once our search is complete, we'll meet back in the lobby to assess the situation. Our time is limited, so if everybody's done eating, then let's move."

I cleared my throat a little louder than normal, and suddenly Collins' memory improved.

"Oh, almost forgot..." He rubbed his spikey hair and cleared his throat. "Agent Johnson's gonna take over onsite. Deputy Administrator Farrell will arrive in a few hours, so let's make sure he gets a damn good situation report, okay team?"

"Let's do it, man," said Slade.

"Alright guys your call signs and COMSEC protocols are in your packets," said Collins. "Any questions...? Good, dismissed."

Everyone left the table, folders in hand. I stayed behind to wait for the coat man. Once I had finished another coffee, a well-dressed gentleman walked in. He wore a dark grey suit and shiny black shoes with sharp pointed toes. And, there was no smiling with that guy—he was all business.

"Ms. Johnson?"

"Yes?"

"Excellent, I'm Charles from Saks Fifth Avenue." He waved at the entrance of the dining room and a second man wheeled in a rack full of coats.

"Could you please stand up for me?" Charles asked.

I sprang to my feet and straightened myself, so he could have a good look.

Charles stepped back and gazed up and down my body for a moment. He just kinda side-stepped left and right as he sized me up. Then, the slightest of smiles emerged on his face. "That's very lovely," he complimented.

I was wearing a chocolate-colored Diane von Furstenberg suit with a white blouse and high-heeled boots. Apparently, Charles approved. "Thank you," I replied.

"How about this one...?" Charles reached over to the rack and touched an all-black, three-quarter length Marc Jacobs coat. He removed it from the hanger and held it up against me.

Charles was the cutest little gay white man on the planet. Everything on him was just right, and his nails were well manicured, far better than mine actually. I was tempted to call him Charlene, but he was so serious and well-refined, I figured making fun of him wouldn't go over well. Besides, with all my recent prison yard lust, it would pretty much be like the pot calling the kettle black.

I studied the coat front and back before trying it on. Then, Charles opened the coat and held it up. I spun around and stuck both arms into the sleeves. He pulled it up onto my shoulders and smoothed out the back of the coat with both hands, simultaneously. Then, he turned me around and grabbed the front of the coat. He tugged it into place, fixing the collar just right. I examined my new look carefully in the full-length mirror on the side of Charles' mobile coat rack. The coat fit like a glove. It was double breasted with a fly collar. Being the "experienced" shopper that I am, it didn't take any time at all for me to decide it was the right one. Once I saw that coat on me, I had to have it.

"I'll take it," I told Charles.

I slipped off the coat, and Charles handed it to his assistant, who then began prepping it for me to wear. He carefully removed the tags, which he placed neatly in the inside pocket. Then, he helped me put it back on.

"Please sign here," said Charles.

I couldn't help but smile. Charles was either good or he got lucky. Either way, it didn't matter to me. I was gonna be warm and in style that day. If Charlene wasn't so gay, I'd kiss him right on the lips. He was the man ... or woman ... whatever.

"We appreciate your business, Ms. Johnson. Here's my card. Do call and tell me how this fine coat works for you. If you desire another, we can arrange that."

"Thank you, Charles. I will."

"Good day," said Charles. Then, he snapped his finger and darted for the door with his assistant rolling the cart behind him.

I ran the palms of my hands down the front of my shiny new coat. I left the dining room, satisfied I'd made a good purchase. My early morning shopping success was almost a good remedy for my lapse of common, damn, fool sense—almost. I grabbed my things and strutted my stuff through the lobby. Outside in front of the hotel, Sullivan was waiting for me by my car. I can't say I didn't see that coming.

"Looks like we're carpooling!" she exclaimed. "Damn, gurl, that's a nice coat. Didn't I tell you they'd hook you up? You go baby—I mean Ms. Johnson." She made a fake, serious-looking face.

"Thanks," I replied softly, unlocking the car. I opened the driver side door and climbed into the car while Sullivan eagerly jumped in on the passenger side. I looked over and gave her a few more well-deserved frowns, and then started the motor. I adjusted the mirrors and pulled off behind the surveillance van.

We used our lights and sirens to cut through traffic. It took about an hour to reach the Williamson-Clark building. Dr. Hughes was driving like a bat outta hell. I did all I could do to keep up with him, and I am one of the fastest drivers in New York City. We turned off the sirens and went silent a block away from our destination. We slowly crept, inconspicuously, into the parking deck across the street.

We took our time and observed the target location from level two of the deck while Rodriquez and Hughes moved into position. I carefully scanned each floor with my binoculars, looking for any signs of trouble. Everything looked normal except the windows on floors five and six. Floors one through four were all busted out, but five and six looked brand new. In fact, there were people walking around inside, and they didn't look like a bunch of crackheads either. If I was thinking straight, I probably would've aborted the mission, but it was the closest I'd gotten to anything credible, so desperation was in the driver seat.

"Mobile One, over," came Rodriquez's voice over the radio.

Collins depressed the talk button on his radio. "Go ahead Eagle One."

"I'm in position with activity on five."

"Give me a count," he commanded.

"Four tangos plus at least 10 civilians."

"Roger that, Eagle One, hold your position. Command, what's your status?"

"In position and running facility scan now."

"Copy that." Collins dropped his radio to his side and held his head down while he waited for a response from Hughes.

"Mobile One, Command."

"Go ahead Command."

"Be advised there are six confirmed tangos, I repeat six tangos confirmed … two on the elevators and four posted at secondary entry points on floor five … plus I count 23 unknowns."

"Status of the U.K.'s?"

"Unattended, over."

"Okay Command, what about the building?"

"Full power … looks like they are running some kind of lab on five … recommend abort and regroup, I repeat, recommend abort, please advise."

I gazed at the building for a moment.

"Agent Johnson…." Collins hustled over to me. "Ma'am, we got too many variables and we're outgunned and outnumbered up there … we need to abort and see if we can get some local law enforcement to back us up. This thing stinks. It just don't sit right with me. Could be a setup, but if we got enough NYPD boys, we ought to be able to serve this warrant and get outta there with our balls still attached, no offense."

It didn't necessarily feel like a setup to me. It looked more like we had caught somebody red handed. If there were Alluvion operatives up there, then they were guarding something serious. I figured it just might be the break we needed. Our chances of stumbling on an opportunity like that again were slim to none. Plus, it would take far too long to get NYPD to cooperate and show up, so I ordered him to proceed with the raid as planned.

Collins just stared at me for a moment. I could tell he wanted to protest, but he didn't. He just shook his head and complied.

"Green-light all units," he radioed, "I repeat Green-light all units."

"Copy that, Mobile One," Hughes responded, "give me a comms-check."

"Check," Parrish replied.

"Comm-check," said Collins.

"Comm-check," radioed Rodriquez.

"Comm-check," said Sullivan

"Comm-check," Slade responded.

"Comm-check,' said Stratton.

I held my radio up to my lips. "Check."

"Copy that," said Hughes. "Green-light all units. Proceed with caution and radio silence."

"Johnson, I don't think this is a good idea," Collins said again.

I stared at him for a moment. "I agree."

"We could shadow them, maybe turn a worker," he suggested.

"Too long, cowboy. Besides, that's too high of a risk if they screw up ... nah, we gotta move on this now. Prep the team and get them ready to hit the lab up on five."

"Yes, ma'am," he replied reluctantly.

Collins and I walked back over to the team.

"New mission," Collins announced. "According to Hughes, the building has power and there're more than twenty people occupying a fifth-floor laboratory."

"Hostages?" asked Sullivan.

"If I had to guess, no," I replied.

"Could be civilian workers," said Slade.

Stratton sighed heavily. "Uh yeah, and they just happen to not notice the men walking around with all the guns?"

"I agree Stratton, we need to play it safe," replied Collins. "Detain the workers, but don't engage them unless they're armed."

"And, if they become hostile?" interrupted Parrish.

"She's in charge now," Collins pointed to me.

"Respond with non-lethal force," I replied. "The four of us will split up, each take a stairway up to the fifth floor. Take down the guard nearest you, no sound, and no kills either—we need to grab these jokers and get one of 'em to talk. Collins and I will take the two elevator guards. Once the perimeter's secure, we'll move to the lab and detain the workers."

"You want me to go up with you guys?" asked Slade. "No," I replied, "stay on the rear entrance. We don't wanna get suprised from behind."

"Copy that," he replied.

"So, we're busting up a drug lab?" Stratton asked, sarcastically.

"We don't know what's up there," I replied.

"Then why are we going in?" she asked, "shouldn't we be calling the FBI?"

"Nothing changes," Collins replied. "Look guys, intel says there are drugs up there. I don't like it either, but it ain't my call. Bottom line, if they're using this place as a depot, and it's connected to all these DTP attacks, we really can't afford to let jurisdiction, or some gut feeling, prevent us from doing our job and making this bust. We're DTP ... we're better than that."

"I don't like this," Stratton mumbled.

"What's the problem, Stratton?" asked Parrish. "You act like you know somethin' we don't."

"Those ain't crackheads up there, man, we need to come back with more guns."

Deep down, I felt the same, but the clock was ticking, and something told me there was a CIA Black Site with my name hanging over a very small, dark cell. Collins was about to respond, but I jumped in first to squash that noise.

"Get ready, we're going in," I commanded.

Collins pulled out his tactical map. "Let's move to plan B," he said. "New point of entry is side entrance Charlie."

I stuffed my map back in my pocket and opened the trunk of my car. It was full of gear just like the good doc said it would be. While Collins continued convincing the crybabies to hike their skirts up and get on board with the program, I passed out flares and bullet proof vests. I offered Slade a vest, but he refused it.

"Your lack of faith is disturbing," whispered Slade, tapping on his chest with two fingers.

Slade and I had history. I knew he was paranoid, but even I found it hard to believe he'd been wearing Kevlar under his clothes all morning. Then again, knowing Slade, he'd probably worn it to bed.

I closed the trunk, took off my coat and strapped on a vest. It was cold as hell, so I quickly put my coat back on. Collins walked over to me to check my vest.

"Team ready?" I asked.

He reached inside my coat and tugged on my vest. "Ready as we gone be, but I still think you better shut this one down, Chief."

Parrish, standing only a few feet away, heard Collins, and yelled, "Come on Tommy, tighten up yo' bra strap, son! Let's do this!"

"Am I good?" I asked. "Yep," replied Collins.

"Alright, take us in, Slade." I commanded.

Slade nodded, but he had this look on his face as if to say, *sure lady, but it's your funeral.* Soon as I gave the order, he instantly went back into Navy Seal-mode and stealthed across the street. Slade was swift and silent and apparently still loyal. He knew my name wasn't Johnson and he probably suspected I was most likely full of shit, but he played right along without blowing my cover. If I'd thought about it just a little harder, I would've stayed far away from Slade and DTP altogether. It was too risky, and I knew it, but I was desperate to find Tesh, which meant at that point, no risk was too great.

We followed Slade across the street and crouched behind him at the bottom of the stairs right in front of the side entrance. With our weapons drawn, we covered the street while Slade tricked the alarm and unlocked the door in record speed. Then, he put away his tools, pulled out his pistol, and moved backwards down to the bottom of the stairs.

"Move in and spread out," I whispered.

One-by-one, we entered the building. My heart raced as we cleared the first floor. The lobby was pitch-black, so we had to use our flashlights. It looked like an old battle field in there with all the broken furniture and debris scattered about. What's worse is it reeked of dead animal carcass—too bad for Slade and Stratton since they had the unlucky job of staying down there to guard the entrances and exit. I signaled for them to take their positions, and then motioned for the others to begin their climb. Sullivan and I moved to the west side of the building and split up.

"See you on five, babe," she said.

I rolled my eyes at her. "Watch your six."

She nodded, smiling at me like we were familiar.

I shook my head and darted into the northwest stairwell. I glanced upstairs and started my climb, skipping as many steps as my long slender legs would allow. Up on the fifth floor, I slowly crept out of the stairwell and moved around the corner, crouching with my gun straight ahead. I came up on my guard quickly. He was patrolling the hallway. He had a black communications device strapped around his neck and an AR-15 flung over his shoulder. He looked and moved like a mercenary. I crept in behind him, waiting to strike at the perfect moment, but he stopped in his tracks, so I had to make my move. I held my breath and closed in on him, staying as low as possible. When I got within arm's reach, I heard a noise in the stairwell behind me—the damn door clicked shut. The guard heard the noise too, and he spun around. The jig was up.

I stood straight up and locked eyes with the guard for a split second. I'd startled him. I could tell he was not sure what to make of me at first, but then he reached for the radio on his neck to signal the others, I knew I couldn't give him a chance to use it. I swung with all my might and swatted him across the face with my gun. He immediately dropped. He was disoriented, but not quite out, so I hit him again, and then again, and again. Thankfully, the final blow did the trick. He went down on the floor. I checked his pulse. He was still alive, but unconscious.

Taking that guard down brought back memories I'd worked hard to forget. It had been some time since I was facing down danger, but it was like riding a bike. I zip-tied my guard's writs and ankles. Then, I removed the black ski mask from his head, which I used along with an extra zip-tie to gag his mouth. Satisfied he was secure, I drug him into a nearby utility closet. That man was heavy. After I got him in there, I needed to take a second to catch my breath, but daylight was burning, so I had to keep moving.

I continued down the hallway and peeked around the corner at the elevators. There were no guards in sight. Either they were goofing off or somebody on the team was an overachiever. I walked past the elevators to check the adjacent hallway and was not surprised to see Collins in action. He closed the door to a small room on the right and signaled, *all clear*. He was such a cowboy, but maybe he was actually good at his job too. He had already taken out his guard plus the other two near the elevators in the time it took me just to take down one of them. I dared not complain. His haste was necessary.

Collins and I stared at each other for about a minute, waiting for the others. He quickly became impatient, and so did I. He looked down and tapped his watch a few times, so I gave him the nod. Time was short and radio silence meant we couldn't get an update from Sullivan and Parrish. They may have run into trouble of their own. We couldn't wait any longer.

I leaned in close, "Let's get in there, secure the lab and call it in," I whispered.

"Cover me, I got the door," replied Collins.

We ran full speed up to the lab door. Collins positioned himself to kick the door down, and I got ready to move into the room. He put three fingers in the air and started counting down... three... two... suddenly, Rodriquez broke radio silence.

"MOBILE ONE... ALERT, ALERT! Hostiles in route to your location. Preparing to engage!"

Collins clinched his fist in the air, and we took cover against the wall on both sides of the door.

I grabbed my radio. "Eagle One, hold your position," I said softly. "Mobile Two, Command... come in Command."

"Go ahead Mobile Two."

"Requesting confirmation of inbound hostiles."

"I've got nothing on thermal," replied Hughes, "nothing on the scanners. Stand by for communications check."

"Attention all units, break radio silence and check in with stat-rep immediately."

"Mobile One here, all clear on five," Collins radioed. "Mobile two and I are at the lab."

"Mobile Three here," Parrish radioed, "I'm on my way out of the North stairwell on five—all clear."

"Eagle One here, get ready, they're getting organized three floors down near the elevators. Multiple tangos, heavily armed."

Neither Sullivan, Stratton nor Slade checked in. They were all off the grid.

"Mobile Two, Command."

"Go ahead Mobile Two."

"Do we have a 20 on Four, Five and Six?"

"Negative Mobile Two, I can't reach them. Switching to microwave ... Oh shit, Mobile Two, Command, Mobile Five and Six are down, I repeat Mobile Five and Six are down on the first floor, multiple hostiles on floor two, I can't locate Mobile Four. Tangos are on the move. It's too many of them, you gotta get outta there now! ALL UNITS, ABORT, ABORT, ABORT!"

Collins and I didn't hesitate. "Mobile Three," he radioed, "hold your position we're coming to you now."

Collins and I ran back down the hallway to the other side of the elevators. We made a left around the corner and ran into Sullivan.

"The fuck were you?" asked Collins.

"Trouble with my guard." Sullivan had this funny expression on her face like she'd just ate the canary.

"You alright?" I asked.

"Yeah."

Collins looked kinda confused. "Well, how come you didn't check in?"

Sullivan held her radio up. "It's fucked," she whispered.

He just shook his head. "We got company."

"Uh, could you be more specific?" she asked.

"Hang on," said Collins. He held his radio up to his mouth. "Command, Mobile One, how many hostiles are we talking about here?"

Doctor Hughes responded, "Too many to confirm and I can't pick them up on thermal. BLOW OUT, GET THE HELL OUTTA THERE NOW, GODDAMMIT!"

"Roger that Command, get to the side entrance and get ready to get us the hell outta here."

"COPY THAT, MAKE YOUR EXIT NAV-POINT CHARLIE, ALL UNITS EXIT THE BUILDING THE WAY YOU CAME IN!"

"COMMAND, EAGLE ONE, I'M RELOCATING FOR VISUAL CONTACT. PREPARING TO ENGAGE."

"NEGATIVE, HOLD YOUR POSITION," commanded Collins, but Rodriquez did not respond.

"Mobile One, Eagle One, I have visual contact with four hostiles, rear exit ... requesting permission to engage."

"Negative," I radioed, "DO NOT ENGAGE! HOLD YOUR FIRE AND STAY OFF THE AIR! WE'RE COMING OUT NOW, COVER OUR EXIT!"

"FUCK THIS SHIT!" she snapped, then I heard a click.

"Eagle One, come in Eagle One ... Eagle One!"

Rodriguez had turned her radio off.

"Shit!" I mumbled.

"Johnson, we gotta move," reminded Collins, urgently.

I nodded, and we took off down the hall. The three of us—me, Collins, and Sullivan—met Parrish on the other side of the elevators.

"Sleeping on the job?" asked Collins.

"Gettin' old, old friend?" Parrish responded, grinning.

"We gotta go man!" Collins exclaimed.

"Yo, fuck that," said Parrish, "they know we're here, they'll just follow us into the stairwell and have an elevated vantage point. They'll pick us off one by one or drop a flashbang down in there. We gotta push 'em back, man."

Collins shook his head. "No, we're gonna-"

"Collins, they are in the elevators, what the fuck are you guys ... OH SHIT!" Dr. Hughes' radio went dead too.

"THE FUCK!" exclaimed Collins.

"I'm with Parrish," said Sullivan, "we gotta do something up here. We don't know shit. They could have all the exits covered. At least up here we know what we're working with. We can hold them back right here in this hallway."

"This is a bad idea," Collins said. "What about the civilians?"

"We don't have any other choice!" she exclaimed.

"Fine," Collins conceded. "Sullivan, take the wall on the inside near the elevators and cover Johnson, don't let anything happen to her."

"I can hold my own," I reminded, "we can work together."

"Whatever," Collins snapped. "Parrish, you and I will take them from this side. I'll move up. As soon as I get a few of 'em in my sights, I'll fire a few rounds and draw 'em back here. Then, I'll move in behind you, man. When I'm clear, open fire. You and I will move back while I reload and pull 'em further back in. Sullivan, we're counting on you. We need your top shot. Keep sharp and take down as many as you can. Stay away from the walls and cover each other on reload, got it?"

We all nodded.

Collins checked his weapon. "Hey man, I'm gonna start moving in okay? You got me?"

"Yeah cowboy," replied Parrish, "I gotcha back, now let's do this thang."

They slapped five and we all split up, Parrish and Collins on one side of the hall and Sullivan and me on the opposite. We didn't know what happened to Slade and Stratton, we'd lost contact with Hughes, and that dumbass Rodriquez turned her radio off. If that wasn't enough, we heard a thud and the building started vibrating. We all gazed at each other with a frightful look, all except Sullivan, who seemed a little too calm all things considered. I've been in a lot of sticky situations, but I didn't wake up that morning expecting to be in one with a bunch of people I barely knew and damn sure didn't trust with my life.

"Hey, hey," whispered Parrish, "Stay focused ... you good?"

I nodded and pointed my gun down the hall. The bells for all the elevators sounded one after another, and I became even more anxious, holding my breath and anticipating the worst.

Collins had a clear view of two of the elevators, but we were positioned around the corner out of sight. I could tell when the men stepped out of the elevators because every inch of Collins' body tensed up. It seemed like we were all frozen in time, trying to find the strength and courage to advance, but it became clear to me we were out gunned the minute Collins lowered his weapon and started shuffling backwards. He didn't even fire one shot. He just waved us back, swinging his hand down near his leg as if to say, *run for your fucking lives.*

An army of men wearing black from head-to-toe poured out into the hallway like a deadly flood. They didn't notice us at first, so we still had a chance to move. Sullivan was crouched in front of me, aiming straight ahead. Collins was retreating fast. Parrish was already several steps behind me. Our plan was not robust enough to accommodate that many hostiles. We didn't have a snowball's chance in hell of surviving.

I tapped Sullivan's shoulder, still aiming for the men down the hall. I just knew she'd get up and start moving back with the rest of us. Boy, was I wrong. With no warning—without uttering a single word—Sullivan lunged forward and opened fire. She hit one in the head and he went down. I watched in disbelief as the assailant immediately got back up. Then, he and his buddies unleashed hell on us without hesitation.

Collins was right. We were outnumbered and outgunned even before the men in black showed up. We tried to stand our ground, but their fully automatic rifles were overpowering. The rounds that were kicking out from their weapons blasted concrete from the walls and shredded up the carpet all around us. Thankfully, all the gun smoke actually worked to our advantage because it made visibility low in the hallway.

"RELOADING!" exclaimed Sullivan as she spun around behind me.

I moved forward and unloaded into the open area. We were leapfrogging backwards down the hall, returning fire, wildly, but whatever body armor those jokers had on was something like I'd never seen before. They were impervious to our gunfire. When they went down, they just shook it off and got right back up. I tagged one straight in the face, but after a while, he got back up too. The bad guys were digging in hard and advancing on us.

"RELOADING!" I yelled.

Sullivan stopped shooting for a second, and I spun around behind her to reload. As soon as I was out of her line of fire, she resumed shooting.

I pushed the release button on my gun and the magazine slipped out of the bottom of the handle. I caught it with my left hand and snapped it into the empty slot on my belt. Then, I loaded a full clip into my gun and pushed the slide release lever down with my thumb. The slide snapped forward into place, moving the first round into firing position, but before I could get back into the firefight, the worst happened.

"RELOADING!" Sullivan yelled. As she turned to move in behind me, blood splattered all over me and the wall, and Sullivan collapsed onto the floor.

"SHIT!" she screamed in agony, clutching her side.

"SULLIVAN!" I fired a few shots into the hallway. "SULLIVAN'S HIT! PULL BACK! PULL BACK NOW!" I fired again.

Collins rolled over to help pull Sullivan back out of the line of fire. Parrish drew his back up weapon and laid down cover fire for us. Collins and I drug Sullivan halfway down the hallway towards the stairs. Collins crouched low and continued firing while I wrestled Sullivan's hand away from her side. There were so many bullets still zipping by our heads it felt like we were in Baghdad. Sullivan got clipped on her side. The bullet went straight through the side of her Kevlar vest and she was leaking badly. I put pressure on the wound.

We were desperately trying to get out of there, but the men were getting closer and they showed no mercy. I took two shots to the chest. The impact knocked me against the wall, and I doubled down over onto the floor. It felt like I'd been stabbed. I coughed and wheezed, trying to loosen my vest. It was burning and I almost passed out. I felt under the vest. Thank God the bullets didn't go through. I couldn't get my vest off, so I sucked it up and reached for Sullivan. I started dragging her down the hall again towards the stairwell. Collins covered us, firing several more shots down the hall.

"ALONZO!" screamed Collins.

Parrish fired as he backed down the hall to us.

"GET THEM OUT OF HERE!" shouted Collins, pulling the pin on the only flash grenade he had, "MOVE BACK, I'LL COVER YOU!"

"NO, WAIT!" I screamed.

But he didn't listen, and he didn't wait. He rolled the flash bang down the hallway, and we all took cover. As soon as it blew, Collins drew his backup gun, jumped to his feet, and began to engage the enemy head on. "MOTHER FUCKER!" he yelled as he charged down the hallway, dual wielding his guns and drawing enemy fire away from us. He fired round after round, spinning, ducking, and maneuvering wildly to avoid being shot. Collins knocked down several hostiles. The men retreated back towards the other side of the elevators, and Collins kept charging towards them. That kid had balls for sure. The whole time, he never backed down, not once. He blasted past them and leaped into the stairwell on the opposite end of the hallway.

The enemy recovered quickly, and they gave Collins chase—all except one, who turned and pointed his rifle right at us. Parrish and I froze dead in our tracks. That man had us, but he didn't fire—he just waved his finger in the air and shook his head as if to taunt us. Then, he turned away and ran to catch up with the others.

"GET HER OUT, I GOTTA GO HELP COLLINS!" I exclaimed.

Parrish grabbed Sullivan by the arm. "That guy had us dead bang," he said, pulling Sullivan up onto his shoulder. "Why didn't he...."

We looked at each other and both said it at the same time. "OH SHIT, BOMB!"

Parrish was damn near down the hall by the time I blinked. I took off running behind him as fast as I could. Collins was on his own. The shooter wasn't being merciful at all. He didn't need to waste any more ammo because he knew we weren't gonna make it out of there in time.

"HANG ON SULLIVAN!" Parrish yelled, running full speed with her slumped over his shoulder.

I was moving as fast as I could but could barely hold my head up. My chest was pounding from the shots I took in my vest. All I could do was just follow the trail of blood Sullivan left behind on the floor.

Inside the stairwell, I stopped at the top of the stairs and tried to contact the rest of the team. "Shots fired, agent down," I radioed, "I REPEAT AGENT DOWN! HUGHES, WE NEED YOU IN THE LOBBY WITH A MED-KIT!" But there was no response, only static.

The lights flickered off, and then I felt like someone doused me with gasoline and set me ablaze. I got launched, face-first down the stairs, and that was all she wrote.

I don't know how long I was out, but I woke up under a bunch of rubble on the platform between floors four and five. I struggled to break free but couldn't. No matter how far I pulled myself, I was still pinned down. After an exhaustive fit of wiggles and squirms, I finally freed both legs and sat up. I fumbled around in the dark on my hands and knees, but then Parrish lit up a flare, and I stopped dead in my tracks. The neon glow from down below showed me just how close I was to death. The blast took out the stairs between floors four and five. One more move and I would've reached the third floor a lot faster than desired.

I leaned over the edge for a closer look. Parrish was down there, kneeling beside Vanessa's still body. My vision was blurry, but I could tell he was waving at me and trying to tell me something. His lips were moving, but I couldn't hear a damn thing.

I rubbed my tearing eyes and fumbled around for my gun. Then, I realized I'd just crawled from under what used to be the fifth-floor door. The blast had knocked it right off the hinges. I sifted through some debris and hot ash, and finally found my gun. The ceiling above was engulfed in flames, and the stairwell was filling up fast with thick, black smoke along with water from the fire suppression system on five. It was hot as hell and I could hardly breathe. My ears were ringing. I thought my eardrums were ruptured. My earlobes felt wet, and I'm pretty sure it was blood. Fortunately, my hearing slowly returned, and I could finally hear Parrish.

"HEY!" he yelled.

"What?" I coughed, uncontrollably.

"She's losing blood fast. WE GOTTA MOVE, RIGHT FUCKIN' NOW!"

"Can you still carry her?"

"Yeah, I got her," he replied.

"Go! I'll catch up."

I lit up a flare and dropped it down between the stairs. It bounced all the way down to the first floor. Parrish flung Sullivan over his shoulder again and took off running downstairs. I carefully lowered myself down to the fourth floor and hustled to catch up with him.

"Where the hell is everybody?" he asked, breathing heavily and looking back over his shoulder as he continued zipping down the stairs.

"MY RADIO'S DEAD!" I yelled breathlessly, pouring on the speed to run past him and take the lead.

We continued down the dark stairs, our path illuminated by the fire above and the dim glow of the flare below. I navigated quickly and carefully down each flight, clearing a path floor-by-floor for my teammates. Parrish followed closely behind with Sullivan over his shoulder. She hadn't moved one bit, and Parrish's back was soaked with her blood. I feared the worst. It sounds crazy, but I cared for her. The woman who just touched me that very morning in ways I'd never been touched before was slipping away, and there was nothing I could do about it. I felt some kind of way about that, but all I could do was keep moving.

Halfway down the last flight of stairs, the first-floor door swung open. Parrish leaned Sullivan back against the wall out of harm's way and aimed for the door.

"IDENTIFY YOURSELF!" I crouched and prepared for a headshot.

"IT'S ME! COLLINS!" he screamed, coughing loudly, "HOLD YOUR FIRE DAMMIT!"

"HOLSTER YOUR WEAPON, PUT YOUR HANDS ON YOUR HEAD, AND SLOWLY MOVE INTO THE DOORWAY!" commanded Parrish.

Collins complied, stepping into the doorway covered with dust and debris. "We ain't got time for this!" he exclaimed.

Parrish lowered his weapon. I couldn't really stand that mothafucka, Collins, but I couldn't have been happier to see his country ass.

"Is Sullivan okay?" asked Collins.

I shook my head. "It's bad. She's lost a lot of blood. Help Parrish get her out. I'll run ahead and grab a medical kit from the van, and I'll meet you in route."

He nodded, and Parrish ran back to grab Sullivan. I took off and ran towards the side entrance. The air was thick, and visibility was low. It was almost impossible to breathe and even harder to run, but I moved as fast as I could through all the garbage on the first floor.

With my gun still pointed ahead, I kicked the doors open and took a breath of fresh air. My eyes adjusted to the sunlight, and then I looked down at the street where Doctor Hughes should've been. He wasn't there, so I made a right and cornered around to the front of the building. My heart dropped. Our surveillance van was in a million pieces, scattered all over the street. The shell of the van was all that was left, and it was just a smoldering mess, flipped over onto the sidewalk. It was full of bullet holes, and Hughes was nowhere to be found. I heard gunshots in the distance, and civilians were panicking up and down the street, running in every direction and taking cover. Oddly, they'd abandoned their cars right in the middle of the road.

I felt like I was moving in slow motion. By the time I reached the bottom of the stairs, Collins and Parrish had made it out with Vanessa. The building was all ablaze near the top, and smoke was filling up almost every floor down below. Charcoal black smoke billowed out of the front doors as they exited the building.

"WE LOST HUGHES!" I yelled, my eyes tearing up.

But Agent Collins and Parrish didn't stop for a second—they kept moving across the street and laid Sullivan down on the grass a safe distance from the building. I ran along to help.

"Stay with her Parrish," Collins commanded, removing his coat and putting it down over Vanessa.

"Where you going?" asked Parrish.

"Back to look for the others. Keep her warm and try to get that bleeding under control, I'm going back in."

"I'll cover you," I said.

"Okay," he nodded, "let's go."

Collins and I ran back inside to search for Stratton and Slade. We cautiously sifted through the debris. As we neared the back of the lobby, we heard a faint voice in the distance.

"...I repeat, agent down. Do you copy?"

"Terence, where are you, buddy?" yelled Collins.

We followed the sound of his voice and finally found him kneeling near the back door. We both rushed to his aid. He was struggling to remove his vest while still trying to get someone on the radio. His coat and shirt were on the floor, full of holes. He kept talking into his radio. He didn't seem to have it all together. I shook him a couple of times.

"Slade, you okay? SLADE!"

"What?" He was disoriented.

I pulled one of his eyelids up with my thumb and shined my penlight into his eye. "Are you okay, sailor?"

"I'm fine," he replied. He shook his head a couple of times and pulled himself together.

He was okay, but Stratton was still on the floor. I got down and checked her vitals. She was definitely breathing, but she had a big bruise on her head. She'd been hit hard and was completely out.

"I got a few rounds off before they hit me," Slade said, coughing and trying to stand up. "I swear I hit at least one of those bastards, but that fucker just got right back up. Where's Nikki? I-"

"She's banged up," I replied, sighing, "might be a concussion. I don't wanna move her until a medic checks her."

Slade continued coughing, trying to catch his breath. "Well get Doc in here goddammit! I can't get anybody on the radio. Where is he?"

I didn't have the heart to tell him.

"Radios are down," I said, "Collins, go ahead and get her out of here."

He picked up Stratton, and I helped Slade to his feet. "Ready?"

"Yeah, I'm good," said Slade.

I pulled his arm up on my shoulders and together we limped outside. By the time we reached the front, Slade was walking fine by himself again. He was tough as hell. If I'd taken five shots in the vest front and back, I'd be crying like a bitch. I was still about ready to crawl up in a corner just from the two bullets that gingerly skipped across me.

The only thing rolling around in my head was a bunch of unanswered questions. *Who were those fuckers? How'd they even know we'd be here? Most importantly, where the fuck are they now?* I looked up and saw a chopper taking off to the east. *Well, that answered one question.* I just stared for a moment in sheer disgust and watched them escape because there wasn't a damn thing that I could do about it. Whoever they were, they were heavily armed and well organized. With a single attack, they damn near took out the entire DTP team, or what was left of it. They were too far away for me to see the numbers on the tail of the bird though. All I could do was try and help pick up the pieces with the rest of the team.

I stood at the bottom of the front steps and watched as everyone made their way across the street. Then, I saw Rodriquez appear from the back of the building. Her clothes and face were covered in debris and black smut. She was struggling to run towards me.

"You okay, Rodriquez?"

"Yeah, what happened?" she asked.

"Hughes is M.I.A," I replied, "and Sullivan and Stratton are down."

Rodriquez ran right up to me. "Shit is that your blood?" she asked, pointing to my face.

I touched my cheek and pulled back a red palm. "We need an ambulance," I casually replied. I knew it wasn't my blood.

She pulled out her cell phone, but it was dead just like all our radios. I checked mine and it was blank too. I removed the battery for a second and put it back in, but that didn't help. In fact, every digital thing I had on me was dead as a doorknob. Something strange was going on. I checked a few cars parked on the street, and they were dead too. Nothing electronic on the block had survived. Even the traffic lights were out.

Rodriquez drew her sniper rifle, wrapped the strap around her wrist twice and pointed it up the street. "I think I see a payphone," she said peering into the scope, "about four blocks up."

"You need backup?"

She shook her head.

"Listen, I saw a chopper, and-"

"Yeah, the black one," she replied, "I got the numbers off it. That's how they came in. I tried to tell you. They landed in the back out of sight."

"Get NYPD on it, alright?"

"Yeah, I got it." She strapped her rifle to her back, drew her sidearm and took off full speed up the sidewalk.

I turned towards the others across the street and couldn't believe my eyes. Dr. Hughes was alive and well, working on Sullivan.

"SLADE!" I yelled.

"Yeah?"

"Can you move?"

"I'm good, Top," he replied.

"GO COVER HER!" I yelled, pointing up the block to a barely visible Rodriguez. She was moving like a bat outta hell.

"I'm on it," he said, springing to his feet. He sprinted up the road to catch up with Rodriquez.

I hustled over to the team. Parrish was man handling one of the assailants. By the time I got over there, he had him cuffed and was expressing himself by repeatedly slamming the man's head face down on the grass. Parrish removed his mask and pressed a gun to the man's head. He was going to put that man's lights out for good, and honestly, I would not have protested, but I'll be goddamned if the man wasn't wearing one of the missing demolition suits. *That explains a lot.*

"DON'T KILL HIM PARRISH!" I screamed, "WE NEED HIM ALIVE!"

Parrish frowned and yelled, "YOU LUCKY MOTHAFUCKA," loudly. It took him a moment, but he finally lowered his weapon and stood down.

I was instantly relieved—we had a suspect—something to go on—someone to interrogate. Maybe there was some hope after all for us to salvage that cluster-fuck of an operation. I walked over and kneeled next to Hughes.

"How's she?" I asked.

"It's as bad as it looks," he said, "she's in shock. I've slowed the bleeding. I've done what I can, but she needs a real doctor."

"Hughes, you're hit too," I said, coughing.

His shirt sleeve was torn and covered in blood. "Yeah, well your face is a lot redder than before," he said, laughing, "so don't worry about me."

I grinned. "Okay, tough guy."

"Give me a second and I'll take a look at that cut on your head," said Hughes. He taped some gauze packs over Sullivan's wounds, and then turned his attention to me. He started by wiping my face clean with a medicated cloth.

"Ouch," I shrieked as he pressed on my cut.

"Hold that," he ordered.

I held the cloth and pressed as hard as I could, but it hurt like hell. Hughes dug around in his medical bag for more bandages.

"I see we got one," I said.

"Here, hold still." Doctor Hughes applied a bandage to my forehead. "I backed up over one of his buddies, and this genius opened fire on the van. I made out with a med pack before the fuel tank blew. The van exploded on top of his partner. Believe it or not, the guy survived, and get this ... bastard didn't have a single scratch on him, far as I could tell. He got away, and that one tried, but I chased him down. He doesn't speak English, and his suit is damn near indestructible—some kind of exoskeleton. Son-of-a-bitch is bullet proof and fire retardant. Never seen anything like it, but we didn't stand a chance against 'em that's for damn sure. Just what the hell is going on?"

"I don't know," I replied softly, still lying through my teeth. "Look, we're sitting ducks out here, Doctor. Can we move them into the parking deck?"

"Probably best," he said, picking through my blood-soaked hair for injuries.

"Come on," I urged, "There are more supplies in the trunk of the car."

"Give me a hand, Tommy," said Hughes.

They picked up Sullivan and Parrish carried Stratton.

"Get up!" I exclaimed, grabbing our prisoner by his long hair. That man was larger than life, about six-foot-five, with blonde hair and blue eyes. He rambled on while I moved him forward at gunpoint. We went back up to the second level of the parking deck where our day had begun. Unfortunately, the deck had lost power too, so the elevators were offline. We had to take the stairs up.

I secured the prisoner in the back of my Crown Vic. Soon as I closed the door, he fell on his back and kicked at the cage and windows from inside, yelling and trying to break free. I walked around and unlocked the trunk with my key.

"Parrish, Collins."

"Yes...?"

"Yo...?"

"What are we gonna do about all the screaming people down there?"

"Probably need to do some crowd control," said Collins, "can you handle this?"

"Yeah," I replied, "I'll stay with Sullivan and Stratton. Slade and Rodriquez should be back soon to lend a hand."

"You sure you'll be okay?" Collins asked. He seemed genuinely worried about my safety.

"I'm a big girl. I can handle this. We'll be fine."

"Alright," said Collins. "We'll send the paramedics up once they get here."

"Thanks."

"Hey Johnson, hand me a couple of med kits if you got 'em," said Parrish, "I'll see what I can do to help the injured while the ambulances are in route."

"Good idea," I replied, "trunks open. Watch your ass down there, guys. Could still be some hostiles in the area. You need backup, you holla, loud as you can, okay?"

"We're cool," said Parrish, "just take care of the girls."

I nodded, "I got 'em, now go!"

They grabbed as many supplies as they could carry and ran back down to street level. After about 10 minutes, paramedics, NYPD officers, and firefighters arrived on the scene. I had the police take our prisoner into custody, and we prepared to leave for the hospital. I climbed into the back of the ambulance with Sullivan, and Hughes rode along with Stratton. The others followed in a police van. All I could think about was that we fucked up. Scratch that, I fucked up. I almost got everybody killed. I should've aborted like Collins said.

"Blood pressure's dropping," said a paramedic, "Miss, Miss! Hold on!"

"Her name's Vanessa."

"Hang on Vanessa," he said.

"We're almost there," I whispered, squeezing her bloody hand.

The bandage on my head was seeping. One of the paramedics wiped my face clean and redressed the cut while the other focused on keeping Sullivan stable. My chest was really burning. I took off my singed coat and unfastened my vest. The paramedic helped me pull it off.

"You were lucky," he said.

"Kevlar did its job," I replied. I was still hurting so bad, my hands were shaking, and I could barely get my shirt unbuttoned. "Here, help me out of this."

He got my shirt open and looked at the bruise on my chest. He pressed on it in several places.

"Does it hurt when you breathe?"

I shook my head.

"Looks like it's just bruised," he speculated. "I don't think anything's broken. You can get something for the pain at the hospital after you get checked out."

I nodded. "Thank you. I'll be alright."

"I'm gonna help with your friend now. You hang in there and sit tight." He turned back around to help his partner with Sullivan.

It didn't take long for us to make it to Mount Sinai Hospital. The ambulance backed right up to the emergency room entrance. I hopped out and watched with my stomach in a knot as they rolled Nikki and Vanessa inside. Vanessa had lost a lot of blood, and Nikki showed no improvement at all—she was still unconscious and most likely concussed. It was all my fault. I walked us right into a trap.

Inside the E.R., one of the nurses gave me an ice pack for my head, which by then was spinning around the room. I pressed the pack to the side of my head and sat down with the rest of the team. We all sat still and speechless in the waiting area, hoping for the best. After about an hour, a doctor came out to talk to us.

"Hello everyone, I'm Doctor Hall."

Collins got up and shook his hand. "Agent Collins, DEA."

"Miss Stratton suffered a severe hematoma," said Hall, "the swelling has gone down, and I've prescribed medication for the pain. She's conscious and doing well. We expect a full recovery, and she'll be released shortly. She's been asking for you now. She's a little shaken up, but feel free to go in and see her. I'm hoping you can calm her down. Any questions?"

"Yes, another Agent was injured," Collins said. "Agent Sullivan ... how is she?"

"I'm not sure," Hall replied, "I know Doctor Smith is in with her now in the O.R. He'll speak with you as soon as possible. I'm sorry I don't have any more information for you."

I stood up. "Thank you, Doctor."

He nodded and left. I felt somewhat relieved to hear Stratton was alright, but apparently Sullivan was still fighting for her life.

We returned to our seats and continued waiting. Each team member went back, one at a time, to see Nikki. After a few hours, I finally grabbed some coffee, which just ran right through me. As soon as I took the last sip, I instantly had the urge to pee. When I got back from the ladies' room, another doctor in scrubs was on his way into the waiting area, so I followed him. Sure enough, he was there to speak with us. The team crowded around him as he introduced himself.

"Good afternoon, my name is Doctor Smith," he said. "I need to talk to you about your colleague, Ms. Sullivan."

"How is she?" asked Collins, "she gonna be okay, right?"

"Hang on there," said Smith, gesturing with both hands. "She's stable, but not out of danger yet."

"I don't understand," said Parrish, "the bullet went straight through her side."

"Yes, but she was struck with more than one bullet," said Smith. "Unfortunately, one of the bullets impacted her lower ribcage before exiting through the back. Shattered bone fragments caused trauma to her left lung. We performed surgery to re-inflate her lung and repair the shattered bone-"

"So, she'll pull through?" interrupted Collins.

"I'm sorry … it's just too early to tell," Smith said, shaking his head, "she's in critical condition in ICU. She's not breathing on her own yet, and she lost a lot of blood. Best we can do is to continue to monitor her progress and update you with any changes in her condition."

"Thank you, doctor," I said. I don't know why, but I was extremely emotional about the situation. I quickly turned around to try and hide the tear streaming down my cheek, but the team caught me slipping. As Doctor Smith walked away, they huddled around me as if they were preparing for a group hug.

"It's not your fault," said Stratton, "we just had a fucked-up day."

"V's tough," Parrish assured me, "if anyone can pull through this, she can."

"I just came back from Nikki a few minutes ago," said Collins, "and she's asking for you now. How 'bout we go see her?"

He put his arm around me, and we walked together down the hallway so I could see Stratton. I entered her room first and sat down on the chair beside her bed. Collins entered after me and stood nearby.

"How are you doing?" I asked.

She replied, "I've been better."

"You gave us all one hell of a scare," I told her.

She shook her head. "It's like they popped up out of thin air. We didn't even have time to move or even think." She started tearing up.

I touched her arm and said, "it's okay. It's over now."

"I'm glad Terence is okay I thought we'd lost him," she whimpered, "but what about Vanessa? I heard the nurse say another DEA agent was in critical condition. Have you heard anything yet, Collins?"

"Yeah, a Doctor Smith just came out and talked to us," he said.

"And?" She tried to sit up.

Collins shook his head and was about to say something, but all he managed to do was stutter. He didn't want to tell her Sullivan might not make it through the day. I couldn't blame him either.

"Just relax," I cleared my throat and put my hand on her shoulder. "She's down the hall, but she's in good hands, and from what I understand she's a fighter, so-"

"She likes you," Stratton said, smiling.

Collins and I looked at each other and all of a sudden, I was the one stuttering. "Uh ... uh, I...."

Nikki reached over and grabbed my hand. "Don't let her die."

My mouth was wide open. "I... I don't know what to say, Nikki."

"Vanessa doesn't like anybody," she said, sniffling, "you can't let her die. We need her, and she needs you."

I pulled my hand away and tried to compose myself. "I'm glad you're feeling better," I said, and gave her a half-assed smile.

Nikki was about to say something else, but then a nurse popped into the room just in the nick of time.

"How are you feeling now, Miss Stratton?" She started checking the equipment near the bed.

"I'm... I'm fine," she replied, whimpering.

"You need to rest," said the nurse. "How about we bring your visitors back when you've had a little more time to feel better?"

Stratton frowned up. "No, please ... I want them to stay."

"Only if you take it easy, sweetie," the nurse bargained.

"I will. I promise"

"Everything's going to be alright." The nurse gave her some pills and a little cup of water to take them with.

"Thank you."

"She's right, Nick," said Collins, "everything's gonna be fine."

I stood up. "Look guys, Deputy Administrator Farrell will be here soon, and I'm scheduled to brief him. I gotta run back to the hotel."

"I'll go with you," said Collins.

"No ... stay with the team, they need you now."

He hesitated for a second, but then he agreed. "Yeah, you're right ... go. We'll be here."

"Take it easy, Nikki."

I touched her shoulder and she smiled at me.

I turned around and walked out. Collins came busting out of the room after me.

"HANG ON!" he yelled.

I turned around. "What's up, Collins?"

"You tell me," he replied, "what was that about?"

"What are you talking about?"

"Vanessa likes you?" He raised an eyebrow. "You've known us a few days and she *likes* you? Look, Vanessa likes two kinds of folks, her teammates and people she's fucking ... so, you fucking her?"

I frowned. "You know, you got some fuckin' balls, kid."

"Did you have something to do with all this?" he asked, moving in closer.

I got right in his face. "Look, dumbass, I got shot too, and I'm the one that helped drag her ass outta harm's way after she blatantly disobeyed an order and gave away our position in the hallway. If she hadn't, then we could've slipped out the back unnoticed."

"Lower your voice!" he commanded.

"Fuck that, you got Rodriquez just doing whatever the fuck she pleases and shit. This is one lunatic team you're running, cowboy, and you wanna stand here, get in my face, and question my loyalty to my country? Have you lost your goddamn mind?"

"What are you talking about?" he whispered. "They fired on us first."

I shook my head. "No cowboy, I tapped Vanessa and signaled for her to move back with me, but she advanced and opened fire. That's how they knew we were there. You got a leak in this department. You better hope it's not her, 'cause you don't even know what she's been into all this time while she was undercover. It's gonna be your ass too, big boy. If I were you, I'd start praying to whoever the hell you pray to that she pulls through, so we can get some answers."

He got quiet. "She couldn't have...."

"You willing to bet your job on it?" I asked. "Your life? Tell me this, professor ... what were they doing while you and I were taking down guards? Her and Parrish? Why where they so late getting up to the fifth floor?"

He sighed. "I dunno."

"Hell, I push pencils all day, but you guys train for this constantly. No reason in hell it should've taken them longer than me to get up to the fifth floor and you know it."

"Fuck you, Johnson," he said angrily, "you need to get the hell on away from me right now."

"Collins, your ego is fucking unbelievable. Look, forget it. Take your chances if you think I'm bullshittin'. I got no dog in this fight. Just remember what I'm here to do."

He rolled his eyes at me.

"Whatever." I shook my head and asked, "And, what about security?"

"What are you talking about now, Johnson?" He was clearly irritated.

"Is someone watching Sullivan's room?" I asked slowly. "Look, whether you wanna consider it or not, if she's playing for the other team and she gets well enough to run, she'll run, unless somebody gets to her first. I strongly suggest you put somebody on her door or it's gonna be a long fuckin' night."

He scratched his head for a second. "HEY!" he yelled at a nearby police officer, waving his hands.

"Agent Collins, special task force, DEA..." he flashed his credentials. "Oh, and this is Agent Johnson with Justice."

The officer removed his hat. "Sergeant Capra, NYPD," he said with a very distinct New York accent.

We each shook hands.

"What happened out there?" he asked.

"Two DEA agents were wounded today," replied Collins, "I need an officer down in ICU for Special Agent Vanessa Sullivan."

"Yeah, we can handle that," Capra said.

"Nobody gets in unless my people give the okay. I'm Tom Collins ... here's my card. Tell 'em to come see me or check with Special Agent Parrish. We'll both be right out in the waiting area, okay?"

"No problem," said Sergeant Capra. "Glad to be of help."

"Thank you, Sergeant."

"Thanks for your help," I said to Capra, "I also need a ride back to the hotel."

"Give me a minute," Capra replied. He grabbed the radio that was affixed to his crisp, clean, blue uniform. He leaned his head over and pushed the button to talk. "Walter...."

"Yeah, Sarge?"

"A young lady's headed out front. Make sure she gets to her hotel safely."

"What she look like?"

Capra looked at me for a quick second. "White lady, long hair wearing brown."

"10-4, I'll pull around."

I waved a thank you to Capra and headed back to the waiting room. I walked up to Rodriguez. "You mind walking me to the car?" I asked.

She looked a little puzzled. "Uh, yeah, no problem."

We headed towards the exit.

"What's going on?" she asked.

"I have to go brief Jack, so I need to know what you saw back there."

"Okay...?"

"Why'd you leave your post, Rodriquez?"

"I wasn't going to sit on my ass and watch everyone die! I engaged because you-"

"Collins gave you a direct order," I interrupted. "So did I, and you disobeyed both."

I checked around for Walter once we got outside, but he hadn't pulled around yet, so we continued talking on the sidewalk a few steps away from the entrance.

"Rodriguez, your job was to watch our backs and cover us. What were you thinking?"

She dropped her head. "I don't know," she replied.

I lifted her chin up and looked her straight in the eyes. "'I don't know' is the new fuck you ... I need an answer."

She grew angry and swatted my hand away. "LOOK LADY, YOU DON'T KNOW SHIT ABOUT ME! WHO THE FUCK ARE YOU TO DRILL ME?" She was very defensive.

"I'm the one ready to shut DTP down for good if I can't get some answers. Like I said, I need an answer, an honest answer, and I need it now."

"Honestly, I didn't feel I could trust your judgment," she snapped, "you damn near got us all killed."

"And, what about Collins? He ordered you to hold your position."

She sighed. "What about him?"

"Look, the bottom line is you had a birds-eye view of the situation. If you'd stayed in place, you could've helped us escape undetected, and all this would've been avoided, but you decided to break team."

"It happened fast. I made a call!"

I shook my head. "There will be consequences."

All of a sudden, she got really loud. "NOT FROM YOU! I REPORT TO AGENT COLLINS, AND HE ALREADY TOLD ME HE'D BACK ME UP, SO GO FUCK YOURSELF, JUSTICE! Find somebody who doesn't do their job and piss all over them. Now," she cocked her head to the side, "you done disciplining me?"

I rolled my eyes. "Far from it. Now, tell me about the choppers."

"Stupid bitch," she mumbled under her breath.

"SAY AGAIN!" I yelled.

"NOTHING!" she replied, angrily.

"Assume I won't stomp your ass into the curb and tell me about the goddamn chopper."

She tensed up. After staring each other down for a minute, she threw her hands up and laughed.

"Whatever, mami," she chuckled, shaking her head, "I saw the helo touch down in the back. There was a whole ass of soldiers pouring out of that thing. I asked for permission to move, but you and Collins acted like y'all were scared, so I did what I had to do." She backed down a little. "I left my post and made my way across the street. By the time Doc radioed, Nikki and Terence were down, and I was already in the back of the parking lot. I needed an elevated vantage point, so I slipped past the four men guarding the back and ran into the parking deck. Two of the men circled around to the side of the building. I heard gunshots and then an explosion. When I got set up, I couldn't see anything with all the fire and smoke, but I figured they hit the van 'cause I couldn't get Doc on the radio."

"Then what?" I asked.

"The two men in the back were fucking around with some device. The pilot shut the chopper down. I thought they were setting off a bomb, so I engaged. I took them both down, but they got back up and one of them detonated the device."

"No explosion?"

"Nah," she replied, "it was definitely some kind of EMP blast. All my gear went dead immediately."

I rubbed my forehead. "Okay, so then what happened?"

"Somebody blew a hole in the side of the building, and a bunch of men in black repelled down the side. I fired on them, but they all made it back to the chopper. I tried to ground the chopper, but that was a waste of time. When the top of the building blew up, I laid down some heavy fire, but their body armor was trippy," she shook her head, "I mean head shots didn't even do it. They all eventually got back up.

They were impenetrable. They closed in on me and launched an RPG at the deck, so I ducked behind a concrete post."

"That it?"

She replied, "I didn't see the chopper take off, but I got the numbers."

I stuck out my hand. She pulled out her note pad, thumbed through it, and then tore a page out. "Here."

I held the note up for a second. "Keep it," I said, "I'll remember."

She smirked. "Is that so? I guess all Justice Agents have photographic memories."

I just looked at her.

"You know what's going on too don't you?" she asked.

"What are you talking about, Rodriquez?"

"I'm talking-"

"Hold on," I interrupted, "you need to lower your voice." She had drawn attention from nearby people.

"I'm talking about those men," she said. "What exactly was stolen from Customs?"

"I can't say right now."

She seemed to calm down a little. "Is Terence in some kind of trouble?"

"What makes you think that?"

Rodriguez looked frustrated as if she knew I was lying. "Navy CID brought me in. They said he was a person of interest in some high-profile U.S. Customs case. They offered me a deal to roll on him."

"What?"

Rodriquez nodded. "Yeah, he's been MIA a lot recently. I found tickets to Arizona."

"And?"

"And, I don't know," she said.

"Well, maybe he's got family there."

"Nope," said Rodriguez, "and we don't have any active cases in that area."

"I've known Slade for a while ... he's a good man."

"Yeah, maybe," she responded, "funny thing is though, I tried to check his file ... he doesn't have one."

"So, what are you saying?" I asked.

"I'm saying I don't trust you or him," she replied, "he just came outta nowhere months back, and I can't find anything on him. All of a sudden, Navy CID comes snooping around. Something stinks, and you know what, it's you. I think you're playing us ... I wanna see the writ."

"First off, Slade is DEA, so you got a problem with him, take it up with Farrell. Second, Slade was a Navy Seal—he fought and bled for this country. He took a bullet today too you know. You're reaching, Rodriguez."

"And you're full of shit," she said. "I know for a fact you are."

A shiny new NYPD cruiser pulled up in front of us. I stepped down off the sidewalk and just waved her off.

"Play games if you want," said Rodriguez, "I know you're hiding something, and I don't buy this inquiry shit either. You damn near got us all killed and you wanna try to pin it on me? Nah, I ain't fuckin' stupid. Tell Farrell what you want, I don't really like his stuffy ass anyway, but I promise you this, I'm gonna get to the bottom of this shit. We gonna settle this tonight."

"Is that so...? Whatever." I just dismissed her and headed towards the car.

"I have a friend in Attorney General McNamara's office."

I spun around and stared at her.

"Won't be long," Rodriguez said, "I've already talked to him. He's waiting for a callback from McNamara." She smiled really big. "Like I say, we're gonna settle this shit tonight."

"You sure you didn't get hit in the head too, Rodriguez? Get some rest, you obviously need it."

"I'll sleep as soon as I oust your phony white ass."

I gave her a half smile and turned around. I tapped on the window a few times to get Walter's attention. It was extremely cold out and Rodriguez was irking me to say the least. Walter got out and walked around to my side of the car. He was young, maybe in his 30's, but you could tell by looking at him the NYPD nightlife had already taken its toll on him. The incriminating evidence included but wasn't limited to a noticeable doughnut belly and a cloud of cigarette smoke which seemed to form a halo around his head.

"Walter, right?"

"Yeah, that's me," he replied. "You Johnson?"

"Yes I am."

He opened the door. "Watch your head ma'am," he cautioned, guiding me safely into the vehicle.

Walter closed my door and ran back around to the driver side. I watched Rodriguez storm back into the hospital. There's no telling what she'd tell the rest of the team, so I had to do something fast. The writ burning a hole in my pocket was as authentic as a three-dollar bill. I don't know if it was her instinct or dumb luck, but she was about to blow my cover wide open and there wasn't a damn thing I could do about it. I had to play it cool and hope I got what I needed before she made contact with U.S. Attorney General McNamara because at that point, it would be game over for me.

Walter climbed into the driver seat. "Where to, Johnson?" he asked, slamming his door shut.

"Four Seasons."

"Pardon my French, but damn, that's a nice hotel," he said, "down on Fifth, right?"

"That's the one." I leaned back against the headrest, pressed the ice pack to my head that I was still holding on to and closed my eyes.

"Rough day, huh?" He shifted the car into drive.

"I imagine it could've been worse, Walter. Not sure how, but I guess it is what it is."

"Yeah I know what you mean. I needed a break too. Just sit back and relax wit' your little ice. We'll be there in no time."

I smiled and we rode off into the dark city streets of Manhattan. The sound of the roaring engine and constant radio chatter wasn't doing much for my migraine, so I rolled down my window a little just to inhale the smell of the city. There's no place in the world like New York. Truthfully, the air is almost repulsive, but at the same time, it's so familiar, you can't live without it. I grew up in the south, Atlanta, Georgia, but New York is home to me now. The cursing, violence, scandals, and drugs—it just all seems appropriate in an odd sort of way. Despite everything that happened that day, it felt good to be back in the Big Apple—back home again.

Walter continued driving and being chatty, but his minor chit chat was drowned out by the sound of my little voice, which at the time was telling me I wasn't the only one at risk of Rodriguez busting up our little charade. Chances are, Slade was just as full of shit as I was. The first day I walked into the DEA and saw him, he stood out like a sore thumb. Vice President Keller is not the most trusting man on planet earth. For whatever reason, he didn't trust the Army, Marines, FBI, CIA, and maybe not even the President for that matter. Keller was a Navy pilot. He completed multiple tours in Vietnam. A sailor is always a sailor, especially when he needs help—he always turns to his brothers—always.

Slade and I were together for years down in Brazil under this asshole of a Seal Team leader named Riggs. He was an evil son-of-a-bitch, who had nothing but disdain for me and probably women in general. Riggs was a real bastard, but not Slade. Slade was actually one of the good guys. I don't know what Keller had on him, but I can't imagine Slade volunteering for this cluster-fuck. Nobody in their right mind would have.

It's funny because every time I look Slade in the face, I remember how messed up everything was for us. I remember how long I was stuck in those darn favelas down there with no guide and no weapons, surrounded by murderers, money, sex, and drugs. The guys used to say the only good day was yesterday. I guess it kinda stuck with me because I keep getting into all kinds of trouble. One thing is certain, I'll never forget the fact that Slade kept me alive on more than one occasion. I owed him my life.

Rodriguez could say whatever she wanted, but there was no way anyone could convince me Slade was not fighting the good fight. As for Sullivan, my suspicions were starting to grow. It took her way too long to get up to the fifth floor. I think she knew those men in the demolition suits were coming. Having thought about it after the smoke cleared and the dust settled, with all of the rounds she fired, I didn't see her hit anything. I had to wonder if she was aiming at the ceiling. Whether Sullivan was working with those men or not, they didn't just pick those demo suits up at the local army surplus store—they jacked a federal transport for them. That meant they were dangerous, skilled operators. It also meant, whatever was going on, I was getting warm.

Chapter 7

My friendly neighborhood NYPD officer, Walter, and I pulled up at the Four Seasons hotel and I thanked him for the ride. I hopped out and started limping. I must've hurt my leg somehow. The closer I got to the front door of the hotel, the more pain I felt. I tried to shake it off but couldn't. What was worse was my energy seemed to be at an all-time low as if I'd been drained of every ounce of my will to keep moving. I struggled through the double doors and drug myself inside.

Halfway through the lobby, I noticed a bunch of white people staring at me as if I were homeless or had been on the wrong end of an Ike and Tina Turner-style domestic dispute. I tried to fix my clothes a little, but it didn't help. My hair was all over the place, my face was battered, and my brand-new coat was singed all over. I was a mess, but at the same time, I'd just survived an explosion in the middle of the city in broad daylight, so I didn't pay those jerks in the lobby any attention. All I cared about was getting cleaned up. Only problem was I didn't have a room. I'd spent the night with Sullivan, figuratively and literally. I needed to get a room key, so I approached the front desk.

It seemed to take forever for me to limp across the lobby, but finally I made it to the front desk. I dropped my half-melted bag of ice onto the counter along with my I.D. The attendant just stared at me for a moment with the strangest look on her face. After a few more looks, she picked up my I.D.

"Are you alright, Ms. Johnson?" she asked.

It seemed like a fairly silly question all things considered, but I responded anyway. "I'm fine ... I need a room key."

"Did you fall?" she asked.

She was sweet, but she seemed to be a sandwich short of a sack lunch.

"You need me to call an ambulance?" she asked.

"Listen... uh, what's your name?" I glanced down at her name tag. "Rose? Listen Rose, I just came from the hospital, so all I need right now is a key ... please."

"I'm sorry, Ms. Johnson, you just-"

"Just the key please."

She lowered her head and typed frantically on her computer. "Uh, this will just take a moment ... ... what room is it?" she asked.

"411."

"Ms. Sullivan?"

I nodded.

"It's none of my business," she confessed, "but, did you two have a fight or something?"

I cocked my head to the side. "What...?"

"Is she okay?" she asked.

I rolled my eyes. "None of your business. Jesus, just please give me the key."

Rose grabbed a card from a drawer, inserted it into a machine and programmed it for the suite. "Here's your key Ms. Johnson."

"Thank you," I said in a frustrated tone. I snatched the key card and headed for the elevators.

"Give Ms. Sullivan my best," said Rose.

I just frowned and walked off. My head was pounding, and my chest was on fire. I took the elevator up and used the new key to get into Sullivan's suite. I headed straight for the bed. I dropped my burnt-up coat on the floor, kicked off my shoes, and fell backwards onto the pillow-soft mattress. I shut my eyes for a moment, but then the phone rang.

"Shit!" I rolled over and picked up the phone. "Hello," I grumbled.

"Ms. Johnson, this is Rose."

"Rose...?"

"Yes, from the front desk," she replied.

"What is it?" I snapped.

"You have a delivery."

I looked up to the ceiling. "Uh, I'll pick it up later."

"The man said it's urgent," she replied.

"Rose, I was just down there ... wait what-"

"It just arrived," she interrupted, "right after you left. Should I send it up?"

"Yes ... no, wait ... I'll come down and get it." I hung up the phone. My paranoia was getting the better of me. I was tired, but I needed to see who was lurking around the lobby looking for me. I was not expecting a delivery, and I had zero contact from Keller.

I grabbed a pair of sneakers from one of my bags. I didn't even bother lacing them up. I stuffed my gun in the back of my pants and headed back downstairs.

I was so paranoid I took the stairs all the way down to stay out of sight. With everything going on, I couldn't be too careful. It took a while—longer than expected, considering my condition—but I finally hobbled my way down to the first floor. I drew my gun and held it close to the side of my leg as I walked towards the lobby. I felt like an idiot, peering around corners and ducking behind furniture, but after a day like the one we had, there was no way I could take any chances. I moved ahead cautiously and stopped short of the front desk, observing everything from a distance. Honestly, I didn't see anything strange, so I took a deep breath, put the gun away, and went up to the desk.

"Rose, you have a package for me?" I said softly.

"Right over here, Ms. Johnson." She turned around. There was a small package on the counter behind her. She took it and placed it on the counter in front of me.

I leaned in close and whispered, "Who delivered this?"

"I don't know, I-"

"Shh, lower your voice!" I looked around to make sure no one was spying on our conversation.

"I'm sorry Ms. Johnson," she whispered, "I took a call in the back, but was only away for a moment. I didn't see anyone, but when I came back, this box was on the desk. It's addressed to you. Is everything okay, Ms. Johnson?"

I paused for a moment. "Yes ... everything's fine ... thank you." I carefully slid the package off the counter and rushed to the elevators because there was no way in hell I was going to walk back up all those stairs. With the way I felt, I wouldn't have made it anyway.

Up on the fourth floor, I hustled back to the room and locked myself in with the package. I sat down at the desk and cut it open with a pair of scissors. Inside was a slim metal box with a small black oval fingerprint reader on top and a red light directly above it. I pressed my thumb against the reader and the light turned green.

"Identity confirmed, awaiting voice authorization," came an electronic voice from the box.

"FBI Assistant Special Agent in Charge, Denise Alexandria Southerland, authorization whiskey-seven-victory-kilo-bravo."

"...Authorization confirmed."

The box's locking mechanism released. I opened the lid and removed a shiny silver cell phone from it. The phone was powered on and already connected to a caller.

"Go for Southerland," I said.

"Agent Southerland," a woman responded, "I need to do an identity challenge, code in Pelican."

"Response Mayflower."

"And, what is the color of the day?" the woman asked.

"Green," I replied.

"Please hold for Deputy Director Anthony Crane."

The line clicked for a second. "I understand you've had a hell of a day, Alex."

All things considered, I was relieved to hear Tony's voice again. "I've had better days, sir," I said.

"Me too," he said, "no doubt about that. Alex, where the hell are you?"

"I can't say, sir," I replied softly.

"Let me try this another way," he responded, "I'm told you're in the field without my authorization. Your team's covering for you, bless their hearts, but when I look at your file, there's a code in here I've never seen before."

"Really...?" I tried to sound innocent.

"Alex, I saw you on the news today with the DEA, now you wanna tell me what the hell is going on?"

"Well, it's ... it's classified."

"BULLSHIT ALEX! OPR paid me a visit today, and I had to call in a favor at the NSA to get your location and get this phone to you."

"I don't know what you want me to say, Tony."

"Well for starters, who the hell is Justice Department Agent Anna Johnson? And why the hell is she standing outside my damn office door looking in at me like she's got a major gripe?" Tony's low, angry tone was telling.

My little charade was coming apart at the seams. "Tony, if I told you, you wouldn't believe me."

"GODDAMN YOU ALEX!" he exclaimed. "A building in New York gets blown up today, rumors are flying that Federal agents turned Manhattan into a goddamn warzone, you lied to me about your so-called vacation, and now I see you on the 12 o'clock news right in the thick of all this shit. To top it off, Attorney General McNamara wants me in his office tomorrow morning. Now I'm not-"

I nearly jumped up out of my skin when he said that. "YOU CAN'T DO THAT TONY!" I gripped the phone tight in my sweaty palm.

"Alex, what the hell have you gotten me into?"

I sighed. "I can't tell you."

"Hold on, Alex, somebody else's at the door... Alex, Roger Campbell's here with me now I'm putting you on speaker."

"We don't have a lot of time here," said Director Campbell.

"Southerland, a young man in the Attorney General's office and an agent from Justice has just started a shit-storm here after getting a call from the DEA."

"Sir, I'm not authorized to discuss-"

"I JUST GOT BRIEFED ON THE SITUATION BY AGENT BILLINGS, KELLER'S SECRET SERVICE DETAIL!" Campbell yelled. "Now, I can buy you some time with the Attorney General, and I can work with Justice, but you've gotta give me something here."

"Okay, I got tail numbers for a chopper," I replied. "It was carrying the troops that attacked us."

Campbell said, "Give 'em to me now."

"Anybody wanna tell me what's going on?" asked Tony.

"Tony, I promise I'll bring you up to speed as soon as possible," said Campbell.

"Director, it was a UH-60 Black Hawk," I said, "tail number 88 dash 26 041."

"Wait one," said Campbell.

I could hear him repeating the tail number in the background.

"You gotta give me a few on this, Southerland," said Campbell. "We're trying to locate it. In the interim, I need your report, now."

Campbell was extremely curt with me, but I understand why—he and Tony both got blindsided by all this. I reluctantly gave them my status report.

"I've been working secretly ... undercover as a Justice Department investigator, and recently gained access to the Los Angeles DEA office. I'm in with fake orders I forged with the Attorney General's signature to assess the DTP situation using a cover I created with Tony's credentials."

"GODDAMMIT, ALEX!"

"I'm sorry, Tony I-"

"It's too late for that now," Campbell interrupted, "go on, Agent Southerland."

"I didn't have time to fabricate history, so I stole Agent Johnson's identity and put her on paid administrative leave. She's probably there because her access has been revoked and no one can figure out what the problem is ... I hacked up her file pretty good and put a virus in there that keeps changing the security access on it." I heard knocking over the line. Agent Johnson must've been getting really impatient by then. I continued confessing my sins, "Basically, Farrell suspects Pamela Harris is Elena Clark of the Williamson Clark Corporation, but can't confirm. It turns out Tesh may be Dr. Williamson. We checked out the Williamson Clark Corp. building today searching for drugs but were attacked mid operation. It was as if they knew we'd be there. A few DEA agents were wounded. The bad news is the enemy blew up the fifth-floor lab to conceal evidence. The good news is we managed to capture one of the assailants. NYPD took him into custody. I need you to get in there and pick him up. Hold him until I can question him."

"How much time do you need?" asked Campbell.

"At least a week," I replied.

"I can do that," Campbell said.

"Director...?" I paused a moment. "You should know he was wearing a demo suit."

"As in the missing experimental demolition suits?"

"Yes, Sir, the very ones Customs is trying to get back. And, guess who's been hanging around?"

"Who?" asked Campbell.

"CIA Director Pearson."

"You mean ex-Director," said Tony.

I gasped. "What?"

"Yeah Alex, he's private sector now."

"You sure this guy was wearing a demo suit?" asked Campbell.

"I bet my life on it," I replied.

"And, what do you know about him?" he asked.

"Not much," I replied. "Military trained, no ID. He doesn't speak a lick of English either, so line up an interpreter for me."

"Roger that," said Campbell. "I'll have Tony send someone over to bring him in. We'll hold him until you return. In the meantime, we're uploading intel on a warehouse in Queens to your mobile."

"Okay, what's the deal with the warehouse?" I asked.

Campbell cleared his throat. "That location was targeted around the same time as the Will Clark facility. Four more locations around the city were hit simultaneously."

"So, they weren't just after us?" I asked.

"Not likely," replied Campbell, "I doubt they knew you were there. We recently intercepted a transmission detailing each location, technical layouts and personnel. We were formulating a strategy to raid these locations under the Patriot Act. Somehow, they found out, and it looks like they were trying to cover their tracks. We're telling the media it's a potential terrorist attack and the FBI's investigating, so I can contain it for now, but that's pretty thin, and it won't hold for long."

"It's been a long day," I said. "I need to know what I'm walking into in Queens."

Campbell continued. "We have a report from DOD Intelligence of the existence of a central database containing identities, tactical plans, targets, and details of global alliances. Intel suggests the lab workers at the Will-Clark building were connecting remotely to the infrastructure at the warehouse in Queens to develop a new computer virus. The virus, along with the computer power in that warehouse, means Alluvion can launch a major attack on our critical infrastructure, or worse, the military defense network."

"But Sir, they dropped an EMP and leveled the fifth floor," I explained. "Whatever's up there's gone."

"Our sources tell us their work was being uploaded every half hour. If they've got a functioning virus, it's already in the warehouse data center. Tony was trying to reach you with no success, so I had him send two HRT teams to intercept the men at the warehouse in Queens."

"Sir, you should've told me all of this before I sent my men in," said Tony.

"Tony, I apologize," replied Director Campbell, "but even now this thing is still unfolding."

"It's my fault," I said. "I should've trusted you with Keller's secret operation, Tony, but-"

"YOU DAMN RIGHT ALEX!" exclaimed Tony. "I sent our teams in with orders to secure the network and the virus. They took out all but one of the bad guys. He's bunkered himself into an office on the second floor, and we suspect he's armed with explosives, so we can't risk breaching. I have a negotiator on the way. I can't tell you how important it is for us to get our hands on the database and the virus. I don't know if we can trust anybody who's not on the line right now. DEA's got a leak and, who knows, we may as well, but we need to know how Alluvion's planning to attack us. I can bet you that information is in that warehouse."

I was quiet for a second. "Sir, this just sounds like a routine FBI negotiation. With all due respect, what's the catch?"

"Southerland, it's Roger," replied Campbell. "Keller's man told me if you blow your cover the deal is off. Honestly,

I don't know what that means, but I imagine it's not a good thing for you."

"Well, that complicates things," I said.

"I understand," Campbell responded, "and I'm sorry, but you've brought this on yourself, Agent. You made a helluva mess here, not to mention violating at least 15 internal policies and federal law. If Keller's recruited you, I understand, but I have to spend the better part of tomorrow and the weekend trying to clean this mess up, so we need to do all we can not to make a bigger mess."

"I'm sorry, sir."

"We'll deal with it later," he said.

"This is what happens when you go off grid," said Tony. "At this point, if I pull the negotiator off, it's gonna raise suspicion."

"I have to assume you know even better than we do the grave consequences involved here," Campbell said. "Give it to me straight Agent, what are your capabilities on the ground?"

"Tony, who's the negotiator?" I asked.

"Sam's in route," he replied.

"Alright, have NYPD setup a perimeter. Have them search every vehicle on the road thoroughly. The traffic should slow Sam down."

"I can do that," said Tony, "but our guys on the ground will not give you access. They're not privy to your assignment, whatever it is. They are under the impression you're on extended leave, understand what I'm saying?"

"No sir, please be clear," I asked.

"I'm saying you're on your own until I get there," Tony replied.

"Southerland, the political pressure is high and Tesh has the upper hand," said Campbell, "you'll have to find a way to make this happen."

I was silent for a moment.

"Alex...? Alex...?"

"I'm here."

"Can we count on you?" asked Campbell.

"I'm an hour away," I said, "so you guys are gonna have to stall Sam somethin' serious ... I just need a window."

"I'll do my best," said Tony. "And, Alex...."

"Yeah...?"

"Be careful," he said.

"Will do."

"I gotta catch a chopper," said Tony, "so, you're gonna have to brief me in the air, Roger."

"I'll call your cell," Director Campbell told him. "Southerland hold the line a second." Campbell cleared his throat. "Southerland, it's just me. There's one more thing...."

"Sir?"

"The computer virus we're talking about...."

"What about it?" I asked.

"It's been used to compromise security at a number of government facilities," said Campbell. "The core worm was developed by a Russian hacker, Dominika Ivanov. Langley's holding her. The virus extracts information from secure networks and transports itself with the data attached around the world without leaving a trace. It's a serious threat to our national security and a high priority for us all. We can't trace it, but Ivanov has been able to identify specific conditions that exist after the virus is present on a network."

"Where'd it last hit?" I asked.

"We traced it to room 411 at the-"

"Four Seasons," I interrupted. "SULLIVAN!"

"The worm was used to compromise your identity," Campbell said. "Your file's security protocols are being stripped down piece by piece from anonymous servers. We can't pinpoint the source because it keeps bouncing around, but eventually they will have it."

"SHIT!"

"Alex, Ivanov claims Tesh and only one other person has access and the knowhow to effectively utilize the virus."

"So, my cover's blown?" I speculated.

"Maybe not just yet. According to Ivanov, it can take up to 24 hours to complete the process, but others may be monitoring in Sullivan's absence. Either way, we don't have much time. According to Keller, your file was being maintained by Navy Intelligence, and as I understand it, the information in it directly links you to the Vice President and this secret mission of his. I don't want to scare you, but if these people are who we think they are, they will kill you."

"There's not a lot I can do here," I said.

"At this point, unless someone else was in that room, Sullivan is our primary suspect. If she survives, bring her in. Be prepared, we may have to cut her a deal."

"I can bring her into the New York field office," I said, "but I need a warrant."

"You're gonna have to improvise," he replied.

"How do you suggest I arrest her without a warrant?"

"I'm afraid that's going to have to be your call, Agent Southerland."

"Director Campbell, I don't know if this is the best strategy. Maybe we should-"

"What's the problem?" he asked.

I dared not tell him I'd just finished pounding pelvises with that bitch, Sullivan, that morning. "Well for starters, what about Farrell?"

"What about him?" he responded.

"He doesn't know, right?

"He's officially on a need to know," said Campbell.

Unexpectedly, there was a knock at my hotel door. "Wait, somebody's at the door, I gotta go."

"Let me be clear, Agent Southerland," said Campbell, "Your orders are to infiltrate the warehouse in Queens and recover the data and the virus. Upon return to the hospital, detain Agent Vanessa Sullivan, bring her here, and interrogate both her and your prisoner from the Will-Clark building arrest, understood?"

They knocked again. "Yes, I got it, sir," I said, inching towards the door.

"Southerland."

"Sir?"

"The terrorist at the warehouse has hostages ... NYPD officers. Kid gloves, understand? You get on site, neutralize the bad man, and rescue those officers. We need this one alive too. Do not, under any circumstances, exceed your orders. There will be consequences for all of us, got it?"

"I understand."

"I hope so," said Campbell. "You've been warned. Don't let us down, and Southerland...?"

"Yes?"

"Godspeed."

The line went dead, so I threw the phone on the bed. Then, I ran out to the door and looked through the peephole. It was Jack and another man standing out in the hallway. I opened the door and invited them in.

Jack introduced the stranger. "Agent Johnson, this is DEA Special Agent Gunter."

"Pleasure to meet you, Johnson," said Gunter.

I shook his hand. "Call me Anna."

"We just landed at J.F.K. a couple of hours ago," said Jack. "I heard the call on the radio. Fire and Rescue's still working to put out the blaze at the Will-Clark building. I checked on the team at the hospital. They said I'd just missed you, so we came right over. You good?"

"Yeah, I'm fine ... what about Sullivan?" I asked.

"Still critical," he replied. "I've got the rest of the team downstairs and we're getting ready to head over to the crime scene."

"Jack, I need to talk to you in private."

He paused a moment, and then glanced over at Gunter. He looked back at me with a confused expression. "Okay," he said. He nodded in Agent Gunter's direction.

Gunter immediately left the room.

"Come on," I said, "we can talk while I get cleaned up." I led Jack back to my room. I walked into the bathroom and turned on the shower. I partially closed the bathroom door, and then ripped off my dingy, tattered clothes.

"FBI's got a break over in Queens—can you hear me, Jack?"

"Yeah," he responded from the other side of the door, "I heard they've got a bomber in a warehouse."

I stretched a shower cap down over my head, opened the glass shower door, and stepped in. I sighed with relief as the scalding hot water pounded against my bruised skin. I pulled off the bandage on my forehead and smeared a soapy washcloth all over my face. "OUCH!" The harsh hotel soap burned all my small scrapes and scratches.

"You okay in there?" he asked.

"Yeah, I'm fine, Jack." I rubbed soap all over my chest, arms and shoulders.

"What do you want to talk about, Johnson?" he asked.

"Jack, I need your help," I said loudly.

"How's that?"

"I have sensitive information about the bomber."

"What kind of information, Anna?"

"He's no bomber."

"What...?" I could hear the surprise in Jack's voice. "He's a decoy," I lied. By then I was covered from head to toe in suds and knee-deep in bullshit. "He's stalling. Word is he's planning to signal a bomber in the crowd once high-level FBI agents arrive on site."

"Who's your source?" asked Jack.

"I can't say, but it's credible." I started rinsing the soap off, twisting, turning and manipulating my body parts to get all the soap out of the cracks and crevices.

"I don't know, Johnson, I mean exactly how credible is this source?"

"Top-level White House," I responded, "and I'd swear my life to protect him. Look Jack, we gotta take this guy down. We can't let him kill innocent people."

"Okay, I'll call it in, and get the team on a-"

"CAN'T DO THAT, JACK!" I exclaimed.

"I don't follow, Johnson."

"Hang on."

I turned off the shower and dried off. I slipped on a terry cloth robe and opened the door. Jack respectfully moved out of my way, averting his gaze. Considering the situation, I was prepared to use my feminine charm, but for some reason, I figured Jack wouldn't go for that. He was very old fashion—a real gentleman—which deep down I think made him even more attractive to me.

"What I'm saying is I need your help to take him down before he can signal the other bomber."

Jack crossed his arms and frowned. "And you're sure about this?"

"I bet my career on it, Jack. My source is concrete."

"How much time do we have?" he asked.

"Hour, maybe two at the most before the FBI negotiator arrives on site."

Jack rubbed his face with the palms of his hands. "This is bad, Johnson. If we interfere, and it goes south, we'll be obstructing-"

"Jack, I don't think I can do this alone. This is not what I do. I'm Justice ... this is not what I do, but I'm going in with or without you."

He held his head down for a moment. Then, he held up his radio. "Gunter." Jack turned around when he saw me start taking my robe off. "Take the team back to the Will-Clark site," Jack ordered. "When the Fire Marshal clears entry, get in there and check for evidence. Call me if you find anything."

"Where are you going to be, sir?" asked Gunter.

"Don't worry about me."

"But, Jack I-"

"JUST DO IT, GODDAMMIT!" exclaimed Jack.

"This doesn't make sense man what's the deal?"

"Agent Gunter, we all have our orders ... call me if you get anything."

"Yes, sir."

Jack clipped his radio back onto his belt. "You decent now?" he asked.

"I'm good," I said pulling a black t-shirt down over my head.

Jack turned around as I pulled my jeans up. He kinda looked off into the corner while I finished dressing. I think he was the first guy I'd met in a while, who didn't take high speed mental photographs of my 34 B's while we were talking."

"Toss me those," I pointed to a pair of black socks on the other side of the bed.

He walked over and handed me the little ball of socks.

"So, you're in?" I asked, pulling a sock onto my right foot.

"I've got a truck with equipment out back. So, what's the plan, Johnson?"

"No plan," I replied. "I figured we'd park a few blocks up and find a way in."

"God, I must be out of my mind," said Jack, rubbing his hair with both hands.

I chuckled a little. "Well, I could lie to you if it'll make you feel better."

"Don't stress yourself on my account," he retorted. "Look, finish up and meet me down at the car in 10." Jack turned and started walking towards the door.

"Thank you for trusting me, Jack."

He didn't turn around. "I don't," he said, "but, I can't risk being wrong about you and just sitting on the sidelines. Hurry please."

I was surprised Jack went along with everything so easily. He was acting so strange the day before. I wasn't complaining one bit though. There's no way I could make it in and out of that warehouse alive if I didn't have somebody watching my back. I was in deep water, and the powers to be seemed all too ready to feed me up to the big shark. My cover is pretty much blown, I nearly died earlier, and once again I would be walking blindly into a dangerous situation. My day was getting worse by the moment.

I laced up my boots and threw on a black sweater. It was athletic looking and made out of a stretchy material, but thick enough for a cold, New York Autumn night. I stuck my guns into a backpack and grabbed the cell phone off the bed. I turned out all the lights, left the room, and rushed to the elevator. I reached the lobby and exited the hotel. Outside, I spotted Jack right away. He was loaded up and ready to roll, sitting in the driver seat of a parked dark navy-blue Chevrolet Tahoe with government plates. I ran around to the passenger side and hopped in.

"You got the location?" I asked.

"Yeah, here have a look." He pointed to a side street on the map on the monitor in the middle of the dash. "Could be our way in right there on the side. May run into some road blocks along the way. You got any ideas, Anna, 'cause I'm fresh out?"

"Let me worry 'bout that, Jack."

"Full of surprises, aren't you?" he said, sarcastically.

"One does what one can ... you ready?"

"Yeah." Jack shifted into drive. "Buckle up."

I pulled my seatbelt over my chest and clicked it into place. Jack smashed his foot down on the accelerator, and we burned out of the hotel parking lot. He switched on the lights to cut through traffic. Halfway to Queens it started raining and the streets got slick, but Jack didn't slow down one bit. Time was not on our side. Every time he glanced at the clock on the radio, he sped up just a little more. Whether he bought my story or not, he sure as hell was driving with a high sense of urgency.

Keller and Campbell both had stacked the odds against me. I felt like my freedom and my life was on the line, and that's not my paranoia leading me down the garden path either. Vice President Keller was no boy scout. Deep down, I feared if I failed, he wouldn't have me arrested, it might just be my funeral. The more I thought about it, the more I realized I was the only one other than Keller who knew everything about the operation versus just pieces of it. Everyone knows what happens to people who know too much. But I'd much rather die by my own foolish hands than by that slick devil, so that's what motivated me to continue running full speed ahead into danger.

The closer we got to the warehouse in Queens, the faster my heart beat. I had to slow my breathing and stop my mind from wandering all over the place. Once again, I was plagued by *what if's*, but if I was going to make it through the night, I had to get Keller, Jack, Campbell, Sullivan and everybody else out of my head. The best thing for me to do was to focus on the task at hand—the data, the virus, the terrorist, and the traitor.

The flashing blue lights from the grille of Jack's SUV reflected off the wet city streets. Motorists frantically swerved out of our way as we blasted through red lights and crowded intersections. We pulled up and parked in an alley about four blocks away from the warehouse. NYPD's perimeter was not directly visible, but we could see flashing red and blue lights illuminating in the distance. Jack and I got out and walked around to the back of the truck. He opened the rear hatch, reached in, and pulled out a vest.

"Come here Johnson." He took the vest with both hands and guided it over my head.

I pulled my hair out from under the vest and fastened the Velcro straps on each side around me. Jack put his vest on and opened a lockbox in the back of the truck. Inside were flash grenades, handcuffs, flashlights, two-way radios, and an assortment of handy little gadgets. We decided it was a good idea to have a peek from a distance first, so we moved down the alleyway to get a closer look. I watched Jack as he checked out the scene.

"What are you seeing out there, Jack?"

"Doesn't look good for the home team, Anna," he said, solemnly as he peered into the distance with a small pair of binoculars. "Come on, let's head back to the truck."

We walked slowly back to the rear of the truck. "NYPD's got a perimeter set up a couple blocks away," said Jack, rubbing his chin. "We've gotta get through there ... I dunno, maybe we can approach from the left. Might be able to pass by the road block undetected. We'll have to hike another two blocks up to the warehouse. They've got the place surrounded, so we'll have to enter through the rear ... it's probably less guarded, but we still have to take down the officers back there without killing them or causing a scene. Won't buy us much time, but ... Jesus Anna, what the hell are we doing here, we can't attack fellow-"

"Wait, what if I could get us a window of time?" I interrupted.

Jack squinted at me. "How?"

"I know a guy on the force who owes me a solid."

Jack handed me a couple of grenades. "See what you can do. I want to help, but if we can't do this without hurting cops, I can't be a part of it. I'm sorry."

"Just hang on," I said. "Let me make a call." I stuck the explosives in my backpack and walked a few steps away from Jack. I used my new little silver cell phone to dial Tony's mobile, but it went straight to voicemail. I redialed a couple of times and finally got him.

"Crane," he answered. The noise from the chopper he was riding in made it hard to hear him.

"HEY, IT'S ME," I yelled, being careful not to say his name.

"Alex, I'm ready for you," said Tony. "Tell me what you need."

"A small window," I replied, "west side perimeter and then the rear entrance of the warehouse right after."

"Wait one," he said.

I waited for a couple of minutes, all the while watching Jack from the corner of my eye as he finished suiting up. He walked over to me and frowned. His impatience was showing.

"Gotta go," he whispered.

I put a finger to my lips and whispered, "Shhh, give me a minute."

After about another minute, Tony came back to the line. "Southerland, you there?" he asked.

"Yeah, I'm still here."

"I called in a request to transition security from NYPD officers to FBI Agents on the west side perimeter. It's going down in precisely five minutes. You'll have exactly one and a half minutes to clear the perimeter. Then you got two minutes to get into the warehouse before the team in back is in position. I'm sorry, but that's the best I could do. Good luck." Tony disconnected the line.

"FUCK!" I yelled, shoving my phone back in my pocket.

"What?" Jack asked.

"I got us a window, Jack, but it's in five minutes, and we got even less time to get from the perimeter into the warehouse. Come on, we gotta hustle."

"Alright." Jack tugged his vest to make sure it was on tight. "Look Anna, when we get in there, let's split up and take him from both sides." He handed me a radio. "I've got you set to channel three."

"Jack, you know you don't have to do this."

"You armed?" he asked.

I nodded.

"We're wasting time, ma'am." Jack drew his weapon and took off back down the alleyway.

I reached into my backpack, pulled out one of my guns and followed him. We sprinted towards the perimeter and just barely made it in time. The officers had already left their posts and were meeting their FBI contact for new orders.

Jack and I hid behind the bushes on the side of the street near the roadblock. The police officers gathered around a man in plain clothes and a grey trench coat. It was our only chance to get through, so we had to move while they were occupied. We crept out onto the street and ducked down beside a cruiser that was parked behind the blockade. Then, we waited until the coast was clear and ran full speed towards the warehouse.

We stopped midway and slipped around the corner of a building to make sure we were still in the clear. Jack looked at me and tapped his watch. We only had a few minutes to get to the warehouse and get inside, so we threw caution to the wind and hustled.

We reached the warehouse with less than a minute to spare. As Tony promised, there were no cops in sight. We went straight for the back. Jack used his elbow to break one of the glass panes in the back door. Then, he reached in and unlocked the deadbolt. We didn't have to worry about alarms or anything. As usual, the FBI was playing it by the book and had already cut power to the building. We rushed inside and not a moment too soon. I barely had my foot in the door before an agent shined his flashlight into a nearby window. I nudged the door shut with my foot, and Jack and I backed up against the wall to stay out of sight.

"Thought I heard something," said an agent. "What?" asked another.

"Not sure. Probably nothing. By the way, how's Barbara?"

"Same old bitch man, I can't do no right," the agent replied.

They both laughed. As soon as they moved away from the door, Jack and I crawled off in opposite directions. There were stairs on both sides of the warehouse. From a distance, I could see a dim, blue light emitting from a door on the second floor. I figured that had to be our guy. On my way up the stairs, I noticed a motion sensor against the wall. The power was down, so it must have been battery operated or on a backup supply. I stepped over it to avoid detection and continued up, staying low and pushing through all the thick cobwebs on my way to the top.

Up on the second floor, I worked my way around and met Jack in front of the room. The door was cracked open. We listened close to try and assess the situation. The bomber was talking to the cops.

"I tell you one last time," he warned, "I wish to speak with the FBI. I will only speak with the FBI negotiator. You now have 60 seconds to comply."

Jack and I looked at each other. He stood up and got ready to breech, but I motioned for him to wait. I nudged the door open and looked inside. The man was not in sight, so Jack and I snuck into the room and spread out.

The warehouse was a subterranean dump, but the room we walked into was right out of a Fortune 500 company. It was extremely high-tech with endless rows of computer racks and a command console near the front. Despite the fact the FBI had cut the power to the building, all the equipment in that room was still running on backup power. I walked down the middle row and back up the next one on the right. After a few more steps, I stopped in my tracks. The terrorist was standing across the way, facing the window. Search lights illuminated the room, casting the man's shadow across the floor. He was using a cell phone that was laid on top of a nearby desk. He had the phone on speaker, so I could hear the officer on the other end.

"Sir, the FBI negotiator is still in route. I'll try to patch you through to an agent, but I need you to stay calm. We don't want anyone else getting hurt."

"You have 30 seconds," said the man.

I moved in as close as possible without being detected. I peered around the corner and saw four officers gagged, stripped of their weapons and cuffed together. Another officer was face down on the floor, and there were two gunmen nearby. None of them were moving and blood was everywhere. Obviously, things had gone bad fast, and I couldn't let it get any worse. Jack joined me and moved in directly behind me.

"Okay, sir," said the policeman, "I have the FBI negotiator online. He's almost here, but he's going to talk to you over the phone, alright?"

"Sir, this is Special Agent Samuel Robinson, FBI. I'll be your negotiator, but I want you to understand I'm not the man in charge. I run your requests up the flagpole, but I don't make the final decisions ... I want you to think of me as your champion. I'm here to help. I understand you gave our officers time to get me on the phone without taking further action. I appreciate that, you being reasonable, and I'm confident we can both make it out of this thing okay if we continue to be reasonable and keep our heads about us."

"If you are not the one in charge, then why are we talking, Special Agent Samuel Robinson?"

"Call me Sam."

"Why are we talking if you are not in charge, Agent Sam Robinson?" the man asked again.

"I'm the only one who's interested in getting you what you want. The rest of these guys are ready to take you down, and no matter the situation, I don't think either of us want that to happen."

The man was silent for a moment. "Perhaps you are right Agent Sam or perhaps not."

"Well, let's pretend just for a moment that I am right, and let's talk, just you and me. What's your name?"

"I have no name," the man replied, "but I have five, I repeat five hostages."

"How 'bout I call you Bob?" Sam said.

"It is irrelevant."

Sam was a very skilled negotiator. He knew exactly what and what not to say. "Stay with me, Bob, we're making progress here. Tell me, what's going on up there?"

The assailant's tone changed. "I will die soon," he said, slowly and remorsefully.

"Bob, nobody's going to die," Sam promised. "Listen, I can help, but you gotta give me something to work with ... is anybody hurt up there?"

"DO NOT HANDLE ME, AGENT ROBINSON!" he exclaimed.

"Look, I'll be honest. It sounds to me like you're a smart guy, Bob, so you must know how this thing works. How about we skip through some of the formalities ... I need to know about the hostages, Bob."

The man started pacing back and forth. "There are five police officers, one wounded, one dead. They are all prisoners of war."

Sam lowered his tone. "Bob, you know I'm gonna need proof those four officers are alive and well up there before we can move on. I need to speak with one of the officers."

Bob grabbed the phone from the desk and walked over to the officers sitting on the floor. One had a gunshot wound to the chest. He was slumped over, but still breathing. The gunman pulled the female officer's gag down and put his gun to her head. She started crying.

"SPEAK BITCH!" Bob commanded, holding the phone up and grinding his pistol against her temple.

"Th... thi... this is off ... officer Williams," she stuttered.

"Williams, this is Sam, I'm with the FBI, are you okay?"

"Yes," she replied.

"Is everybody alright up there?" asked Sam.

"There's an officer down, another with a gunshot wound to the chest. The suspect is armed with explosives and he has our guns."

The assailant replaced her gag and put the cell phone back on the desk.

"Their lives are in your hands Special Agent Sam Robinson."

"How can I help, Bob?"

"I work for a Holy man," Bob replied. "He has a message I must deliver."

Sam asked, "What's the message?"

"You have 10 minutes to locate Assistant Special Agent in Charge Denise Alexandria Southerland with the Domestic Counterterrorism Unit of the FBI. Find her and bring her to me. I will deliver the message to her and her alone. You have 10 minutes Agent Sam Robinson, 10 minutes starting now."

"Okay I can do that, but I need more time. You have to give me-"

"DO NOT ATTEMPT TO CONTROL THE SITUATION, AGENT ROBINSON!" exclaimed the man. "I will destroy this building and kill everyone in it. I am here to die today, AND I AM PREPARED TO RIGHT NOW! I have made peace with God. Do not make a fool of me."

"Listen Bob ... Bob, I'll get Southerland here, you have my word, but I need you to promise me you won't harm her or the hostages. I need your word that you won't set off that bomb you got up there. You promise me that, and I'll get Southerland on the line."

"NO!" said Bob, angrily. "BRING HER TO ME OR I WILL KILL EVERYONE! You have 10 minutes Agent Sam Robinson."

"Okay, okay, just calm down here, I-"

"NINE MINUTES, 50 SECONDS!" yelled Bob.

"Bob, we're locating Southerland now, but she's no longer with the Bureau, so I need more time."

"BULLSHIT!" he screamed. "DO NOT FUCK WITH ME! BRING HER TO ME OR THE DEATHS OF THESE POLICE OFFICERS WILL BE ON YOUR HEAD!"

"You're right, Bob," said Sam. "I'm sorry, I'm not trying to mess with you. Honestly, I'm just trying to locate her now. You gotta give me more time to find Southerland and get her onsite. I told you I'm not the decision maker. I gotta run your request up the chain. We talked about how being reasonable would get us through this thing. Now's the time for us to be-"

"NINE MINUTES!"

The terrorist walked to the window again. His back was to me, so I took a chance. I stepped out and motioned for the officers on the floor to my right to get down. "FBI," I shouted, "DROP YOUR WEAPON AND LIE FACE DOWN ON THE FLOOR!"

Jack leaped out of the shadows and covered the man from the left side.

The man dropped his gun and turned around. He smiled. "Agent Southerland?"

"THAT'S RIGHT ASSHOLE, NOW DROP IT!"

"Agent Southerland?" Jack asked, his weapons still trained on the hostile.

"LONG STORY, JACK!" I exclaimed.

Bob held up a detonator in his left hand, so we could clearly see it. He had enough C-4 strapped to his chest to vaporize the entire warehouse. From a distance, the bomb looked sophisticated, and unfortunately, the timer was on final countdown.

"DON'T MOVE MAN!" I yelled. I noticed Jack out of the corner of my eye.

"Johnson, what's going on here?" asked Jack.

With all that was going on, I couldn't help but notice how conflicted Jack seemed. He had this spooky look on his face like he was trying to figure out just who he should turn his gun to—the bad man or the woman who was answering to a name he'd never heard before.

"SHUT IT DOWN!" I yelled.

The terrorist did not comply. He slowly started advancing toward me.

"What's going on up there, Bob?" asked Sam, over the speakerphone.

"Sam, it's me," I replied, "you gotta give us a second here."

"The hell...?" Sam was just as confused as Jack.

"Okay Bob ... it's Bob, right? Look Bob, you wanted me here, so I'm here," I said.

"Johnson, what the fuck's going on?"

I could hear frustration and confusion in Jack's voice.

"HANG ON A SECOND JACK!" I waved at him. "JUST HANG ON A SEC!"

Bob held his fist up higher with his thumb positioned directly over the red button on the detonator. A cluster of braided red, green, and black wires ran from the bottom of the detonator into the back of the device on his chest. The timer was down to 16 minutes and 30 seconds. Bob took another quick step forward.

"DON'T FUCKING MOVE MAN!" I shouted.

"Agent Southerland, I have message for you," Bob said.

"SHUT THE BOMB DOWN FIRST AND WE CAN TALK!" I replied.

"The bomb will blow in less than 15 minutes, but I press this button and it will explode right fucking now. Hear me and live but defy me and die. Now, lower your fucking weapons."

I paused for a moment. Then, I lowered my gun. "Put it down Jack," I said.

"I've got a shot," said Jack.

"No Jack, wait."

"PUT THE FUCKING GUNS DOWN NOW!" Bob yelled, shaking the detonator in the air.

I slowly kneeled and put my gun on the floor. "Kick it over to me Agent Southerland," he said.

I complied and so did Jack, reluctantly.

Bob picked his gun back up. He moved in and pointed it at my head. "If you move, I will kill you," he said.

"Alright, Bob you got my attention," I said softly, "now what?"

Suddenly, he turned his gun to Jack. "You ... get them out of here."

Jack didn't hesitate. He ran over and uncuffed the officers.

"I SAID GET OUT!" shouted Bob.

The female officer dashed for the door. Jack and another officer carried the wounded and the dead man out. At that point, it was just me and Bob left in that server room.

"What's going on up there?" Sam asked over the cell phone. I could hear the distress in his voice.

The moment Bob turned his attention back to the phone on the desk, I pulled my backup weapon out of my backpack and drew down on him. "DROP IT, MOTHAFUCKA!"

The terrorist spun around, and I instinctively fired. His gun hit the floor, he dropped the detonator, and grabbed his throat with both hands. He fell to his knees and collapsed down onto the ground.

"SHOTS FIRED! SHOTS FIRED!" Sam radioed.

I ran over, kicked his gun away, and rolled Bob onto his back. I pressed the barrel of my gun against his temple. I thought to myself, I just can't seem to catch a break. I was aiming for his shoulder, but he moved. The bullet caught him right in the throat. He was hurt bad.

"De fucking folk dør!" he murmured, squirming around on the floor, blood spewing from his neck.

"What...?" I leaned in.

"De vil all dør!" he yelled, spitting blood everywhere. "DEN STORE FLOMEN REGNER NED PÅ DERES FAMILIER, MEN DE VUNNET'T LEVER SE DET!"

The timer on the bomb was ticking away.

"SHUT IT DOWN NOW, AND I'LL CALL FOR A MEDIC!"

"ARRGGHHH!" he screamed out in agony. He was literally drowning in his own blood.

"How do I shut the bomb down?" I asked.

He coughed violently.

I ground the barrel of my gun on the side of his head. "How do I shut the fucking bomb down man?"

"YOU BITCH!" he murmured, blood spilling from both corners of his mouth. He looked over and tried to grab the detonator, but I pushed it away.

"IT'S NOT TOO LATE!" I yelled. "Tell me how to shut it down and I'll get a medic up here."

He looked me in the eye and smiled as if he knew something I didn't. He started gasping for air, his eyes rolled into the back of his head and he was gone. I locked my eyes in on the timer on his chest. I'd wasted damn near five minutes on his dying ass. The timer was down to five minutes, ten seconds, and counting. Carefully, I shifted the device around on his chest to look under it and try to trace the wires. I studied the device for almost a minute, but I was no bomb disposal expert.

"THE FUCK'S GOING ON UP THERE?" asked Sam. "Fuck it, I'm coming up!"

I sprung up and grabbed the cell phone. I took it off of speaker and held it to my head with my right shoulder.

"Sam it's me."

"Seriously, Southerland? The fuck are you doing up there? How'd you-"

"Sam, listen to me ... the terrorist's down, but we got about three minutes before this bomb goes off."

"TALK TO ME, SOUTHERLAND! TELL ME ABOUT THE DEVICE!"

"Shit, uh, it has multiple triggers ... I don't see a ground or anything, hell I don't fuckin' know-"

"What kind of explosive are we talking about?" Sam asked.

"C4—a lot of fucking C4!"

"THERE'S GOTTA BE A GROUND!" Sam yelled.

"I'm looking for it, but I don't see anything," I replied, becoming more frantic with every second that passes.

"CLIFF, GET THE BOMB SQUAD UP THERE!" yelled Sam.

"No time Sam ... I'm coming out. GET YOUR PEOPLE BACK!"

"What?" Sam starts yelling, "Fuckin' shit, CLIFF FORGET THE BOMB SQUAD, GET EVERYBODY BACK NOW! COME ON, GET EVERYBODY BACK!"

I hung up and stuck the man's cell phone in my backpack. Then, I ran out of that room like my life depended on it, because it did. I tripped the motion sensor at the bottom of the stairs, and an alarm sounded, but I couldn't have cared less about a few flashing red lights—I had to get the fuck outta dodge. I hustled out back, through the parking lot and headed straight for a small patch of brush I spotted in the distance. I ducked down in that trench and covered my head with both my arms.

When the bomb exploded, the blast was so loud it was like putting your ear right over the muffler of a backfiring car. Glass, debris, smoke, and God knows what else spewed out all over the place. The shockwave from the blast sent me airborne. I flipped over a couple of times and landed shoulder-first on a pile of rocks. I felt heat on my back and realized my sweater had caught fire, so I rolled around in the dirt, wrestled off my sweater, and kicked it away.

"FUCK ME!" I yelled. Then, I sat up and watched the entire building, or what was left of it, collapse into a pile of rubble and dust in less than a few seconds. I crawled back to the edge of the parking lot. Visibility was zero, but I could tell the warehouse was toast. I'd be surprised if the foundation was still intact.

I lay on the pavement for nearly 10 minutes just trying to pull it together. Two explosions in one day was too much for one person to handle. It was like a horribly written "Bad Boys" movie. Once my ears stopped ringing, I pushed myself up to my feet and circled around to the front lot, cautiously. The windows of every car out front were shattered, but the cars parked closer to the building had been overturned and damn near melted by the heat from the blast. The entire block was covered in a blanket of dust and debris. I walked about ten more paces and surprised a crowd of NYPD officers. They all pointed their guns directly at me.

"FREEZE!" yelled an officer.

"DON'T MOVE GODDAMMIT!" exclaimed another.

"GET DOWN!" I heard one shout.

"DOWN ON YOUR KNEES RIGHT NOW!"

I put my hands up quickly and dropped to my knees. "AGENT JOHNSON, DOJ," I yelled, keeping my hands visible. "I'M WORKING WITH THE DEA." I looked over at Jack who was leaning against a police car. A paramedic was checking him out, but I knew he saw me.

"NOW, GET ALL THE WAY DOWN ON THE GROUND!" exclaimed the closest officer to me. "GET DOWN OR I'LL SHOOT."

"I CAN'T MAN, I'M FUCKED UP!" I exclaimed.

He hesitated for a second. "WELL, JUST DON'T FUCKING MOVE!" he shouted.

They all advanced towards me. One of the officers circled behind. He snatched off my backpack, grabbed both my arms, and twisted them together. Then, he cuffed me with absolutely no regard for my busted shoulder.

"SHIT!" I yelled as he yanked me up to my feet. "TAKE IT EASY MAN, I TOLD YOU I'M A FEDERAL AGENT!"

"YEAH, AND I'M THE PRESIDENT OF THE UNITED STATES," he replied, sarcastically, "GET HER UP AND OUTTA HERE!"

I felt like an idiot—like a bank robber who forgot to put gas in the getaway car. Why on earth did I walk to the front of that building. I should've just snuck off and caught a cab. What was I thinking? I was just thankful I'd made it out of there alive. That was too close for comfort. One of the officers locked me into the back of a squad car. I was hurt, but like I say, I was alive, and that's gotta count for something. I leaned my head back and just tried to relax as best I could, handcuffed in the back of a police car.

About a half hour passed, and the car door opened. It was Sam. He leaned his head inside the car. "Southerland, what the hell's going on?"

"Sam, you've just gotta trust me on this, I-"

"Trust you...?" he interrupted, "I had orders to secure this facility. You charged in and fucked that up. You got no credentials, hell you're not even supposed to be here, I thought you were out on vacation in a goddamn third world country and-"

"Sam, I could use a little medical attention right now."

"Yeah, well   I could use some answers, Southerland!" he replied, sharply.

I looked up at him and frowned. "Really Sam? All my years with the Bureau and you're treating me like a suspect?"

He rolled his eyes and sighed heavily. He pushed me forward, reached down and uncuffed me. "If you run-"

"Sam, why on earth would I run? I wouldn't be here if I wasn't ordered to be. You know me."

"Yeah, I know you alright, but I also know people, and everybody runs." He stood up. "I NEED A PARAMEDIC OVER HERE!" he yelled.

A young man in a dark blue jacket with an EMT patch and matching cap rushed over to the police car. I turned my body to the left until my legs hung out of the car. My shoulder was busted up pretty bad. It hurt just to move.

"Where are you hurt ma'am?" he asked.

"I fell on my shoulder," I replied.

"Let me have a look at you," said the paramedic. The left sleeve of my t-shirt was soaked in blood, so he cut it straight up the side to get to my injury. "I can treat the cuts, but you're going to need to get this x-rayed. Can you walk?"

"I think so."

"Okay." He reached out both hands. "Here, let me help you up."

Carefully he pulled me to my feet. I followed him to the back of an emergency vehicle.

"Sit down right there on the edge for me," he said.

I took my time sitting down on the bumper while the paramedic searched for a few medical supplies inside. Sam stood right by me to keep an eye on me. The paramedic hopped back down out of the ambulance, and then cleaned my shoulder with a medicated pad. Then, he pushed the little pad into my shoulder and worked it around in a circular motion. It hurt like hell. After strapping on a few bandages, he fitted my left arm with a sling.

"That too tight?" he asked. "No, it's fine ... thank you."

He smiled. "Just doing my job, ma'am."

"Brian, I need you over here!" yelled a man in the distance.

"Be right there!" he responded. "Listen Miss, I want you to get to the hospital as soon as possible ... you can rest right here as long as you need, but then get to the nearest hospital, got me?"

I nodded.

"Good. My name's Brian. I'll be right over there if you guys need me." He gave Sam a nod.

"Thank you," said Sam. He patted Brian on the back.

"No problem, sir," Brian said. And then he ran off to help someone else.

Sam put his right foot up next to me on the bumper of the ambulance. "Talk to me kid," he said, resting his arm on his knee.

"Sam, I can't explain what's going on, but you gotta trust me ... I'm under orders ... and, I need you to do something you're not going to like."

"What are you talking about?" he asked.

"Agent Jack Farrell arrived with me ... I need you to detain him."

"DEA Deputy Administrator Jack Farrell? NO FUCKING WAY KID! ARE YOU INSANE? Did you bump your head too?"

"Listen to me Sam, you do this for me, and I'll give you whatever you need to make all this right, whatever you want me to say I'll say."

Sam dropped his eyes and shook his head. "You know, you've come through for me in the past Southerland, but right now I gotta take you into custody until we can sort this out." Sam turned and gestured to a group of nearby officers.

"Sir?" responded the nearest cop.

Sam waved him over. "Could you come over here for a second?"

"Yes, sir." The officer sprinted up to us.

"Listen, my team is a little preoccupied, so I need you to book this woman for me."

"What's the charge?" asked the officer.

Sam looked me right in the eye. "Obstruction."

"SAM, DON'T DO THIS!" I yelled.

Sam didn't budge.

"You know Crane lands in five minutes," I told him. "You can do your job now or get ass fucked when he lands."

Sam turned and pointed his finger at me, "YOU KNOW WHAT, FUCK YOU SOUTHERLAND!" he yelled. Then, he turned to the police officer. "Book her and get her out of my sight!" he commanded.

The officer gave me a confused look, but then he just shrugged his shoulders and went to work. He searched me, and then picked up my backpack. He unzipped it and shifted around the contents. He took note of my guns and grenades in the bag before dragging me over to his police cruiser. He opened the door, put cuffs on my wrists and put me in the back. And just like that, I was back in the one place I knew my cover wouldn't last long—police custody.

"You're making a mistake officer ... don't do this man!"

"Ma'am, I'm just doing my job," he said. Then, he slammed the car door shut. He got into the driver seat and grabbed his radio. "Dispatch, this is 10 David."

"Go ahead 10 David," came a voice over the radio.

The officer held up my false ID and said, "I need outstanding warrants on a Johnson, Anna, 36 years-old ... eh, black? Well, she looks Caucasian, but her I.D. says black female."

"Copy that, 10 David, hang on...."

"Listen officer-"

"Believe it or not it's Roger," he said in a dry tone.

"Roger...?" I chuckled a little. "Roger, I know you're just doing your job, but I'm a Federal Agent. Give me 10 minutes, and my boss will come here and clear this thing up."

"I don't know, I-"

"Hey, if he doesn't show, take me in. What you got to lose?"

"10 David, Dispatch," said the woman on the radio.

"10 David here," said Roger.

CONTAINMENT

"No warrants. Anna Johnson is a Federal Agent ... United States Department of Justice."

"10-4, I've been instructed by the FBI to bring her in on obstruction charges."

"Roger that 10 David, over.".

Roger hung up his radio and started the motor.

"Roger, come on, five minutes? You can wait five minutes, can't you?"

Roger sighed. "Listen, whatever's going on, you can work it out at the station." He shifted into drive. "Right now-"

Out of nowhere a blast of debris flew up on the windshield of Roger's police cruiser, and he diverted his attention away from me. The distinct chuff of whirling helicopter rotors got my attention too as Tony's FBI-branded UH-60 Black Hawk slowly descended onto the parking lot.

"WAIT!" I exclaimed. "Look, he's here now."

We both looked up like little kids searching the night sky for a UFO. As the chopper descended, the wind from its propellers cleared away the smoke and debris in a circle all around it. Everyone grabbed hold of their hats, paperwork and anything else of importance light enough to get blown away. Roger looked back at me in the rearview mirror.

"Stay right there," he said, "I'll be back." He shifted back into park and opened the door.

"CRANE!" I yelled. "My boss is FBI Deputy Director Anthony Crane. You tell him I'm here, okay?"

He just looked at me for a moment. Then, he spun around, grabbed his hat and jumped out. After a few moments, Roger returned to the car with a crowd of men. He walked up to the car and opened the door. Roger moved out of the way, and there stood Tony in the flesh. I couldn't have been happier to see him. It'd been so long.

"You alright?" he asked, leaning in.

"Get me out of these," I said, raising my arms just high enough for him to see my restraints.

Tony seemed agitated that I was locked up like a criminal. He stood up and moved out of the way. "HELP HER OUT OF THERE AND GET THOSE CUFFS OFF, NOW!"

"Yes, sir," said Roger, who eagerly complied. He uncuffed me while I was still sitting in the back, and then helped me to my feet. "Sorry 'bout this," he said.

"Thanks Roger."

"No problem," he replied. "Uh, again, I'm real sorry, I was just following orders." He gave me back my bag and stood there with a shameful expression on his face.

I pulled my backpack up on my shoulder and looked around. Tony got there right in the nick of time. I looked around and saw FBI H.R.T. agents putting Farrell in the back of an unmarked car. I was struggling to come up with a good reason to hold him. I knew in my heart it was wrong, but I had to do some serious damage control, and I didn't have time for a bunch of lame questions from anybody, especially Farrell.

"Let's go," said Tony. He and the four FBI agents with him escorted me over to a Chevy Suburban. I threw my backpack in and climbed into the back seat. Tony got in and closed the door. The other agents stood guard outside.

"Tony, I'm freezing."

He reached down and turned up the rear heat using the switch in the middle console. "Alex, you were told to neutralize the terrorist, not take him down."

My jaw just dropped. "Tony, what's your problem?"

"Oh, you mean besides the fact you used me to break the law, you killed a man, and blew up a city block all while you're out on a bullshit, so-called leave that happened to be part of a top-secret operation you failed to inform me—your supervising officer—of? To top it off, now we've got nothing."

"I got his cellular...." I took the phone out of my bag. "Get it to the lab and let me know what you turn up."

"Now, you're giving me orders?" Tony shook his head and sighed, but he took the phone from me anyway. Then, he cracked open the door. "Hey, George...."

"Sir?" an agent responded.

"Got this off the terrorist," Tony explained. "Get it to the lab ASAP. Make sure they understand it's their new number one priority. Nothing else matters right now!"

"Yes, sir!" George took off with the phone.

Tony shut the door again. "I see you managed to piss Sam off." He reached in his pocket and pulled out a black leather badge holder. He flipped it open, "Here, I found this in your desk. Thought you might need it."

I took my shield and rubbed it against my shirt to wipe off the fingerprints. "Thank you, Tony."

"So, all this stuff about you going out on leave because of what happened in the consulate was just a bunch of bullshit?"

I nodded.

"And you couldn't've said anything to me?" he asked.

"I was trying to protect you."

"Alex, this isn't protection," exclaimed Tony, "I'd be willing to rank this one as your worst cluster fuck yet! You just toasted the best lead we had."

"Tony, he drew down on me, what was I supposed to do? I tried to hit him in the shoulder, but he moved, and I accidentally caught him in the neck. I didn't mean to—"

"Yeah, I've heard that before," he said, sarcastically.

I gasped and shook my head in disbelief that he would say such a thing about me. I was highly offended

Tony just frowned and rolled his eyes. "You don't make it easy, do you?"

"What do you want me to say, Tony?"

He rubbed his hands through his hair. "I want you to say, don't worry, I've got everything under control. And then, I want you to tell me how you're gonna get the job done!"

"Don't worry I'm on it," I replied in a monotone tone.

"Alex, my ass is on the line," said Tony. "I need something concrete. Oh, and Sam's in my ear right now ... ... why the hell are we holding Farrell?"

I raised an eyebrow. "You mean, he's actually holding him this time?"

Tony frowned again. "Until I say otherwise."

"I went in with his team today at the Will-Clark site. My cover's still intact—maybe—but I need a couple of days to get back and debrief them. If Jack's out of the way, I might be able to get one of them to talk, you know, give me something to work with."

"ABSOLUTELY NOT!" exclaimed Tony.

"Why not?"

"Can you give me a legitimate reason to hold him?"

"Well, no, but-"

"Then, you got as long as it takes Sam to get Farrell's statement. I can delay Sam and give you a head start—three, maybe four hours max, but that's it. You need to get that team on a plane back to L.A. immediately. Debrief them in the air, but then you get your skinny little ass on the next flight back here to New York. Campbell briefed me on the situation." Tony shook his head, "It's worse than even I can imagine, isn't it?"

"You could say that," I said, nodding.

"OPR wants to eat you alive, and I'm tempted to let them have at you."

"Tony, I need more time because-"

"Look Alex, I need you here to question the man in custody and make no mistake about it you're Sullivan's handler if she pulls through."

"TONY, I AIN'T GOT TIME FOR BABYSITTING!" I exclaimed.

"You and Keller left me no choice, kid. VP gives a bunch of wild ass orders, suddenly he's nowhere to be found, you run off like a wild ass idiot, and now I gotta clean up all the mess. I've got a warrant with Sullivan's name on it. She's a material witness now."

I sighed heavily and even growled a bit, I think. "I need a few more days in California. Colonel Hammond's team is running forensics for Long Beach. They may find something. I wanna check with them and see what they turn up."

"NOT ON YOUR LIFE! I need you right here in New York, Alex."

"I don't really have to ask, you know."

Tony shook his head. "You're gonna be the death of me." He rubbed his face with both hands. "Fine, work from the L.A. Field Office next week, but you wrap up quickly and bring your ass home. Rest assured Farrell won't be happy about us charging Sullivan, so we need to get her to roll on Peter Tesh ASAP before he gets all worked up about it and tries to intervene."

"Fine, I need a vehicle."

Tony frowned. "Whatever," he replied. "Take this one ... anything else, your highness?"

"Yeah, the guy up there spoke Norwegian, I think ... said something about a great flood. That mean anything to you?"

"No," Tony replied, "did he speak any English at all?"

"Yeah, he said he had a message for me, but he didn't tell me the message, or maybe that was the message. Hell, I don't know, Tony maybe they were just trying to kill me. I don't think he really had anything to tell me." I thought about it for a moment. "Nah, they were just fishing."

"You mean he didn't get a chance to tell you before you shot him in the neck?"

I frowned, squinted, and then threw both hands up.

"Wait, you speak Norwegian?"

I cocked my head to the side a little and just stared at him for a moment.

"Never mind, how does this guy know you?" asked Tony.

"Beats me," I replied. "Never seen him before, but stranger things have happened this week. I can't put my finger on it, but my gut says somebody's playing us. This is firefight number two in one day. I mean, this is some Alex Southerland shit and beyond."

"GODDAMN RIGHT!" Tony bellowed. "I still don't understand how Keller even pulled you in for this or why. What's the deal?"

I frowned and shook my head. "I can't tell you."

Tony's lips curled up. I could tell my answer completely disgusted him. "YOU PISS ME THE FUCK OFF, ALEX! SOMETIMES YOU JUST MAKE ME...." Tony put both hands up and squeezed his fists until I could see the veins bulging on the back of his hands. Then, he calmed back down. "Look, I trust you, you know I do, but I'm worried."

"About?"

"You and me," said Tony.

I raised an eyebrow. "I don't understand."

He took a deep breath. "Before you took your bullshit leave, I ... this is the most you and I have really talked one-on-one since you ... since the shootout at the consulate."

I rolled my eyes. "Paranoid much, Mr. Crane?"

"Last thing I want to do is give in to paranoia, but I'm worried Alex ... I don't trust Keller."

"Newsflash," I replied, chuckling.

"I'm serious," said Tony, "our family is disappearing. Your dad, David .... You're all I got left. You gotta be more careful."

I touched his hand and smiled. "You and I are good. I love you. We're fine, I just ... look we're good, I promise. Let me finish this thing and we'll talk, I swear. I'll tell you everything."

The door swung open, and an agent stuck his head in. Without skipping a beat, Tony put on a bit of a show for his benefit.

"Listen, no bullshit this time okay, Alex, I want your report by next Thursday." He turned to the agent at the door. "What is it?" he snapped.

"Sir, they're asking for you over here," said the agent.

Tony nodded. "Okay ... give me a moment."

The agent closed the door again.

Tony sighed. "Don't give me this classified, jurisdiction shit, Alex, okay? I know this isn't an FBI investigation, but you and Keller have sucked me into it. My ass is on the line. It'd be different if it were just mine, but Director Campbell's got his neck on the chopping block too."

"I don't want to hurt you, I-"

"Doesn't matter now," said Tony. "We just played our last card when you made a Jackson Pollock with the bad man all over the warehouse walls. We got nothing unless you can turn up something with DTP, Sullivan, or the guy in custody from the Will-Clark building. I'll update Director Campbell and try to smooth things over short term, but like I say, it doesn't look good for the home team. We'll do what we can on our end, but do what you got to do and then get back here fast, got it?"

"Done."

Tony locked his gaze in on my arm sling. "You sure you're alright?"

I nodded. "It'll be fine. Just a precaution."

Tony shook his head. "Alex, don't make me come looking for you."

I smiled and gave him a double thumbs-up.

He chuckled a little. "Be careful out there. Assume your cover's blown. Keep a low profile, and don't waste any time fucking around. Get those people out of New York."

"Yes, sir."

"One last thing..."

"What?"

"Director Campbell told me the nature of your mission," said Tony, "he told me what Keller gave you authorization to do, but you're still one of ours. We don't execute Americans. We bring the criminals to justice. Innocent until proven guilty, remember? We do have a Constitution to uphold."

I shook my head. "Tony, I'm not gonna shoot anybody else."

"I'll believe it when I see it," he replied. "Just keep us off the front page. Can you handle that?"

"I got it. Now get outta here and go see that pretty Sicilian wife of yours."

"I wish," he said, frowning, "thanks to you, I'm up to my ass in paperwork. Let me go deal with Farrell. You sure you don't need anything else?"

"Yeah, just one more thing?"

"What?" he asked.

"Do I look white to you, Tony?"

He curled his upper lip, looking like he wanted to take a bite out of me and not in a good way.

"Too soon after a cluster fuck to discuss race?" I asked. I paused for a moment. "Okay fine, I'll ask when you're in a better mood."

Tony rolled his eyes, grumbled a few times, and complained under his breath before swinging open the car door. He hopped out and headed straight for Sam, so I figured that was my cue to get out of there. I climbed up into the driver seat, shifted into drive and started rolling.

My shoulder hurt like hell and the pain seemed to be moving down to my back and side, but I didn't have time to think about it. I had to get the jump on Farrell and the rest of the team. I remembered to pull my seatbelt on and click it into place as I slowly and carefully pushed my way through the crowd of police officers, FBI agents, and emergency response units. Once in the clear, I put the pedal to the metal.

I made it back to the Will-Clark site within the hour. The entire block was spilling over with paramedics, cops, news crews, and a boat load of curious civilians. It was all eerily familiar to the scene I'd just left, only unlike the warehouse, the building was still standing. As I pulled up, I thought about what Tony said. Maybe he had a point about being extra careful. Danger and destruction of property seemed synonymous with *Denise Alexandria Southerland.* On top of that, I couldn't help but wonder if I was actually getting anywhere with my investigation at all. The more I tried, the more it seemed I was only making things worse.

I turned my flashing blue lights on, honked my way through the crowd, and parked across the street. I got out and checked the back of the truck for anything useful. The temperature had dropped big time. It was officially cold as hell, and all I was wearing was a half-torn t-shirt. I needed a jacket or something. Luckily, there was a blue coat folded up under the third-row seat. One look and it reminded me of how nothing in my life's ever easy. The jacket had *FBI* stamped across the back in big yellow letters. Talk about blowing my cover. The FBI logo was Velcroed on, but my shoulder was hurting badly, and my strength was low, so I couldn't pull the damn thing off. I thought about just doing without the jacket, but I would not have survived up there with the building blown half open. The wind would have cut right through me, and I was already chilled to the bone, so I had no choice. In the spirit of maintaining my cover, I turned the jacket inside out. I stuck my good arm in the sleeve, but between the sling and my busted shoulder, there was no way I was getting that coat all the way on, so I just draped it over my shoulder and held it in place with my fingers.

I closed the back doors, locked the truck and crossed the street. There was a police officer right behind the line, waving his flashlight at people and barking orders. He seemed to know what was going on, or at least it looked that way from a distance, so I approached him.

"Who's in charge?" I asked, softly.

"Who the hell are you supposed to be lady?" he yelled, rudely.

I missed home, but I didn't miss all the attitudes. "FBI, asshole," I flashed my badge in his face.

Suddenly his demeanor changed. "I'm sorry, I didn't-"

"Your boss, officer," I snapped, frowning.

"Yeah, uh, Chief Moore's over there." He pointed to a crowd of camera men behind the caution tape, and then moved to the side.

"Thank you." I headed over in that direction.

Chief Moore was literally surrounded, stuck in the middle of reporters. As I approached, I heard him telling them he was unable to confirm or deny their speculations about the explosion. I couldn't wait for him to finish pacifying the press, so I pushed through the crowd and walked up to him.

"Chief Moore, Agent Johnson, Justice Department," I interrupted.

"I've been expecting you," he whispered. He turned back to the reporters and said, "Thank you ladies and gentlemen, I'll make a full statement as soon as possible." Then, he motioned for his officers to move the crowd back.

As Moore's men executed crowd control, he shook my hand and said, "Thanks for being here, Agent Johnson."

"You're welcome, Chief."

Moore smiled. "Agent Gunter told me you and Agent Farrell would arrive soon."

I leaned in closer. "Yes, actually Farrell's still with the FBI over in Queens, so I came ahead. We'll catch him up later."

"Alright then, your team's already inside. My men are at your disposal. Channel your needs through Lieutenant Garrison, but if I can be of assistance, don't hesitate to ask. Firefighters put down the blaze. There's still a ton of water up there, so watch your step. We suspended efforts to bring down the bodies, so you folks can conduct your investigation. Let us know once you're done so we can get back in there. You gonna be okay with that arm?"

I nodded, "I'll be fine ... so, what's the situation up there?"

"Over 15 dead so far in the lobby," he replied, "more up on five. I been up there, and it's not a pretty sight."

"No survivors?"

Chief Moore replied, "We found a man tied up in a utility closet. He was still breathing, but he suffered from third degree burns and smoke inhalation. He also lost a leg in the blast. We rushed him over to county about a half hour ago, but he's banged up pretty bad. I doubt he'll make it."

I shook his hand again firmly. "Preciate the heads up and the support Chief," I said, "let me catch up with my guys."

"Be careful up there, Johnson."

"Will do," I said, walking off.

I crossed the police line and went up to the front entrance. I moved in slowly looking around the first floor. It was dark in there. Even with all the glow-sticks floating around it was still pitch-black. Luckily, I still had my trusty backpack, so I reached in and pulled out my flashlight. As soon as I switched the light on, my eyes instantly zoomed in on a row of body bags against the far wall. Those poor people didn't have a chance. They never even knew what hit them.

Dirty water dripped down from cracks and holes in the ceiling. I moved through the waterlogged first floor back to the stairwell on the left. I took my time, cautiously navigating my way upstairs. I figured the team was on the fifth floor checking out the lab, so I headed straight there.

The firemen were kind enough to leave a ladder in place between floors four and five, so I used it to climb up. It was a challenge getting up with only one working arm, but I made it without plummeting to my death, which was a plus. The floor was buried under several inches of water and there were half-singed documents floating around on the surface. I heard voices around the corner, so I headed down the hallway. I made a right past the elevators, which were also twisted up and mangled. In fact, the doors were blown right off the hinges, and the actual elevator cars were history—no cables dangling or anything. The bomb they set off, whatever it was, produced one helluva blast.

I hung another right at the end of the hallway and proceeded to the lab. As I neared the door, the stench became unbearable. Inside, I found a box of latex gloves and some masks on the desk to the left. I quickly put on a mask and used my teeth to pull a glove on my right hand.

I heard the team in the distance, sifting through the soaking wet mess. There were bodies all over the place, face down in the water. I noticed a dead man with a rifle fused to his hand and moved in for a closer look. His back was a charred heap of mess. I kneeled down and tried to turn him over onto his back, but my shoulder made my left arm damn near useless. I repositioned myself and finally managed to roll the man over. His face was burned beyond recognition. I tried to check his vest and pockets, but it was useless. What wasn't burned up was literally fused to his body. I pushed him a few inches away and stood up.

"Who's there?" asked Agent Gunter.

"It's me, Johnson." Our voices were muffled by the masks.

"Johnson, you okay?" he asked. "Where's Jack?"

"Tied up with the Bureau boys in Queens," I lied. "He told me to come and give you guys a hand."

Gunter nodded and looked down at my sling. "You hurt?" he asked.

"I'm good." I nodded my head towards the man on the ground next to me. "He had a bad day though."

"That's an understatement," Gunter replied

I moved in closer to Agent Gunter. "So, give me the rundown."

"Workers are dead. One guard survived-"

"Yeah, I spoke with Chief Moore," I interrupted.

Gunter said, "I'm hoping he'll live long enough for questioning."

"Find anything useful yet?" I asked.

"No, but there are over twenty half melted hard case laptops in the other room. They're lined up on this steel table inside the lab. I gotta warn you though, some of the chairs still have bodies."

"Nasty!" I shook my head and frowned. "Wait though, they set off some kind of EMP. Any data's gone, right?"

"Look around, Johnson." He shined his flashlight around the room. "This whole area is shielded with some type of strange metal."

"Maybe that's why they had to blow it up then."

"Probably. Look." He shined his light up near the ceiling at a group of wires, still partially connected to a twisted metal box.

"See that?"

"Yeah."

"Place was wired to blow," he said.

"EMP would've taken out their gear too, right?"

Gunter scratched his head. "Maybe."

"So, how'd they do it?" I asked.

He shook his head. "Honestly, I don't know, but talking to the team ... I'm guessing these guys came up to kill the lab workers, but when they ran into you guys, they probably decided to do it remotely. Then again, maybe somebody inside triggered it, who knows. I've got the NSA helping with satellite footage. Hopefully we'll find some answers there."

"Okay." I shook my head and paused for a moment. "Gunter, how's our team?"

"Should be about finished sweeping the lab," he replied. "I'm about to get them to try and pull apart these laptops."

I lifted my sling a little. "I'll help as much as I can."

"You gonna be alright to work like that?" he asked.

"I'm fine, it's just a scratch. Many hands make light work."

Gunter smiled. "Okay, let me see where everybody's at ... team, I need a sit-rep," he radioed.

"Parrish here. Everything's toast, we're wasting our time."

"Nothing down here either," responded Collins.

"I'm here, boss," said Rodriquez.

"Got anything?" asked Gunter.

"Zilch," she replied.

"This is Stratton... same here, boss man."

"Ditto," said Hughes.

"Alright, the laptops are a long shot, but let's see what we can find if anything, over."

"Copy that," said Collins, "we're on the way."

I followed Gunter further back into the lab. Even with my mask on, the smell of dead people, melted flesh, and pools of body parts was too much to bear. That place was a real biohazard. Gunter and I walked into the room and were met by flashlights shining in from all directions.

"Johnson," said Parrish, entering the room, "What's up!"

"Hey guys," I replied.

Rodriguez rolled her eyes when she saw me. "Where's our boss?" she asked.

"Still in Queens," replied Gunter. "We'll finish up here and wait for him at the hotel."

"Actually, Jack asked me to get you guys back to LA soon as we finish here. Agent Gunter, he wants you to meet him in Queens."

"Well ... okay," said Gunter, "if that's what he needs us to do ... alright, let's see what we got here."

"God, that's repugnant," said Stratton, moving a body away from the table. "This guy's melted to his chair."

Alonzo pulled back and turned his head hard right. "They smell worse than they look!" he exclaimed.

"Not a very nice thing to say about the dead, Parrish," I said.

"So, you're saying you like the smell of dead people?" he asked, sarcastically. "I knew you were strange."

I walked over to him. "No, but it's better than acting like a little girl about it."

"Hmm." Parrish nodded in agreement. Then, he took out his pocket knife and pried open a laptop. The case was almost completely melted, so he chipped away as much of it as possible. It didn't take long for him to confirm what we already knew. True they were all hard-case laptops, and yes, they were built tough, but they were not fire retardant—not by a long shot. All the internal components had been liquefied.

We continued working for at least another hour, moving dead bodies and dissecting mangled laptops. Finally, Collins hit the jackpot.

"HEY, I THINK I GOT SOMETHING!" he yelled.

We rushed over. He was kneeling down, looking at the edge of the table.

"You see that?" he asked running his finger along the edge. "Something's in there."

"Can you get it?" asked Gunter.

"Hang on." Collins pulled out his utility knife and started scraping around the outline of the little secret compartment. "Fuck, I can't get it."

"Maybe it's just part of the table," said Stratton.

"No way in hell," replied Collins, "look." He knocked on top of the table just left of the compartment. It sounded solid, but then he kept knocking as he moved his hand to the right. The table top over the compartment was hollow. Collins was right, something was in there.

Clearly excited, Parrish crawled under the table. He lay on his back in the water for a while, studying the compartment. "Ah, a fingerprint reader," he said. "Hey, there was a guard out front ... bring him in here."

"What...?" Collins looked like he was going to be sick.

"Just trust me," Parrish said.

Collins and Gunter reluctantly ran out of the room. After about a minute, they came back in, dragging the dead guard into the room with them.

"Now what?" asked Gunter.

Parrish crawled out from under the table and moved a chair up to it. "Set him in here," he said.

They struggled to get him into position. Rigor mortis had already set in. They damn near had to break his limbs to get him down.

"Everything in this room is in pieces from the blast except this table," Parrish reasoned. "It seems it was designed to withstand the holocaust, so you gotta ask yourself why."

"Okay, why?" asked Collins.

"This is an ideal slick. You know, so investigators come through and won't even notice? Then the bad guys send somebody in to retrieve whatever's in there after the place is vacated and all taped up?"

We stepped back and let Parrish do his thing. The man's left hand was pretty much useless, but he had at least one finger with an intact one on the right. Parrish forced the guard's right hand, palm facing up, pressing his index finger under the table top near the secret compartment. He moved the man's hand around a couple of times and then we heard a click. Parrish pushed the guard out of the way, and we watched as a piece of the table retracted and opened like a CD-ROM drive, revealing the contents to us.

"Bingo!" Parrish exclaimed. He reached into the small compartment and pulled out a flash drive. He held it up so we could see it. "Give me one of those damn evidence bags, Nikki, and let's get the fuck out this bitch!"

Stratton handed Parrish a bag. He placed the flash drive inside it and wrote the time and the location on the outside label.

"Good work, guys," exclaimed Gunter, "now like my man Alonzo just said, let's get the hell out of here, and find out what's on that drive."

We headed back to the hotel. I followed Gunter and the team in Tony's Suburban, which no one questioned why I was driving it or where it even came from. I guess they were just as tired as I was. We took FDR Drive to 63rd Street and turned left onto Fifth Avenue. Then, we made another left onto 58th Street. It took a minute for us to get back to the city, but we finally made it. We drove around to the back of the hotel and got out.

Gunter pulled up and rolled his windows down. "Hey, I'm gonna go help the big dog wrap up with the Bureau. Remember to check on Sullivan on your way out. Get her home if you can. If you can't, let me know and we'll take care of her. I'll see you guys back in L.A."

"Take care," I responded.

Everyone said their goodbyes to Agent Gunter. Then he pulled out of the parking lot, headed for what was left of the warehouse in Queens, which wasn't much at all. I knew as soon as he got there, he'd know what was up with me, so as always, the clock was ticking.

Collins waved both hands and whistled loudly. "Guys, Johnson got us through this thing almost in one piece. It's still her watch."

"I want everyone checked out and ready to roll in 10 minutes! We'll check on Sullivan on the way to the airfield."

The team followed my order without question. I think they were just as ready to get away from there as I was. I didn't need to check out of Sullivan's room, so I changed fast, grabbed my gear and ran back out to the truck. After everyone else checked out, we loaded up and headed back to the hospital.

The bright headlights from oncoming vehicles made it feel like my brain was expanding inside my skull. I had a migraine. I was starting to think I'd broken my shoulder the way it throbbed every time I moved. I was a piping, hot mess. After an entire day of pure, unadulterated, nonstop abuse, I was running on empty. As bad as I felt though, I couldn't stop thinking about Sullivan. Despite how foolish it was, I had to see her again. After seeing her performance at the Will-Clark building—her giving away our position and all—my gut told me she was guilty on all charges and then some, but I didn't want to talk to her like a cop. I needed to know if she was serious about us or if her blowing my mind that morning was just part of her sick strategy to throw the hunter off her scent.

If there was a mole in the department, Sullivan was a prime candidate. She had been in the field without a leash for a long time, and she had that expensive hotel suite she kept year-round—like who pays for that on a government salary? But there I stood with my pussy wet for a woman I didn't know from a can a paint—an obvious slut and probably traitor to our country. Who knows what I was thinking? All I can say is I felt something for her, something real. Guess this was a new record low for me. Forget about her being a woman—I knew her all of a few days and we were already in the sack. It was either magic or another dumb scene from this epically stupid play I call my life. Everything in my entire being told me we should've headed straight for the airport, but I ignored it. I had to stop by the hospital and check on Sullivan first—I had to see her.

Every one of us was covered in cuts and bruises from head to toe—some more than others. It had been a rough day. We walked back into the ER for the second time in 24 hours, but this time, we were all barely standing, so everyone scrambled for a seat. Of course, they elected me to inquire about Sullivan's status, so I did my best to hide my excitement, and drug myself up to the receptionist station.

"Miss, you have a huge gash on your forehead," said the woman at the desk, "are you alright?"

"Yes, listen, I'd like to visit an ICU patient."

"Name?"

"Vanessa Sullivan," I responded.

The woman started to check the computer, but then she stopped. "I'm sorry, I forgot Agent Sullivan's no longer here."

"They moved her to a room already?"

"No," the woman replied, "I mean she's gone. She was checked out of the hospital."

"What do you mean she was checked out? Was she transferred to another hospital?'

"I don't know, I just remember they came in and took her," she replied.

"Who?" I asked.

The woman shrugged. "I don't know!"

"So, somebody comes in and leaves with a DEA agent, and you don't know why or where they took her?"

"No, I don't!"

I got livid. "HOW THE FUCK CAN SOMEONE COME IN AND REMOVE A PATIENT FROM THE ICU AND YOU NOT ASK WHAT THE FUCK'S GOING ON?"

"Ma'am, don't take that tone with me!" she exclaimed.

"ARE YOU OUT OF YOUR FUCKING MIND?" I yelled, "GET YOUR SUPERVISOR!"

"Ma'am, I-"

I slammed my badge down on the desk in front of her. "Justice Department lady. If I'm short with you it is because a Federal Agent may be in danger, so don't take it personally just pick up the phone and-"

"I understand," she interrupted, "but I think you-"

"NO, DON'T THINK! GET YOUR FUCKIN' SUPERVISOR, NOW!" I slammed my fists down on the counter. "GET YOUR FUCKIN' SUPERVISOR!"

She rolled her eyes, and then picked up the phone. "Doctor Tucker, I have a situation up here ... It's a woman from the-"

I snatched the phone and started yelling into the receiver, "THIS IS SPECIAL AGENT JOHNSON, U.S. JUSTICE DEPARTMENT. PUT DOWN WHATEVER YOU'RE DOING AND GET OUT HERE, NOW!"

I tossed the phone onto the desk and walked over to the automatic doors leading back to the triage. The doors opened slowly and a woman in blue scrubs came hustling around the corner.

"Agent Johnson?"

"Yes."

"I'm Dr. Karen Tucker," she grabbed my hand and shook it, "how can I help you?"

"Doctor, a team member was in critical condition down in the ICU. There were two NYPD officers guarding her door."

"Yes, I remember ... Sullivan, treated for a gunshot wound," said Dr. Tucker.

"Where's she now, Doctor?"

"Karen," she replied. "The FBI took her into custody ... I thought they would've informed you and your team."

"Karen, are you sure it was the FBI?" I asked. "It's important."

"Yes," said Karen, "the Agent showed me his badge, and he had a warrant."

"What was his name?" I asked.

She looked up and to the right. "I don't remember off the top of my head, but I-"

"Karen, I need that name."

"Come with me, Agent Johnson. He gave me a card."

I followed her through the doors and back to her office. She opened her desk drawer and retrieved a business card. "Here," she said, handing it to me.

She was right. An FBI agent did take Vanessa—Victor Torrelli, the worst apple in the bunch, and there was no telling what he had up his sleeve.

"What was her condition when you released her?" I asked.

"She was doing quite well," Tucker replied. "She'd regained consciousness. We were in the process of moving her to a room."

"You should have contacted me before releasing her," I chastised.

"I'm sorry, I didn't know," she replied.

I hung my head down and sighed. Then, I nodded a few times. "It's okay," I said. "Thank you, Karen."

I walked away feeling completely defeated. Just when I thought I'd seen ground zero of my bottomless pit, my cell phone rang, and things got even worse.

"This is Johnson," I answered.

"CUT THE BULLSHIT!" exclaimed Jack. He sounded furious.

"Jack?"

"THEY WARNED ME, BUT I GOT INVOLVED ANYWAY. I KNEW YOU COULDN'T BE TRUSTED!"

I played dumb. "Jack Farrell, what on earth are you talking about?"

"GOT A CALL FROM A VICTOR TORRELLI," he replied. "TORRELLI BLEW YOUR COVER, JOHNSON, OR SOUTHERLAND, OR WHATEVER THE FUCK YOUR NAME IS!"

I was silent for a moment.

"I trusted you with my best agents," he said, "you nearly killed them all, and all the while, you were just putting on a big show for your FBI buddies."

"Where's Sullivan?" I asked.

"Torrelli took her into custody. Claims you two been building a case against her. Bastard wouldn't even tell me what the charge is."

"Jack, where are you?"

"You had me detained?" he asked in a frustrated tone.

I asked again. "Jack, where are you now?"

"I CAN'T BELIEVE THIS SHIT!" he yelled. "You did, didn't you? You had me fucking detained. I need to know what's going on out there."

"Jack I can't talk right now, but when we get back to L.A., we'll sit down and-"

"NO, YOU KEEP THAT PLANE ON THE GROUND!" he screamed. "DEA agents are on the way to JFK right now, so you stay put."

"Can't do that, Jack." I started walking backwards towards the waiting room. "They have to come back with me for debriefing."

"YOU LISTEN TO ME, YOU LITTLE-"

"JACK I GOTTA GO!" I hung up. Before walking back out into the waiting area, I stopped in a vacant room and called Tony.

"Hello?" he answered.

"Tony!"

"Hang on ... keep me updated on your progress. No mistakes this time. Okay, I'm back, go ahead."

"Tony, it's Alex," I said.

"Southerland, I-"

"It's over, Tony," I interrupted, "Torrelli screwed me."

"I don't understand, what happened?" he asked.

"He took Sullivan into custody and blew my cover. Tony did you authorize this?"

"No, no I didn't!" he replied. "I'm still in Queens."

I hoped with all my heart he was being honest with me. "I need you to deal with him!" I exclaimed, "I don't want him questioning her."

"Hang on a sec ... ... Alex, it looks like Victor's been reassigned to the White House. He doesn't work for the Bureau anymore from what I'm seeing here."

"What the-"

"Yeah, I just looked him up in Discovery Directory."

"FUCK ME!" I exclaimed. "That son of a bitch is gonna get us all killed!"

"We can't let that happen," Tony said, "you got a new priority. One way or another, you gotta deal with Torrelli and get Sullivan back. Hang on ... ... H.R.T. is saying Torrelli's on his way to LAX right now with a prisoner. Alex, you and I both know this guy's bad news. You gotta get to him before Sullivan has an "accident" like the last witness that was in his custody. Has Farrell been released?"

"He just called my cell, and he was pissed."

"That was faster than expected. What do you need from me?" asked Tony.

"If he's been released, he's headed for JFK. I need a jet— private airfield."

"When?" Tony asked.

"Like yesterday!" I responded.

"Hold on."

I waited on the line for about a minute.

Tony came back on the call. "Alex, I've got a jet on standby right now. Pilot's waiting on a destination. You go where you need to, but you gotta get wherever you're going fast. I'll try to do some damage control with DEA Chief Carter before you get back to California. Maybe I can get him to agree to a joint operation or something. It'll take some doing, but I'll sort it out. Find Sullivan and bring her back here."

I walked out of the room I was hiding in and headed back to the waiting area. "Thanks Tony, look I gotta go."

"I'll check in with you later," he said.

I pushed the button for the doors and waited as they slowly opened. I stuck my cell back in my purse and hustled back into the waiting room. The entire team lunged at me.

"Where's Vanessa?" asked Collins.

"Is she alright?" Stratton looked like she was going to start crying.

"Can we see her?" Parrish asked.

"Wait, calm down," I said, "she's been moved to a more secure facility, but she's doing extremely well. Her condition is stable and she's conscious now."

"That's good news," said Parrish.

"Did she ask about us?" asked Stratton.

"They say she was very tired, but she's in good hands now," I lied. "Farrell called ... boss man says we gotta get in the air right now. I've got a jet fueling as we speak."

"I can stay behind and catch a flight with Vanessa," said Rodriguez.

"Negative," I replied, "we have our orders. We don't have a lot of time, so let's get moving." I turned towards the exit.

"You sure you feel like driving with that arm?" asked Hughes.

"I'm fine," I replied. "Come on, let's go guys."

We walked out of the ER together and piled into my SUV. Rodriguez, still suspicious, took her time studying my license plate before getting in. My arm was killing me. I didn't feel like driving, but I also didn't feel like trying to explain why we're going to the airfield in an FBI vehicle.

"Going back to Cali, to Cali, to Cali," Parrish rapped. He was just a cool ass brother.

Rodriquez temporarily pulled the wooden post out of her ass and joined in, beat-boxing with precision.

"What the hell is that?" asked Collins.

"Tommy, you've never heard that song?" asked Parrish, clearly offended by Collins's musical ignorance.

"That's a song?" Collins frowned. "Whatever you say, dude."

"I know you heard of LL Cool J," exclaimed Rodriquez.

"Can't say that I have," he replied.

"You concern me, man." Parrish laughed.

"Lonzo, we gotta sing the Beatles or some Beach Boy, country western shit for him to identify with," said Rodriquez, giggling uncontrollably.

I watched in the rearview as they interacted with each other, seemingly relieved by the thought of Sullivan recovering well, even if it was a boldface lie. It was inspiring to see it though. Despite all that occurred, they were still holding it together. They were a pretty tight-knit crew, which was good in a way, but it also meant at least one of them knew more about Sullivan than they were letting on. I didn't realize it then, but I think I was already placing my bet on Stratton. Who else knew Sullivan and I had fucked? If Vanessa confided in her with that little detail so quickly, they had to have some kind of bond that was more than just professional.

I felt terrible about lying to them, but I didn't have much choice either. We'd been on the receiving end of a two-for-one sale on cans of whoop-ass since we first got off the plane Friday night. I'm sure everyone was feeling the effects, but my injury seemed severe. I couldn't concentrate on anything. It felt like an eight-ton bull had spent the day pouncing on my shoulder. Every time I turned the steering wheel it burned deeply, and the uncomfortable sling I was wearing wasn't helping either. I sucked it up and pressed on, but I knew I was gonna have to get to the hospital at some point.

We pulled up to the airfield around 9:15 p.m. and boarded the jet. We took off after a few more minutes. Despite the pain, I had almost fallen asleep when Collins sat down next to me.

"Johnson," he said.

"What is it Collins?" I tried to sit up, but the pain shooting through my shoulder was excruciating.

"You alright?" he asked. "You don't look so good."

I sighed. "I'm just a little tired ... what's up?"

"Let me take a look at you." he insisted.

"If I do, will you please let me go to sleep?" I started unbuttoning my blouse a little so that he could look at my shoulder.

"I'm a little concerned," he confessed.

"Why?" I struggled to undo another button.

"I know this isn't a DEA flight, and Jack's been calling me back-to-back."

I unfastened another button. "What'd Jack say?"

"I don't know," he replied, "My phone's still dead, but I checked messages back at the hotel. I had a bunch of empty voicemails, but I couldn't reach Jack. His phone just kept ringing. Your phone still working?"

"Not well," I replied. "I just got a call in, but I still can't dial out for some reason," I lied.

"Well, I guess I'll try him when we land," Collins said. "I just figured you might could tell me what was going on."

By then I'd unbuttoned my shirt halfway. Collins pulled it down off my shoulder and leaned in a little.

"Holy shit is it broken?" he asked. "Can you move it around?"

"It's a little stiff," I confessed.

"HEY, HUGHES," Collins shouted, "COME HAVE A LOOK AT THIS!"

"This better be good, Collins," said Hughes, yawning as he unbuckled and walked over to us. That don't look good, champ." Hughes had a disgusted look on his face.

"Tell me something I don't know," I replied, smiling.

He put his hand on my collar bone and gently applied some pressure.

"THAT HURTS!" I shrieked in agony.

"That answers my question," he said, "Doesn't feel like anything's broken, but it may be fractured. You've got a lot of swelling and discoloration here ... you need to have a real physician take a look at it ... HEY SLADE!"

"WHAT?" yelled Slade.

"Get the stewardess to bring some aspirin and a cup of water, maybe some ice."

"SHE'S NOT A STEWARDESS ASSHOLE, SHE'S AN IN-FLIGHT SPECIALIST!" Slade retorted.

"GET , THE, GODDAMN, ASPIRIN!" Hughes shouted, tensing up and waving his finger at Slade. "GET THE ASPIRIN! GET THE FUCKIN' ASPIRIN!"

Slade laughed loudly. "Okay, okay, no need to get nasty about it."

"Thanks, Doc," I whispered, giggling a little.

It didn't take long for Slade to pop back over with a small paper cup. In it were two little Motrin pills. He even brought me a bottled water.

"Only two?" I asked, being ungrateful

"You don't need to take more than two," Hughes said.

"Can you give us a minute guys?" asked Slade.

Collins and Hughes looked slightly confused, but then they nodded and walked away.

Slade grinned at me and held his fist over my little Motrin cup. He opened his hand a little and I heard something drop down in the cup. When he pulled his hand back, I looked down and there were four more pills in my cup for a total of six. I smiled really big and took the Motrin in one big gulp of water. Slade sat all the way down in the seat to my right. He had a solid ice pack with him too, which he politely cracked up and placed on my shoulder.

"Thanks, brother."

"Anytime," he replied. "Listen, we gotta talk," he said softly.

I nodded and he leaned in close.

"You know why I'm here, right?" asked Slade.

"You're my backup from Keller?"

"Yes, but not exactly," Slade responded. "Not anymore. Things have changed."

"Slade, we've known each other for years ... just cut to the chase."

"I just got a summary execution order for anyone suspected of being an Alluvion operative."

I shook my head as much as my shoulder would allow. "I don't understand ... what does that mean exactly?"

"Vanessa Sullivan is on the list," said Slade.

I squinted at him and shook my head again. "No."

"When we touch down, I have orders to find her and...." He gave me the kind of nod that can mean only one thing.

"No ... no, Slade, you can't do that. She's a Federal witness now. I'm supposed to be her handler and-"

"FBI's in the dark on this," Slade interrupted. "Alex, unless you got a better plan, it's going down, and you know I don't miss."

"Goddammit, Xavier, why didn't you tell me this shit before now?"

"You know the answer to that," he said. "Orders come minute-by-minute. This just happened."

"Fuck!"

"There's more," Slade warned.

I stared into his eyes. "What more?"

"Your name is on my list too," he said.

"What the fuck are you saying?" I asked.

Slade said, "Vice President Keller's office issued the order."

At that point I realized why Tony had not been able to get in touch with Vice President Keller. This whole thing stunk from the beginning. I was starting to doubt Vanessa had anything to do with Alluvion at all. Keller had his hands in the cookie jar, and he was trying to cover his tracks, using my friend to do it. I'm sure he knew I would have my guard down with Slade. My heart sunk into my stomach and a tear streamed down my cheek.

"Are you gonna kill me?" I asked.

Slade sighed and gave me a funny look.

I closed my eyes. "Just do it right here and get it over with," I whispered.

"Alex, if I wanted, you'd be dead, and I'd be on my way back to the Pentagon. Remember the day we took down Santos?"

I giggled a little. "I did so much coke I was seeing pink bunny rabbits."

"Yeah, that was fucked up," he said, laughing. "Remember all that gunfire? It was a goddamn bloodbath and what happened to you?"

"I was laughing the whole time, half naked and coked up, but I didn't get hit once. You kept me safe."

Slade nodded. "Fuckin' right I did. Look, I don't give a shit what Keller says, we don't turn on our brothers. You sacrificed everything back then to get us into the cartel. Doesn't matter what the report said, you were the real hero then and you are now. Keller sent you on a suicide mission. I respect authority, but I can't understand why he made you primary on Tesh. I have the resources to see this thing through to the end without all the interagency backroom bullshit and games. Everything may seem fucked, but we're gonna turn this thing around, and don't worry, you're gonna be fine. I have trouble taking orders from a text message. I tried to confirm all this shit with Keller, but he's still M.I.A. I get taking Sullivan out, she's a traitor—maybe—but you?" Slade shook his head. "Nah, that doesn't make a damn bit of sense to me."

I stared at Slade and wiped the tear from my cheek. Collins walked by and we both looked up. He paused for a second, but then he moved along back towards his seat.

"This is still a DOD operation," Slade whispered, eyeballing Collins. "When this plane touches down, my men are gonna take everyone into custody, Torrelli too. Meanwhile, I'll sort this mess out with you and Keller's office. Don't worry for a second. I'm not going to let anyone touch you. If Keller wants you dead, he picked the wrong fucking guy for the job." Slade paused and thought for a second. "I think the V.P. is foul," he said.

I shook my head. "That's what I thought at first, but this has gotta be the President. Think about it. I've been asking around and Keller is supposed to be a standup guy. He was a manipulative old bastard with me, but I don't see him as a traitor. Keller's sneaking around like this for a reason. If all this came from the President, then-"

"No, you're wrong, Alex," said Slade. "Keller's a fucking snake. Trust me."

I replied, "I don't see it, and I'm a pretty good judge of character."

"Look, forget Keller for now," he said. "Army Intelligence is analyzing the data on the thumb drive we found in that table back in the Will-Clark building lab. They'll let me know if they turn up anything. Soon as I debrief these folks, my team is going to re-tool and get back out in the field for a nationwide manhunt. We need to find Tesh and put him out of his misery."

"What about Sullivan?" I asked.

"I'll have her and Torrelli sent to the FBI Los Angeles field office. I understand you'll be there for the foreseeable future, right?"

I nodded.

Slade continued. "I suspect Torrelli's mixed up in this thing one way or another, but I can't prove it, so at this point, he's not my priority. I can't give you much time, so you better break Sullivan fast. FBI won't be able to hold Torrelli for long. When I'm finished with Tesh, I'm coming back for Sullivan. I have enough evidence to justify taking her out, so if you don't find her valuable, I'm going to complete my mission. She's a terrorist, a murderer, and she's guilty of treason, at least that's what they're telling me-"

"Okay, but who?" I asked.

He shook his head. "I don't know."

"You can't just kill this woman and not know...."

He sighed heavily. "I'll give you a head start on her, but that's the best I can do."

My eyes watered up, and I'm not really sure why, but they did. I guess I did have feelings for Vanessa—enough to not want her murdered like a dog in the street. "Thank you, Xavier."

"Don't thank me," he snapped, "get the job done. By the way, your perp never made it back in FBI custody. His transport got hit and he escaped."

"I just talked to Tony, are you sure?"

Slade pointed to his ear. "I'm getting it straight from the top," he replied. "Yes, I'm sure. Sullivan's all we got, and they want me to shut her up. I'm not sure who to trust, but my gut says this is all bullshit, so I'm counting on you to get something credible out of her that helps me call the dogs off. We all got enough innocents on our conscious. I'd like to be able to sleep at night at some point in my life."

"I'll go to the L.A. office immediately, and-"

"No!" Slade shook his head. "You gotta get to Long Beach first."

"What are you talking about?"

Slade replies, "You visited a man, who calls himself Malik ... prostitution, grand theft auto ... you know the one."

I repositioned the ice on my shoulder. "You been surveilling me?"

He dropped his head for a second. "I have."

"What about Malik?"

"Alex, these Alluvion folks are entrenched in every part of our government. Word is you gave your buddy Malik something you shouldn't have. Whatever it is, they want it back. Somebody tipped off the Long Beach Police Department. There's a raid planned tonight."

"No, I talked to LBPD, they're not going in until next week."

Slade shook his head. "They're gonna kill him, Alex. Whatever you gave him, it'll be in their hands if you don't get there before they do. What was it?"

I sat up in my seat a little. "I don't know," I replied, "I don't know what it was, if anything, I ... I traded cars with him so he could pull it apart. L.A.P.D Homicide said the car belonged to Jeremy Taylor."

"That kid got killed in custody," Slade said.

"Yeah, Jack told me."

"Listen, he may have hidden something important in that car. Could be the next big piece to this puzzle. You got plenty of time. Your boy works pretty much through the night. They're not planning to go in until 2 a.m. Get down there, get your friend safe, and secure whatever Taylor didn't want Alluvion to find. Give me your number, and I'll send a rendezvous point to your phone."

I whispered my number to him, and he put it in his phone. Then, he helped me button my shirt back up.

"Get to Long Beach," said Slade. "Then, get back to Sullivan as fast as you can. I'm going fishing."

I nodded. I felt relieved after Slade shared everything with me, and he still cared enough not to blindly follow orders. There was something strange going on in Washington. Evidently, I was in someone's crosshairs, but I couldn't waste time thinking about. There was no way I'd let politics get in the way of me keeping the people I care about safe. We were already in the air, but that plane couldn't land fast enough.

"Keep this ice on," said Slade, loudly, putting on a show for all the nosey folks on the plane to hear.

I just looked at him for a second and smiled. All sorts of thoughts were flying through my head.

Slade touched my knee and kissed my forehead. "Be careful," he whispered.

I grabbed his hand and squeezed it for a moment.

"Need anything else?" he asked, standing up.

"No. Thank you." I said, smiling.

Slade returned to his seat. After a few minutes, the Motrin I took started to kick in, and the pain didn't seem to be as bad. I leaned my seat back, turned off my cabin light, and fell asleep on my good shoulder.

I awoke hours later to a hazy vision of a paramedic hovering over me. The passenger cabin and everything in it seemed to be spinning.

"Can you hear me, ma'am?" a man asked.

I was completely groggy. "What'd you give me?"

"I've given you something for pain," he said, "you may continue to feel some discomfort, but please let me know if it gets worse. We're going to take you to the hospital, okay?"

"No, where are we?"

"You're in Los Angeles," he said.

I struggled to sit up. "No, I have to go ... where are the others?"

"They're gone," he replied. "Some weird DOD guy took them all. He told me to stay here and make sure you were alright."

"What time is it?" I asked.

The paramedic looked down at his watch. "It's after midnight."

"Listen, what's your name?"

"Harry."

"Harry, I'm an FBI agent, and if I don't get to my car right now, a man is going to die. Can you get me to my car?"

He shook his head. "I'm not sure you're in any condition to drive, ma'am."

"I'm fine," I replied. "I'm just a little dizzy. Here, help me up." I raised my arm.

He locked his arm under mine and helped me up to my feet.

"You got a ride here?" I asked.

"My partner is down in the ambulance. Where's your car?"

"I'm not sure. Get me down off the plane so I can have a look around."

Harry helped me off the plane. We walked to the rear of his ambulance. He sat me down in the back to check me again. I felt weak, but luckily the meds he gave me were doing their job and the dizziness was wearing off. All I could think about was Malik. I should've been there hours ago. The clock was ticking, and I was running out of time. I blinked and focused in the distance, I could see my black AMG Benz parked over a few hundred feet away.

"HARRY! THAT'S MY CAR!" I pointed with my good arm.

Harry spun around and hopped down out of the ambulance. He took a few steps forward towards the car for a better look. "Okay, we'll get you over there," he said. He turned around and climbed back up into the ambulance with me. He told the driver to back up. Then, he put his arm around me to keep me safe, and we backed right up to my car.

It was hard to believe it was still parked where I'd left it, especially since it seemed to be the focus of LAPD's investigation. I just knew the minute our wheels were up, it would've magically disappeared, but the car was still there waiting for me. My bags were a different story though.

"Harry, I'm sorry to ask, but my bags?"

"I saw they unloaded the plane," he said. Harry pointed to a group of airport workers standing nearby. "Let me ask one of those guys over there." He jogged over to the men.

I struggled to get down out of the ambulance, but I finally made it out and over to the car. I took the keys out of my pocket and hit the unlock button twice. I lifted the trunk open. By then, Harry had returned with one of the airport workers, who had all my bags.

"We got 'em," said Harry.

I smiled. "Thank you for everything."

"Glad I could help," he replied. "Good luck."

The young man with my bags placed all three of them down in the trunk.

"No, sweetie put that one up front with me," I said before he had a chance to close the trunk.

"What, this one?" he asked.

"No, that one." I pointed to my laptop bag.

He walked around, opened the passenger door and placed the bag on the front seat.

I took notice of his nametag. "Brandon?"

"Yes, beautiful?" he replied.

"Thank you for your help." I pulled $20 from my pocket and gave it to him.

Brandon held up the cash and smiled. "Thanks! Have a good night." He ran back over to the crowd of guys he had been chatting with when we first pulled up.

I turned back to Harry.

"Don't even think about it!" he exclaimed. "We don't take tips."

I smiled and touched his shoulder. "I gotta run. Thank your partner for me, okay?"

"We're just doing our job, ma'am. Please be careful driving. And get to the hospital soon as you can. Let a doctor have a look at your shoulder."

I nodded. "Will do."

Harry helped me sit down on my driver seat, and he even put my seatbelt on for me. He was the perfect gentleman, and he was fine as hell in his little EMS gear. I started the car and left the airfield, thinking about Harry and his partner throwing me around the back of their ambulance, strapping me down on a gurney and filling my holes with their hot, sticky, first responder cum.

By the time I got out on Century Boulevard, I realized just how bad I was fucking up again. I should've been devising a plan for how I would approach the Long Beach situation, not fantasizing about Harry's medic balls. My pussy was soaking wet, and I was driving slow as hell. I can be so stupid sometimes. I needed to put the hammer down. I don't know what was wrong with me. Maybe subconsciously I didn't want to go down there at all. It was 12:30 a.m., and I was tempted to turn around and go home. The way I felt, Malik could kick rocks right along with Lady Liberty. The only thing was though, Malik was right—I still loved him, and I still loved my country. I had to pick up the pace.

I turned on my warning lights and floored the car. I blasted onto the 405, cutting through traffic and coming within a hair's breadth of having a fatal accident. It didn't slow me down one bit though. As soon as I made it out of the dense traffic, I placed a call on my cell. "Come on Malik, pickup!" I yelled, but his phone went to voicemail. I redialed a few times, but he still didn't answer. I just tossed my phone down on the passenger seat and drove faster.

The tires screeched as I swerved from lane to lane, passing everyone in sight. I was tired and worn down, and every time I turned the wheel my shoulder was on fire, but I focused and made it into Long Beach by 1:15 a.m. I arrived early, but I couldn't celebrate just yet. I had to find Malik and fast. Luckily, time was on my side, and there was still enough time to make it to Malik well before 2 a.m.

I continued blazing down the road, running red lights and cutting people off on my way to the warehouse. When I pulled up, my heart sunk. Slade told me they weren't going in until 2 a.m., but much to my horrific surprise, Malik's place was crawling with LBPD officers and the SWAT team. Every single one of them was pointing their guns at the warehouse. I pulled up on the curb and got out. I could hear gunfire in the distance. I snatched off my arm sling, drew my weapon and moved over to a crowd of officers, staying as low as possible.

"FBI, what's going on?" I asked, showing my badge.

"DEA needed help on a drug bust," said an officer, "we're here backing them up."

My eyebrows shot up. "DEA?"

"Yeah, we got a tip this guy's got a helluva lot of guns and drugs in here. We're securing the perimeter, but SWAT's already in there."

I dropped my head. "Shit."

"The hell's the FBI doing here?" he asked.

I shook my head and shut my eyes tight for a second. "I'm going in."

"NO WAIT, YOU CAN'T!"

I completely ignored his warning. I jumped up and maneuvered around his squad car. I took a deep breath, and then ran full-speed all the way to the side of the warehouse. The frequency of gunshots increased the closer I got to the firefight. All I could hear was automatic gun fire. I was about to move in, but then out of nowhere several bullets ripped through the sidewall right next to me. I dropped down and took a few deep breaths. I had to get in there. I started counting down in my mind, tensing up and getting ready to bust in through the door. I had to get in there fast, find some cover, and get Malik out. Three ... two ... I stopped counting and was about to hop to my feet and take off, but suddenly I didn't hear anymore gunfire. I waited a moment and then stood up. I kicked the side door open, and charged in, gun first. I lunged ahead and rolled over next to a nearby car, which was riddled with bullet holes.

"BACK THERE!" someone yelled.

I popped my head up for a split second and saw a line of automatic weapons pointed at me, so I dropped down and stuffed my head between my knees as they lit up the entire length of the car with automatic gun fire.

"FBI!" I screamed, but they kept right on shooting. "FBI! HOLD YOUR FIRE!!"

"HOLD YOUR FIRE!" a man yelled. "HOLD YOUR FIRE, GODDAMMIT!"

Eventually, everyone stopped shooting.

"COME OUT WITH YOUR HANDS UP!" said a man's voice.

I put my gun away and held up my badge as I slowly climbed back up to my feet. The building was full of gun smoke and as I looked around, I was hard-pressed to find a single object that wasn't partially see-through. They just shot everything that moved and everything that didn't. The mob of SWAT officers, who I assumed were responsible for all the holes, moved in and circled me.

"FBI!" I yelled, holding my badge up high.

"THE FUCK ARE YOU DOING HERE?" asked an officer, walking up to me.

"I'm Special Agent Southerland, FBI, New York field office, Counterterrorism Unit."

He looked confused. "Okay, so what the hell are you doing in Long Beach, Agent Southerland?"

"What's your name?" I asked.

"I'm Lieutenant Gibson, LBPD SWAT Commander."

"Gibson, I've got a C.I. in here. I need to take him into protective custody."

"What?"

"I GOT A CONFIDENTIAL INFORMANT HERE!" I yelled. "Can't let you arrest him."

He shook his head. "Who's your guy?"

"Christopher Young a.k.a. Malik."

Gibson pointed his finger in my face. "NO FUCKIN' WAY!" he yelled. "We got an interagency tip and we did this by the book. Who the fuck are you coming in here now?"

"Look, I'm sorry, I'm sure there's some way we can work this out. I'll talk to your Captain, but right now I gotta get in there and-"

He shook his head again. "Lady, whoever's in there just stopped shooting. My team's going in, but it's not safe right now. I understand you need your C.I. out, but I can't let you in there until we've secured this facility."

I looked him right in the eyes. "I'm going in."

He rolled his eyes. "Hey, this is my bust. You can stay, but you'll have to stick with me. I can't have an FBI agent get killed on my watch. We're going in now to assess the situation and make some arrests. You good?"

I could hear his men in the distance, yelling *clear*, one-by-one. I pulled my gun out and gave Gibson a head-nod.

"Alright then, come on," he said, "stay close to me." He held up his radio. "Ethan, I'm coming back. Are we clear?"

"Yes, sir, we've cleared the area," said Ethan.

"I'm coming back with an FBI agent, so hold your fire."

"Roger that, sir," Ethan radioed.

I followed Gibson back to the office where I'd met up with Malik before. Gibson's men were all standing around, scratching their heads. There were bodies everywhere—young boys—most of them facedown and riddled with bullets. It was hard to tell, but some of them looked like they'd been shot from behind. I didn't see a single one with a gun in his hand.

I pushed past Gibson and walked towards the office.

"You can't go in there," said the officer, guarding the door.

I held up my badge. "FBI, GET OUTTA MY WAY!" I exclaimed. I looked back at Gibson and he nodded. The officer moved and I stepped in front of the door, which was still shut. There was glass and shell casings all over the floor. I heard Gibson radio and tell his men to search everything. While they shuffled around the warehouse looking for drugs, I stood at that office door frozen stiff. I didn't want to go in there, but I knew I had to.

"Ma'am, we need to get in there," said an officer behind me.

"I need a few minutes," I replied.

"Well, you got two."

I didn't even feel like arguing. All the fight in me was gone. I closed my eyes, took a deep breath and slowly pushed open the door.

Malik and his girlfriend were laid up on the couch together murdered. Their bodies were swollen from multiple gunshot wounds—tens, maybe hundreds of bullets. They didn't even look human anymore. SWAT had opened fire on them. They didn't even give them a chance to get up. I dropped to my knees and cried. I cried there on the floor for almost a minute in a pool of debris and bullets. Nobody deserved to die like that, not even Malik.

Before my tears could dry up on my cheeks, I pulled it together and did what I had to do. It was all bullshit. Malik was done with drugs the minute he realized how much money he could get for a chopped-up Toyota Camry. He was no drug lord, and I was willing to bet my life they wouldn't find a single ounce of anything anywhere. I did however see Taylor's Benz shot up back there on my way in. It was in a million pieces, which means Malik had done what I needed him to do. Only question was, did he find anything?

Malik wasn't your average criminal. He was smart. Despite his chronic thuggery, he got a perfect score on the SAT. The reason he always stayed one step ahead of the law is he was a thinker—a heavyweight in the brain department. He was also a helluva clothes horse, rest his soul. He was always fly from head to toe. So, why did he have the same pair of work boots from 10 years ago in his office? Because in each hollowed-out heel, he was able to stash a couple thousand dollars and anything else he needed to snatch up fast to make an escape. Unfortunately, he didn't have a chance this time.

I crawled over to his boots near the desk and picked up the right one first. I pulled at the heel and twisted the cover off. There was just money in that one, so I grabbed the other and checked it. The left boot had money in it too, but there was something else—an extremely small USB thumb drive.

"I don't understand," came Gibson's voice.

I glanced back and saw him standing in the doorway behind me. I inconspicuously shoved the little drive in my pocket and stood up.

"Something wrong?" I asked, solemnly.

My source said there'd be guns and dope here," he replied, scratching his head, "we got nothing."

"Lieutenant, you killed a bunch of kids, chopping cars. You didn't even know what they were doing here did you?"

"I... I..." he stuttered and scratched his head.

"Who told you there were drugs here?"

Gibson just kept shaking his head. "I don't understand, I-"

"Who called in the tip, man?"

"DEA," he said, staring at Malik and his girlfriend on the sofa. "AWE, FUCK ME!"

"Who at the DEA?"

"What?" he snapped, covering his mouth with his hands.

"Who at the DEA told you there were drugs here?" I asked, sternly.

He shook his head. "I... I don't."

"WHO CALLED IT IN GODDAMMIT?" I yelled.

He looked me in the eye. "Jack Farrell, DEA, Los Angeles. Big guy, mid-forties. He came into my office. He said they'd been working this case for months. Said his task force was low on resources, and he needed us to conduct the raid ... he called the tip in tonight. Goddammit, there's no way we did this."

"What are you talking about?"

"They were firing on us," he replied, "they were wearing all black, my men said they looked like ninjas."

"What?"

"Yeah," Gibson said. "I thought they were just some kind of militia running drugs in here. I swear, Agent Southerland, they opened fire on us, and my sharpshooters took them down. We didn't do this." He just kept looking at Malik and the girl. "SERGEANT!" he yelled.

Another man came running in. He took off his tactical helmet.

"Yes, sir?"

Gibson grabbed him by the shoulder and turned him towards Malik on the sofa.

"DID YOU FUCKING DO THIS?"

He shook his head. "No, sir we barely got a shot off. We saw about six or eight guys back there and we took cover. I may have fired a few rounds, but they were towards the back door. We never fired into the office. We took cover and when those guys stopped shooting, we turned and fired at this lady here, but we didn't know she was FBI."

"YOU TOLD ME THE SUSPECT WAS DEAD!"

"No sir, I said the suspects were down, and they were, but we can't...."

"Can't what?"

"Well..." He shook his head and stared up towards the ceiling.

"CAN'T WHAT SERGEANT!"

He shook his head again. "I don't know how to say this, sir, but they're gone."

"And the kids?" I asked.

"Dead when we got here," he replied. "It's hard to say, but they look like they been dead for hours."

"Gibson," I said.

"What?" he replied.

"You sure Jack Farrell sent you in here?" I asked.

"I swear on my dead mother's grave he did. Kid, get me the Captain on the line."

"Wait, Sergeant," I interrupted.

"Yes, Ma'am."

"You check the back?" I asked.

"I sent a few units back there," he replied. "They report in?"

"Not yet."

"Listen, these men are heavily armed and have some kind of special body armor," I explained. "They attacked us back in New York earlier today. You better send some more men back there."

"Do it," said Gibson.

The Sergeant ran off.

"Sir, it's Allen," said a voice over the radio. Gibson held up his radio. "Go ahead, Allen."

"Uh, I got a DEA Agent Farrell here requesting access."

"Send him back," said Gibson. "Tell him he's got a bunch of dead kids in here and a goddamn FBI agent wants to know why her informant's dead."

I didn't wait for Jack to come back. I walked out of the office and met him at the door. I squinted, staring him right in the eyes.

"Johnson...?" He looked confused. "What the hell is going on here?" he asked.

"You tell me, Jack ... are you Alluvion? That why you killed my informant?"

"HEY, I DIDN'T KILL ANYBODY!" he yelled.

"CUT THE BULLSHIT JACK, YOU FUCKIN' SON-OF-A-BITCH, I SHOULD KILL YOU RIGHT WHERE YOU STAND, YOU FUCKING BASTARD!"

He shook his head. "Your guy Torrelli told me you were holding Sullivan here."

I nearly hit the floor. "What?"

"He said you were here with Sullivan," Jack explained. "Said you attacked an officer and broke out of the hospital with Sullivan."

"So, you didn't tell LBPD to come in here tonight?"

"I swear I didn't," said Jack.

Jack seemed sincere, and Gibson's description of Jack didn't match, but I still didn't trust Jack as far as I could throw him. At the same time, none of this made sense, unless Torrelli orchestrated it all—I wouldn't put it past his fat ass.

Jack looked over my shoulder. "What the hell happened?"

"I don't know. When I got here, it looked like SWAT just came in and killed everyone, but they claim they barely fired a shot. I don't know what's going on Jack. They killed my guy."

"I'm sorry," he said.

I shut my eyes for a second.

"What about Sullivan?" he asked.

"FBI issued a warrant for her arrest, and-"

"You mean you did?" he retorted, angrily. "And, where the hell is Xavier Slade?"

I shook my head and sighed.

"Where is he, Johnson? Southerland? Whoever you are?"

I kept shaking my head. None of it made sense. "I'm sorry Jack. Slade works for the Pentagon. He's gonna take her in." I sighed.

"NO, YOU CAN'T LET THAT HAPPEN!" Jack exclaimed.

"I... I don't know what you're-"

"Look, she's no terrorist," he interrupted. "Somebody's trying to kill her, and you put her in danger. Now, I'm sorry about your man, I really am, but this is on your fucking head!"

"The fuck you want from me, Jack?"

"I don't know," he said, "I don't trust you, hell I don't even know your real name, but I got nobody else. FBI wants to take her into protective custody, fine, but you do it. Stratton says you care about Sullivan. If you do, then you'll do this for me. You can't trust anyone, you hear me!"

I just hung my head low and pushed past him. I walked outside.

"YOU HELP HER!" screamed Jack from behind. "YOU FUCKIN' HELP HER GODDAMMIT! HER BLOOD'S ON YOUR HANDS!"

When I got back to the car, I had several messages on my cell—all from Slade, so I called him back.

"Go for Slade," he answered, loudly. "It's me."

"Alex, you get down to Long Beach?"

"Yeah, but I got delayed at the airfield ... I was too late ... Malik's dead."

"Shit," said Slade. "I'm sorry, Alex. Were you able to get in there and look around?

"Yeah."

"Did you find anything?" he asked.

I was looking at the USB thumb drive in the palm of my hand, but I didn't hesitate to lie. "No ... what about you? Did the evidence we recovered from the lab back in New York pan out?"

"It was a righteous find," he replied.

I cranked up and pulled away from the curb.

"That drive had personnel dossiers, plans and facilities—everything we need. We made several arrests and uncovered a cache of weapons, synthetic drugs, lab equipment and about $50 million in cash. Oh, and the demo suits ... Alex, we got 'em all back."

"No shit!"

"Yeah," he replied.

"Are you sure?" I asked.

"Positive. NSA helped us launch a nationwide search. We turned up a couple of unidentified choppers fueling at a remote location in Virginia. My guys on the ground intercepted before they could take off. We detained four top Alluvion lieutenants. They're in custody as we speak. This was a serious blow to their network. These guys are finished."

"So, we got 'em?"

"HELL YEAH!" exclaimed Slade. "It's over. Suspects are on the way to Langley for interrogation. They'll roll on Tesh and it's a wrap. Rest easy babe, we did it."

"Good," I replied. "What about Sullivan?"

"I don't need her now, but keep her close, just in case. Make sure she stays alive. Get close to her and get her talking. See if you can make a deal, but definitely stash her someplace safe."

"Where's she now, Xavier?"

"I sent her to the LA field office like I said I would. Don't worry, she's safe there. I've got a doctor I trust looking after her. All is well."

"Okay, good ... look, somebody hit Long Beach hard. Who else knew about it other than you and me?"

"Nobody," he replied.

"What about Torrelli?"

Slade paused for a moment. "I don't know ... maybe ... my guys intercepted him, and he gave Sullivan up without any resistance, but I don't know anything else. He's way above my paygrade."

"So, Sullivan's okay? You sure about that?"

"Yes. I signed her custody transfer myself. She's fine, Alex—well, I mean she is in a coma, but the doctor says she's got a very good chance of pulling through."

I started tearing up. "Look man, I gotta get some rest. I'm gonna go to my place. I'll go see Sullivan in the a.m. Soon as she's better, I'll take her someplace remote."

"GOOD FUCKING JOB, SAILOR! The Pentagon thanks you for your service."

We shared a moment of uncomfortable silence.

"Xavier ... you be careful out there."

"No worries. Check in with me later."

"Will do." I hung up.

I locked Slade's contact information into my phone. Meanwhile, I was trying to put all the puzzle pieces together in my head. First and foremost, I know LBPD SWAT didn't kill Malik. Based on Lieutenant Gibson's story, our mysterious men in black had struck again. But what were they doing there? Who sent them? Were they looking for the drive I took from Malik's place too? I didn't tell Slade about Jack or the drive because, well, who gives a shit about Jack, and I had no clue what was on the drive or if somebody was tapping our call for that matter. All in all, Slade was in a good space for the moment. Sounded like he'd be reporting back to Keller that all was good, which meant I was off the hook at least for a while. No matter how bad I just wanted to take the win and move on though, my little voice said I was not out of the woods just yet. The way Gibson's man described the bad boys in black, they were wearing demo suits, which means Slade hadn't recovered them all, and the hunt was still on for the truth.

Chapter 8

I got home just before dawn. When I pulled into my space at the apartment, I couldn't get the sight of Malik's girlfriend out of my head. It's not like I was torn up Malik was gone. Despite what happened, he sealed his fate a long time ago. He and I both knew one day he would die by the same violence he purported all those years. I just didn't think it would happen so soon. That little girl on the other hand—and all those boys in that warehouse—they didn't deserve it. I just thought about Malik and hoped he was in a better place. Even if he was a complete asshole, maybe, just maybe, the big man upstairs would show him some mercy. My heart might've been broken about the situation, but I ran low on tears for him years ago, and I'm certain I cried my last few back at the warehouse. Malik could have done anything he put his mind to, but he chose to live by the sword.

I got out of the car, pulled my laptop bag up onto my good shoulder, and took one of my bags from the trunk. I was so tired, I figured I'd come back down for the other bag later. I drug myself upstairs, opened the door, and walked in.

It felt good to be home, even if it was my home away from home—the home that wasn't really my home. I went straight to my room and stretched out on the bed, kicking my shoes off onto the floor. I rolled over on my back and wrestled all my clothes off. It was amazing just how hard it was to get undressed with one arm, but I managed to make it work. I sat up on the edge of the bed for a second to take a breather. Then, I went into the bathroom to get cleaned up.

I opened the shower door and turned the hot water on. When I turned around and looked in the mirror, I realized just how much of a hot mess I was. My hair was terrible, and my body looked like I'd spent the day rolling down a hill in a barrel full of bricks. With all the swelling on my face, I didn't even recognize myself. At least everything was matching though. Both my arms had cuts and scrapes—same for my legs. Also, the big bruise on my chest from the impact of the gunshots I took in the vest perfectly matched my swollen and completely discolored shoulder. All and all, I guess it could've been worse. After all, I was still alive.

I put my shower cap on and jumped into what I would describe as a hot, hard-pounding piece of heaven. I spun around, sticking my face right up to the shower head, being careful not to bump my shoulder against the wall. After I got used to the pressure from the jet stream, I positioned myself so I could slowly push my shoulder into the water. It hurt like hell, but the extreme heat seemed to do me some good.

I finished showering, got out, dried off, and pulled off my shower cap. I sprayed on some deodorant, stuffed a little baby powder in all the right crevices, and then rubbed a sweet-smelling lotion from Victoria Secrets all over my body. The lotion definitely helped. As bright as I was, after oiling up, I barely noticed the bruises. After brushing my teeth, I took what was left of my make-up off, washed my face and finished with a smile because at that point it was officially naptime.

I still have one rule for bedtime—no clothes. If we're stranded on an island inside a deserted hotel with only one bed left in the place and we have to sleep together, you have a few options: accept the fact you may accidentally roll over onto my bare ass in the middle of the night; sleep on the dirty, nasty floor; or get the hell out. I know if I ever have kids, they'll be completely messed up—a bunch of pale-skinned, violent, angry nudists. I doubt they'll fare well in society, but I remain hopeful. Then again, maybe I just shouldn't have any and save everyone a ton of heartache.

I crawled under the covers and looked over at the clock on the nightstand. It was already 5:30 a.m. It felt like I'd lost an entire week. I closed my eyes, tossed and turned for a while, but then finally fell asleep.

It would seem not even a weekend of gay sex and violence could cure my insomnia. I barely slept an hour. I was so exhausted. I lay in bed for a while, but my body gave me absolutely no indication it'd let me get back to sleep. I knew if I stayed in bed, I'd just get pissed, so I got up and turned the news on while I got ready to leave for the office.

"Good morning Los Angeles, I'm Harold West, the time is now 7:00 am, and this is the news. Our top story this morning, the financial crisis."

Immediately, my ears fixed in on the television. I didn't know what the hell he was talking about, but I'd also been so deep undercover I hadn't had a second to stay current.

"The DOW dropped 800 points again yesterday, marking the 10th straight day of massive losses on Wall Street. Markets around the country have been devastated for a number of reasons, but most importantly we've learned this week that the credit market has all but shut down. Economists say this is the worst financial crisis since the depression. Our correspondent Elizabeth Cooper has been following this story from Wall Street ... Elizabeth?"

"Thank you, Harold. I'm reporting live from Wall Street where the opening bell is about to ring in just a little while. As you know, the stock market can go up and down, but recently, we've seen a trend where both the DOW and the NASDAQ have hit record lows and it's impacting both Wall Street and Main Street. People all over the Nation have watched their 401(k) and long-term savings disappear in a matter of weeks and it seems for the moment, the government is ill-equipped to respond to this crisis. Treasury Secretary Gene Colbert is scheduled for a press conference later today where he'll be talking about the crisis and what Washington will be doing to restore confidence in the financial system. This comes after Japan and Europe's markets crashed yesterday. After weeks of frozen credit, job losses, and record low retail sales, the effects of the U.S. economy seem to be felt around the globe. We'll be following this crisis and speaking with White House officials, who we hope will be able to shed some light on the President's position regarding this crisis. Back to you, Harold."

"Elizabeth, can you tell us what we can expect to happen if … are we talking about some kind of government bailout here for Wall Street banks? If not, then what? And, what happens if nothing's done, I mean are we just in a low point here and things are going to rebound? Tell us more about that."

"Well, Harold, the honest answer is I just don't know about a bailout package for Wall Street. There are many who would argue they are the cause of the problem, and as economist Bruce Mattingly said, it would be like giving more chickens to the fox in the henhouse. At the same time, individuals and business owners are unable to get loans right now for payroll, equipment, cars and other critical items, so even though we don't know what's going to happen, we do know something has to be done about it.

"Thank you, Elizabeth, we'll continue to follow this story and bring it to our viewers"

I turned off the TV, ran into the living room, and went straight for my laptop. I fished it out of the bag and powered it on. I damn near bit my fingernails off waiting for the internet to come up. Finally, I was online. I clicked the shortcut for my benefits management account and logged in. The news report was right. It looked like my 401(k) had been robbed at gunpoint. I grabbed the phone and called my financial manager, Josh. As always, he picked up on the first ring.

"Hello," he answered.

"Josh!"

"Alex, my girl!"

"Tell me I'm safe and my little sexy Jewish banker man is all over this thing."

He laughed, but his laughter was not without a grim undertone. "Alex, I-"

"No, Josh, don't say it! Don't you dare!"

Josh laughed. "I haven't said anything yet, Alex."

"Yeah, but I know what you're gonna say. You're gonna say I'm broke and have to cut back."

"Well, wait, let's be clear now," he said, "you're not broke. It'd take a helluva lot more than banks on Wall Street falling apart to bankrupt you. You've got treasury bills, solid investments, real estate-"

"Uh huh, real estate that's not worth shit now. Come on Josh, give it to me straight."

"Listen, I won't lie to you," he said, "each of the companies have reported significant losses. All your properties ... just forget about them for now. We have to look at the fact your discretionary funds are gonna disappear fast, if they haven't already."

"Brass tacks, Josh."

"The bottom line is you're fine. You are still extremely wealthy, and you've got that big government salary." He laughed an annoyingly loud, high pitched laugh.

"Ass!" I exclaimed, jokingly.

"Alex, you're gonna have to ignore the bank statements for a while. This isn't like your 401(k) for work, I mean, we've got solid investments, but it's the hold and wait game. You don't wanna sell anything right now. We'll keep an eye on everything and move some investments around if we need to, but you're young and you have plenty of time to recover."

The other line rang. "Josh, I gotta go." I hung up on him and switched over. "Go for Southerland," I answered.

"Southerland, Nick Rhodes."

"Hey, yeah, I remember you," I said. "Nicholas ... Austin, right?"

"Yep, that's me," he replied. "I'm in the L.A. Field office now."

"What's going on, Nick?"

"We got a situation here," he said.

"Okay, I was going to head that way in a bit. What's up?" I stood up and started pacing around.

"It's Victor Torrelli."

I stopped in my tracks. "Torrelli?"

"Yeah," he replied. "He came in with a group, but we couldn't hold him, so we let him fly, but then he came back— said he had a transfer of custody for an Agent Sullivan, but the paperwork wasn't in order. Federal Police wouldn't go for it...."

"Okay, and?" The suspense was killing me.

Nick cleared his throat. "He killed three guards and one agent ... ran off with the prisoner. He's holding her hostage. We got him blocked off down in the holding area and the place is locked down. He's got nowhere to go and wants to negotiate. He's asking for transportation or he says he's gonna kill her."

"How the hell-"

"I know what you're going to say, but he had high-level clearance from the White House," Nick interrupted. "That's the only reason they let him back. Listen, I spoke to Tony Crane—he said he couldn't reach you—told me to keep trying till I got you. He wants you to negotiate."

"I'm on the way. Keep the area locked down till I get there. If you need me call my cell."

I hung up, grabbed my gear and darted out to the car. I peeled out of the parking lot and headed straight for the field office. As I sped down the street, all I could think about was seeing Sullivan's face again. Between that and wondering what was going on with Torrelli, my brain was on 10. Talk about all the wrong stuff—Torrelli never passed a single physical test after the academy, far as I know. And, I don't think he ever made a single criminal arrest either, but somehow, he got promoted over and over again all the way up to the White House? My phone rang as I merged onto the 405.

"Go for Southerland."

"Alex, it's Tony."

"Sorry I missed your calls earlier."

"Forget it," he replied, "listen I just got off with the White House and the Pentagon. They say Torrelli's been off the grid."

"Say again?"

"Neither the White House nor DOD is backing him up," said Tony. I could hear the frustration in his voice.

"So, what are you saying?" I asked.

Tony was quiet for a moment, and I knew exactly what that meant.

"No, hell no Tony, I just-"

"Alex, we need that witness ... I'm sorry, but you-"

"No Tony, I'm sorry!" I exclaimed. "What am I supposed to tell this man's wife, his kids? Huh?"

He was quiet again.

"Uh, hello...? Tony...?"

"Alex, we all have orders to follow. Do what you can, but your priority is the witness. Sullivan is a valuable asset for the FBI now. I don't know shit about this guy Torrelli. I had a look at his file, and it was less than stellar. We either got a mental on our hands or a cowboy that's wandered off the range. Either way, I'm authorizing lethal force. Take him down quickly. We can't afford to take a chance with this guy."

"Are shooters in place?"

"Negative," Tony replied, "he's bunkered himself in the holding area. You're gonna have to get in there and create a window of opportunity."

"And, what if I can just talk him down instead?" I asked.

"Too risky," he replied. "White House's throwing him to the wolves, but they'll protect him if they have to. He kidnapped our witness once already, and now he's threatening to kill her ... take him out."

"Tony ... I ... ... I don't wanna do this anymore. I can't-"

"Alex-"

"Why can't you send in a team? I ... when I saw Malik and his girlfriend shot up like that, I just-"

"ALEX, GET YOUR MIND RIGHT!" Tony shouted. "Torrelli's coming apart at the seams, but he's asking for you, so-"

"Did Nick say that?"

"No," replied Tony.

"Then, how do we know-"

"Alex, that came from Washington."

I sighed. "It doesn't make sense, Tony."

"None of it does, Alex, but frankly, I don't care. We need Sullivan alive. If we give this Torrelli guy more time and our only witness ends up dead, we are back in deep shit. We can't take that chance."

"This is fucked up," I mumbled. "Be straight with me Tony, is this absolutely necessary? We're the FBI ... we arrest people, right? We have a Constitution, remember? Isn't that what you told me? What are we doing here?"

Tony sighed. "Alex, I don't know anymore. This is bad for everyone. I've given you the order that was given to me, but you and I have been doing this for years. I trust you'll make the right decision."

"I'm not gonna kill him, Tony."

"Do what you gotta do," he said, "but you get that woman out of there alive, you hear me?"

"Yes, sir." I ended the call.

By the time I hung up with Tony, I was two minutes away from our Los Angeles field office, so I called Nick back.

"FBI, Rhodes," he answered.

"Nick, it's Alex ... I'm almost there. Where are you?"

"We got a command station set up right outside the detention area," he replied.

"You got eyes in there?" I asked.

"Yes," replied Nick, "but he's staying outside the camera view."

"Only one way in?"

"Roger that," he confirmed. "It's a secure facility. He's holding her in a cell, but he's got a good line of sight on the point of entry. We already got a man down in there bleeding out. We need to get him out now."

"I'm pulling in right now, Nick. Can you get 'em on the line?"

"He's not picking up anymore," said Nick.

They'd evacuated the office. I moved through the crowd outside and parked in front of the building. "Nick, I'm hanging up ... I'll see you in a minute."

I clipped my phone back on my belt and ran inside. I flashed my badge at the security station and asked where the holding cells were. Then, I high-tailed it back to Nick.

He locked eyes on me as soon as I walked through the door. "Southerland?" he asked.

I ran right up to him and we shook hands. "Hey, Nick, call me Alex."

"Alex, meet Agent Jones and this is Bobby, one of our analysts. That's my SAC over there, Mike Rhodes."

Mike saluted me and the others just nodded.

"Alex, they're telling me we have to take this guy out," said Nick, "but he's one of us, and I don't think we need to be making that kind of call."

I shook my head. "Nobody's dying today, gentlemen." I picked up Torrelli's file and thumbed through it, looking for the names of his family. Then, I took my cuffs, gun, and cell phone off and placed them down on the table next to Mike. I looked up at the ceiling for a second and collected my thoughts. "Okay, can we get this guy's family in here or at least on the phone?" I asked.

"We're working on that," said Bobby.

I rubbed my chin a few times.

"You're not going in there are you?" asked Mike.

"Mike, you gotta die of something." I took three deep breaths. "Somebody give me a radio."

"SHIT!" Mike jumped up and grabbed a radio. He checked it and handed it to me. "It's fully charged," he said, drawing his gun. He gave me a quick head nod. "Come on."

I followed Mike up to the door. He opened it and stuck his head in a little. Torrelli fired two shots that came within inches of Mike's face.

"FUCK!" Mike yelled, quickly backtracking into the safety zone. "HOLD YOUR FIRE GODDAMMIT! HOLD YOUR FIRE!"

I peeked in and saw the injured officer down on the floor in the hallway. He was still moving, but he was swimming in a puddle of his own blood.

"When I get in there, drag him out," I whispered.

Mike nodded.

"VICTOR, IT'S ALEX," I yelled. "I'm unarmed ... don't shoot, I'm coming in to talk."

Torrelli didn't say a word.

"YOU HEAR ME VICTOR? I JUST WANNA TALK, BUT I DON'T WANNA STEP IN HERE AND GET A BULLET FIRED UP MY ASS, YOU COPY?"

"JUST YOU!" he commanded.

"You got it buddy. It's just one thing though, Victor ... Victor, I need to get that officer on the floor out of here. I'm gonna drag him back a little and let them take him out, okay?"

"Make it quick," Victor snapped.

I didn't hesitate. I swung the door open wide and hustled down the hallway. I kneeled down and put my hands under the officer's arms, lifting him up a little, but then I stopped dead in my tracks.

"You planning on doing something with that?" I asked, calmly.

Victor was aiming his pistol right at my head. "You don't like me do you, Southerland?"

I didn't move an inch. "What makes you think that, Victor?"

He grinned and twisted the gun in the air a little. "Oh, a guy can tell. I changed my mind," he said, "DROP THE COP!"

"That's not how this works Victor, you know that."

He side-stepped into a holding cell, still pointing his gun at me. With the other hand, he rolled Sullivan out in a wheel chair. "This what you want?" he teased.

"All I wanna do is make this thing work out for everybody," I replied. "I'm here to make sure everybody gets what they want."

He chuckled. "Well, like I said, I changed my mind."

"Think about your wife, Linda, and your daughter, Nancy."

"I am," he said solemnly. "Tell your man back there to get this guy some help. But, if he brings a gun in here, if more than one of them comes in here, I'll fucking shoot you."

I nodded. "I'm just reaching for my radio, alright? DON'T SHOOT!"

"SLOWLY SOUTHERLAND!" he gripped his gun with both hands and trained it on me.

I held my radio up to my lips. "Mike, take off all your gear and get in here now."

"What?"

"Take off your gun, knife, vest ... anything you got on and come get your man out of here. He's bleeding out." I touched the side of his neck. "He's barely got a pulse. Hurry!"

"Copy that I'm on the way in," he radioed.

After a few seconds, Mike ran in with his shirt off. He didn't even bother to look at Torrelli, he just grabbed the officer up off the ground and pulled him back out to safety.

I was still kneeling down right next to all the blood on the floor. "Can we talk now?" I asked.

"Take your jacket off," he commanded.

"Victor, I'm unarmed."

"TAKE IT OFF!" he yelled, shaking his gun at me.

I slowly removed my jacket and dropped it behind me. Then, I put my hands up. "See, my holster's empty. I wasn't lying. I'm unarmed."

"I'M NOT STUPID, SOUTHERLAND!" he said. "Turn around."

I stood up and made a full, slow circle. I kept my hands up the entire time and continued turning until I faced him again.

Victor looked me in my eyes and just sighed. "You don't understand what's going on here, do you?"

"Help me understand, I'm here-"

"SHUT UP!" he yelled, "JUST SHUT YOUR FUCKING MOUTH! You don't know what you're doing. This has to be done." He lowered the gun to Vanessa's head. "I'm a goddamn patriot," he said. "I'll do whatever it takes to protect this country. I'm not like those cowards in Washington."

"Victor, there's gotta be a way to work this out, man."

"SHUT UP!" he screamed.

He pushed Vanessa's head down into her lap and pressed the barrel of his gun against the back of her head. I just kept my hands up.

"Come on Victor, please talk to me. You called in the raid in Long Beach, didn't you?"

Torrelli smiled. "I'M A PATRIOT!" he exclaimed again. "I follow orders."

I shook my head. "But why? Why did you kill all those boys? Who are the men in black? Talk to me, Victor. Are you Alluvion?"

"You think all of this is just happening?" he asked. "Nothing happens just because ... nothing you think is how it is, hear me?"

I stood in complete stillness. "Yeah, I hear what you're saying, but I don't understand why we can't work together to resolve this, just you and me. It's just us man, it's just us. Are you Alluvion?"

He laughed. "Please! Alluvion is a big fucking joke. You just don't get it."

"Okay but tell me what I'm missing. If somebody is messing with you or your family, we can do something about it. You don't have to do this."

"There's no turning back now, Southerland. You have to do what you are here to do, and so do I."

"Don't talk like that, Victor. Think about your family. Look you asked me to come in unarmed and I did that. You asked me to take off my jacket and I did that too. I'm not trying to trick you. This isn't a game. Just talk to me ... nobody else has to die today. I swear to God I am unarmed. You got the upper hand. You can end this without any more bloodshed. I'm not here to hurt you."

"Southerland, you're a good liar. I know too much. They want me dead and they sent you in to do it." Torrelli kicked the guard's gun right in front of me. "PICK IT UP!"

I shook my head. "No, we're not doing this."

"PICK IT UP SOUTHERLAND OR I'LL BLOW THIS BITCH'S BRAINS OUT!"

"Okay! Okay! Be cool!" I slowly reached forward and picked the gun up. I gripped the handle and pulled back the slide. It was already chambered and had been fired so a round popped out and hit the floor.

Torrelli shook his head. "Of all the people in the world, they sent you. Ain't it ironic?"

My left eyebrow instinctively shot up. "That's the second time you said that, Victor ... you asked for me, so-"

"THE HELL I DID!" he exclaimed. Victor looked so confused.

"Victor, I told you-"

"It doesn't matter. It's too late for me." Victor pulled back the hammer on his gun. "Washington won't back their own play. You have any idea how that feels?"

I sighed, and slowly lowered the gun down by my right thigh. "Victor, you're right, I don't understand what's going on. I thought I knew, but obviously I don't. I tried to do what Keller asked me to, and the only thing that happened is a lot of people got hurt, and people I don't even know now have a reason to not trust me. This shit's not fair, and I don't know you that well, but I can see you and I are being jerked around by the same assholes." I stepped over the puddle of blood and advanced down the hall a few steps. "We can figure this thing out, you and me. No more violence. I'm so tired man. I don't even know if I want to do this anymore. They told me I had to find Peter Tesh, but I-"

"Tesh?" Victor laughed again.

"Yeah, Peter Tesh, the terrorist."

Victor just shook his head. "Terrorist...? And you believed that? I thought you were some kind of super star genius." Victor turned Vanessa loose and moved ahead of her wheelchair. "It's always "they" ain't it? They tell you this and they tell me that. They told me she was a traitor. A terrorist. Said she had to be terminated. Said she was a threat to national security."

"Who?" I asked. "Who's they?"

"It's always the same shit, Southerland," he said, looking down at his gun.

"Alex ... call me Alex."

"So predictable, Alex," he said. "Still doing your job. Talking me down, eh? You know that's why he wants you because even when you're breaking the rules, you're still playing by them. I admire you," he admitted calmly.

"Victor, what are we doing here? Who is he?"

"Well," he wiped the sweat off his forehead with his shirt sleeve, "What we're doing is ... you're going to help my family get what they need now. And, then you'll have to decide about that whore back there. Maybe she's a traitor, maybe not. Hell, by now I don't know what's the truth, but Sullivan does, and she's still in a coma. Maybe she'll stay asleep, but nobody in Washington wants to take a chance on it, so what does that tell you? She's a witness, but they want her taken out? I should've seen this coming. Honestly, I don't want to kill her, but I have my orders, and unlike you I follow my orders."

I took another step towards him. "Victor, help me ... that's all I'm asking, just help me."

Torrelli teared up. "Ever do what you think is right even though you know you've been had? I don't want this to be the last thing I do on this earth, but I'll fucking do it, so it's gotta be on you."

"It's not too late for her," I said. "It's not too late for you. Hell, it's not too late for any of us, Victor."

He nodded. "Yes, it is. They fucked me. They lied to me. They knew I wouldn't make it out of here alive. They were counting on it."

"Who?"

Victor chuckled and shook his head. "Look at me." He pinched the side of his big belly. "They knew what they were doing when they came to me at the FBI. I knew it too. I just wanted to believe I could be something better."

"It's politics Victor. We are dangling around like puppets for these guys in Washington. You can't trust them, but you can trust me."

Victor pointed his gun at me. "I'm going to make you kill me now, Alex."

I shook my head and put my left hand up. I kept the gun down by my right side. "You're not going to-"

Victor fired right by my head.

"SHIT! OKAY, OKAY! JUST SLOW DOWN HERE!"

Victor gripped his gun with both hands. I could tell he was serious this time.

"I may be old and fat and ugly," he said, "but I'm still a crack shot, Alex. The next one won't miss."

In a split second, I drew down on Victor and shot him right in his left knee. He hit the wall and fell to the ground, screaming.

"FUCK!" he yelled, "GODDAMMIT, SOUTHERLAND!"

I rushed over and rolled Sullivan away from him to get her out of the line of fire, but when I turned back around to take Torrelli's gun, he fired again—this time at his head. His brains and blood shot up all across the side wall, and his body dropped to the floor.

Torrelli's last gunshot woke Sullivan up out of her coma. She screamed, jumping out of her chair and falling over onto the floor.

"SHIT! MOTHERFUCKER!"

I ran up and tried to do something for Victor—anything—but he was already gone. He'd blown his head half off. I stepped on the gun and slid it away from his hand. Agents piled into the hallway, guns first. I stepped to the side as they converged on Victor's body. I didn't say a word. I just helped Sullivan back up into the wheelchair and rolled her out of the detention area.

Vanessa was awake, but completely disoriented. She didn't seem to know who she was or what was going on, and she damn sure didn't recognize me. I touched her shoulder and tried to calm her down.

"Just relax Vanessa," I said, "it's gonna be okay, I promise."

She pushed herself all the way back in the chair and looked up at me. Then, she smiled and closed her eyes. And, just like that she was out again.

"WE NEED SOME HELP DOWN HERE!" I yelled, wheeling her up the hall.

A few agents darted over to us. They made sure we got to the right place. The holding area was officially a crime scene at that point, which meant Sullivan couldn't go back in there, so they set up a makeshift triage area in an empty office. They wheeled a small bed in there, and the doctor who'd been working on her moved all the medical equipment inside. They finally got Vanessa back into bed and reconnected all the monitoring equipment.

"She was conscious a few moments ago," I told one doctor, "will she be okay?"

"It's too early to tell," he replied. "She could've slipped back into a coma. We just don't know. Her wounds were severe, but she seems to be holding on. We'll keep an eye on her and do all we can."

"Can I stay in here with her?" I asked.

He thought about it for a moment. "Yes, that'd be fine."

"Thank you."

He nodded. "You're welcome, Agent Southerland."

I sat down in a chair on the other side of the room and got comfortable. After some time, Vanessa showed brief signs of improvement, but she looked like she was still in bad shape. As always, I hoped for the best, but like the doctor said, it was too early to tell.

I hung around for days, keeping a watch on Sullivan and researching anything I could that might have given me a clue to what Victor was talking about. Slade claimed everything was good, but where was Tesh? Why would Vice President Keller just say, *hey no worries, let Alex live free as a bird* with Tesh still walking around? Was he even really a terrorist or was this all just more bullshit?

I needed answers. I still had the drive I took from Malik's office, but I dared not check it there inside the FBI. If the men in black that kept popping up everywhere were as good as they seemed, the moment I loaded the drive, they'd storm the place just like they did Malik's and kill me and everybody in the place. I couldn't take that risk. In my mind, I was still trying to connect the dots between the dead kid, Jeremy Taylor, who had the drive in the first place, and everything else that was going on. Why did somebody kill his father? Hell, why did they kill him? And, how do these assholes know so much about everything before anybody else does?

It turns out Sullivan really had slipped back into her coma. It didn't seem like she would snap out of it anytime soon. I was spending every waking moment in there with her, so I was getting a little stir-crazy, but I did whatever I could to help keep her comfortable. One day, I was about to read the newspaper to her when my phone rang. I had been ignoring it, but this time I recognized the number.

"Southerland," I answered, softly, standing up and walking over to the window.

"Hey Alex, it's Tony."

"Hey, what's up?"

"Your guy from the Will-Clark incident died in custody," he told me.

"The hell you mean he died?"

"I don't have details, but he's beyond terminal," said Tony. "Sullivan's all we got now. I wanted you to hear it from me. We're looking into it, but at this point it doesn't matter what happened."

"This is ridiculous!" I exclaimed.

"I agree, but whenever cases overlap like this, COMSEC deteriorates fast. Do you need more resources?"

"No, the guys here in L.A. are helping, and I don't want to overcrowd the office."

"Alex, hang in there, and keep me posted."

"Will do, but Xavier Slade told me they were wrapping things up, so what are we doing here, boss? What am I doing here? I miss home, Tony and-"

"Something's not right. I can't reach Keller. I know I need to let this go, but I can't. None of it makes sense. Why would Keller pull you into all this?"

"Cause, I-"

"You're not that fucking good, Alex," Tony interrupted. "All those resources at the VP's fingertips and he blackmails you? Why not call in the military? Why not Secret Service or Homeland?"

"What are you saying, Tony?"

"I'm saying with all this shit going on, a global economic meltdown, little black ninjas running around killing people, plus drug lords, terrorists and every other kind of scum pulling off impossible stunts ... the President seems completely absent on all of this ... it just doesn't make sense to me. Keller was all over the map, I mean you couldn't walk down the street without him popping up out of the bushes, but now we can't even get the guy on the phone? We need someone who knows ... we need someone on the inside, and I'm willing to bet everything I own that Sullivan knows way more than we do. What if Keller did all this to orchestrate a coup?"

I thought about it for a moment. "So, he makes things chaotic, makes the President look incapable of leading the nation through all the crisis, and-"

"And then, he makes a move on the Presidency," said Tony. "Invokes the 25th Amendment."

"Seriously...?"

"I can't put my finger on why I feel that way, Alex, but I do. He's doing all this below the President's radar, and I can't tell you whether it's to the President's benefit or not. And you-"

"Wait, what did I do?"

"I'm just worried about you is all," he said. "You've been pushing and pushing, and no offense, but when things get crazy, sometimes so do you. I spend more time trying to convince leadership to let you keep your badge than actually doing my job. I just need you to keep your nose clean on this one. Can you do that?"

"No," I replied softly.

"What?"

"Tony, I'm sorry ... I fucked up ... a little ... again."

"Look, don't worry about it," he replied. "Just make sure we handle this witness by the—wait, what are you sorry for exactly?"

"You're going to be very angry with-"

"JUST SPIT IT OUT!" exclaimed Tony.

"I ... uh ... I may have slept with her."

"What...? Who?"

"I slept with the witness," I said softly. "Sullivan. I just ... I don't know how it happened...."

There was complete silence on the line for at least a minute.

"Look Tony, if you think I'm putting this investigation in jeopardy then-"

"Shut up kid. You're so much like your father it hurts." Tony sighed. "Jesus Christ."

"That's not fair."

"I don't even know what to say," Tony replied.

"Tony, I have no words. I am ... I'm ashamed, maybe? There I said it ... I'm ashamed of myself." I just shut my mouth and stopped talking.

"You still there?" asked Tony.

"Yeah," I replied, sheepishly.

Tony cleared his throat a few times. "I feel stupid asking this, but do you love this woman?"

"I don't know what you mean, I-"

"Alex, I'm asking as a friend, not the boss."

"Off the record...?"

"Just answer the damn question," he ordered.

"I ... I don't wanna see her die," I said slowly.

"Alex, you have really fucked this thing up. Every time I think you can't drag me down any lower, you manage to dig our hole even deeper."

"I know Tony, I am ... well, I just am, and you know I am. But-"

"But I love you," he interjected, "and I keep letting you screw me and the Bureau over because I do love you."

I sat quiet for a moment. Then, I whispered, "I love you too. And, not like ... it's just like I need you, and I want to be with you, but you're married, and I feel like I'm just left to be alone forever, and she touched me like I never been-"

"ALEX, STOP!" he exclaimed. "Don't ever tell anybody-"

"I know, I know! Tony, I know you don't feel the same about me, but I can't keep-"

"ALEX, SHUT UP! You don't know what you're talking about."

"Huh? What do you mean?"

Tony sighed heavily. "It doesn't matter. We have a job to do. You're going to have to either make nice with Sullivan and the two of you lie your way out of this or you're going to have to find another way to get credible intel on Tesh. Maybe Keller has called the dogs off, I don't know, but one thing I do know, he hasn't sent me any official communication and he hasn't called you back to the White House, has he?"

"No," I replied.

"Hell, we haven't heard a peep from him at all, and that's not a good sign for you," said Tony. "I doubt it's a good sign for me either. Campbell spent the last few days chewing what little ass I had off after the Attorney General chewed off half of his. There's no telling what Campbell had to do to get McNamara to not bring charges against you. So, you do what you gotta do, understand? Lie. Hell, lie your ass off, you do it to me all the time."

"Yeah, maybe, but I'm tired of lying," I replied. "Tony, I don't want to do this anymore."

"I'm sorry, kid, but you don't have a choice. You need me, and I need you. At the end of the day, we have to cover for each other 'cause nobody else has our backs. They could spin this thing any number of ways and put your and my head on the chopping block. Sullivan's testimony or something else credible is the only way we can cover our asses, okay?"

"Yes, sir ... I understand."

"I think you know what you have to do."

"I do."

"Goodbye, Alex." He hung up.

I could tell Tony was mad as hell with me. He didn't even give me a chance to say goodbye. He usually always waits for me to say goodbye before he hangs up. I clipped my phone back in the holster and turned back around, facing Vanessa. Even though Tony was mad at me again, I really didn't care. I just stared at her gorgeous face, her lips, and ... I just wanted to walk over and run my fingers through her hair, but I couldn't—not there. It would just make things worse.

Sitting around and doing nothing gives you all sorts of time to think. Maybe Tony's instincts were more on point than I initially thought. Maybe I was in love with Sullivan—I don't know. It's crazy to me. Somehow, I'd gone from all but hating gays to justifying my infatuation with Vanessa. Maybe I'd always been bi-sexual and didn't know it. I'm still repulsed by the thought of it, but there's something about this gorgeous woman that I think could make Mother Theresa give in and spread her thighs wide open. I'm no Mother Theresa, so it would seem, at least for the foreseeable future, I'd be digging the hole Tony was talking about even deeper.

Yes, I was crushing on Sullivan hard, but maybe that was all part of her plan—fuck Alex and then fuck Alex over to get what she wanted. Maybe she was just playing me, and I was just another thing she used on the way to completing her mission. Maybe when she wakes up, she'll be the evil, cold bitch she has to be to continue betraying her country. I needed to put my little stupid feelings aside and deal with that bitch, forcefully, until I got some real answers.

A full month passed, and I continued staying with Sullivan around the clock. By then, I'd all but moved into that little room. It was uncomfortable, but I needed to be the first person Sullivan saw when she came out of her coma. I needed to gain her trust, or at least threaten her into cooperating. There's no telling what kind of state she'd be in when she woke up, but her learning I was not who I claimed to be most likely would not end well.

I was off leave, done with my self-proclaimed undercover cluster-fuck, and finally accessible again, so I talked to my family a lot more during that time. My little brother, Chris, and my ex, Bill, of course were ecstatic to hear from me, but my sister Theresa still hated me and wouldn't part her lips to say a word to me. I still loved her anyway. Sometimes, you just gotta love family from a distance—like from another continent.

After a few more weeks of watching Sullivan, it became clear just how stupid and desperate I was for love. It was pathetic. And, why on earth would I tell Tony about Sullivan and in the same sentence tell him I wanted to be with him. *Fucking Blondie!* I knew it was just a matter of time and OPR would surely have a field day with all this. Just when I thought I couldn't get any more stupid, I actually told my family. I mentioned that I may be in love with a woman to my little brother Chris, and he thought it was cool, but oh why in God's name did I say anything to Bill? Before I could hardly spit it out, he acted like I'd insulted his manhood. He was seriously pissed as hell. Men ... can't live without 'em 'cause ... well, you just can't, and you can't live with 'em 'cause like Bill they'll knock up your little sister, marry her behind your back, and of course you can never fuck a hot sexy babe after, or they'll get all up in their feelings about it like you just chopped their balls off.

Even when Bill and I were together, after all those years, Mr. High School Sweetheart never understood the first damn thing about me. I'm not as sinister as he claims I am. I don't do crazy things just to spite him. I just wanna live my life in the moment, and I don't want a bunch of assholes lined up to tell me how guilty I should feel about every little fucking thing. Is that too much to ask for? I haven't found a single man who gets that. Deep down, I think that's why I liked Sullivan so much. It's like she could look inside me and see all the dirt and grime and she didn't care—not one bit. I wanted to feel that in my life more than anything.

My mind told me I needed to hard-case Sullivan the second she woke up, but every other part of me just wanted to climb in bed with her. True, in her state, that would have been a bit creepy, but that's how I felt. Honestly, I didn't know what to do. I was starting to hope she'd never wake up. That would make my life easier, but my need to find out whether this entire operation was real or not outweighed my fear of being alone for the rest of my life.

Chapter 9

I did a lot of things to pass the time waiting for Sullivan to wake up. I spent my time working out, reading, writing, and basically whatever I could think of to not get bored out of my mind. However, there's one thing I didn't dare do—I didn't think once about the secret flash drive no one knew I had. It was in a safe place, and until I could get my arms around the Sullivan angle, that's where it was going to stay. David Chandler, rest his soul, always said a good field agent should have at least one hiding place so secret it would take at least 30 minutes to remember where it is. I never had the need for one until then, but I had a feeling if I did anything with that drive other than keep it stashed away, they'd find me and splatter my ass all over the walls. I had to wait and be patient, which is the next thing David taught me. He'd say, "An opportunity always presents itself, so don't rush, just be patient and ready, kid." I miss that old man.

The days were long, and the nights were even longer. My insomnia was really getting the better of me. I couldn't even force myself to sleep anymore, and I looked a piping, hot mess. I had bags under my eyes and dark circles around the bags. I couldn't get through 15 minutes without yawning uncontrollably. All the waiting was killing me. It wasn't like being in the hospital. When you're in the hospital, you can get up and walk around, hit the candy machine or the cafeteria, meet some new people, and feel normal, but not in that field office. I felt like I was just wasting away for no good reason.

Everything in the Los Angeles field office looked just like my office back home. The only difference was I wasn't working. I didn't have a desk or anything, so I had to beg and borrow just to do a few web searches. I guess I could've just kicked back and chilled, but all I kept hearing in the back of my mind was Tony's paranoia, and it was beginning to make more sense to me as the days passed. The way Keller had been carrying on with me, threatening to lock me up at every turn, there's no way he would just drop it all and move on. And where the hell was he anyway? Nobody knew.

More than three months off the calendar, and I wasn't the only one ready to give up on Sullivan. She wasn't showing any signs of improvement. The doctors were beginning to wonder whether she actually even did anything at all that day Torrelli tried to kill her, and truth be told, so was I. Maybe I made the whole thing up in my mind, but I know what my eyes saw. The only thing I really have going for me now is my memory. There are things I wish I could forget but can't. Despite all my imperfections, my memory is flawless. I remember visual and audio, and I remember how Sullivan looked up at me that day. I remember her smile.

Another week passed and still nothing from Sullivan. It was Saturday night, and I was exhausted, but as usual I couldn't go to sleep. I sat down on my favorite chair and pulled a blanket up over me. It was really cold in the room, but I was way too lazy and far too tired to get up and ask someone to turn the air conditioning off and the heat on. Ironically, the cold was exactly what I needed to fall asleep. I squirmed around a little in my chair and next thing I know I was out.

I woke up hours later feeling something cold pressed against my face. I thought the air was on again, so I reached for my blanket, but it wasn't there. I opened my eyes slowly. I thought I was dreaming at first, but it was no dream.

"Johnson," whispered Sullivan, shaking me awake and touching my face with her big, ice-cold hands. "Hey, Johnson."

I opened my eyes and just stared at Sullivan. She put her hands on my shoulders and lowered herself down on my lap, straddling my thighs. Then, she wrapped her arms around my neck and leaned in close. She held her lips right up to mine and breathed heavily for a moment before she kissed me passionately.

"Am I too heavy?" she mumbled, flicking her tongue around in my mouth, beckoning my tongue to come out to play. She ran her fingers through my hair.

"No, but you should be in bed," I said softly, pulling back a little, "and why doesn't your breath smell? I thought all patients had bad breath."

She giggled and squinted her eyes. "Is that what you thought?"

"Uh huh," I kissed her back.

"Well, I used your toothbrush," she replied seductively.

I pushed her up off me a little and frowned. "Sullivan, you ... OH SHIT!" I exclaimed, looking down at my shirt.

"What?" she asked.

My shirt was soaked in blood. "Vanessa, you're leaking, bad!"

"GODDAMMIT!" she exclaimed. She hopped down off me and walked over to the mirror, lifting her gown up to have a look at her side. "Whelp, this ain't good."

I got up and ogled her, conspicuously. I couldn't help but look at her body. She was just as fine as I remembered.

"I'll call-"

"NO, WAIT!" she exclaimed, smiling deviously. Sullivan ran up and pulled me close, kissing me like I've never been kissed before and pressing her body against mine. She took my hands and moved them down to her lower back. Naturally, my hands found their way all the way down to her ass, and I gave her soft cheeks a nice firm squeeze, pulling her into me. It was in that moment I realized two things—first, I was actually falling in love with that woman, someone I barely even knew, and second, it could never, ever happen. I abruptly let go of her booty and stepped back.

"You need to lie down," I said in a very serious tone, wiping my mouth with the back of my hand.

She looked confused. "Oh, so it's like that?"

"No, but Vanessa, there are some things we need to discuss. Let me get somebody in here first to take a look at this, okay?"

She nodded. Then, she slowly walked over to the bed and sat down.

I stuck my head out the door and asked the guard to send someone in. Then, I came back and sat down on the chair by the bed. I leaned in close to her.

"What do we need to talk about, Johnson?" she asked softly. "And, what hospital is this? Are we still in New York? I'd like to go back to the hotel and pick up some things. God, I'm thirsty. Do me a favor and-"

As soon as she heard the click, she looked down and pulled her arm up. She tugged at the handcuffs and looked at me with a very confused expression on her face. "What the fuck, Anna?"

"Let me explain," I said.

"Take the cuffs off, I'm not playin'," she said, angrily.

"My name isn't Anna Johnson," I confessed.

She cocked her head to the side. "What?"

I cleared my throat. "My name is Alex Southerland. I'm an agent with the F, B-"

She didn't even let me get the "I" out. She punched me square in the nose and jumped all over me. We fell onto the floor and she just kept slapping me with only her right arm since her left arm was still cuffed to the bed.

"YOU FUCKIN' BITCH!" she yelled.

I grabbed her arm. "STOP IT SULLIVAN!"

She struggled to break free. She was a strong woman, but she was still weak from her injuries, so I had the upper hand.

"You're under arrest," I said sternly, "now I need to get you back up in bed so my people can look at your wound ... you gonna be cool?"

"FUCK YOU!" she exclaimed.

"Look, you can calm down and get some medical attention, or you can get it down in holding. The choice is yours."

Sullivan dropped her head back and sighed. "I FUCKING HATE YOU, YOU FUCKING GODDAMN CUNT!" she exclaimed. "I HATE YOU! I'M GONNA FUCK YOU UP!"

"Yeah, well get in line," I replied.

Sullivan screamed loudly and spit at me, but she missed. I stood up and checked my nose to make sure it was still attached. I shook my head and stepped back a little. Sullivan looked like she wanted to jump back up and punch my lights out again, but she didn't have the strength to stand. I reached down to help her back up, but she smacked my hands away. Eventually, she gave in, and I helped her back up on the bed. She leaned back, closed her eyes and rolled over away from me. I just gave her some space until the doctor came in.

After a few minutes, the doctor arrived. Sullivan was bleeding pretty badly, but her side was not as bad as I thought. The doctor stopped the bleeding and redressed her wound.

Sullivan was livid. She did not want to be in there with me at all. To be honest, I didn't want to be in there with her either, but like Tony said, I had to do what I had to do. Sullivan kept kicking around and pulling at the cuffs I put on her, so I had a few agents help me fully restrain her.

After we locked Sullivan down, she and I sat in silence for the rest of the day. She refused to eat or do much of anything at all. I just gave her as much space as the situation allowed. It was too soon to try to talk about anything. It took months for her to wake up. The least I could do was give her time to get her strength back.

Over the next few weeks, Sullivan's condition continued to improve. I took my time and kept my distance because whenever she saw me, she went completely ape shit, trying to tear everything around her apart to break free and get to me, meanwhile reinjuring herself in the process. By then, she'd been moved to a holding cell and was brought out several times a day for interrogation. They pushed her hard, but she was solid as a rock. They couldn't break her, and they were trying everything in the book. She was cold, bitter, and just all around pissed about everything. I watched her in her cell every day. All she did was workout, curse, and kick at the walls. I didn't know how I was going to get through to her, but I was determined. My ass—and more likely Tony's ass—was on the line.

Several more weeks passed, and I was digging my heels in, getting ready for the long haul. I kept Tony informed. Of course, he was pushing for me to get in there and grill Sullivan on the hot seat under the spotlight, but I knew if we pushed her, she'd just shut down, and I couldn't afford to lose her. I know it sounds twisted, but she was all I had. Tony was off living it up with his little Italian broad, with a warm meal every evening and the touch of someone who loved him all night. But me, all I had was a snack machine and an incarcerated angry, tall bitch, who wanted to beat me like I owed her money. Now, that didn't sound like much, but it was more than I'd had in a long time. So, even though I said *yes sir* every time Tony told me to get all in Sullivan's shit, I had no intentions of doing so.

Sullivan kept her lips tight through interrogation after interrogation. One day, I was in the observation room, watching and listening, while Special Agents Joseph Owen and Jessica Clark questioned her.

"Let's talk about Jeremy Taylor," said Owen. "You were impersonating a DEA agent, but we know you're not DEA."

Sullivan just smiled.

Owen continued, "With DTP, you were tasked with drug investigations and raids. You were undercover with Alluvion operatives, is that correct...? You were there the day Taylor was killed, weren't you? Can you tell me what happened that day in your own words?"

As usual, she sat quiet.

"Sullivan, what happened that day, and do you know the whereabouts of Pamela Harris?"

Sullivan turned and looked at the big glass mirror I was watching her through and finally broke her silence. "I'm ready to talk," she said, "but I will only speak to Agent Johnson."

"You mean, Agent Southerland," replied Clark.

"WHATEVER!" she exclaimed, frowning.

"That's not gonna happen," replied Clark.

"Then, go fuck yourself 'cause I ain't talking to nobody else, bitch." She rolled her eyes. "That's right, I called you a bitch! The fuck you think you dealing with, sending a couple of punk ass bitches in here, wasting my goddamn time?"

I looked over at ASAC Brown, who was in the observation room with me. He nodded, and I stepped out into the hall. I took a moment to gather my thoughts and then pushed my way into the interrogation room. I propped the door open with my back.

"Can you guys give us a second?" I asked.

Clark and Owen stood up and walked out. I shut the door behind them and walked slowly over to the table. Sullivan just sat and stared as I sat down across from her.

"We're running out of time, Sullivan-"

"Don't call me that!"

I smiled. "Alright, what would you like to be called?"

"The betrayed," she snapped.

"How about Vanessa?"

"FUCK YOU!" She shot me a bird but couldn't get it up very high since she was cuffed to the table.

"You have something to tell me?" I asked.

Sullivan smiled. "Pamela Harris is not Elana Clark of the Will-Clark Corporation. She was just a pawn and she's dead now."

"And, you know this how?"

"I know everything," she replied.

"You help me, and I'll talk to the D.A. and-"

"NO FUCK THAT, YOU HIGH YELLOW WHORE! You don't have shit without me. I've been at the top of the Alluvion network for 10 years. If you want Tesh, I'm the only way you'll get him, but you will give me what I want first."

I sighed heavily. "You know it doesn't work that way. You're a traitor and a terrorist."

She smiled.

I just shook my head. "You don't get it do you? Look, you are a-"

"I'm the bitch who has everything you want, and don't pretend like what I got ain't valuable." She chuckled. "But hey, it's your call baby. We can spend the next five years going over the same ole shit in this shit hole, or you can give me the small, insignificant little things I need, and you get to save the day."

I just looked at her.

"They're going to kill him," she blurted.

"Kill who?"

"Oh, I think you know the answer to that."

"Why don't you tell me, Vanessa?"

She laughed loudly. "You don't have any clue what's going on here." She shook her head. "You're a dumb bitch."

"Be that as it may, why should we trust the word of a traitor?" I asked.

"I don't have anything to lose," she replied. "I remember that day, the Torrelli guy, he was going to kill me, wasn't he?"

"I don't know."

She frowned. "My ass! You know he was coming to kill me. He works for Tesh. He was gonna kill you too."

"Let me say it again, Vanessa. You're a traitor. Your crimes are punishable by death. What makes you think I won't take you out back and put a fucking bullet in your brain?"

She smiled really big. "You're here because you got nothing else. You're losing, Southerland, and you know it. You also don't have shit on me. Yeah, you keep calling me a traitor and all this shit, but you don't have a goddamn thing on me, or your boys back there would be charging me with all sorts of shit. What did I do? All I did was my job ... the one the United States government paid me to do."

Sullivan was right. Everybody knew the reason we were holding her was paper thin. We suspected she was the DEA mole, but we had no real proof. It was all on Keller's word—the word of perhaps the real traitor—one who still had not resurfaced anywhere. Maybe he was out building his militia and plotting to take over the throne. Either way, I was losing ground, and as much as I wanted to bash Sullivan's skull into that mirrored, glass window, she just might have been able to tell me what I didn't know. I looked up at the ceiling and rolled my eyes. "What do you want?" I asked.

"Immunity, of course," she replied.

"Hell no, ain't no fucking-"

"I'M NOT FINISHED!" she yelled. "Immunity, witness protection and relocation out the country, and..." she licked her lips, "and I want you to kiss me right now."

I sprung up to my feet. "Let me know when you get serious." Then, I stormed out and went back into the observation room.

"You gotta get back in there," said Brown.

I all but jumped back and smacked him. "What...?"

"Southerland, I don't care if you gotta fuck her in the broom closet, you better get back in there and seal this deal. I'm on hold for the President."

"You can't be serious, Don?"

He held up his cell and showed me the number on the screen. It was the White House. "GO!" he exclaimed.

"FUCK!" I slammed the door on my way out and busted back into the interview room. I was steaming. Once again, Sullivan was manipulating me, and I was fit to be tied about it. I removed her handcuffs and slid them across the floor to the other side of the room. "We're contacting the White House on the immunity and witness protection request," I said, "but I need to know what you know, and I need to know right now!"

She shook her head.

"This ain't no fucking game, Sullivan!"

"No, it isn't," she agreed. "What about my other request?"

"No! How 'bout hell no!"

She sat up tall in her chair. "What do you mean, no?"

I was being stubborn as a mule, and the funny thing was it wasn't as if she was asking me to do something I hadn't done willingly and enjoyed. I was pissed but looking at her sexy full lips made me horny at the same time. I was so fucked up. I looked down for a second, stamped my right foot and let out a frustrated groan. All my professionalism went right out the window.

"Fuck you, whore!" I screamed.

Sullivan laughed an evil laugh.

I rushed up to the desk and leaned over. I closed my eyes and moved my head in a little closer, poking my lips out. Evidently, Vanessa had gotten her strength back because next thing I know, I was lying on my back on the table and she was on top, grinding her pussy on my leg and sucking my tongue, right there in front of all the other agents. I fought her at first, but hey, been there done that. Eventually, I gave in and caressed her back and played in her hair as she passionately kissed my lips. She sucked my tongue and pushed hers damn near down my throat.

Sullivan finally finished giving my teeth a tongue bath and sat up straight, still rubbing my breasts. "I wanna stay with this one while we wait for confirmation on my deal," she said. "YOU HEAR THAT BUREAU?" she yelled, looking over at the mirrored observation window, "I want to stay with Agent Southerland while you work my deal, that's the only way this is gonna happen."

I tried to get up, but she pushed me by my shoulders back down on the table.

"I have the upper hand," she whispered.

"GET OFF!" I exclaimed.

She just smiled, wiping my lipstick off her mouth.

"GET OFF!" I yelled again. "DON, GET SOMEBODY IN HERE!"

Finally, Owen and Clark came running back in. Sullivan immediately hopped down off me and moved back into the corner, giggling and smiling like a little school girl.

I got down off the table, wiping my lips and straightening my clothes. Even after tasting her again and feeling all that pleasure zip up my thighs, I was still mad. I rolled my eyes at Vanessa, and then went back into the observation room to let Brown have it. I walked in and slammed the door behind me.

"The fuck, Brown? This is some-"

"Get her ready to move!" he ordered.

"Hell, no, what the-"

"HEY, DON'T FUCK WITH ME ON THIS KID!" he yelled, "YOU GET YOUR HEAD IN THE GAME."

"This puts our investigation in jeopardy, and you know it! She could say-"

"I DON'T CARE!" Brown exclaimed. "You get the same phone calls from Deputy Director Crane I do, don't you? Lives are at stake. I'll send Owen and Clark with you, but you take her back to your place and make sure she doesn't fucking kill herself, you got me?"

"No, I don't get you, goddammit! My place?"

"This ain't New York, ASAC Southerland!"

"AND THIS AIN'T YOUR CASE!" I yelled.

"The fuck are you talking about?" he asked. "Somethin' change in the last 24 hours? 'Cause last time I checked you're out of your jurisdiction!"

I just stood there quiet.

"That's what I thought!" said Brown. "Now, the President was unavailable, so I just briefed the Chief of Staff. He says he needs 48 hours. You think you can watch one damn unarmed woman for two days?"

I frowned. "I guess."

"WELL, GET YOUR FUCKING ASS IN GEAR, SOUTHERLAND!" he shouted.

"Look Don, you don't have to talk to me like that, this is some fucking bullshit."

"Well, you didn't seem to be complaining in there!" he replied.

I put my hands on my hips and gave him my evil death stare. "The fuck man?"

He put his hands up. "Okay, I'm sorry, that was unnecessary ... listen, we're almost there, Alex ... just take her to your place and try to get her to talk. Can you handle that?"

I rubbed my hands through my hair. "Jesus Donald, my place is no safe house."

"That's why I'm sending two of my best agents," he replied. "That makes three highly trained law enforcement agents for one witness. Look, my SAC's already onboard as is the White House. You need me to clear this with Crane?"

I shook my head. "Nah, I got this. Do I need any paperwork from you?"

"Nope," said Brown. "This ain't happening till it happens. Like I say, keep her alive and try to get her to talk. The more we get upfront, the easier it will be to get her immunity. Send Joe and Jessica back in on your way out. I'll brief them. They'll catch up to you."

I gave Brown another evil stare, and then turned around and walked out.

Back in the interview room, I think I was finally starting to calm down a little. I took a deep breath, and then announced, "Joe, Jessica, they need you in there."

"Alright," Jessica replied. They both walked out.

"Stand up," I said, emotionlessly.

Vanessa complied.

"Turn around!"

She did.

"Put your hands behind your back," I said as I walked over to cuff her.

"Hey take it easy-"

"SHUT UP!" I jerked her wrists towards me and slapped the cuffs on her. I tugged at them to make sure they were secure.

"Aren't you so glad we met?" she said, sarcastically.

I leaned in close behind her and whispered, "Say one more goddamn word and you'll be taking the short way down the stairs."

She giggled. It all seemed to be a big joke to her. I pushed her out the room and down the hall.

"You trippin', baby girl," she said as we walked past the elevators towards the stairs.

I just smiled and kept shoving her forward, hard.

"Hey, I need my stuff!" she exclaimed.

"Shut up, Sullivan."

"Bitch," she mumbled.

I ignored her and just kept shoving her towards the parking garage. Outside at the car, I switched her cuffs to the front and helped her get into the passenger seat.

"Damn, you smell good," she said as I reached around to buckle her seatbelt.

I pulled back and slammed her door closed. Then, I walked around, got in and slammed my door too. Sullivan was really pissing me off. I cranked up the car and turned the radio off. Then, I pulled out of my parking space and sped off. I hit the accelerator so hard I was kinda hoping she'd just fly out the window and over the side of the parking deck. That would've made my life far less complicated.

When we got to my apartment, I pulled around back and parked. I checked to make sure no one was watching, and then I drug Sullivan out of the car. We took our time and made our way upstairs. As far as I could tell, we were clear, so I unlocked the door to the apartment, and we walked in together. I slammed the door shut, and then locked the deadbolt. I have a habit of leaving my door unlocked, but after all that had happened, I couldn't be too careful. Forty-eight hours doesn't sound like a long time, but if the bad guys caught wind of what we were up to, that two days would turn into an eternity. I couldn't take any chances. I ran around and closed all the blinds and even checked under the beds and in the closets. The coast was clear. I went back to the entryway where Sullivan was still standing.

"I take it this is your "undercover apartment"," said Sullivan, laughing and holding up air quotes.

I just ignored her. "Second master is over there," I said, pointing to the right side of the apartment, "shower and do whatever you gotta do. There's plenty of stuff in there and you can get something to wear out of my closet. I'll be in my room. We'll get some takeout in here soon. I shouldn't have to tell you no phone calls, emails—no contact of any kind. I swear, I catch you trying to get a message out and I'll fucking shoot you myself, understand?"

She held her bound hands up and gave me a head nod.

"Any questions before I take these off?" I asked.

She shook her head.

"I know how criminals like you operate," I said as I uncuffed her. "Don't think for a second, just because you tasted my pussy, I'm gonna be some kind of punk bitch. I will fuck you up! Now, get outta my face."

She turned and walked slowly towards her room. "Southerland, huh? So, what's your first name?" she asked over her shoulder.

I continued to be catty with her. "And that would be none of your fucking business!"

She turned around. "Come on, this will be over soon," she said softly, in a sweet, inviting tone. She smiled. "Look, don't get it twisted, pretty girl, I tasted your pussy, but I tongue-fucked your ass too and made you squirt, so don't act brand new. Least you could do is tell me your real name."

I sighed and shook my head. "This is stupid ... ... it's Alex ... my name's Alex."

"BULLSHIT!" she exclaimed.

I sighed again and rubbed my forehead. "Denise, but nobody calls me that."

Sullivan asked, "So, where does Alex come from?"

"My middle name is Alexandria."

Sullivan smiled big. "Damn. Denise Alexandria Southerland." She put the tip of her finger in her mouth for a moment, and then said, "Hmm, I think I'll call you Denise. I bet your boyfriend calls you Denise, huh?"

I just rolled my eyes and headed towards my bedroom. As I walked in, I grabbed the doorknob and yelled, "I DON'T HAVE A FUCKIN' BOYFRIEND!" Then, I slammed the door shut.

After about 15 minutes, Jessica and Joe called to let me know they were close. I had them stop and pick up some Chinese food, so we didn't have to order delivery. I just waited and chilled in my room until they arrived. I told them to come in through the back entrance and to call me, so I could cover them. A few minutes later and my phone rang. It was Joe.

"What's up, Joe," I answered.

"We're here," he replied softly. "Coming up the back now."

I walked out of my room and walked to the front door. I heard Sullivan in the kitchen rummaging around but didn't pay her any attention. I just unlocked the door and let my coworkers in.

"Hey Southerland," said Jessica.

"What's up guys," I replied, "thanks for the backup."

"That's what we're here for," said Joe. "Hey we ended up...." He stopped talking abruptly, and his jaw hit the floor.

I looked over at Jessica and her mouth was wide open too. I turned around and saw Sullivan in the kitchen, butt-ass-naked from head to toe—titties and ass all out on display with her nipples on hard. If that wasn't offensive enough, she was drinking my scotch too.

"GODDAMMIT!" I stormed past her and into my room. I came back out with some shorts and a top and threw them at her.

"No underwear?" she asked, giggling. "It's all good. I don't even wear any, but you already knew that, didn't you?"

Jessica and Joe both had this look of surprise plastered all over their faces.

I just shook my head. "Get dressed, Sullivan. There's food here if you're hungry."

"Oh, you ordered for me? That's my girl!" she winked at the agents and took her drink and the clothes I threw at her into her room.

She was so extra. I was still shaking my head. "Just ignore her," I told them. "You can put the food down over there on the table, Joe."

"Oh, okay," he replied, still seemingly confused.

"The third bedroom is available," I said, "and one of you can take the couch if need be."

"I got the couch," said Joe, enthusiastically, just the way a gentleman should be.

"Thank you, sir," said Jessica. She was so stiff and crisp—typical Bureau rookie material.

Sullivan came back in dressed, and we all sat down and ate. It was almost as quiet at the table as it was at dinner time in my house growing up. My family could get through an entire Thanksgiving Day feast without saying a single word to each other.

I doubt any of us wanted to be there all piled up in my apartment. I'm sure Joe and Jessica had better things to do with their time and careers. Sullivan seemed to be the only one who was happy to be there, and I didn't really have a good word to say to her, so silence was probably the best option.

I finished my food and went back in my room. I stretched across the bed and turned the TV on. I tuned straight to CNN. They were still talking about the financial crisis. Basically, everything and everybody was fucked from households to small businesses and big Wall Street banks like AIG. I never thought I'd see the day when slave money was no good, but that day had come. AIG had been around since before the Civil War. How's that for your nightly news? Big insurance companies were screwed royally, I mean the entire credit market, consumer and commercial, was frozen according to the experts, and no one, not even world governments were able to get loans. I always knew this country was going to hell in a hand basket, but who in God's name knew it would be so soon? I hadn't prayed in a long time, but based on recent events, I figured one was in order.

So, I put my hands together, bowed my head, and whispered a little prayer.

"Dear Lord, thank you for the day and for the food, and the blessings you give to me. Thank you for keeping me safe, even though I don't deserve it. Please forgive me for becoming a lesbian slut, and please help me stop doing wrong ... and please don't turn me into a pillar of salt ... and, please keep this bitch in the other room away from me, so I don't crack her skull and lose my job. In your name I pray, Jesus ... amen." I nodded and felt very satisfied with my prayer. In fact, I felt at ease and no longer had the uncontrollable urge to go across the hall and bludgeon Sullivan with a golf club. I just kicked back and settled down on my nice plush pillow and enjoyed watching television— one of my favorite pastimes.

It was late. I'd been watching TV for hours. During the Larry King show, there came a soft knock at my door. I can't say I didn't expect it.

"Come in," I said, yawning.

I just stared at Sullivan as she crept in. She looked at me for a moment, and then pushed the door shut. She didn't get halfway to the bed before Joe came busting in the room.

"Everything alright in here?" he asked, his hand gripping his holstered weapon.

"It's cool, Joe," I responded, "she's fine."

He nodded and backed out of the room, but left the door cracked. Sullivan went back over and closed the door all the way. Then, she came and sat down on the edge of the bed across from me.

"Something on your mind?" I asked.

She nodded, and then shook her head. "I don't wanna fight ... I almost died, and ... I need you."

"What are you talking about? Look Vanessa, you-"

"Back in New York, he called me."

"Who?"

"Peter Tesh. He wanted me to run a virus for him on you so he could find your family, but I told him I didn't want to do this anymore."

"Is that so?" I curled up my lips and rolled my eyes. "Well, it wouldn't have worked anyway. My cover was solid."

She tried to touch my hand, but I pulled away. "Listen," she pleaded, "I know I've done some pretty fucked up things, but ... but I-"

"But what?" I squinted my eyes and shook my head. "No, uh uh, we are not doing this, Sullivan!"

"Haven't you ever wanted to be close to someone?" she asked. "I mean really close?"

I shook my head. "I was close to someone once, and all he did was break my fuckin' heart into little pieces so no, fuck that."

She frowned. "Okay, have you thought about being close with me?"

"It's getting late," I replied, callously. "I have to get some sleep."

"I'm not like your old man or that lowlife piece of shit in Long Beach. I'd never-"

"What?" What she said about Malik set me off, and unfortunately, I lost the cool I had collected after my prayer time earlier. Without saying another word, I leaped across the bed, grabbed her by the throat with both hands, and slammed her down on her back. I hopped up on top of her and squeezed with all my might. "FUCKING BITCH!" I yelled angrily, choking harder and harder. I didn't let go until her hands dropped by her side and her eyes rolled into the back of her head. She coughed as I released her neck. I didn't give a shit she'd been shot and spent months in a coma, I was filled with rage, and I didn't see any other option but to kill her with my bare hands.

I slugged her as hard as I could. Then, I hit her again and again, pulling her head up by her hair and jabbing her in the mouth.

Joe and Jessica busted into my room.

"WHAT THE HELL?" they yelled in unison.

I rolled over and drew a gun out of my top nightstand drawer. I pointed it at them. "GET THE FUCK OUT! NOW!" I snatched the slide back, placing a round in the chamber.

They didn't hesitate. They backed up out of the room.

I ran to the door and locked it behind them. All I could see was red. I gripped my pistol with both hands and put my finger on the trigger. I crept slowly back to the bed, where

Sullivan was squirming around trying to catch her breath and pull herself together. She climbed up onto the bed. I walked right up to her and aimed for her head. She mumbled something, but I couldn't make out what she was saying.

"What, Vanessa! What the fuck could you possibly say to me?" I gritted my teeth and pressed the gun to her head.

"I love you," she said, coughing. "I fucking love you."

I closed my eyes and started crying. Then, I pulled the gun away from Sullivan's head and backed up. I pressed the barrel to my right temple. Vanessa moved off the edge of the bed down onto the floor. She crawled on her knees over to me, reached up, and pulled me down. She put her hands on my face and pushed the gun away, pulling me close and kissing me passionately.

"I'm sorry," I said, kissing her back.

"No, don't do that!" she exclaimed.

"I don't know why I love you, but I can't I can't ... Vanessa, I can't lose anyone else, I...."

She wiped my tears. "When the time comes, they will kill me or put me away forever, but until then, I just wanna be with you. It's over for me, I just want to have something good in my life right now. Please don't kill me."

She kissed me, and I kissed her back, pulling her close to me. I dropped the gun on the floor, and we started ripping each other's clothes off. I opened my mouth wide and took in her tongue, sucking it and moaning, breathing heavily. Vanessa squeezed my ass and rubbed my lower back. I melted at the touch of her hands. There was nowhere under the sun I wanted to be other than right there with her.

Before I could get my top over my head, Vanessa was sucking my nipples and squeezing my breasts, licking between them and making me feel just like she did back in New York. I pulled her t-shirt off, exposing her huge, perfect breasts. Her nipples stood up, inviting me down for a taste, and I obliged. She rubbed my pussy while I tasted every inch of her gorgeous tits. By then, we'd forgotten all about the suffocating drama that seemed to be waiting at every corner to snuff us out.

"Fuck me!" I moaned. "Please, fuck me!"

Vanessa pulled my hair and guided me over to the bed where she picked me up and laid me down on my tummy. She buried her face in my ass, licking hungrily all around my asshole and squeezing my cheeks. She spit on me several times, making it very wet, and that turned me on. It wasn't like the last time. I wasn't all curious and shy anymore. I wanted her to do everything to me she knew how for as long as she could. I wanted her to bring me to ecstasy. I squirmed as she tongued my ass and pushed two fingers into my slippery, wet pussy. She hunted around inside me, searching for my G-spot, and I'll be damned if she didn't find it again. She hit it over and over, bringing me to an unbelievable orgasm. Vanessa held me down as I came, still fingering me and licking my ass until my legs stopped trembling. Then, she rolled me over and aggressively sucked my clit, still fingering my pussy.

"Yes, just like that baby," I said softly, biting my bottom lip and trying to keep from screaming.

She replaced her tongue with her fingers on my clit and rubbed it while she gave my love tunnel more much needed attention. First, she licked and sucked my juicy pussy lips, and then she spread them and pushed her tongue inside. It was so hot, wet, and nasty. You could hear my juices each time she flicked her tongue around in me. When she smacked her lips on my pussy, I almost completely lost it. She continued licking and rubbing, but then she slid a thumb in my ass, intensifying the experience. She made me cum two more times before moving up and mounting me. She tongue-kissed me and rotated her hips, grinding her pussy on mine, clit-to-clit. It was so amazing.

We made love until we exploded in a simultaneous climactic orgasm, clawing at each other and pulling our bodies together as tight as possible. I shivered and shook, and Vanessa kissed my tearing eyes.

"I love you little girl," she said, "I swear I do."

I shook my head and rolled out from under Vanessa. She laid down on her back, and I crawled up and rested my head right on her chest, still breathing heavily.

"Don't say that if you don't mean it," I whispered.

Vanessa played in my hair and rubbed my back. "I mean every word. Just be mine, pretty girl."

I was quiet for a second and almost cried, but I managed to hold it in. Vanessa made me feel special, like she really loved me, even if she didn't. We were sharing a special moment—one like I hadn't had in a very long time. I wanted to just lay there with her and enjoy it, but with orders in hand, I would've been stupid not to take advantage of the situation.

"Vanessa," I said, softly.

"Yes?"

"You have to tell me everything."

She didn't respond.

I looked up into her eyes. "They tried to kill us. You gotta help me take these fuckers down."

She nodded. "Okay, I'll tell you what you want to know, but not tonight."

I nodded too.

"Can I...." Sullivan shook her head and said, "never mind."

"What...?"

She hesitated a moment, and then timidly asked, "Can I stay in here with you?"

I smiled. "Yeah ... but, hang on, I'll be right back." I got up, put my robe on and cracked my bedroom door. Joe was pacing around the living room, and Jessica looked like she was ready to call in the National Guard.

"Everything's fine," I said.

Joe gave me a strange look and walked over to me.

I stuck my hand out and stopped him from busting into the room. "Joe, you gotta trust me on this one, okay?"

He scratched his head. "Alright, but-"

"Hey, I got this man."

He looked confused. "If you say so, Southerland."

I smiled. "I say so ... we're fine. You guys get some rest. I'm okay, I promise."

He nodded, and I ducked back into the room, closing the door again and locking it. I picked my gun up off the floor, unloaded it, and secured it back in the nightstand. Then, I disrobed, and climbed back into bed with Vanessa.

CONTAINMENT

We cuddled and talked as if we hadn't just had a knockdown, drag out fight. I felt like I was turning into my dad—just sweep it all under the rug and keep on moving. It felt so good to be lying there in her arms with the TV running in the background—almost as good as when Bill and I were together. He'd hold me like he was afraid I'd somehow slip away. Bill was kind of an angel compared to my unholy self, but Vanessa was the complete opposite of Bill. I was convinced she was the devil, and I was a complete sinner. Or, maybe it was the other way around—I don't know. All I know is she made me feel whole again, and I didn't want that feeling to ever go away. Eventually, I fell asleep, and I slept extremely well that night.

Chapter 10

The next morning was probably the most awkward breakfast in the history of mankind. Joe and Jessica were up early, and so was Sullivan. I got up, brushed my teeth, showered, and threw something on. When I walked into the kitchen, I damn near burst into laughter. I'm not sure if it was the fact that Joe and Jessica had the same weird look on their faces or that Sullivan was walking around with a black eye, happily fixing breakfast for everyone. It was an odd way to start the day to say the least.

"Good morning," greeted Sullivan, smiling big.

"Morning everyone," I replied.

I sat down at the table with Joe and Jessica. Sullivan already had a plate out for me. She'd made bacon, grits, and toast, and she'd cut up some fruit too. I didn't know what to say, so I kept my mouth shut and dug in.

Joe leaned over to me. "What the hell is going on?"

"You don't wanna know," I whispered.

He looked up to the ceiling as if he was praying to Black Jesus. "Southerland, I-"

"Joe, it's just one day," I interrupted, "one day is all I'm asking for."

"What are you guys over there whispering about?" asked Vanessa.

Joe cleared his throat. "This is very-"

"We're just surprised you can cook," said Jessica, saving Joe from embarrassing himself.

"I grew up in a big family," Vanessa responded. "With four older brothers—you know they could eat—so I had to get in there and help my mother out."

"That's sweet," said Jessica, smiling.

"Thank you," replied Sullivan. "You want anything else?"

"No, I'm fine thank you," Jessica responded.

"You talk to Don this morning?" I asked Joe.

"Yeah," he replied, "but no change in status. Don's still not able to get hold of the Vice President, but he's in communications with the White House Chief of Staff."

"So, you think we're looking at more than 48 hours?" I asked softly.

"Nah, if ASAC Brown says it's getting done, it's gonna get done. I'll check back with him and let you know soon as I know more."

Sullivan sat down with her plate.

Joe and Jessica quickly finished and got up from the table.

"We'll give you two some space," said Jessica.

Sullivan smiled. "Do I make them nervous?" she whispered as they walked out of the room.

"Forget about them," I said. I touched her face softly. "Look, I'm sorry about your eye, I just-"

"It's fine," she replied.

"It's just that when you talked about ... well, he was...." I sighed heavily. "I lost a friend, and I don't know if I can say he was a good friend, but he-"

"Denise, it was wrong of me to talk about-"

"No Vanessa! I shouldn't have hit you like that. It doesn't matter what you said, it's not right."

"It's fine," she said, "I promise. Seriously, I'm a tough girl, I can take it. Honestly, I rather liked you dominating and manhandling me."

I did a double take. "Uh, I don't know what to say ... look, it wasn't right, and I'm sorry. Listen, all bullshit aside, I'm so tired of this job." I shook my head. "I can't do this anymore."

Sullivan raised an eyebrow. "What are you talking about?"

"What if this was the last thing I did for the government? Made sure you get your immunity deal, and then we'd be free."

"We...?" Vanessa was shocked.

"Yeah, you and me," I replied. "We could leave and go anywhere like France or-"

"Bora Bora?" interrupted Sullivan.

"Why not?" I replied. "Anywhere but here. My family hates me. I don't have anyone. I got money, so we wouldn't have to want for anything. My dad set me up before he died and that money has been growing really big, I mean, I'm just sayin' a bitch is rich, okay! I just ... I'm sorry ... I was angry at myself more than anything, and I lost some good friends, not just Malik. I haven't even had a second to think about them or ... I just saw you, and ... I'm sorry for hitting you."

We sat in silence for a moment.

"You have plenty of time to make it up to me, Denise," she said, seductively.

"Stop calling me Denise!" I laughed.

Sullivan giggled uncontrollably. "I can't help it, baby," she said. "It's so sexy the way you react every time I say your real name." She leaned in and whispered, "Makes me wanna take you from behind with my strap-on and-"

"Oh my God!" My eyes got big and I shook my head. "Change the subject! Change the subject!"

Vanessa laughed, loudly. "What do you want to talk about other than strap-ons and whips and chains?"

I rolled my eyes. "Jesus! Uh, the grits are really good!" I exclaimed. "Yes, let's talk about grits ... how'd you make them?"

Vanessa laughed again, and replied, "Lots of butter, lots of cheese, salt, and pepper."

We chatted about the financial crisis and a few other things while we finished eating. I made a point to avoid open-ended questions and statements that could lead to her saying things that made my pussy wet. Soon as we finished breakfast, I got back on the clock and started pushing Sullivan to open up to me.

"Vanessa, last night you promised me something."

She lowered her head. "I did, didn't I?" She looked back up at me.

I nodded. "Are you gonna make good on that promise?" I asked.

"Yes," she replied, reluctantly. "Where would you like for me to start?"

"Why Alluvion?" I asked.

"Alluvion...?" She laughed. "I took this mission because I got tired of taking it up the ass, getting passed over for promotions, and being stuck, holding the bag over and over again. I'm a highly educated, intelligent black woman, and my C.O. was pissing on my head and calling it rain. He acted like I was the maid."

My left eyebrow shot up to the ceiling. "C.O.?"

She smiled. "Yeah, I'm not DEA."

"You're Alluvion, right?"

She shook her head and chuckled a little.

"Why the hell do you keep laughing every time I say that?" I asked.

"You don't understand ... there's no Alluvion, sweetie...." Vanessa sat up straight in her chair. "Sergeant Major Vanessa Sullivan, United States Army, Special Forces." She stuck her hand out at me.

My jaw dropped. I shook her hand, but at that point I was even more confused than before.

"See Denise, they got me either way ... conduct unbecoming, treason, terrorism—take your pick. This FBI witness shit will only last so long. When they find me, and they will find me, they will lock me up forever, or more likely just bury me. If you're serious and you're not just shining me on ... if we're going to make a run together, as soon as I get that paper, we really have to go."

"Wait, I don't understand," I said. "What do you mean no Alluvion?"

"Alluvion is not a terrorist group," she explained. "It's a black bag operation ... a mission template ... a regime shift."

"If you're Army, then why...? How'd you get mixed up in all this? I mean pretending you're DEA and all?"

"Well, I wasn't the only one pretending," she said, smiling.

I rolled my eyes. "Hey, fuck you!" I laughed.

"Look, it's simple," explained Vanessa, "my brother was up to his neck, drowning in half a million dollars' worth of gambling debts, and I was swimming in credit card debt trying to float his ass around the country, so the Vegas mobsters didn't kill him. It was a mess. One day I was driving some brass around, and we ended up at an off-base meeting. I didn't know all the men there, but they were hot shit, and their goal was to get on the inside of the joint DOD DEA taskforce. They weren't shy about talking in front of me either. Turns out, I was their way in. They told me it was some kind of secret interagency audit, but I soon learned what a crock of shit that was. I was tasked with counterintelligence and sabotage, and that's exactly what I did on every DTP joint operation. They paid off the guys trying to put my brother in a hole in the desert, and they said they would keep him safe as long as I played ball. I soon came to realize that really meant they were watching his every move and would kill him if I didn't comply with their every command."

"So, Alluvion is a military operation?" I asked. "Off the books?"

"Yes," she replied. "The primary objective of Alluvion is to make the administration look inept, incapable of defending America against drug dealers and terrorists, financial crisis, and a lot of other adverse conditions."

"Tony was right, it's a coup," I said.

"Who's Tony?" she asked.

"My boss," I replied. "And ... a really good friend. I mean, like good. He's been there for me, taking chances on me and taking care of me in and out of the Bureau since I started back in Atlanta. He was actually friends with my Dad. Tony loves me, and I love him, I really do. He's sharp too. Made his way all the way up to Deputy Director."

"And he's your boss?" Sullivan asked.

"Yup," I replied, proudly.

"Oh, so you're the woman sitting next to the man at the FBI, Mr. Anthony Crane himself. I didn't realize you worked for the man, Denise." She smiled and slapped my arm. "So, you call him Tony, huh? So, that means you two are really close. Future is looking a little brighter now baby girl." She smiled. "So, Tony saw this coming?"

"Yeah, he speculated Keller might be pulling a coup, and I had my doubts, but I'm starting to think he's right."

Vanessa ran both her hands through her hair. "What else could it be? The President and Vice President front like they're friends, but nothing could be further from the truth."

"So, you work directly for Tesh?"

"Yes and no," Vanessa replied. "Even when I met with him, it was like having supervised visitation or some shit. I had to talk to him through a proxy. I know you think I am bad, but he's Satan in green, and his reach is far and wide. Tesh isn't his real name. He's at the top of the food chain in the Army—maybe a general. Hard to say. I never got his real name. Everything was all cloak and dagger, but he directly tasks the men in the black fallout suits. They don't move without his say."

"They killed Malik," I said.

"What?" Vanessa looked surprised.

"The men in black ... they went in before LBPD SWAT could raid the place and killed everybody. Victor Torrelli, used to be FBI, but he was working for the White House when he tried to kill you ... he must've called Tesh, because the demolition suits showed up and wiped everybody out. When I got there, Malik and his girlfriend were on his couch ... they were up to their necks full of bullets. No way LBPD would've done that. I know it was Tesh's men."

"I'm sorry, I didn't know," replied Vanessa.

"How could you? You were in a coma."

"But, why would they?"

"It's like you say, Vanessa, they think I have something. They obviously thought he had it, and they killed him for it."

"That's why you slugged me last night?" she asked.

"When you talked about Malik, it just all came rushing back, and I ... ... can we get back to the demo suits?"

"What do you want to know, pretty girl?" Vanessa smiled and touched my hand.

This time, I didn't pull away. I turned my hand over, palm up, and squeezed hers. "My boss said the guy we took into custody, the one from the Will-Clark building, is dead. The only saving grace is Slade told me all the demolition suits have been recovered."

"Well, that's good, but they're not demolition suits," Vanessa explained. "They're fallout suits, designed to withstand a surface nuclear detonation."

"Well that explains a lot," I replied. "How much do you know about them?"

"I know Tesh's men mastered them. I know they are technically advanced. They use artificial intelligence and nanotechnology to maintain clean air inside during a biological attack. They can sustain your body for years. They even have a waste management system. No telling how the hell that works, but the point is they maintain an airtight seal so nothing unwanted gets in. They're like ghosts in plain sight, unstoppable. You can't detect them with satellite or radar. They don't give off any heat signature whatsoever. They are undetectable and indestructible. If a nuke goes off, a guy could be standing right next to it in one of those suits and survive the detonation and the radiation completely unaffected. You could go to hell and back in one of them."

"So, they use these suits to launch attacks and wage a fake war, so the President looks bad? Vice President Keller's behind this isn't he? He's trying to take the Oval. That's why we can't reach him?"

"I don't know," replied Vanessa. "Maybe ... it's impossible to know for sure. Tesh is a master at compartmentalizing. Nobody knows everything except him. I got a little excited to know you and Crane are tight, but thinking about it, it'd probably be a miracle if I see any immunity deal before I die a horrible," she air quoted, "accidental death." Vanessa sighed.

We both sat quiet for a moment. Finally, I asked, "What's so important about Jeremy Taylor? Why'd they kill him? Wait, did you kill him?"

She shook her head. "No, I didn't kill him! And, I dunno why he's so important. Word is he found something—something that puts the entire operation in jeopardy. That's why they wanted his car. They think Jeremy left something in it. I hear they got to the FBI agent who gave you the car. How'd he get involved?"

"Who, Tom?" I shook my head. "I don't know. He tried to tell me something, but I didn't listen. I was too busy trying to play Farrell, and now Tom might be in trouble—maybe even be dead. I hope not thought. He's one of the few good ones. It's all my fault, I swear if something happened to Tom, I'd-"

"Stop it! It's not your fault, sweetie," said Vanessa. "They know someone took something from Jeremy Taylor's car, and they're not gonna stop until they find it. Denise, listen, here's what you need to understand ... these men are committed, and they have people everywhere, I mean law enforcement, local governments, the White House—everywhere. They don't trust the rest of the world. They believe the United States should control all of the resources, assets, finances, security, and everything else for every other nation."

"Global domination," I said, solemnly.

"Exactly!" she exclaimed. "One government, one currency, one constitution, one rule, all American. You wouldn't believe how powerful they are."

"Help me understand, Vanessa."

"Let me give you an example...." She pushed her plate to the side, picked up her glass, and sipped some of her orange juice. "In my heart, I know this whole unexpected financial crisis is complete bullshit. Mark my words, all the nations will come together because, suddenly this banking problem will miraculously affect the whole world. They'll take over the big banks and insurance companies, make them part of our government in some insane, tax-funded bailout, and then someone will have the bright idea that it's better to have a single point of governance for all these institutions. The Alluvion protocols will shape the future. Tesh is connected at the top of the U.S. and Israeli governments and military, and whatever he's planning, you're at the center of it."

"What do you mean?"

"Infiltrating the DEA wasn't my mission," Sullivan said, smiling. "You were."

"I don't understand," I responded.

"Alex, all the sabotage, the DEA busts gone bad, the so-called terrorism was designed to lure your team at the FBI in, so I could capture and turn you. I am embarrassed to say, but that's why I was coming on so strong with you."

I just looked at her in sheer surprise and disbelief. "I don't understand."

"Remember your embassy incident? They knew everything. If the tax threats didn't hold up, they would've charged you with the death of your partner, Dominic, and Ivan Ashby. I saw that brief with my own two eyes. Who knew Keller was in bed with Tesh? I didn't even know he was involved, and I can't ever see him going along with the program."

"Keller threatened me with tax evasion," I said.

Vanessa shook her head. "Well, if Keller is in on it, he damn sure double-crossed everyone, sending you on a secret mission of his own. Maybe he got greedy and wanted Tesh dead but didn't have the balls to do it himself."

"So, if you knew who I was, why wouldn't you tell them-"

"I did," she interrupted. She lowered her head a little and shook it. "I'm sorry Denise, I told them the first day you showed up. CIA Administrator Pearson knew. Farrell was clueless, and the rest of the team, but the Will-Clark building is where they were supposed to take you. I just ... I didn't expect what happened between us to mean anything, but it did, and when I saw Tesh's men, I couldn't let them take you and hurt you. That's why I opened fire. They would've killed you ... I couldn't let that happen."

"So, my cover was blown the entire time?"

Vanessa nodded. "Yeah. I'm sorry. Look, it's gotta be Keller. That's the only thing I can think of. He gave you the mission. He threatened to put you in jail with the same tax evasion charges I saw in a brief my C.O. gave me. It's gotta be him. Tesh has the V.P. in his pocket."

"Maybe...." I said. "So, you really think somewhere in a dark smoke-filled room, somebody's manufacturing this whole financial issue to bring all the governments together?"

She nodded.

"I can see Israel, the UK, and maybe a few others, but what about Middle Eastern countries like Saudi? No way with all their money and resources they'll go for that."

"You know, that reminds me of a joke," said Sullivan, "you want to hear it?"

I frowned. "Yeah, I can't wait," I replied sarcastically.

"Okay, okay," she said smacking her hands palms down on the table, laughing. "This lady was walking on the beach, and she tripped over a lamp. She thought it might be a Genie lamp, so like she picked it up, rubbed the side of it, and boom out popped a Genie. She was so excited. She asked if she got three wishes, but the Genie told her due to inflation and a slow economy, she had only one wish. So, she pulls out a map, points at the Middle East, and says, "You see these two countries? They're always fighting, so I wish for peace in the Middle East." The Genie takes a look at the map and says, "Lady, these countries have been fighting for thousands of years. That's impossible. You need to make another wish, so-"

"Is this gonna be a long joke?" I interrupted.

"No, wait, this is good, trust me!" Sullivan exclaimed. "So, the Genie tells her to make another wish. She tells him that she's always had trouble finding a good man, and that she needs a man who will treat her well, pay the bills, get along with her family, and a bunch of other shit. So, she says, "that's what I wish for, a good man." Then, the Genie sighs and says... let me have another look at that fucking map!"

Unfortunately, I was trying to sip my juice when she delivered the punch line. I almost hurt myself laughing. I covered my mouth to prevent spewing O.J. all over the table. "Girl, you crazy," I said, still laughing.

I sat for hours, drinking more than just orange juice and listening to Vanessa spill her guts. She didn't know much more about Jeremy Taylor, but she told me she'd heard that Taylor's father, the scientist, was working on some kind of munitions system with a triggering mechanism that uses DNA or some other genetic coding to arm the bomb. I guess he died before he could finish it though. Whatever he did, he must've pissed off the wrong people to receive the classic "fatal car crash" treatment.

Vanessa told me Tesh was always talking about interconnectivity. She said it's the reason he chose the DEA to infiltrate. Under the auspices of waging a war on drugs, they could play things anyway they wanted, and no one would suspect any foul play. The black super soldiers were mixed up in everything too, and Sullivan had been giving up all the intel she'd gathered from her undercover activity to them, which explains why they were always a step ahead of us and everyone else. The whole situation was bad, and it was impossible to know who to trust. I wanted so hard to trust Vanessa, but like David Chandler used to say, believe half of what you see and none of what you hear. Maybe she was telling the truth about everything, or maybe not. I couldn't be sure, but I had no way to corroborate or discredit her, so I had to take everything at face value.

Vanessa claimed Jack and the rest of the DTP team were all innocent, but I wasn't convinced. Farrell was one strange, squirrely bastard. After everything she shared, the only thing I could think of was that thumb drive I had. Not everything she said made sense, but I was convinced the missing piece of the pie was on that drive. It was still too risky to access the data on it though, so I stuck to my guns and kept it hidden. I figured I would wait at least until we got Sullivan her deal and she and I got off of U.S. soil. Then, I could try and find out what was on that drive. By then, it may not matter anymore, at least not to me. All I wanted was to finally be happy, and at the time, I believed I had a fighting chance at that with Vanessa.

Sullivan talked until I had a throbbing headache. I ran my fingers through my hair and yawned. "This is out of control," I said. "But we haven't even scratched the surface, have we?"

"Not even close," she said. "I can tell you shit that'll make your head spin."

"Why on earth would you follow Tesh so blindly?" I asked.

Vanessa rolled her eyes. "I was a soldier, a good soldier," she replied. "Tesh has a gift. When he talks, he can convince you things make sense that you would never do in a million years, and he's an idealist. He believes he has the moral compass and spiritual guidance to deliver this earth into the next millennium—no poverty, no hunger, no social injustice, only peace and harmony. He says the blood he sheds paints a roadway for a brighter future for the whole world."

I thought for a moment. "How do we stop him?"

She shook her head. "I don't know. I don't know if he can be stopped. He is a very powerful man. No one can touch him, and I mean no one—not even you, Denise. You either do what he asks, or you die. That's it. I learned that the hard way. Look, they know something's up, and I know they're going to kill my brother—I've accepted that—but I'm not ready to die, and I don't want to be without you."

I smiled, and my eyes teared up. We kissed a while and just held each other as tight as we could stand. We were completely screwed up together, but somehow, we were really good.

We continued talking through the afternoon. Hour after hour, Vanessa spilled the gory details of all the dirt she'd done with Tesh and the Alluvion project. A lot of people say they're bad or evil or naughty, but that bitch was the devil incarnate. I sure can pick 'em. There was no religion on earth that could grant her salvation. Oddly, I couldn't possibly judge her. Even with all her flaws—all her compromises—from dishonorable soldier to disgraced criminal, I still felt like we were meant for each other.

Vanessa and I grew closer as the months passed. We vacated my apartment in Los Angeles and made a habit of moving around just about every other week. It sounds excessive, but with all my money it was easy. I was the poster child for Western Union, making the occasional withdrawal whenever we needed money, and we paid cash for everything just to be on the safe side. We stayed far away from Los Angeles, laying low in quiet spots—old retirement communities up the 101 North—places like Oxnard, Camarillo, and Santa Barbara. We skipped from city to city, leaving stuff behind and buying new things once we got settled in to a new place. With all the shopping we had to do, it was actually fun for a while. Money can't buy you everything, but it can damn sure keep you from getting your head chopped off when you're on the run. The only person I talked to was Ira, and only when I needed information on one of my accounts because there was no way I was logging on to a banking website.

I hated sitting around waiting, but that's all we could do. We waited so long for Vanessa's immunity deal to come through, I damn near forgot about it. Our security protocols were getting lax too. I came to the conclusion if someone really wanted Vanessa dead, they would've done it by then, so we stopped running and hiding. Against Joe and Jessica's strenuous recommendations, we went back to my apartment in Los Angeles. I was tired of running around, buying stuff and giving it away, all the while trying to cover our tracks. It was so wasteful and a waste of time too. I thought, *just kill us and get it over with if you're gonna do it.*

It was hard to believe, but Vanessa and I were a real couple, and we were good together. It felt like I'd known her my entire life. She made me laugh so hard sometimes my sides would hurt, and then she would get on my goddamn nerves, preaching about what an insensitive, racist, homophobic hypocrite I was. In her defense, we would be out hugging and kissing each other, and then I'd see a gay couple and start talking bad about them. I guess I really was the "pot calling the kettle black" she accused me of.

Turns out Vanessa, in all her sexy glory, had never had a single man in her life. She was a total lesbian. She could have any man she wanted, but she never wanted any of them. It made me feel special in a twisted way that no one had ever made me feel before. All she wanted was me, which was crazy because we were polar opposites. I'm pretty sure I offended her 40 ways from Sunday, but she never turned on me—she never cast me aside—she would just kindly, and sometimes not so kindly, point out my bad behavior and educate me about the LGBT community, its history, and all her struggles growing up. It was touching and sad at the same time. A lot of her friends turned on her and hurt her really badly, but I bet those bitches would be jealous as hell if they could see her fine as wine and rich as hell.

I tried to be better with my thoughts and reactions to everything gay, but I couldn't help it. In my mind, I was this huge exception to the rule, but Vanessa was right. I was a hypocrite and sadly a bit of a bigot—a bisexual bigot. I knew I was wrong, but I couldn't shake the feeling in my mind that Vanessa and I were just plain ole wrong for bringing each other from the starting line to the illustrious finish of ecstasy every chance we got. It was amazing and emotionally disturbing all at once.

Vanessa didn't talk much about her family, and I didn't press the issue, but when we passed through certain towns, we stopped, and she proudly introduced me to some of her friends. They were all gay, and some were like, I don't know, dressed up in leather? The first time I saw that I freaked out, but I swear they were the nicest men I've ever come into contact with, and they were a real hoot. We had a blast, drinking and just being together. Vanessa had the best friends in the world. They were so much fun. The more I tried to stop being a hypocrite and accept who I had become, the more I realized they were just people too. True, they were into some different shit, but I guess I was too.

After a few more visits with Vanessa's gay friends, I stopped reacting like an utter asshole to what I perceived as abnormality. When I saw the lesbian couples together, I was trying to take notes so I could be a better mate for my girlfriend, but it wasn't working, and I think Vanessa could tell how conflicted I still was about us. After every time we were together, I felt guilty about us until she touched me again. I'm pretty sure that, once she realized this, she purposely started touching me a lot more. I don't think she wanted us to end for any reason, and truthfully, I didn't either.

Vanessa couldn't seem to keep her hands off me, and she kept asking me to "dominate her" as she called it. I liked it though—probably more than I should've. Daddy, Mr. Non-violent Law Man (however that worked), was probably turning over in his grave every time I face-slapped Vanessa, but the feeling of sexual power gave me one hell of a rush. She wouldn't tell me everything she was into, but I could tell she was into some creepy, dark shit because I caught her on a BDSM website a few times. Even though I wanted to know more about that side of her, I really didn't want to know more. I was okay with our playtime. Honestly, I just wanted to stay as normal-ish as possible, but she never had to tell me to get kinky and violent twice. Blondie and I went all in.

Vanessa and I settled into my apartment in Los Angeles again and got very comfortable real fast. We had no worries whatsoever. We went to the movies together, shopping at the mall, appointments at the nail and hair salon—I mean I was literally walking around in public with this woman on my arm, introducing her as my girlfriend, using my real name and hers, and no one showed up to whack us—not one. It was all rather disappointing seeing as I was all amped up and ready for a fight, but I got over that fast.

Joe and Jessica continued hanging around to provide security, but even they were pretty much off duty while on duty. None of us went into the office. We just reported to our superiors periodically and enjoyed our downtime together. It was hard to believe, but Joe and Jessica eventually warmed up to Vanessa. As odd as it sounds, we were kind of like a family. We all did things together, and we actually had a little fun. It was good—life was good. Every now and again, we'd talk more about the Alluvion program, and we would check on the status of Vanessa's immunity request, but we got the same response over and over again—it had not been denied, it was still under consideration, and we needed to keep her safe, so we did.

Vanessa's body was amazing, and I soon discovered why because that bitch was the ultimate nutrition-Nazi. After moving back into my apartment, she religiously cooked a real breakfast for all of us, but after that, she and I drank our meals for the rest of the day. God only knows why I was letting this woman tell me what to eat, but as sure as the day is long, she was telling me, and I was doing it. I got so sick of it too, it was all kale this and almond milk that with agave nectar. *What in the holy fuck is agave nectar anyway?* I was ready to tell her to shove that smoothie shit up her ass, but I was too busy living my life on the toilet. I wasn't regular anymore—I was super premium with Techron. I swear I was going like 10 times a day. Thank God I had my own bathroom.

One day, around three o'clock in the afternoon, I had a breakdown—a momentary nutritional lapse. Truth be told, I blame society—the clown, the big fuckin' golden arches—all of these things are burned into the minds of children every day in America. No sane person can resist the power of hot, salty, golden French fries, and it had been ages since I had a taste. You need to understand what I'm saying here—at McDonald's, even the French fries are golden, and who doesn't like gold? I tried to resist the urge, but it was a waste of time and energy.

Vanessa was a little miffed with me, but I wasn't going to lie to her. I needed a fucking burger and a break from all her constant "eat this and eat that, so you can have a bikini body" crap. This venture was the first one we didn't go on together. She told me if I wanted to screw up months of progress, go ahead, but she was sticking to her diet, which consisted of kale smoothies and salads—a bunch of rabbit food nobody wants to eat. I needed flavor, so McDonalds was about to have my blackass in there ordering the whole menu within just a few moments.

Joe and Jessica were smart enough not to even try Vanessa's crazy diet. They'd been feasting on steaks and tacos the whole time, of which I made them eat in their rooms or out on the deck. I didn't want to even smell it. I asked them both if they wanted anything from McDonalds, but they said no, so I went ahead and left.

I hit the freeway, and for the first time in a while, my mind was clear as if I had no worries whatsoever. I jumped in the fast lane and gunned it for a few miles, then I clicked on my right blinker and proceeded to cut off about three or four other drivers as I changed lanes all the way over from the fast lane to the slow lane. What can I say, I'm a New Yorker at heart? If you see my blinker, I'm not asking for permission. I'm coming in your lane, so brace yourself.

A few miles up the road, I slung the car off the exit and made a right turn. There was a squad car ahead in the left lane. Everybody was driving slowly, acting all scared behind him. I'm pretty sure the police do this on purpose just to see if you've got enough balls to pass them, but no one ever does. *Chickens!* I tried to be patient, but I'd become more desperate for real food than a crack-whore needs a hit in rehab, so I jammed on the gas, whirled around the car in front of me, and almost took the cop's front bumper off. I think I pissed him off, but by the time he was ready to do something about it, I'd already whipped into the drive thru lane. I didn't care at all. I sat and looked at the menu for a minute trying to convince myself to get something halfway decent, and finally, I did.

"Welcome to McDonald's would you like to try a value meal today?" said a woman's voice over the drive thru speaker.

"Yeah, let me have a Big Mac combo, super-sized!"

"What to drink with that combo?" asked the drive-through window attendant.

"Oh, a diet Coke," I replied.

"Thank you ... I have a Big Mac combo, value-sized with a diet Coke. Please drive around for your total."

I pulled around waiving a $10 bill at the first window. "Come on this is supposed to be fast food," I mumbled.

The lady in the first window took my cash and gave me change. I darted up to the second window to retrieve my pure, unadulterated greasy surprise. The guy at the window handed me my drink, which happened to be a lot bigger than I remembered. I looked at it and laughed but didn't hesitate to partake of it. I removed the straw from the paper wrapping and jammed it down through the plastic top into my big vat of soda. The cup barely fit into my cup holder, but I made it work.

The guy came back to the window. "It's going to be about a minute on fries," he said.

I threw my hand up. "Whatever."

When he finally gave me my bag, I was more than ready to go. He tried to tell me to have a nice day, but I was already pulling off, and damn near took his arm with me. I couldn't wait to get home, so I started eating in the car, swerving all over the road, alternating between driving and fumbling around in that little brown bag.

"Shit!" I yelled, scalding my fingers and nearly burning my lip off from a fist full of crisp golden fries. Those suckers were straight outta the grease. I burned myself, but it was nothing another sip of coke wouldn't take care of. I slowed down a little and leaned over to take a sip. "Man, that's good!" I exclaimed. "You guys do it right!" I kept on eating as I drove back home.

I pulled up at the apartment and ran upstairs, clinching what was left in my little brown bag like a fiend. I climbed to the top of the stairs and saw the little boy from across the hall, Corey, standing there. I froze. It was as if he knew I was coming with fries—like he could smell them a mile away. I wanted to cut his little cute ass. In my mind I was thinking, *They're mine goddammit, all mine!* like Daffy Duck and his buried treasure. I could tell by the look on Corey's face he wanted whatever I had in the bag, and I wasn't feeling that at all. However, I was certain saying, *get a job and buy your own fries you little bastard*, was just not the right kind of response, so I decided to share, but only if he asked.

"Hi Ms. Anna," he greeted.

"Hey sweetie. What are you doing out by yourself?"

"Just chillin'!" he replied.

He was only six-years-old, and he was just too much, looking like a little old man and cute as ever. He had a gang of hair too, but it was neatly trimmed. He must've just come from the barber shop. He wore a Sean-John t-shirt, baggy little jeans, and the cutest basketball shoes. He was adorable.

"Chillin', huh?" I smiled.

"Yeah." He looked at my McDonalds bag and grinned from ear-to-ear. "Can I have a fry?" he asked, pointing right at the bag.

"Here baby." I put down my drink and reluctantly held the bag open so he could take a few fries out. "Be careful, they may still be hot."

He stuck his little hand in the bag and pulled out a fistful. "Thank you, Miss Anna."

"You are so welcome baby." I closed the bag and rubbed his head.

"Ah man, you're gonna mess up my fro. I gotta be fly for the ladies!"

"Ladies...?" I poked his side a few times, and he started to giggle. "Boy, get yourself in there, and tell your momma I said hey!"

"Yes ma'am," he replied. "Thank you for the fries!"

"My pleasure. Now go on in, baby." I watched to make sure he got back inside okay. Then, I busted into my apartment to finish eating. I flung my bag onto the table and sat down. I unwrapped my burger and took a bite.

"Mmm, damn!" I exclaimed. Then, I proceeded to take bite after glorious bite, just pausing long enough between bites to swallow. I couldn't eat the whole burger, but I sure as hell tried. Needless to say, I was completely satisfied, and it was time to chill. I headed for the sofa, but the phone rang before I could sit down. I ran back and grabbed the cordless off the table.

"Hello," I answered, walking over and stretching out on the sofa.

"Hey girl!" said the caller. It was my neighbor, Corey's mom.

"What's up, Donna?" I held the phone to my ear with my shoulder.

"Where the heck you been, Anna?"

I almost tripped and replied, *who the fuck is Anna?* I have so many aliases, sometimes it's hard to keep up. Every time I meet someone, I have to make up a new story about what I did for a living and remember what I say. Even though Vanessa and I had been all out in the open, we were still trained operatives, so we'd been careful to get in and out of the apartment without being seen, especially by Donna. That woman was a total gossip.

"Girl, I been working," I replied, "I had to leave town for a while."

"Still with that software company?" she asked.

"Story of my life!"

Donna asked, "Was my son just over there, begging?"

I giggled. "He wasn't begging ... well, maybe a little."

"That boy know not to be bothering people."

"It's okay. I shouldn't have been eating that junk anyway. He actually helped a sistah out."

"He's always on the move," she said, "I'm gonna have to put a satellite tracker on his little ass in a minute."

"Is it that bad?" I laughed.

"Girl, he all over the place, but he's my little man. I love him."

"He's precious. By the way, any word from James?"

"Shit, I'll have to stop by and tell you about his triflin' ass," she whispered. "I don't want lil J hearing all this mess. You getting your hair done this week?"

I heard a knock at the door. "Hey girl, let me call you right back, somebody's at my door." I hung up and walked towards the guest bedrooms.

"Joe? Jessica?" They were nowhere to be found. I went back to my room and Vanessa was in there lying down.

"Vanessa," I whispered, "wake up!"

"Huh?" she rolled over and rubbed her eyes. "Where's Joe and Jessica?"

"They didn't go with you?" she asked, yawning.

"No. Look, somebody's at the door. Stay in here and keep quiet."

She nodded.

I grabbed a gun from the dresser, cocked it, and put it in the back of my pants. Then I went to answer the door. Whoever it was, they were still knocking and ringing the doorbell when I came out the bedroom as if they just knew I was home. I looked through the peephole and was surprised to see Detective Marshall of the L.A.P.D standing outside my door. I have to admit, I wasn't prepared to see him. I pulled myself together and opened the door.

"Ms. Johnson."

"Detective, so good of you to drop by. To what do I owe this pleasure?"

"Well, you never called," he said.

"No, you were supposed to call me, remember?"

"Oh yeah," he said, smiling, trying to look inside. I stepped out and pulled the door up.

"So, what can I help you with?" I asked.

"We found Jeremy Taylor's vehicle," said Marshall.

I crossed my arms. "Really?"

"Yeah, it was down in a chop shop in Long Beach ... you mind if I come in for a second?"

"Now's not a good time."

"You got company?" he asked.

"No, I just have some things I need to take care of," I replied.

He looked strange. "It'll just be a minute," he said, pushing past me.

I scratched my head. "Well, come on in, Detective." I shut the door and turned around and Marshall had the oddest look on his face, but I just dismissed it.

"So, about the kid Taylor?" I asked. "What happened to him again?"

"Yeah, we're starting to think maybe he was carjacked," he said.

I put my hands on my hips and shifted my weight to the left. "Oh, really?"

"Yeah, I understand the crew down there in Long Beach were some real bastards."

"Is that what you heard, Detective?"

He nodded.

"So, you've made some progress. What can I do to help?"

He looked up towards the ceiling. "You have something I need."

"Say again, Detective?"

Without saying another word, he grabbed my neck and started slamming his fist into my face. After about the fifth continuous blow, everything got blurry. I scratched his face, but that made him angrier. He reared back and landed a crushing uppercut blow that knocked me out of his grip, up off the floor and down on to the glass top coffee table. My body cracked right through the tabletop. I felt broken glass pierce my back, arms and legs. I lay there dazed and hung up inside the steel frame of the table. I couldn't move an inch.

Sullivan came running out yelling and swinging, but he pistol-whipped her down onto the floor. She was out, instantly. Marshall holstered his weapon, straightened his suit and kneeled down next to me.

"Dumb bitch," he mumbled, picking glass off me and moving my hair out of my face. "I bet you don't feel so smart now, do you! Now, where's the thumb drive?"

I was breathing hard and fast. I could taste blood and my skull was vibrating.

"We're going to find the drive!" exclaimed Marshall. "We're going to find it if we have to cut that bitch open and show her own fucking heart to her. You hear me? You want that Southerland? We're gonna find it, and then I'm gonna find your family and kill every last one of them!"

He pulled my hair and raised up to hit me again, but a man walked through the door and interrupted him.

"WAIT!" he commanded.

Marshall seemed disgusted. He slammed my head back down. Before I blacked out, I saw them drag Joe and Jessica's body into the apartment. They'd both been shot in the head. My eyes rolled back, everything went dark, and that was that. I woke up in a cell days later, naked, alone, and scared out of my mind.

Chapter 11

Present day, back in the court room. It had been a long, tiring day in court. Judge Scott had spent most of the day scratching his head as I unraveled my story for all to hear. He seems to be getting more frustrated with me by the moment, but I really am doing the best I can. I stopped telling my story when I got to the part about Detective Marshall—if that was even his name—attacking me in my apartment in Los Angeles, killing my teammates, and kidnapping the woman I love. Scott sat straight up in his seat and took his glasses off again. Each time he did that, I knew he was gearing up for a big speech or a bunch of questions I had absolutely no desire to answer.

"Lieutenant Southerland, you've given this panel one incredible story today," says Judge Scott, "but you seemed to have omitted some very important details."

"I'm not sure what you mean, sir," I replied.

"First, let's talk about FBI Deputy Director, Anthony Crane. He's still M.I.A. There's a nationwide search going on for him as we speak. No kidnapper or terrorist group has taken responsibility for his disappearance. There's no reason to believe he would simply pick up, abandon his position, and leave. So, what happened?"

"They took me to a place way out in the desert," I reply. "I endured extreme torture ... for a long time. I lost count on the days, but I held out as long as I could. They wanted me to do something. At the time, I had no idea they were holding other prisoners. If I'd known, I would've ... it all happened so fast. I'll never forget that day inside a secret U.S. Army controlled facility in Mesa, Arizona...."

I continue telling the panel my story. I remember being so badly beaten, I wanted to die, but I was still alive even after the Colonel and his henchmen did their worst. To my surprise, it would seem Dr. Lerner, my one and only angel, finally got her wishes. Who knows how that happened? I had no clue what day it was or the time, but I lay on a hospital bed, hooked up to a ton of equipment. I had an IV in my left arm, and they were pumping me full of liquid, but I still felt dehydrated. My back felt a little funny too. I knew my arm was broken, but I was feeling a lot of pain in my spine as well. Up to that point, I'd been betrayed by nearly everyone I ever knew or so I thought. It didn't matter at that point though because I was all alone once again.

I was weak, but I knew I had to take action—it was the only way I was getting out of there. Unlike in that torture room, I was completely unrestrained. I zoomed in on a nearby nurse, who was doing something in the room, but it wasn't what she was doing that caught my attention—it was her Blackberry. I closed my eyes and mustered up every ounce of strength I had. I waited until she was closer to my bed, and then I threw myself down out onto the floor.

"Help," I cried, "please help me."

She hurried over and kneeled down, trying to help me back up, but I took my good elbow and beamed her right in the eye. I hit her hard enough to knock her out, and she went down. I drug myself over and unclipped her phone. Then, I scrolled through the menu. She had a lot of programs installed, but the one I needed was the map. The phone had GPS, so I was able to use the map to get my coordinates, which I sent with the word *Containment* along with my full name in the body of a broadcasted interagency message. I pushed send and watched to make sure it actually went out. Maybe Keller was behind all the treachery or maybe he wasn't. Either way, I had a 50/50 chance the alert system he put in place for me was still active.

After a few minutes, two guards checked in. They saw the nurse knocked out on the ground, and me beside her with the phone still in my hand. They immediately rushed me and started slamming me around, trying to wrestle that phone away from my grip. It hurt each time they kicked or slammed me, but I didn't let go of that thing until my message was sent.

"GET THE COLONEL IN HERE!" yelled one of the men.

The other man slammed me onto the bed and strapped me down. "FUCKING BITCH!" he yelled.

I spit at him, which prompted him to slap the snot out of me. My head was ringing like a bell. Having been smacked with the back of his fist, I passed out again.

Later, I woke up to the sweet smell of a Cohiba cigar. I leaned my head to the side a little and slowly opened my eyes.

"It breaks my heart to see such a beautiful lady go through all this," said the man sitting next to my bed. But he was not just a man—it was Peter Tesh in the flesh.

"You do not seem afraid of me," he said puffing his cigar.

"I don't scare easy," I whispered.

"Indeed," he said, chuckling, holding up his cigar and looking down the side of it. "What my men have done to you is unacceptable. You're a soldier like me. You shouldn't be punished for work you're sanctioned to do by our government. I am sorry for the treatment you have received here."

"Let me go and we'll call it square."

"Sure," he replied. "But first, I need to know something."

"What?"

Tesh smiled. "Unfortunately, I cannot find someone else to do what I require. I need your DNA and your cooperation, so you and I are joined by the hip. My operative was to bring me a disgraced agent, but it seems failure is more common these days than not. You have interrupted my plan with your distress signal, but it matters not. We will reacquire you soon. Right now, I just need to know if I am safe to let you live ... so, where is the flash drive you took from me?"

"They took it," I replied. "Your men killed everyone in sight in Long Beach and took whatever was there."

"No, no, no," he said, shaking his head, "you took the drive, and you hid it. Maybe not in your apartment, but somewhere in Los Angeles, yes...? Listen, it's okay ... I know how it is ... you need leverage, right? The thumb drive you took gives you that, so keep it for me. Just tell me what Taylor had on it, and who you've shared it with."

"I DON'T HAVE ANY GODDAMN THUMB DRIVE!" I yelled. "You got your facts wrong on a lot of things."

"Is that so?" he asked.

"You're a terrorist ... turn yourself in, and I'll make this easy on you."

He laughed out loud, slapping his knee. "You are too much. Now, who'd you share the information on the drive with?"

"No one," I replied. "I don't have any drive. I never met Taylor-"

"But you had his car, did you not?" he asked.

"Your men killed my guy before he found anything. If there's something there, it's still in the car." I coughed, hard.

"Here, let me get you some water," said Tesh. He walked over to the sink and filled a pink plastic cup with water. He came back over to the bed and helped me drink.

"Thank you."

"You're welcome," replied Tesh. "You don't look well."

"I think my arm is broken."

"Wait one," he said. He got up and walked out into the hall. After a few minutes, he returned with a doctor.

"Set the bone," he commanded, "and clean up all those wounds, she's leaking all over the place. Just what the hell were you people thinking? GET HER SOMETHING FOR THE PAIN, IDIOT!" He looked down at me and touched my shoulder. "We can talk while he works."

The doctor got right to work, fixing me up.

"Your name isn't Tesh is it?" I asked.

He smiled.

"What's your real name?"

He kept smiling but didn't answer my question. "I know your name is not Johnson," he boasted. "So why don't we talk about Vanessa Sullivan...."

"What about her? Ouch, easy with that!"

"Sorry, ma'am," the doctor replied.

"I understand you two are close," said Tesh.

I shook my head.

"No? Hmm, that's funny ... she says you were planning to leave the country together."

"She's a material witness in FBI custody."

"Not anymore," he said, smiling.

I shook my head again. "Don't you dare hurt her."

"So, you are close," he deduced.

"Whatever."

"There are a few things that need to happen here, Alex ... may I call you Alex?"

I rolled my eyes at him.

Tesh continued talking. "Unfortunately, you have forced my hand, and we don't have much time left. The first thing I need is to believe you about this missing drive. I need to feel confident you're telling the truth. The second thing is I have a group of gentlemen who need to visit the Middle East and they need a guide. I'm hoping I can count on your expertise. My brother was brilliant. He understood biotechnology and nanotechnology like none before him. He was a renowned scientist, and he promised to do something very important for me, but he betrayed me—he and his son. As a result, there is now a device that can only be triggered by you, and it cannot be activated under duress, which means you have to be willing. I don't know what he was thinking. Perhaps he lost his nerve. Perhaps he thinks you will not lose yours—that you will be strong enough to refuse me—but everyone has a price, Alex. I need your word that you will do this for me, and I swear to God there will be no more bloodshed. I will leave you and your family and friends be. I swear on my life. So, what will it take for me to be able to count on you? What is your price? I promise, we will leave you and your people unharmed. You have my word."

"I DON'T BELIEVE YOU!" I yelled. "You're going to kill me anyway."

Tesh smiled again. "Well, let's take it one step at a time ... Sergeant!"

A soldier came in, dragging Sullivan across the floor. She was all messed up. It looked like they'd been beating her all night. She was barely recognizable.

"NO!" I yelled.

"Hold her!" said Tesh.

The doctor pulled me back by my shoulders and tightened my restraints.

"I DON'T ... SHE'S NOT IMPORTANT TO ME!" I screamed. "SHE'S NOBODY!"

Tesh walked over to a soldier and stuck out his hand. The soldier relinquished his weapon to Tesh, who checked it to make sure it was loaded. Tesh kneeled down, took two fingers and ran them across Vanessa's bloody face. He held his fingers up to his lips and tasted her blood. Then, he shook his head. "Soldier, you were given a task," he said calmly, "but you botched it up. You were given a second chance, and you botched that up too. What on earth are we going to do with you, Sergeant Major?"

Vanessa spit in his face. "GET IT OVER WITH ASSHOLE!"

"NO, NO, NO, PLEASE NO!" I shook my head violently, pleading for him to just leave her alone, but he didn't.

Tesh wiped Vanessa's spit off his face and looked me in the eyes. "Alex, your filth is all over her now. She's no use to me."

"You don't own me!" murmured Vanessa, "I love her, I defied you and there ain't shit you can do to me to make me give a fuck about you, you bastard!"

"I'll do whatever you want, just let her go, please," I begged.

Tesh chuckled. "Now, I'm the one who doesn't believe you, Alex. A single grain of rice can tip the scale, can't it?"

Vanessa began to cry. "Baby, I love you," she said, whimpering. "Don't you ever forget I love you, pretty girl."

Tesh snatched her head to the side, pressed the gun to her temple and pulled the trigger. Vanessa's brains shot out all over the floor and the side wall.

I started screaming and kicking, but Tesh didn't flinch a muscle—he had zero emotion or remorse about killing her. Vanessa was right—he was a black-hearted mothafucka. I couldn't help it. I burst into tears.

Tesh wiped Vanessa's blood off his hands with a handkerchief and casually walked back over to me. "Leave her there so she can see the body," he commanded.

"Yes, sir!" the soldier replied. Then, he exited the room.

I couldn't stop crying. "You motherfucker I hate you, motherfucker!"

"We've got a serious problem, Alex," said Tesh. "Two teams of Navy SEALs are headed this way. You've been a bad girl. You called in the cavalry. Believe it or not, even I have to play by the rules, so I can't touch you now, but I can help you make your decision. Will you help me...?"

I shook my head.

"Bring him in!" Tesh commanded, loudly.

The same soldier reappeared, this time dragging a man with a hood over his head. The soldier drug the man right up beside me and removed the hood. It was Slade. Like Vanessa, he was badly beaten, and he had duct tape covering his mouth. Tesh reached down and snatched the tape off.

Slade shook his head and looked at me. "I was wrong, Alex," he confessed. "Kill 'em all," he said, sniffing blood up into his nostrils. "Goddammit, you kill this fucking asshole, Alex!"

I shook my head. "Please!"

"This one here is a killer," said Tesh, nonchalantly. "A loyal killer. He kills and doesn't even know why, so he is a most valuable asset. And, since you're so fond of this murderer, I'm going to give you the opportunity to save his life. Tell me where the drive is, tell me what you know, and promise me you'll do me the small favor of escorting my men to the Kingdom ... you do these things for me and you will have saved his pathetic life."

"Slade I'm sorry I-"

Tesh fired a shot straight down into the top of Slade's head and his body dropped down on the floor like a sack of potatoes.

"SON-OF-A-BITCH! LET ME OUT THIS MOTHAFUCKA AND FACE ME LIKE A MAN YOU FUCKIN' PUSSY," I yelled, spiting at him.

"You can stop this Alex, you know what I require."

"FUCK YOU! MOTHERFUCKER FUCK YOU! PIECE OF FUCKING SHIT!"

The doctor was just as fucked up as I was with all the killing. He was shaking, still trying to work on me.

Tesh pointed his gun to the doctor's head. "GET IT RIGHT DOCTOR!" he yelled.

"YES, SIR!" The doctor's voice trembled, and his hands began to shake even worse.

"BRING THE NEXT ONE IN!" yelled Tesh.

Once again, the soldier went out and dragged another prisoner into the room.

"Alex, don't you say a fucking word," said Tony as the soldier pulled him towards me.

I fell apart. "NO, NO ... NO, NO, PLEASE NO!" I cried.

"I've never seen an FBI agent like this man before," said Tesh. "If I didn't know better, I'd say he had this whole thing figured out. You know where we found him? At a checkpoint less than a mile up the road. How'd you know about this place, Deputy Director Anthony Crane?"

"Listen, you don't wanna do this," said Tony, "I'm a high-ranking government official-"

"And, I am not?" asked Tesh.

Tony looked confused. "I don't know what you are, but I know who you are."

Tesh laughed. "You see Alex, not even your highest-ranking official knows how Washington works. Look around. You think I just happened to stumble upon a bunch of boys in green, willing to wander off the reservation? This is a U.S. military facility. You Alex, me, we're all the property of the United States of America, and we are all expendable. Terrorist...? Oh, please!"

I just shook my head and wept. "I told you everything," I said, softly. "I'm not lying."

"I believe you," Tesh replied. "I believe you don't have any information to give me. The slut, maybe, but no way you'd let me kill your man like that. The things he said about you—such honorable things. Thank you for your help. Now Alex, you have about an hour before we leave. I'm going to do for you what no one would do for me. I am sorry, but this man cannot live, he knows too much. I am going to leave you this gun." He took the magazine out of the pistol and put it in his pocket. "There's one in the chamber. If you kill him, then I will have your answer. If you do not kill him, eventually you will watch me rip his guts out slowly. If you kill yourself, I will kill Mr. Crane, his lovely wife, and the rest of his family, one-by-one. The choice is a simple one, and the choice is yours. Let's go, Doctor."

The doctor fled the scene, frantically. Tesh laid the gun down on the counter on his way out the door. Then, they locked us in together.

Tony removed my restraints, and then leaned up against the bed close to me. He looked into my eyes and smiled a nervous smile. "Kid, I'm sorry ... sorry I didn't take care of you the way-"

"Shhh," I put my finger to his lips. "I'm not going to hurt you."

"You don't have a choice," he said.

"Please, Tony."

"Alex, they're going to kill the President. We should've done something to stop Vice President Keller before it got this far. This is on me."

"Are you sure it's Keller?" I asked.

"I bet my life on it," he replied. "He's mixed up in all this somehow with Tesh. There's nothing we can do here. You have to find a way to stop this. The ball's in your court now. I'm old, and I-"

"I don't wanna talk about it, Tony," I interrupted. "I just want to hold you. Come here...." I scooted over to make room for him, and he moved all the way up onto the bed beside me. "I just want to be with you, Tony. I ... I love you."

He put his arm around me, kissed my forehead and ran his fingers through my hair. "I love you too," he whispered.

We didn't talk after that. We just lay together, looking into each other's eyes. I felt safe with him, and I knew in my heart we'd find a way out of the mess I had gotten us into. I couldn't let anything happen to Tony because I needed him. With Vanessa and Slade's body laying just a few feet away from us on the floor, he was all I had left.

The pain medication that doctor gave me was very strong. I dozed off after a few minutes, laying there with Tony. I slept peacefully in his arms, wrapped up in his tender, loving care. I was sleeping so hard, I didn't even hear him get up, but I did hear the gunshot.

"LIEUTENANT SOUTHERLAND!" A sailor in blue camos shook me awake. "I'm Lieutenant Holt. We're here to take you home, ma'am."

I opened my eyes and the first thing I zoomed in on was Tony's body on the floor. He'd killed himself to save me. The sailor helped me to my feet, and we started moving towards the door.

"Package is secure," the soldier radioed, dragging me towards the exit.

"Wait," I said, trying to break free and get to Tony's lifeless body.

"WE GOTTA GO MA'AM!" the sailor yelled repeatedly.

I finally gave in. I nodded and stopped struggling. The Calvary had arrived just like Tesh said. Keller may have been M.I.A., but my rescue squad was still on duty. Someone sent two platoons of eight Navy SEALs, each armed to the teeth. They'd secured the area and detained some of the rogue soldiers. Half the team loaded up with me in one of the helicopters, and we ascended off into the night sky.

I was still shaken to my core. I didn't know what day it was or how long I'd been down in that hole. All I knew was the people I cared for most were dead and someone was gonna pay.

My rescuers took me to a Navy hospital, Camp Pendleton in San Diego, where I was checked in under an assumed name and treated for stab wounds, broken bones, malnourishment, and pneumonia. I stayed in the hospital for what seemed like an eternity. I received a ton of treatment and rehab over several months. Finally, they were ready to release me, but that day, I had an unexpected visitor.

"Stephanie Jordan? Well that's an interesting name," came a man's voice.

I turned around and it was Jack Farrell, standing in the middle of my room.

I just shook my head. "You're taking a big risk coming here, aren't you?"

He nodded. "Yeah, but this is all I got. Took me six months to find you, Stephanie ... it is Stephanie, right?"

I smiled and nodded. "Just Alex. Why are you here?" I asked.

"I took a leave of absence," he replied. "They told me Sullivan is missing in action. Said she was really Army and she went AWOL. You believe that?"

I sighed. "I don't know what to believe anymore, Jack."

"Slade's missing too," he said. "DTP has been shut down and the team scattered. They wanted me to take a promotion."

"Why didn't you?" I asked.

"Instinct," he replied. "You know, if they'd just said Sullivan was killed, I might've bought it. But, this whole story about her missing...?" Jack shook his head. "I don't buy it."

"I don't know what to tell you, Jack."

"You know who told me?" he asked.

"Chief Carter?"

"No, Carter's dead," Jack replied, emotionlessly.

"What?" I responded, shocked to hear the news.

"Unexpected "heart attack,"" Jack said as he paced around my hospital room. "So, either I was both the unluckiest and the luckiest man on the planet all at the same time, seeing I lost my team and was suddenly up for promotion, or I am extremely slow on the uptake. Point being, I didn't take the job. Instead, I started poking around, and you know what I found?"

"What?"

"I found your apartment," he replied.

I squinted at him a little. "Found, huh?"

He nodded. "I was able to get Sullivan's last GPS location from her phone. And, you know what I found inside in your place?"

I shook my head.

Jack reached in his pocket and retrieved a USB thumb drive. "She was recording every single intimate moment between the two of you on this thumb drive," he said.

My jaw nearly hit the floor. "Say again?"

"Yeah," Jack replied. "A camera right over your bed. Now, lie to me again, and I swear to God I will-"

"I loved her," I interrupted. "We ... we loved each ... we became close, Jack."

"Yeah, I saw," he replied. "Where is she? What did you do to her?"

I shook my head.

Jack moved in close to me. "ANSWER ME, GODDAMMIT!"

I started crying. "She's dead, Jack ... Tesh killed her right in front of me. We were captured, and ... it doesn't matter ... ... she's gone ... Slade too."

A tear streamed down Jack's cheek. I tried to put my arms around his neck, but he stepped back.

"Don't touch me!" he exclaimed.

I cocked my head to the side. "Jack, what's going on?"

"So, they just let you go?" he asked.

I stepped back a little. "No, they didn't just let me go, they tried to kill me too, why you think I've been in here, asshole! What a shitty thing to say, Farrell!"

He nodded. And then he shook his head. Then he rubbed his face a few times. "I'm sorry," he said.

"How'd you find me?" I asked.

"Sullivan," he replied. "She left a trail of breadcrumbs a mile long. Apparently, no one checked her for the little micro cameras we had, courtesy of the CIA. She put one in your room, and when you weren't in there, she used it to record a host of information, like all your aliases. I've been checking every hospital for every name she gave on that recording."

I smiled and just shook my head. "She was one sly bitch."

Jack burst out laughing. "Yes ... yes she was. You two were together ... was that ... real?"

I smiled and tried to stop myself from crying. I nodded. "It was good, Jack ... we were good man, I swear, it was like ... it was real. For me it was real, and she ... I mean all the goddamn smoothies—my asshole was on fire."

I thought Jack was going to split his side he laughed so hard.

"We got sloppy, Jack," I said. "The White House promised her immunity. She and I were going to leave together, but they got to us first. An LAPD Detective, this guy Marshall caught us off guard. He killed two FBI agents and took Vanessa and I to this secret military base. I barely made it out with all my parts attached. If it wasn't for a team of SEALs...." I shook my head and closed my eyes. "I'm just lucky to be alive. I miss her, you know."

"Yeah, me too," Jack said. "I found something else though."

"What?"

Jack reached in his other pocket and pulled out another thumb drive—the one I'd hidden so well—or so I thought.

"Jack, what are you doing?" I asked.

"You wouldn't believe what I had to do to find this," he said. "You're one sick lady, but I gotta hand it to you—hiding this thing inside a vibrator? Seriously?"

I grinned an evil grin. "You're more resourceful than I thought, but you should've left it where you found it."

"I know that now," Jack replied. "I should've walked away. I shouldn't have led them here to you."

"What?"

"They're coming," he said.

"Jack, if you're being followed, why would you come here?"

"I needed you to know what's on this drive, and I couldn't risk trying to call or send a message. They would've just intercepted it, killed us both, and no one other than me would know the truth. Listen, we don't have a lot of time."

"What's on the drive?" I asked.

"You," he replied.

"I don't understand."

"Everything on the drive is all about you, Alex. It's your DNA sequence, but in the form of some kind of advanced program. It's like a simulator. When your DNA is presented, it returns a positive, and if any other DNA sequence is introduced, it locks the program down. It's not compiled either. Whoever made this thing put every piece of code on this drive and a tracking worm to locate every interface that uses this security technology. Somebody wanted you to get this drive, and I think whoever it was, they wanted the bad guys to find you. I think you might be able to use this to stop them from doing whatever they're trying to do."

"It was Dr. Taylor," I said, "it had to be. Tesh said Taylor and his son betrayed him. He gave this to his son Jeremy. Jeremy hid it in his car and gave his car to Tom at the FBI— my friend, Tom—oh, fuck me."

"There's more," said Jack.

"What?"

"I used the program to locate a device," he replied. "Alex, it's nuclear, and I tracked its movement from a facility in Arizona all the way to its current location. I went to the Arizona facility … there's nothing there anymore. When I hit the go button, something started transmitting. This thing has some kind of security protocol."

"So, you shut it down, right?"

"Yeah, about that," Jack replied. "I can't. I unplugged it, plugged it back in, and even stuck it in water. No matter what I do, it won't power down, and it's still transmitting. It's gotta be some kind of special internal battery or something. Either way, I know it's just a matter of time before they catch up to me. I'm a dead man."

"DON'T SAY THAT!" I exclaimed. "Wait, where is it, Jack?" I asked.

"Alex, I've been running from these jokers since I found their bomb, and I'm tired of running."

"Where's the bomb, Jack?"

Jack pulled out his gun. He walked over and sat down on the bed. "There's a black GMC pickup truck parked out back. It's clean." Jack threw the keys at me, and I caught them, midair. "You need to get out of here Alex, NOW!"

I heard a commotion out in the hallway. "Where's the bomb, Jack? Just tell me, man!" I started walking backwards towards the door.

Jack chambered his weapon. "Goodbye, Alex. If you don't leave now, I will shoot you." He trained his gun on me.

"BASTARD!" I yelled as softly as I could. I backed myself up behind the door and stood there as quietly as possible, hidden in the shadows.

Two men in black entered the room and went straight for Jack. I hesitated to leave, but I knew what he was doing. They were still tracking him. It was over for him, so he was trying to give me a fighting chance. The men asked Jack something, but it was hard to make out, I just slipped around the door and snuck out.

A few steps out into the hall, and I heard all hell break loose back in the room behind me. I stopped in my tracks as two security officers ran towards me, but they both went around me, so I kept moving down the hall. God knows what happened back there, but I couldn't wait around to find out.

I picked up the pace and made my way outside the hospital and around the back where I found Jack's truck. I climbed in, said a little prayer for him, and then sped out through the parking lot and onto the main street.

I drove for as long as I could, until I felt like I was going to run off the road. I pulled off the freeway and stopped at a gas station. Jack had some cash stuffed in the ash tray, so I used it to pay for fuel and filled the truck up. At that point, I had a full tank, but nowhere to go seeing as Jack wouldn't tell me the location of the bomb. I don't know what that was about. Maybe he was trying to protect me. Or, maybe he left me a clue. I immediately started rummaging around through the truck. I searched through all the junk in the back of the cab. It looked like Jack had been living out of the truck. There was trash and a bunch of pre-paid cell phones lying around on the floor. I checked the middle console, under the seats, and finally looked in the glovebox. I was a complete idiot for not looking there first. Inside, I found a map of Washington, D.C. Only one location was circled in red on the map—the Naval Observatory—the residence of the Vice President of the United States of America. It was Keller after all. It had been the whole time.

Tony was right. Keller was starting a coup. He put everything in motion from the very beginning. He set me up. He targeted me after Dr. Taylor screwed them by coding that bomb to my DNA. There was no telling how many bombs there were out there, Jack just found one. If Taylor knew Tom well enough to trust him, then he had to know I wouldn't go for it, and they gave me the tool to find those bombs and shut them down. Tesh said the trigger would fail under duress. That's what this was all about. That's why Tesh tried to beat me into submission. I was his patsy. The minute Tesh found out what Taylor did, he and Keller started scheming on me, the crafty bastards. I'm the one who would set off a nuke in the Middle East and put the icing on their bullshit world crisis cake to make President Wood look completely useless. It would be all on me—the rogue FBI agent with the violent, fucked up past. I can see now that Tesh worked for Keller the whole time. The bad guys knew everything about me because Keller told them. They were a step ahead of us at every turn, and Keller was the only one with access to both my file and my secret mission. Keller had Tesh kill Vanessa and Xavier in cold blood. He made Tony kill himself, and he was planning to use me to kill a bunch of innocent Muslims, oust the President, and take over the world. Considering all that happened, I came to a single, logical conclusion—that motherfucker, Keller, had to die.

Chapter 12

I had every intention of starting up Jack's truck and driving straight to Keller to put two in his chest, but unfortunately, I didn't get that far. In fact, I didn't get much farther than a parking spot on the other side of the gas station. I thought, *just sit for a few seconds and then go*, but a few seconds turned into half the night. It would've been the entire night had it not been for the knock on my driver side window, which nearly made me jump up out of my skin. I rubbed my eyes and focused on the people outside my window. The woman knocked again. It was dark, so it was hard to make out her face. I didn't have a gun, and to be honest, I was tired of fighting, so I rolled my window down halfway.

"I knew something was wrong with you," said the woman. I cocked my head to the side. "Huh?"

"You never looked like an Anna to me," she said.

"Rodriguez?"

She stepped back a little and stood straight up. "They killed Vanessa."

A man stepped forward out of the shadows. "They killed Xavier too," said Parrish.

A short woman pushed him aside. It was Stratton. "And, they tried to kill Jack, fucking sons of bitches!" she exclaimed.

Jack stepped forward to my window, bloody and bruised. "Surprised to see me?" he asked.

I just shook my head. "You people are crazy."

"OLD MAN'S STILL GOT IT!" he exclaimed.

I was still shaking my head in disbelief. "Jack ... but, how?"

He smiled his perfect, "Jack Farrell" smile. "I've had Nick shadowing you from the day those Navy SEALs drug you into the hospital. How do you think I made it out alive? The gang's all back together again."

"Step back a little," I said, reaching for the door handle. Jack moved back, and I climbed down out of the truck. "I believe this belongs to you," I said, nodding towards the pickup.

"Not really," Jack replied. "Listen up everybody, this is Alex Southerland, FBI. I know we've been through a lot of shit, and it may be hard to trust each other after all this, but somebody took a shot at us—all of us. We believe that somebody to be the Vice President. Now, I don't know Alex all that well, so, I don't want to assume-"

"WE NEED TO KILL THAT MOTHERFUCKER!" I exclaimed.

Everyone erupted into a loud roar.

"The ayes have it," said Jack. "I've had Alonzo shadowing someone as well."

I squinted a little. "Keller?"

"Have a look at this." Jack held out his phone and pulled up a picture. "See anything odd?"

"Is this Keller's family?"

"Yep," replied Jack, flipping through surveillance shot after surveillance shot.

I took a closer look. "Help me out here, I'm sleepy."

"Secret Service," said Parrish.

"HOLY SHIT!" I exclaimed. "VP's family doesn't get a Secret Service detail."

"Yeah, but they're all over 'em in every shot," said Rodriguez. "Like a fucking army, man."

"It's a coup," said Stratton.

"You and Tony were right," said Jack. "We all got fooled by this asshole. And, in case you didn't know, you're all over the news."

"Let me guess, rogue FBI agent gone mad?" I asked.

"Yeah, that about sums it up," Jack responded. "There's a warrant out for your arrest—at least that's what those two assholes back at the hospital claimed. Somebody's trying to cover their tracks."

"No," I replied, "they're trying to recover their asset ... me. They need me to trigger one of those bombs."

"Not gonna happen," Jack said. "Listen, I got us a ride to D.C., but when we hit the ground, we're going to have to cut through literally an army of sailors. Anybody got a problem with that?"

"Yeah!" replied Parrish. "But we can't let that little bitch, Keller, get away with this."

"Just get me there," I said. "I'll find a way in. This is my fight."

"We'll lock down the perimeter and give you enough time to finish this," said Rodriguez, "but if you're not out in 20 minutes, we're storming the castle."

"Fair enough." I looked around at all of them. I stared them right in the eyes. "You don't have to do this, guys," I warned.

"Daylight's burning in China," said Jack.

I laughed and shot him a bird. "Gear?"

Parrish said, "We got handguns, rifles, vests, flashbangs, and everything on the helo."

I hung my head down and shook it. "What the fuck are we doing here? This is treason. What about his family? We can't kill him like this. We need to take him in."

Rodriguez touched my shoulder and said, "He'll beat the rap, and you know it."

"This has to happen," said Stratton. "You and Vanessa may be some lying ass whores, but I loved that girl, and I kind of liked you too, so we gonna do this or not?"

The wind picked up, and I heard a pulsing noise in the distance. It grew louder as we stood in the darkness of that gas station parking lot, plotting a treasonous scheme to take the life of the Vice President of the United States of America. As the noise got louder, the wind grew stronger and I saw strobe lights approaching.

"WE ALL DO THIS TOGETHER OR WE DON'T DO IT AT ALL!" yelled Jack.

I nodded. "LET'S DO THIS!"

The helicopter landed right in the middle of the street. We all climbed aboard. The pilot turned and smiled at me.

"Good to see you again, Agent whatever your name is," he said.

I smiled really big, headed straight to the cockpit, and gave him a big hug. "Doctor Hughes, how'd you let them drag you into this mess?"

"They didn't have to," replied Hughes, "I volunteered! Close the door!" he yelled, "We're out of here." He pulled up on the stick and we lifted off into the night air in a freshly stolen Army UH-60 Black Hawk.

Jack and crew had all the gear we needed in the back of the helicopter. I stripped down and suited up, equipping myself with three handguns, an MP5 sub machine gun, communications gear, a flashlight, and a razor-sharp Gerber tactical knife. We were in the air for more than two hours before reality started setting in, and it hit us all pretty hard.

Stratton pressed the button on the radio strapped around her neck. "They're going to blow us out of the fuckin' sky."

"Just set it down, I can take it from here," I radioed.

A voice came over the helicopter comms. "I can't hear you," said Hughes, sarcastically. "Too noisy in here. We're one hour out."

"Why don't we jump?" asked Parrish. "We got chutes."

Jack shook his head. "They see us coming, and it won't matter, they'll shoot us down. It's a chance I'm prepared to take. We make a stand now or they will just keep sending their goons after us and pick us off one by one."

"Try to get some rest everybody," said Jack. "Might be the last chance we get."

We all nodded and slumped down into our seats. I was amped up, and my mind was running all over the place, but I was dead tired too, so I fell asleep within minutes.

I woke up after having felt what seemed to be turbulence. The cockpit was lit up red, and Stratton was shaking me with both hands, yelling for me to wake up.

"WE'RE FIVE MINUTES OUT!" she told me. "You good?" I nodded and she squeezed my shoulders.

"We're gonna be fine," she said.

"I know."

"LOOK ALIVE PEOPLE!" Jack screamed. He opened the door and cautiously looked down over the side of the helicopter. "We're clear," he announced.

Hughes set the helicopter down right on the street near the west edge of the Naval Observatory. He took his helmet off, powered down the chopper and turned around to us. "This is it," he said. "It's the end of the line for me. I wish I ... actually, I don't, but ... just get in and get out, okay? I'll meet you in the a.m. at the rendezvous."

Jack shook Dr. Hughes' hand and gave him a man-hug. The rest of us piled on top for a group hug. I figured it would be the last time we'd ever see each other. We all climbed down out of the helicopter. Hughes took off in one direction and we slowly crept up the street in the other direction towards the main gate.

We hustled and reached the gate, but to our surprise, there was no guard in sight, and the gate was wide open. We should've been smart and aborted, but perhaps we thought we'd hit the jackpot. We moved past the gate and headed for the big white house, which I expected to be lit up like Christmas and the wide-open lawn thick with Secret Service agents, but for some reason, it wasn't. And for some reason, we didn't care. We just kept charging forward. We should have known it was a setup.

We huddled in front of the Vice President's house to the right of the door, our infiltration attempt still completely unchallenged.

"Alonzo, breech," said Jack. "Nick, Adriana, secure the first floor. Alex, I've got your back."

"Thank you all for this," I whispered.

We all knuckled up and got in position. Parrish pulled out his lock pick kit, but he tried the door handle first, and it was already open. He looked back at us and shook his head. Then, he shrugged his shoulders and pushed his way inside. The rest of us hustled in behind him.

After a few hand signals from Jack, we spread out. Jack and I headed for the kitchen. We crept in slowly, pointing our weapons at every nook, cranny, and shadow in the place. We heard a noise on the other side of the room near the stove. When we circled the island in the middle of the kitchen, we saw a man down on the floor with his hands bound and his mouth covered. He was moaning and squirming around. Jack shined his light on the man's face. It was the President.

"Sir, I'm Jack Farrell, DEA ... are you alright?" Jack whispered.

The President nodded.

"I'm going to remove this," said Jack. He put his finger up to his mouth. "Shhhh."

I kept watch, alternating my gaze back and forth between both sides of the kitchen and President Wood. Jack pulled the tape off of his mouth.

"Sir, where is Vice President Keller?"

The President looked up to the ceiling.

"Upstairs, sir?" Jack asked.

The President nodded.

Jack depressed the button on his radio. "Everyone, back to the kitchen now," he whispered.

The others piled into the kitchen and surrounded us.

"Holy shit!" whispered Rodriquez.

"There's no bomb here," said Parrish.

Jack shook his head in disbelief, but if Parrish said there was no bomb, then there was no bomb.

"Mission's changed," said Jack. "Listen up, the three of you get the President to safety. Alex and I will-"

"No Jack." I shook my head. "Get the President out of here. No questions!"

We heard movement upstairs.

"Now!" I said, quietly. "Get POTUS the fuck outta here!"

Jack nodded.

Parrish reached down and cut the President's zip ties. The girls helped him to his feet. President Wood touched my arm and whispered, "Thank you, young lady."

I saluted him, and he saluted me back.

"We have to go now, sir," said Jack. He took the President by the arm and moved with him out of the kitchen.

One-by-one, the others hugged me, and then ran after Jack and the President. I stood there for a moment, listening to the movement above my head. Once again, it was just me, all alone, facing ridiculous odds. It seemed like a good idea at the time to tell them to get the President out of there, but in hindsight I may have sealed my own fate. Judging from

Parrish's surveillance of the VP, that man stayed surrounded by his own personal army of Secret Service agents. There's no telling what I might face up there, but I had to go anyway.

I did my best to breathe the fire out of my lungs. I tried to shake off my fear, and get moving, but my feet were so heavy. I moved through the kitchen, slowly, and then tripped over something. I nearly fell. I turned back and squatted down. It was a body. I moved my MP5 around towards my back and let it hang from the strap. There was blood everywhere. It was a sailor, and someone had stabbed him to death. His body felt cold. He'd been there for a while. I pulled out my flashlight and turned it on. There was a trail of sailors and staff members all the way out into the hall. They were all dead. "Jesus, I have to stop this bastard, Keller," I whispered to myself, "He's killing his own people." I picked up the pace and hurried out of the kitchen to make my way upstairs.

There were more bodies leading up the stairs. I'm not sure how we didn't notice them before, but I guess we were too busy searching the first floor for the bomb. Whoever did it didn't even care to conceal the bodies—that or they didn't have time. I didn't see a single Secret Service agent among the dead, so I had to assume they were all upstairs waiting to kill me.

Up on the second floor, I turned my flashlight off and headed for the only door I could see light under. They were in that room. This was my only shot at taking Keller down before his goons killed me. I didn't have time to think about all the ways they could take me down before I did what I had to do. All I could do was hit the door as hard as I could, stay low, and take my shot.

I took off my MP5 and quietly set it down on the floor, along with everything else I didn't need. By the time I finished, all I had was my Sig. I gripped my pistol with both hands in an isosceles stance and took off running down the hall towards the room, full speed. When I got close to the door, I lowered my weapon and slammed into the door with my shoulder. The door trim exploded, sending wood fragments into the air, and I did the best roll I've ever executed in my life. When I came to my feet, I saw Keller standing on the other side of the room. From the corner of my eye, I saw a man with a very familiar face down on his knees with Secret Service men on both sides of him, but I couldn't process it all at that time. I had to take my shot because all the other Secret Service men in the room were drawing their weapons. I didn't have time to do a headcount, but there must've been more than 10 agents in that room.

I looked down the night sights of my gun and squeezed off two shots before the agents bum-rushed me. I got tackled, pistol whipped, and I'm pretty sure someone hit me with a Taser because my teeth were grinding, uncontrollably, and my body shook violently. When I hit the ground, so did Keller's body.

I got you, son-of-a-bitch! I thought, but I couldn't speak a word of it because of the 50,000 volts surging through my body. The agents hit me one more time with the Taser, and then they all piled on top of me. I could barely breathe. I just knew they were going to kill me, but oddly they didn't—they just kept beating the hell out of me. Then, the strangest thing happened. I looked up and realized who else they had in custody. They slammed a man down on the floor right in front of me and handcuffed him. It was Secret Service Agent, Stephen Billings, the Vice President's right hand man—the same man I saw they were holding when I first smashed though door.

"What the fuck is going on here?" I struggled to ask.

Then, another man ran across the room to the Vice President. "GET OVER HERE, YOU IDIOTS!" exclaimed the angry stranger, but I don't think he was really a stranger after all. The man dropped to his knees and put pressure on Keller's wounds, which added an entirely new level of confusion to an already chaotically, mysterious situation.

All of it was extremely odd. Vice President Keller, the very man we'd just risked life and limb to take out and save the country from his evil grasp, was being treated like an innocent victim by a man I swear I'd seen before—someone at the very top of our government. My photographic memory started to kick in, and I'm pretty sure I recalled his name, but before I could say a word, I got hit in the back of the head. That last blow knocked me out. I woke up in the brig, hours later, and that was the story of me.

Chapter 13

Back in the courtroom. I finish recounting my story and look around. Not a single person in the place has mercy in their eyes for me. Judge Scott's rubbing his forehead and trying to speak, but he's at a loss for words. "We ... we're going to take a short recess," he says. "We'll reconvene in-"

"FUCK THIS SHIT!" I yell. "Just do it."

The room erupts. People are screaming at me, but I can't make out what anyone's saying. All I know is they're angry. They want blood.

Judge Scott slams his gavel down on his desk so hard the sound echoes throughout the room. "LIEUTENANT!" he exclaims. "ORDER IN THE COURT!"

I leap to my feet and yell, "JUST FUCKING DO IT MAN, JUST KILL ME, FUCK ALL THIS BULLSHIT!"

I keep cursing at the top of my lungs even after two bailiffs slam into me from both sides. Judge Scott yells *order in the court* over and over, but no one cares.

"I DID MY JOB," I scream. "I SAVED THIS COUNTRY FROM THAT GODDAMN EVIL BASTARD KELLER! FUCK YOU JUDGE, KILL ME!"

"CLEAR THE ROOM!" Scott yells.

I struggle with the bailiffs while my lawyer stands back several feet away, horrified at the sight of me. I have never said so many *fuck you's* in my life, but I keep right on saying them, repeatedly. If the bailiffs weren't so strong, I'd be shooting the judge a bird and probably mooning him. I'm out of my fucking mind at this point. Not even my story makes sense to me. They're going to hang me for real. The thought of bringing things to a logical conclusion calms me though, and I stop tussling with the bailiffs. It's hard to breathe, sandwiched between those two big, strong men. I try to slow my breathing and calm down, concentrating on replacing short, hysterical breaths with slow, deep, long ones.

"I'm alright now." I nod to each of the sailors gripping my arms. I nod my head. "I swear, I'm done, I'm good."

They let me go but stay close on both sides while the courtroom is cleared. After a few minutes, it's just me, my useless attorney, the Judge, his band of bailiffs, and the rest of the review panel.

Judge Scott rubs his forehead yet again. He sighs heavily. "Lieutenant Southerland, there will be no more outbursts in this courtroom...." He flips through several pieces of paper. "You say you and your team flew an Army Black Hawk helicopter right up to the Vice President's residence?"

"Yes, sir," I reply, still trying to catch my breath.

"Would it surprise you to know that no helicopter has been reported missing from the DOD, nor has one been recovered?"

I shake my head. "I don't understand, but I swear that's what happened. Maybe someone covered-"

"STOP IT, JUST STOP!" exclaims Scott. "ENOUGH! You say DEA Agents Jack Farrell, Nicole Stratton, Adriana Rodriquez, and Alonzo Parrish accompanied you on this secret, late-night incursion, but each of these individuals were killed on a DTP drug raid more than a month before you say this even happened. They walked into an ambush."

"WHAT!" I exclaim. "No, that's not-"

Judge Scott bangs his gavel again. "There's more, Lieutenant. The report also says there was no big army of Secret Service agents present. Just Agent Billings, who you shot and killed along with the Vice President."

"NO! NO! NO!" I put my face in my hands and almost dig my nails into my forehead. "I swear I-"

"If not for Agent Billings' heroic actions, disabling and detaining you, and calling for backup before he bled out, we wouldn't have a chance for justice here today."

"No, he was ... he ... I just, I don't-"

"Lieutenant Southerland, I believe you are suffering from PTSD. I've read your file, and I see an alarming number of incidents where I'm certain you experienced trauma and you failed to seek the help you needed to get your mental health in order."

I keep shaking my head. I feel like a crazy person.

"For God's sake, I wish I could have met you before all of this," says Judge Scott. "You were a good soldier. You were a good agent, but something snapped. You needed help, and I would've made sure you got the help you needed. Lieutenant, you murdered the Vice President of the United States of America and 25 of your fellow sailors at his residence. He invited you there to discuss your progress on the Peter Tesh case according to the White House Chief of Staff, and you killed the only man in the world who gave you a chance to redeem yourself from all the red in your ledger. They never saw it coming. Whether you had relations with Sergeant Major Vanessa Sullivan or not, the CID investigation revealed you killed her too, along with Victor Torrelli, and your boss, FBI Deputy Director Anthony Crane, who's body has yet to be recovered. There are no words for this degree of treason."

I'm crying now, still shaking my head uncontrollably. "No! Torrelli was ... he killed himself—he was trying to kill her ... he died in the FBI L.A. field office, and I shot him, but-"

"VICTOR TORRELLI'S BODY WAS FOUND IN THE TRUNK OF YOUR CAR!" Scott yelled. "A car you stole according to the report. You stole it from a scientist...." Scott looks down and thumbs through more papers. "Yes, it says right here, Dr. Taylor and his son were car jacked by an unknown assailant. Both killed at the scene. You were in possession of his black Mercedes, which you drove to see the Vice President. It was recovered from the Naval Observatory. The bullet from the head shot that killed Mr. Torrelli was not found; however, ballistics analysis suggests it is the same caliber of the bullet recovered from his leg, which was determined to have been fired from your service weapon. We can't prove it, but the removal of evidence from this crime scene is similar to previous attacks on DTP raids. Was it you all this time, Agent Southerland? Did you just start getting sloppy with Mr. Torrelli? There's no evidence of these black ninjas you claim are running around killing everyone—just evidence of you, murdering people in cold blood."

My mouth drops wide open, and I feel like I'm going to pass out. I just close my eyes and cry.

Judge Scott clears his throat. "We trained you, sailor," he says, "and you took all of those skills to wage war on this country—on this administration—against our Commander in Chief. You struck a blow that will prove hard for us to recover from for years to come." Judge Scott closes his eyes tightly and shakes his head a few times. "Do you have anything else to add to the record?"

I'm still whimpering, with my head down. "I'm sorry. Something is wrong ... ... with me. I'm sorry for what I've done, I just... no, sir. I don't have anything more to add."

I look up and Scott is crying too. He sniffles and wipes his tears.

"Are there any additional remarks from the panel for the record?" he asks.

"Sentencing should be done now," says the woman to his left.

The panel agrees, unanimously.

Scott sits up straight as a nail. "Lieutenant Denise Alexandria Southerland, you have been found guilty of treason as charged under the indictment filed against you. This panel unanimously concluded that the aggravating circumstances involved in this case substantially outweigh the mitigating circumstances. For your crimes, in which you have been and now stand convicted, under the Uniform Code of Military Justice, I sentence you to death by lethal injection. You are hereby remanded into custody until the Court of Appeals for the Armed Forces affirms this sentence at which time the sentence may be carried out. May God have mercy on your soul, Lieutenant." Scott bangs his gavel, and the sentencing is complete. "Bailiffs, get her out of my sight!"

The bailiff to my right handcuffs my wrists behind my back and they drag me out the rear of the courtroom. We walk down a long, empty hallway towards two marines, who open the double doors at the end. Outside there's a black, unmarked van backed up to the ramp. I look closely and determine there is no way it's a military transport. The rear doors are open and there are two men in black shirts and khaki pants with guns strapped to their legs waiting for me. The bailiffs push me out to the van, and as soon as I'm within arms-reach, the man to my left covers my head with a black hood.

"You can leave now," comes a deep, scratchy voice from the right.

I hear footsteps at first, but then nothing. I just stand still. My heart feels like it's going to blast off out of my chest cavity into outer space. After a brief moment of silence, I feel a pinch on the side of my neck, and everything goes dark again.

Chapter 14

I'm not sure what's worse—being sentenced to death and handed over to the CIA or waking up in a country club as if none of it ever happened. I'm looking around and I'm not restrained. I'm not locked in a cell, and the room I'm in is extremely nice—it even has a small library and a computer. I wonder if I'm in a hotel. I also wonder if I have really completely gone crazy. I walk over to the windows on the other side of the room and look out. The lawn is immaculate, and I swear I've seen it before. "Am I back at the White House?" I ask aloud. "The fuck is going on?"

The door opens behind me and in walks a man with two security sentries dressed in a black shirt and khakis right behind him.

"Agent Southerland, how are you feeling today?"

The man's face seems familiar to me. In fact, he was the man running to save Vice President Keller's life at the Naval Observatory that night. I'm not crazy after all. I think long and hard for a brief moment. "CIA Director Pearson," I say calmly. "This isn't the White House, is it? Where am I?"

Pearson smiles. "You know, when we started building a replica of the White House, it was all about terrorism. It was about making sure Secret Service, marines, even the FBI could respond to a real threat on Washington. Active shooter, dirty bomb, it doesn't matter—it would've proved to be a useful training tool one way or another. They had every little detail built exactly like the White House. Impressive, isn't it?"

"Why am I here?" I ask.

Pearson laughs. "Because you're a killer. You've been convicted of treason. They were so sure taking away your freedom, ruining your reputation, and beating you senseless would actually do the trick. We both know better, don't we?"

I roll my eyes at him.

"That's the trouble with you military folks, you got no imagination. You've been detained in a black site for months. Don't you remember?"

I shook my head.

"The things my men did to you were horrific," Pearson says, "but you didn't break. I told them all—I said, "This one is a patriot. This one's committed. It won't work. All the waterboarding...." Pearson nods. "Impressive for such a little woman. I've watched you for a while. You don't value your life or even your name enough to betray your country. I believe there's a more effective way to motivate you to do what's necessary to secure our great nation's future freedom and financial stability."

I sigh heavily and roll my eyes again. "The bomb?"

"I will personally see to it that the whole world thinks you're a traitor," he threatened. "Remember the courtroom? If making an attempt on the Vice President's life is enough for everyone to hate you, wait 'till they get a load of what I've got in store."

"He's dead," I respond.

Pearson bursts out laughing. "Oh, you are a real hoot, Southerland." He walks over to the window and looks out. "You hungry?"

"No."

"Well, maybe later," he replies.

I hear a helicopter outside. I walk to the window, stand beside Pearson, and look out into the yard. We both stand and watch a Black Hawk slowly descend. The tail number instantly grabs my attention, and I lock in on it. It was the same chopper the bad guys fled the Will-Clark scene in. I remember the tail numbers Rodriguez gave me: 88-26041. It's one of two choppers Slade claimed he seized in Virginia when he supposedly recovered all the fallout suits. I know because I saw the report. Now that I think about it, it's the same damn helicopter Doctor Hughes flew us to Washington in the night I shot Vice President Keller. No sooner than those thoughts race through my mind, the chopper comes to rest down on the middle of the lawn, and I see that son of a bitch, Hughes, climb his punk ass down out of it. *That bastard, Dr. Hughes, is one of them, and the CIA's been playing us the whole time.* I want to crush Pearson's windpipe and run outside to pay Hughes a visit, but unfortunately the situation doesn't allow for such pleasures.

Pearson says, "Whole world is experiencing economic crisis now—every nation. The world leaders are coming together to fix the problem and make one government the principal to administer the solution—to govern all nations' financial health. The world is changing, and we all need to stick together—every nation—but the United States must lead the charge. What better way to convince everyone this than you, Peter Tesh, and the rest of your terrorist buddies attacking all the world leaders. You're a bad lady. You don't play by the rules. Won't be much of a stretch for anyone with any amount of sense to believe you're capable of setting off a bomb at the economic summit in Riyadh."

I smile. "Still can't arm the bomb without me, huh?"

Pearson shakes his head. "That Taylor was a real son-of-a-bitch." He laughs again. "Naturally, CIA security and Secret Service will be there to stop your little band of terrorists from killing President Wood. By the way, your family's having dinner in the state dining room. You sure you're not hungry?"

My mouth drops. "You lie!"

"Young lady, I am many things, but a liar...? I told you back in Los Angeles, I'm here to help. I'm your friend. You can go anywhere you want in this facility, but if you try to escape ... well, you know the drill, don't you?"

I nod.

"Good then," Pearson responds. "We'll talk again soon." He walks out and his henchmen follow. They leave the door wide open.

I carefully walk to the door. I stick my head out and peer down the hallway both ways. Pearson and his men disappear around the corner, and I hear voices—familiar ones. I creep out into the hallway and follow the sound. Towards the end of the hall, I find an open door, and I can hear people talking inside. I move my head slightly into the doorway, just enough to see inside the room. Pearson wasn't lying at all. My entire family is sitting at the table, eating, just like he said. I walk inside and stand right at the front of the table, just watching them. They continue eating and talking for a moment. Finally, Bill looks up at me.

"ALEX!" he yells.

Everyone turns and looks at me. Then, they all rush and tackle me to the ground. Bill squeezes me so tight I can barely breathe. Chris kisses me all over my face, and behind them I see my sister Theresa, standing there with a toddler up in her arms. There's another woman, but I have no clue who she is.

"ALEX, OH MY GOD, ALEX!" Chris yells. He shakes his head. "I thought we'd never see you again!"

Theresa casually walks over and puts the little girl down on the floor.

"Go give her a hug baby, that's your auntie, Alex." She looks back at her mom. Theresa gives her a little shove and nods. "It's okay." She smiles.

Bill and Chris finally get up off of me and give us some room. The girl slowly walks up to me. She seems shy. She looks back at Theresa, and then back at me, and then at Bill, who nods and motions for her to go to me. She takes a few reluctant steps towards me.

"Come 'ere!" I say, reaching out and grabbing her with both arms. I pull her into me and kiss her face. "My God you are so beautiful. What's your name, sweetie?"

She looks back at her mom, who nods again. "Tell her, baby."

The little girl smiles and says, "Angie. Come on." She grabs my hand and tugs at me. "You have to meet my mommy!"

"Awe," says Bill.

I look over at Chris and he is grinning like a complete idiot. I pull myself up to my feet, still holding Angie's little hand. "I know your momma baby, I'm her sister. We're family."

We walk over to Theresa, who seems afraid to even look me in the eye.

Theresa closes her eyes for a second and then looks into mine. "I'm ... I-"

"I love you," I interrupt. I nod my head, and then I shake my head. "I really do. I love you."

Theresa springs forward and slams into me, wrapping her arms around my neck. She cries and squeezes me tight. "I love you too, I'm so sorry, I didn't mean to-"

"It's okay," I say. I close my eyes and wrap my arms around her waist and pull her tighter than ever before. "I love you, little girl."

We hold each other until Chris interrupts us.

"Alex, I want you to meet my wife, Teri," Chris announces. He reaches out for the pretty stranger who was patiently waiting, watching our family reunion from a distance. "Teri, this is Alex, my big sister—the one I've been telling you about."

Teri smiles and sticks her hand out. I knock it away and pull her into me for a big, bear hug.

"Welcome to the family," I say.

"Thank you." She smiles really big.

"We're just now eating," says Bill. "Won't you join us?"

We all walk over to the table together. They each sit down in front of their plates, which were piled high with food, and I sit down at the end of the table in front of an empty plate. I watch them eat. They periodically stop and all stare at me like I'm a ghost—or, maybe it's me staring at them. It's all so surreal. I try to put it all together in my mind, but nothing makes sense, so I ask the one question I desperately needed an answer to.

"What are you all doing here?"

Bill cleared his throat. "The President asked us to come here. He said you got wounded, trying to protect the Vice President from a would-be assassin. He asked us to come to the White House to be with you."

"We wanted to be here for you," says Theresa.

Chris wiped his mouth with his napkin. "We met with the Vice President this morning. He says you are a true hero. Asked us to be strong for you. Said everything would be alright."

I put my face in my hands.

"What's wrong, Alex?" Bill asks.

I look up, smile, and shake my head. "Nothing. Everything's fine." I cock my head to the side. "I love you guys."

"We love you too," says Chris.

I see Bill and Theresa hold hands for a moment. They both look at me and smile. Bill kisses the back of her hand, and they resume eating while conducting the seemingly complicated joint operation of making sure Angie gets her dinner in her mouth and not on her adorable little yellow dress.

We continue talking and catching up through the evening. Just seeing them makes me feel human again. Discovering all the things I missed throughout the years is the icing on the cake. Chris' wife is absolutely perfect, and Chris himself has grown into an amazing young man—a business man. He owns his own tax service company and is evidently good at his job. Teri tells me they have 15 offices across the Northeast. I'm so proud of him. He keeps telling everyone I'm rich, and I keep trying to get him to shut up about it. Something tells me if Theresa found out Dad left me all that money, her stripes would change, instantly. She and Bill are doing great anyway though from what they say. Bill actually owns a dealership now, and Angie is so cute. She's so amazing.

We finish dinner and move into Bill and Theresa's room. We watch a movie together, and eventually fall asleep—everyone but me. I want to snoop around, but I feel obligated to wait for my family to tire out before I leave them. Finally, they have, and now's my chance to get some answers. I slowly get up and creep out of the room. I open the door and move out into the hall. I pull the door as slowly and quietly as possible. The door clicks shut, and I turn around.

"FUCK!" I jump back. "Goddammit Pearson!" I whisper.

"Did I startle you?" he asks.

"Would it startle you if I choked the shit out of you, old man?"

He chuckles a little. "Kill me if you want, it changes nothing." Pearson nods his head to the left and says, "Come take a walk with me." He turns and heads down the hallway.

I walk fast to catch up to him.

"Here, have a look at this." Pearson shows me a tablet. On the screen I see some kind of surveillance app with a bunch of small squares. He taps one. "See, that's your family." He taps another. "Look familiar? That's Judge Scott from your military tribunal. Here look, remember the bailiff? So many familiar faces...."

I stare at the screen in disbelief.

"That's right, Alex," says Pearson, "They're all right here with us. They think they are here for a special terrorist training exercise for the CIA to develop tactics and legal doctrine regarding extremism. After we told them how you were connected to Peter Tesh and Alluvion, they were all too ready to sign up. They think they are actually doing some good." He laughs. "You're one of the few people in this facility, who knows the truth, but if you share that truth with anyone—and I mean anyone—I will not hesitate to kill your entire family."

"So that's your play? Threaten my family, and then I arm the bombs?"

"That sounds about right," Pearson replies.

I shake my head. "You think it'll be that easy?"

"I can't kill you, but I can execute every single person in this facility. The Judge, those sailors ... your sister."

"And, what about the Vice President?" I ask.

"Alive and well," Pearson replied. "Right here on the same floor. Keller's such a boy scout. He's a lot like you. Threaten his family, still stubborn. Leak bad intel on him, still stubborn. When we all met in L.A., we kicked Jack Farrell out of that meeting and offered Keller a seat at the table, but he refused. He wanted to go public, so we had to take him out of play. Unfortunately, before we could, he gave your medical file to Doctor Taylor, and instructed him to reprogram the bomb to require your DNA. That traitor screwed us all. Keller knew he wouldn't be able to contact you anymore, but apparently, he was confident no one would break you or stop you from completing your mission.

You're the only thing stopping us from using this bomb the way it was intended."

"Why this bomb?" I ask. "What difference does it make?"

Pearson smiles. "I guess you deserve to know. Taylor designed a bomb that uses so many different technologies— very much like the fallout suits that accompany it. Think of it like a smart, stealth bomb. We're able to use the cutting-edge nanotech Taylor developed to fool investigators, shape forensics, and blame the attack on anyone we want."

I smile. "And, he only made one?"

"Just a prototype, but it works, and although the technology will be lost forever now that he's dead, as you know, we have a very specific use for this one. It'll shape history ... lead us into a new future, a stronger future for America."

"But the program Jeremy Taylor had ... the thumb drive I found was-"

"Fake," Pearson interrupts. "Why on earth would we try and sneak a bomb inside the Vice President's residence? The mission's always been the same. Destroy your name and acquire you through coercion. Those simpletons thought if they made you believe President Wood's life was in danger, they could persuade you."

"You fed us the bullshit that pointed us to Keller," I say. "You and Hammond?"

"Who knew Secret Service would be stupid enough to let you get a shot off in that room. See, everything's about appearance. The facts don't matter. What matters is what people believe. We've been shaping elections with social media. If it's on the internet, the average dumb person automatically believes it. So, an agent with your history, going mad, attacking the Vice President, and then running off to bomb the upcoming economic summit...? Well, that's an easy sell. Even better now we have concrete evidence—I mean you wouldn't believe the mountain of evidence we have against you now. Had you just sat down and done nothing, we'd have nothing, but you couldn't help yourself. You had to solve the mystery. You had to be the hero ... had to save the day."

"Evidence? Please, I've already been tried for treason. I can't be tried twice for the same-"

"Treason?" Pearson laughs again. "Tried? What trial? There's no record of a trial. Why do you think everyone from that courtroom is here with us? Soon as the reports went out about the shooting, we started damage control on the internet, and the news networks recanted their story. Even now, with Keller being held here, we stick him up on the internet or TV and it all looks the part as if he's right there in the White House with President Wood. This replica White House is the best eight million dollars the Secret Service could've ever asked Congress for. Too bad it's been defunded and shut down."

"And, my friends?" I ask.

"All here," says Pearson. "Farrell, Parrish, and Stratton ... they're all right here. What, you think we just run around killing people?"

I grow angry. "You killed Vanessa Sullivan!"

He shakes his head. "I had nothing to do with that. Tesh killed Major Sullivan. She was a fine soldier. Tesh and his people believed violence would force you to undo Doctor Taylor's treachery. After all, all you have to do is put your palm down on a reader and say a passphrase. But I've studied you since the day we first met back in Los Angeles. When you do something, no matter what it is, it has to be your decision. Can't be forced, at least not that way."

"I don't understand what I have to do with anything."

"Taylor gave us a way to verify the bomb was real, everything including the trigger," Pearson reveals. "He gave us all that he developed, but then somehow he found out what we were going to do with it. I suppose Keller had something to do with that. Counterintelligence has been the cornerstone of the Alluvion operation. We told Farrell and Josh Carter that Doctor Taylor was killed, but Taylor was still alive when you went to New York to our fake pharmaceutical company. Keller suspected something was going on with President Wood and was convinced he was sending in the cavalry when he gave you this secret mission. We had to tell him our plans because you were sticking your nose in places it didn't belong. After we met that day and laid everything out for Keller, he refused to back the plan. When we told him Peter Tesh and Alluvion was all a ruse he lost it. We had to contain him, and we had to lead you back to him. I had the thumb drive planted in Jeremy Taylor's car, and I had the car delivered to you."

"Is Tom still alive?"

Pearson nodded. "The only casualties came by Tesh's hands. I knew leaking the existence of the drive would turn him into a raging patriotic animal. He sent his men after you in New York. I knew it would be a mistake putting those fallout suits in Tesh's hands. He let the power get to his head, and he went way off script. I had no idea he would do what he did, but he paid the price for his lack of vision."

"So, you were using Tesh and Colonel Hammond too?"

We turn the corner and continue down the hallway. "They both became liabilities. Tesh was supposed to be an urban legend, but he started believing his own press, and Hammond forgot who he worked for."

"So, you conveniently killed them, and now you're in possession of all the fallout suits?"

He nodded. "SEALs took care of all my problems thanks to you. We already had the suits. We had your buddy Xavier Slade to thank for that, rest his poor soul. We took the surviving elements of Tesh's team into CIA custody."

"To a black site?" I frown.

Pearson shakes his head. "I don't know why people like to use that term so much. They are in our custody. This was a very messy operation, primarily because you kept running around like a headless chicken, and others couldn't seem to keep their mouths shut. Keller, Sullivan, Torrelli—just a big mess all the way around."

I yawn. "Ya know, I don't know why I'm so calm right now."

"Maybe you're ready to actually serve your country?" he replies.

"Maybe I'm saving my energy for the moment I get to cut your fucking head off."

Pearson laughs, loudly, as if I am just there for his complete and utter amusement.

"Pearson, this is stupid," I say. "You went through all this drama and bullshit to get me to do something?" I shake my head. "This is the dumbest thing I've ever heard of."

"CIA can't operate on U.S. soil," he replies. "Well, not legally anyway. When you try to pull strings without letting people know that you're pulling them to become the most powerful man in the world in the one place you aren't supposed to pull a single thread ... let's just say it gets messy."

"So, what now?" I ask.

"Now, you go talk to Keller," he suggests. "You catch up, share a few laughs, and he convinces you that your family and your country are more important than your pride. You strap yourself in one of those suits, and you and my men go set that bomb off at the economic summit. You keep your head low, get out of there safe, and you come back here. We release the," Pearson holds up air quotes, "truth, that you were so distraught from the attack on the Vice President by the terrorists that you took matters into your own hands, and of course, you and your family stay here."

"As prisoners?" I ask.

"It's either this or a black site," Pearson replies. "How long you think that little girl will remain innocent surrounded by mercenaries?"

"FUCK YOU!" I exclaim.

We approach a door with two guards posted on it. Pearson nods to the man on the right, who reaches back and opens the door.

"Vice President's waiting to see you," Pearson says, smiling.

I lean in to him. "If you touch my family, I will put you in a fucking hole," I threaten. "I'll do whatever you assholes want me to do, but when I'm finished, you're gonna let my family go home, and if you don't, you'll wish that whore of a mother never pushed you out of her worthless, funky-ass womb. Look me in the eye...."

We stare each other down for a moment.

"I will kill you," I say. "Now, do you think I'm bluffing?"

Pearson shies his gaze away. "My men will be ready in two days," he says, looking down. "You got 48 hours, Agent Southerland. Do your job, and your family will survive this."

Pearson walks away and leaves me standing between his two goons. I stare into the doorway of the room where the Vice President of the United States is being held against his will, having been shot twice in the chest by a slightly confused, yet dedicated, loyal supporter such as myself. Who am I fooling? I voted for the two guys on the other ticket, but that's not the point. Every scenario running through my mind makes me think that walking through this doorway is just a bad idea. I can only imagine Keller, sitting in there, strapped to a wheelchair, breathing through a tube, judging me like every other person I've come into contact with. How the hell was I supposed to know he wasn't the bad guy? I mean could that asshole have hung a sign around his neck or something? Everything—and I mean everything bad about this whole, twisted heap of a mess—pointed to his guilty-looking ass. But, isn't that how they do it? How they play you? How they played me? I'm not sure who the bigger fool is—me for being hoodwinked by Pearson or Keller for believing I was his only hope. He must've been really desperate to come to me of all people. I bet he won't make that mistake again.

I take a few steps forward and stop right in the middle of the doorway. I look back over my shoulder at one of the men guarding the door. He doesn't budge, he's still facing the hallway. I turn back and stare at both the men. There are so many places I'd rather be, and so many people I'd rather be with. Don't get me wrong, seeing my family is—well it just is, but I miss Vanessa. In hind sight, after all that's happened, I know I loved her. It wasn't just a fling. I wish we had more time. Love is so strange. I'm pretty sure she was my first love, or maybe Tony is if I'm being honest. I miss him too. I don't know if it's possible to love more than one person at a time, but they both have my heart. I put them right up there with David Chandler, rest his old, grouchy soul—and along with my dad and my little brother Chris. Pearson was right. I would destroy the entire earth to stop him, but not if it meant me losing any more of the few remaining people I love. Vice President Keller doesn't have to convince me of anything—I'm in.

"Change your mind?" comes a voice from behind.

I'm almost scared to turn around, but I do, and there he stands, Vice President Keller in the flesh, looking amazing. I start to wonder just how long they held me in that black site because if I'm to believe the man I shot twice in the chest is standing before me, I'm thinking I've been fooled yet again.

"Sir, I-"

He raises his hand. "Alex, shut up, and come here."

I slowly walk further into the room, and when I get close, he reaches out with both arms. I flinch a little, still afraid he wants to kill me with his bare hands, but he pulls me in for a big hug instead. He presses his face against mine and sighs heavily.

"Alex, I already know what you're going to say," says Keller. "Don't waste your or my time with it. You may have made mistakes, but you didn't fuck up ... I did."

I step back a little, shocked to hear him utter the words. "Mr. Vice President, I-"

"Surprised?" he asks.

I nod and reply, "A little. I don't think I've ever heard anyone say that to me before."

He smiles and rubs both my arms. "Well, it's true. Come on in."

Keller leads me back into his room, which looks just as nice as the real Oval Office. He offers me a seat and we both sit down on sofas facing each other.

"It was unfair of me to put the fate of the world on your shoulders," he says. "When I saw you back in Los Angeles, I thought we had a clear mission, but as soon as I left you in Jack's office and went back to meet with Pearson, it got nasty. They told me something I couldn't bring myself to believe, and now they think they can bury me here in this abomination...."

"It was all a game," I say. "One big global CIA operation run off the books."

He nodded and rubbed his hands together. "I should've seen it coming. All the bad raids and the missing suits. It was all so grandiose a scenario, it just kept everyone jumping back and forth, and at this point I believe that was part of the strategy. No two threads came together in any reasonable way, so why not believe it was some big terror network that was chipping at the heart of America and her allies?"

"Sir...."

"Yes?" he replied.

"I thought it was ... ... I'm sorry for shoot-"

"Do you know why we're here, Agent Southerland?" he asks.

"I'm not an agent anymore."

Keller smiles. "We're here because you shot me." He slowly raises his right index finger in the air. "DISRUPTION!" He smiles even bigger and snaps his finger. "They wanted to make a big mess and point it all to me, but you disrupted that plan, didn't you?"

I cock my head to the side a bit. "I guess?"

"You run off to New York and get closer to Tesh than the enemy ever dreamed you would. Hell, you convinced their operative to give you intelligence on how to go after them. You became the threat they overlooked. And, when they thought you would just go along with their ridiculous stage play, you shot the living shit out of me."

I burst out laughing, covering my mouth. "I'm sorry, I didn't mean to shoot you, I swear I thought you were doing all this to me, to the country. But, it's really President Wood isn't it? That's who Pearson is doing this for, am I right?"

Keller fiddles with his tie a bit, and then takes a sip of water from the mug on the table between us. "I can't figure why he would do this. There are so many other ways we can make change around the world, but I can't figure it to be anyone else."

"I was sure I'd killed you," I say.

"Young lady, I am a voice, a voice shared by many," he replies. "I stand for freedom, and no matter how hard you try, you cannot kill freedom. That night, while Secret Service tried to crush the life out of you, CIA Director Pearson saved my life, and I've been here ever since—a prisoner in my own country. Apparently, he has a use for me as well. Only time will tell what that truly is."

I shook my head again. "Terence Slade told me you gave the kill order to terminate me, and I-"

"Alex, I gave no such order," he interrupts. "I know Slade. He's a good man, but I gave him no such order. They cornered me the minute I said no and brought me here. After that I imagine they were just putting my name down on briefings in case they end up needing another patsy."

"That explains why no one could get in contact with you," I say. "I'm sorry for thinking you were-"

"Stop apologizing," Keller demands. Then, he sits up and clears his throat. "Sailor, I gave you a job to do," he bellows, officially.

I sit up too. "Yes, sir!"

"Did you complete the mission?" he asks.

I shake my head. "No, sir, but the true enemy has revealed himself."

"We need to complete the mission!" he says sternly.

I look confused. "But, Mr. Vice President, if I don't do what they ... they're gonna kill you and my family and everyone else here." I put my hands on my knees and look down. "We've lost ... I've lost more than I can stand, sir," I say softly.

Keller stands up and walks around the table. He sits down right next to me and puts his arms around me. He leans in and whispers, "Doctor Taylor did more than just give you a way to prevent the bombs from being armed, and I have a friend waiting for you on the outside. Go along with Pearson but be ready."

"I don't understand, I-"

"Be ready," he says. "How long did Pearson give you?"

"Forty-eight hours," I reply.

"Remember Agent Billings?" he asks.

I nod. "They slammed him down in front of my face back at your house."

"Billings was my detail," he whispers. "He was never on board with all this either. He's still alive and on the run. You need to find a way to break from your team, find Billings, and do what one of us should have done ages ago.

"What?"

Keller removes his lapel pin and with both hands he places it in mine. He closes his hands around my hand and stares me straight in the eyes. "Kill the President."

I remain silent, pressing Keller's pin between the palms of my hands.

Keller gives me a stern look. "You get your ass back here safe," he says. "I want my pin back, and this country will need a leader, sailor."

I nod. I let go of his hands and stand up. I give him one last look, and then head for the door.

I walk out of Keller's room and make my way back down the long corridors towards my family. I want to spend every minute I can with them right up to moment I'm forced to leave this spooky tomb that's masquerading as the White House. I know there is no way I can tell them I'm off to do the CIA's dirty work. Once again, I have to lie to the people I love. With all that has happened up to this point, my brain should be so full it's ready to explode and pop right out of my head, but strangely, I'm not thinking about anything at all. The issues haunting me up to the point when I walked into Keller's room are all off my radar now. The only thing I'm thinking about is the six months of pain and torture creeping out from the darkness of my memories into the forefront of my mind. I remember exactly what those bastards did to me after that phony trial. They took my life away from me. Pearson can blame Tesh all he wants, but Tesh was his junkyard dog, and he took Vanessa, Tony, and Xavier from me. Now he wants to take my family too? Keller's right, the mission has changed, but it's not just President Wood who's in my sights now. Before I leave this earth—before the devil claims his little star child—I'm going to watch CIA Director Pearson die, screaming like a little bitch.

www.ingramcontent.com/pod-product-compliance
Lightning Source LLC
Chambersburg PA
CBHW030600180626
46816CB00005B/1614